JUST MY LUCK

Lelia Coles
&
Rosilyn Seay

ISBN 978-0-9985576-5-6

Library of Congress Control Number: 2020902771

Printed and Bound in United States of America

PicBooks Publishing

http://picbookspub.com

DEDICATION

This book is dedicated to the memory of Corrine Banks, our mother and our rock. She was a strong woman with a lot of faith, a lot of character, and a lot of love. She, by example, taught us that you can make it through life with kindness, integrity, honesty, humility, and hard work.

ACKNOWLEDGMENTS

We've been truly blessed to have family members and friends who support and encourage our many creative endeavors. I, Rosilyn Seay, thank Robert Seay, Nathanael Seay, and Kevin Seay who never waiver, but patiently put up with this and my many harebrained projects. I am eternally grateful to them and other members of my extended family—Dorothy McClinton, Constance Hardy, Vanessa Kerry, and Muriel Lee—for providing ideas, suggestions, and a gentle push, every now and then, for me to bring to an end this near decade long project. And of course, my sincere thanks to those many individuals who helped and encouraged Lelia, as she put pen to paper. I don't know all the names, but you know who you are.

PREFACE

Lelia Coles and I, Rosilyn Seay, are sisters. We were best friends from the day I was born until the day she died, in 2011, of colon cancer and subsequent complications. She passed quietly at home, with the love of her life, her husband Arthur, on one side and me on the other, each holding a hand.

Late in life, Lelia decided to pursue her artistic side. She created several poems and wrote and produced several plays. She trusted me to be her editor for all her writings. In other words, she decided. And I had no choice in the matter. She was my big sister. I was used to her telling me what to do.

Lelia's big dream was to write a novel and have it read by millions. When she died, she had the skeleton of her story, but her dream of getting published was still unrealized. Knowing what it meant to her, as a final gift to my sister, I made a pledge to get her story into print. My original intent was to fill in the blanks, cross the t's, dot the i's, produce a private bound version, and give copies to those who loved and supported Lelia.

After completing the basic edits, I decided that would not be good enough. What I really wanted was to make Lelia's dream a reality, if at all possible. I owed it to my sister to try. So, I started over.

It wasn't easy, without her around to talk with. Still, there were times I felt her there behind me, saying, "no, no, that's not what I meant . . ." and I'd make the changes. The hardest thing about the rewrites was staying true to what Lelia was trying to portray. That's why it took so long. I couldn't stop until I felt that I had a product worthy of my beautiful sister.

It was a labor of love and at times it was almost as if we were still holding hands and plotting together.

Rosilyn Seay

PART ONE

Ghetto Girl
(1989-1992)

CHAPTER 1

"ONE MINUTE. MISSED IT by one stupid minute!" Twanie said, as she watched the tail end of the five o'clock bus turn the corner. Out of breath and soaking with perspiration, she knew it was pointless to continue running. Even if she could somehow be fast enough to catch up with the bus, without a doubt, it would be wasted effort. Once the driver pulled away from the stop, he would not open the door to let her in. Not between stops. She'd seen it before.

The frustrating part, for Twanie, was that she had timed everything perfectly, so that she'd be at the stop long before the bus was scheduled to arrive. Now, through no fault of her own, she was sweaty, winded, and her bus was gone.

Of course, she was disappointed. More than that, she was upset and trying hard not to get angry—like any normal person would be—at the idiots, her fellow cheering squad members, the ones who'd played the prank that made her be that one minute too late.

They had been pranking her for months. But all the previous ones had been petty annoyances—like a scary fake spider dangling by a sheer thread outside her locker; or a locker filled with rolled up dirty socks set to tumble out on her as she opened the door; or the contents of her deodorant stick replaced with some awful smelly cream that she almost rubbed under her arms. All of which were silly things that middle school kids, not high school teenagers, would do.

Each time, she'd tried patience, believing it was easier to ignore the shenanigans than to make a big deal out of them. And each time she crossed her fingers that the pranksters would tire of the harassment.

For a while, it appeared that they had given up. Then something must have happened. What affront, insult, or slight she could possibly have committed, Twanie had no clue. But for some reason, on the day of their very first end-of-year practice session, the pranking returned with a bang.

The spring practice sessions were new that year, the brainstorm of Twanie and the coach, Mrs. Davis. They both hoped the sessions would inspire the girls to improve and come up with ideas for stunts, routines, and exercises to work on over the summer.

Unfortunately, the idea did not go over well. Even though the entire squad desperately needed the practice, they had better things to do on their Thursday afternoons—like preparing for weekend shopping trips and parties. Being dedicated or skilled athletes was not a priority.

Given their attitude towards the optional practice, both Twanie and Mrs. Davis were relieved that the entire squad showed up for the first of the spring sessions. Happily, it went better than either of them had expected.

Not wanting to press her luck, Twanie didn't ask any of the other girls to stay back to make sure the gym was left as it should be. Instead, she and Mrs. Davis rolled up and put away the couple of matts they'd used, while they chatted about how well the session had gone and made plans for the following Thursday. By the time she entered the locker room, everybody else was gone. And, to her surprise, so were her shoes.

Not ready to accept the obvious, Twanie went through the motion of searching her bag, her locker, and every visible space in the room.

"Now that's just mean," she said, at last acknowledging that the shoes were gone. "Who takes someone's shoes, even as a joke?"

Her only consolation was that they had to still be in the room. Removing or destroying them would cross a line Twanie was positive her pranksters were not willing to cross. Messing with her head was one thing. Pushing it far enough that she'd go to the authorities—in this case, Mrs. Davis—was another. In all honesty, Twanie did not want that either.

In an ideal world, Twanie could go to Mrs. Davis and report that someone had removed her shoes as part of an ongoing pattern of harassment. In that glorious world, Mrs. Davis would bring everybody together. She would wisely explain the true meaning of being part of a team, and get the pranksters to understand the error of their ways. At that point, there would be a Disney movie kumbaya moment, complete with hugs and tears.

Unfortunately, Twanie lived in the real world, where going to Mrs. Davis would be squealing. That simple act would most likely result in her shoes disappearing permanently, while the culprits would never be identified. After that, life for her on the squad would become considerably worse, with the few semi-allies she had on the squad turning against her. In short, it would be a lose-lose situation for Twanie and the entire cheering squad.

She looked at the well-worn white-ish sneakers she'd used for practice. Hopefully, she wouldn't have to wear the dingy things home. They absolutely did not go with the silk blouse—a special gift from her favorite aunt—short skirt, and stockings, that she'd worn that day. It sickened her to think that she'd worn the outfit in an attempt to impress the others on the squad, a decision that she now realized was stupid and sad, in more ways than she could count.

"I just want my shoes . . ." she sighed, taking a breath to calm herself.

She had bought the cute little ballet flats with her own hard-earned money—from a lot of babysitting and running errands for neighbors and church members. If she didn't find them, unlike her well-heeled squad members, she could not afford to simply go out and buy another pair.

"Where would I even start looking?" she said, as she slumped down onto the nearest bench. She let out a sound that was more moan than sigh. She couldn't just forget her shoes, but there was no way she could check through the gazillion lockers that covered the entire room wall-to-wall and get out in time to catch her bus. "I could be here forever . . ."

Like a signal from above, the florescent light, which had been threatening to go out for days, flickered, drawing her attention.

"Hmmm, maybe . . ." she said, looking up. "I never thought about on top of the lockers."

Twanie climbed onto the bench, she had been sitting on, and used her tiptoes to make herself as tall as she could. That way she could see from one end of the room to the other.

"There you are!" she exclaimed.

On top of the set of lockers, the ones directly in front of her, was one pair of black ballet slippers, shoved back against the wall.

Twanie bent down and grabbed the only tool she had to work with, her gym bag. After a few well directed sweeps, she was able to force the shoes to the floor.

"Yes!" she said, and silently thanked maintenance for procrastinating in repairing those lights.

With her shoes safely in hand, Twanie had to admire the pranksters' ingenuity. At five-feet-three inches tall, she would never have seen them from the floor. For a brief moment, she wondered just how far they were willing to go the next time. But, with all the delays and only a few minutes left before her five o'clock bus would arrive, she decided that she didn't have the time or the brain cells to waste worrying about it or them.

CHAPTER 2

THE BUS WAS GONE and there was nothing Twanie could do about it.

"Jokes over!" she said, louder than she intended, and immediately took a calming breath. "Right now, if I saw any of those girls from the squad—don't care who—I'd probably strangle her," she whispered, as she wiped the sweat from her forehead, using the handkerchief her mother always made her carry. For once, she was grateful for her mother's old-fashioned ways.

On top of everything else, her attempts at calming breaths to cool herself down—a technique taught to her by her aunt—were stymied by the unseasonable heat. Twanie couldn't believe how oppressively hot the day had gotten. When she'd left home that morning, it was a comfortable seventy degrees. If the perky weather girl for Channel-6, Rose Marie, could be trusted, it was still no more than eighty degrees. Nothing against either Rose Marie or Channel-6, but from where she was standing, the muggy day felt at least one hundred degrees hotter than that.

"Phew," she said, stepping closer to the skinny bus stop sign, hoping for any little shade it could provide. "It can't be this hot already. It's only May."

Every second she stood there, it got harder and harder to imagine forgiving or ignoring her tormentors' latest prank. Because of them, she was forced to stand outside in the direct sun, on a hot and muggy day, at an unsheltered public bus stop that didn't even have a bench to rest on. On top of all that, since it was rush-hour, there was no way she could predict when the next bus would arrive. It could be anywhere from five minutes to fifteen minutes. Either way, she dreaded the wait.

Twanie turned to face the clouds, hoping someone was listening, and whispered softly, "Please get the bus here soon. Please have at least one free seat. And please-please-please have the air-conditioning working full blast!"

A loud voice, that seemed to come from nowhere, startled her and made her jump. Twanie giggled when she realized it wasn't the voice of God answering her prayer, but the sound of people leaving the school across the street. Some activity or class must have recently ended, and several people were heading in the direction of the parking lot. A few of them recognized Twanie—probably from her being on the cheering squad—and aimed sympathetic nods or waves in her direction. Twanie smiled wistfully back at the wavers and nodders, envious that they would soon be departing in air-conditioned vehicles. She was certain that behind those sympathetic gestures was relief that they didn't have to wait, in the sweltering heat, at the public bus stop with her.

They didn't know the half of it. Once Twanie got on the bus, she still had a long tiring ride in front of her—at least thirty minutes with one bus change in between. Though she'd long ago adjusted to the commute, there were days when she couldn't help but fantasize about how much simpler things would be if she attended her neighborhood school, Frederick Douglas, which was within walking distance from her house. But that ship had sailed. Nothing she did or said would convince her parents to allow her to transfer.

Attending George Washington High had never been her idea. That was the decision of the grown folks around her. They were all enamored with the school's reputation and couldn't understand why she was not thrilled for the opportunity to attend, what they considered, one of the best schools in the city. Maybe it was. It just wasn't best for her.

Frederick Douglas was her school. For years, she and her two best friends, Debbie and Neasha, couldn't wait to go to Douglas. It was like a rite of passage, the symbol that they were almost grown. They'd often talked about what they'd wear for prom night—Debbie would shock everyone in all red and Neasha would wear white with a tiara.

Besides attending the school, Debbie and Neasha could not imagine anything more exciting than being on one of the best cheering squads around.

Douglas had the best cheerleaders, the best teams, and the most loyal fans anywhere. Go Wildcats!

And they had a plan to make it possible. The three of them, who did almost everything together, would first tryout and make it onto the Benjamin Banneker Middle School squad. That would serve as practice and a steppingstone to their goal.

It was only natural that the three of them would do it together, since the girls had been friends and neighbors, in the Delaney Housing Projects, all their lives. When Neasha became a fan of the Pointer Sisters singing group, she started calling their little trio the Delaney Sisters, and soon so did everyone else in the neighborhood.

Twanie loved Debbie and Neasha and truly thought of them as sisters. If they wanted to be on the cheering squad, though she was more academic than athletic, she swore to give the effort her all. Even now, she remembered how much fun it was planning and rehearsing. The best part was when her girls put together dance moves and stunts, and were thrilled when their spastic-nerdy friend managed to master them. They never suspected how she went home and worked on them for hours, just to get close to the skill level of Debbie and Neasha.

What Twanie didn't anticipate was her mother's reaction to her dedication to impressing her friends. Margie took exception to all the effort Twanie was putting forth. She suspected that her overachieving daughter would not stop working overtime, even when and if she made the squad, which was not necessarily a good thing for her daughter.

From the time Twanie was an infant, she stood out from the rest. Margie never had to worry about her baby meeting the expected milestones. Twanie always got there early, mostly because, from day one, she was stubborn and met every challenge head on. At ten months, after jealously watching another baby toddle around in the pediatrician's office, she was walking within a week. When other kids were barely recognizing letters, Twanie taught herself to read and to write her name. In elementary school, she was tapped for the city-wide talented and gifted program, RTAG. What's more, she was not only making all A's in the RTAG required accelerated classes, but she was also excelling in the optional high school level math and science courses.

Margie had high hopes for her daughter. She was determined that her brilliant child would graduate college. She'd get a good professional job that required that college level education. Then she would marry a dependable man and have a family. In that order. It had not worked out quite that way for her.

Margie fell for Twanie's father in high school. Terence Frederick Addison, a charming Smoky Robinson wannabee, was the hope of Wake Forest North Carolina. Certain that he was destined for stardom, right after graduation from Lincoln High, he and Margie headed up north, in his 1969 Chevrolet Camaro. Terence was to join up with friends who had started a singing group in Washington, D.C. Halfway there, they stopped in Richmond to visit his relatives and give Margie a chance to get a handle on her persistent carsickness. When the carsickness proved to be morning sickness, Terence and his Camaro continued to D.C., leaving Margie in the care of her big sister, Dee, who was a senior at Virginia State College.

Dee, a member of Chapel of Hope Baptist Church, on Hope Street in Richmond, turned to Pastor Wright and his wife, Constance, for advice. Before Dee was off the phone, Sister Constance and the ladies of her Outreach Ministry started making calls. The ladies worked, what could only be considered, a miracle. They helped Margie land a job as a kitchen aide in the cafeteria of Richmond General Medical Center. They also helped her get a two-bedroom two story home in the Delaney Court Housing Projects, a short bus ride from her new job.

While Margie was eternally grateful to the caring people at Chapel of Hope, and acknowledged they were a true blessing, she never wanted her daughter to be in a position where she needed that level of assistance.

That's why, when she discovered that Twanie was staying up late and putting so much effort into preparing for the cheer tryouts, Margie felt it was time to step in. She had no choice. To keep her daughter from jeopardizing her studies, her grades, her standing in RTAG, and her future, Margie made her give up any notion of joining the Benjamin Banneker cheering squad.

Debbie and Neasha were disappointed, but they understood. They knew their friend was special, and assumed she was headed for greatness. They did not want to do anything to slow her down. Besides, nothing could break up the Delaney Sisters. They were, and always would be, best friends forever.

Then again, none of the Delaney Sisters were aware of Margie's grand plan for herself. She'd had enough of irresponsible dreamers and prayed nightly for a good stable man to come along to take care of her and her out-of-wedlock daughter. She couldn't believe her luck when she caught the eye of a handsome young deacon from her church, Raymond Samuels. Raymond was literally the answer to her prayers. He was a man of obvious character—after all he was a trusted deacon of Chapel of Hope. He had a good job—he worked as a social worker. And he had ambition—he was studying to be a minister, with plans to eventually start his own church.

So, while Debbie and Neasha were busy teaching their nerdy friend new cheer and dance moves, her mother was in the early stages of courtship with Deacon Samuels. And the summer before they entered eighth grade, while the girls were still giggling at the thought of Miss Margie with a boyfriend, the romantic devil made his move.

He and Margie had stopped for a bite at the Broad Street White Tower Restaurant. While waiting for their food—he 'd ordered the famous burger and she the waffles—the deacon looked over at the beautiful Margie Brooks and couldn't wait any longer. He declared his love and proposed.

They were married a month later in a small private ceremony at the church. After the wedding, Margie and Twanie left Delaney Court and moved into the deacon's cute little bungalow, only a few blocks from where they had been living. For Twanie, it might as well have been a thousand miles away.

Once his new family was situated, the deacon proclaimed to Margie that he'd stand back and leave the raising of her child to her. But there was one issue he felt strongly about, and that was Twanie's continued association with the Delaney Housing Projects. He felt she should stay away and not visit the old neighbors or the neighborhood. "For the girl's own good," he said.

As a social worker, he had seen too many casualties of the housing projects, and he did not want Twanie to "fall prey to the bad influences" in Delaney Court. Margie, who didn't necessarily agree, complied because her main goals in her new life were to keep the peace and not upset her husband.

Naturally, the Delaney Sisters were disappointed at not being able to hang together as before, but they were still not discouraged. They could continue to see each other at Banneker Middle School or talk over the telephone. And, after graduation, they'd be together at Douglas.

Then, towards the end of eighth grade, the girls were dealt the final blow. It happened during the end-of-year awards ceremony. As expected, Twanie was called up several times for group and individual awards. Each time, her friends clapped enthusiastically. Then Mrs. Luck, the eighth-grade guidance counselor, walked to the center of the stage to make a special announcement.

"This year," she began, "Benjamin Banneker has the distinct honor of having one of the 1989 RTAG Special Award winners at our school." Mrs. Luck paused, for effect. Mrs. Luck tended to be a bit dramatic. "Would Antoinette Brooks please return to the stage?"

This was big. No one at Banneker had ever won that award before. The auditorium roared, as Twanie stepped forward. Mrs. Luck silenced them to explain that a big part of the award was that the recipients were placed in a lottery for elite schools in the city. "And . . ." she said, as she again paused for effect, "Antoinette's name has been pulled for special admission to George Washington High School. Congratulations Antoinette."

This time, the Delaney Sisters did not join in the applause. Stunned and broken hearted, they moaned in their separate parts of the auditorium.

* * *

Twanie immediately started on a campaign to convince her mother that Douglas was a better school for her. After all, it was closer. By being only a ten-minute walk from their house, there would be no need for buses or special transportation vouchers—which everybody knew was a pain. She'd be home early enough to take some of the load off of Margie. That way, she could help more with the housework and have food prepared when both parents got off work. And—what she felt was her most compelling argument—in the long run, no matter what school she went to, she would work hard to earn those scholarships her mother wanted for her.

She kept at it until Margie lost patience and snapped at her, "Antoinette Catrina Brooks, you need to stop whining and be grateful for the chance to attend such a good school. Count your blessings and be thankful."

After that, Twanie had no choice. She resigned herself to accepting the school everyone seemed to think was so much better for her, and all that went with it. Instead of counting her blessings, as her mother had insisted, once she was enrolled, she counted the days left until graduation.

The one person who listened and understood, was Dee, Twanie's aunt and Margie's older sister. Being a student of history and a sixties' *say-it-loud* radical, Dee knew a lot more about George Washington High and its surrounding community than either her sister or her brother-in-law. As far as she was concerned, she agreed with Twanie. George Washington was not the right school for her niece.

George Washington High School originally had been one of Richmond's premier all-white schools, one that fought to stay that way, until it was forced to integrate in the sixties. Then, when people of color began moving into Richmond Heights—the restricted area surrounding the school—even though they were just as well-to-do as the current residents, it was just too much. By 1989, when Twanie entered Washington, the school still ranked high among Virginia schools, but the percentage of Caucasians in the school and the surrounding neighborhoods had gone down to less than ten percent.

However, what Dee understood that her sister and brother-in-law missed, was that the transition of the population had not changed the community's overall attitude. It was still restrictive, only it was now unofficially class restrictive. In other words, little girls like Twanie, from the wrong side of the class line, would never be welcomed with opened arms in George Washington High or Richmond Heights.

One thing Dee did admire about the now diverse community was they were much more subtle about their exclusion policies. Unlike the previous residents, there were no mobs with pickets blocking the entrances, and no locked doors to deter undesirable outsiders. Instead, to maintain the character of their schools, they initiated programs with rigorous criteria and set aside a limited number of slots for academically promising young people—like Twanie—from underserved communities in the city. And it worked. It kept the number of undesirables down and the city and bleeding hearts off their backs.

* * *

Twanie could not remember a time when Dee didn't have her back. It seemed that Dee had always been there to provide unconditional love, encouragement, and, when necessary, unfiltered—often unsolicited— counseling. Five feet ten inches and two hundred pounds of all heart, she was a force to be reckoned with. She even taught Twanie how to fight—a requirement for life in the projects.

The weekend before Twanie was scheduled to start in her new school, Dee surprised them all by driving the twenty-one miles from Petersburg to their house. She was on a mission; one she could only do in person. She had a special gift for her niece.

"A present? For me?" the thirteen-year old squealed, as her aunt handed a velvet black jewel box to her. In the box was a black pearl teardrop on a silver chain. Before that day, Twanie had no idea that there was such a thing as a black pearl. The only pearls she'd seen were the white ones in the necklaces of the ladies at church. And very few of those were real.

Inside the box was a handwritten note. Twanie unfolded it and read it out loud:

> *Antoinette, you are a perfect gem in an imperfect world. Always know how much I love you and wish I could be there to protect and remind you. Wear this and never forget that, like this pearl, you are not only black and beautiful, but also rare and of exceptional value.*

"Thanks Auntie, I love it," she said, brightly. "But, Auntie, you do realize that I can't wear this all the time, everywhere I go."

"Yeah, I know, sweetie," Dee, chuckled, embarrassed to be caught out by her thirteen-year-old niece. "I know I can't protect you from all evil, even from the crazy aristo-blacks in Richmond Heights. The least I can do is make sure you realize your value. You know?"

"Don't worry. I'll be fine, Auntie," Twanie said, moved that her aunt cared so much. "If I can stare down gangbangers and wannabes at Banneker, then I can definitely handle a few stuck-up rich kids at Washington."

"I know, sweetie. You are strong and way smart. But, snotty nosed stuck-up kids can get to you, even worse than the gangbangers. If it was just about brains, you'd do good no matter where you went. You're probably twice as smart as any of those kids in that school," Dee said with obvious pride.

Twanie's smile vanished. "I wish the people at Washington saw it the way you, and Mrs. Luck, and the people from RTAG do."

"What do you mean?"

"Auntie, there was only one thing about Washington that I really liked. Mrs. Luck had told me how I'd be a shoo-in for the advanced placement program. She said that it was one of the best in the city. When she showed me some of the stuff they did—things Douglas could never afford—it looked so cool. And she said that by doing well in the program, a bunch of good colleges would automatically offer me scholarships." Twanie paused again as her eyes started watering.

"But, Auntie," she said continuing, "when I got to orientation, there was no mention of advanced placement or the possibility of me getting in. They had me signed up for some of the same courses I had already taken. Wasting time retaking basic stuff pretty much disqualifies me for AP level courses. I could see it if I had failed the courses the first time, but I aced them all."

"What did Margie say? Did she talk with those fools . . . make them understand that you're the damned poster girl for RTAG?"

"Momma did call the school. They made it clear that my doing good in RTAG only got me through their doors. Turns out that the people at the great and wonderful George Washington High don't have a lot of confidence that kids like me can cut it, no matter how good I did in RTAG, or how many A's I got. That's not what they told Momma. But it's what they meant."

"What did they say?"

"They said that it's for my benefit and it's best for me to start out slow."

"Sorry, baby."

"Yeah, me too, Auntie. It's just so unfair . . ."

"Those people are damn idiots," Dee said, with disgust.

Twanie exhaled, happy that her aunt, not only understood, but was as upset as she was.

"Sweetie," Dee said, with a quiet fire building, that Twanie had come to recognize, "no matter what, you can't let any of those bastards get to you or make you feel less than you are. You hear me?"

Twanie replied, "Yes, ma'am."

"And, if any of them mess with you, you give your old aunt a call. If I can't fix it . . . Well, I know some people . . ."

This time Twanie burst out laughing, because she knew her aunt was only half joking. Again, she said, "Yes, ma'am." This time with enthusiasm.

CHAPTER 3

TWANIE HAD READ the books and watched the movies. She knew the fate of the teen misfit who invaded the domain of privileged insiders. She was the misfit, undeniably the outsider. There was definitely no likelihood of blending in. The best she could hope for was invisibility. And that was her plan. She prepared ahead of time to ensure that nothing about her stood out or drew undue attention to herself, especially on her first day at George Washington High School.

The night before, she set the clock to wake her an hour early. She put the few things she knew she'd need in her new backpack—notebooks, pens, pencils, and calculator. Her stepfather, in an uncharacteristically accommodating mood, agreed to drive her to her Broad Street transfer point, so she could arrive a few minutes early. And her first day outfit was carefully considered and laid out.

Coming up with the right look, took several days and multiple iterations. The outfit couldn't be too conservative—she didn't want to advertise to the world that she was totally square. Nor could it be too flashy—the point was to draw attention away from herself. And, heaven forbid she chose something which appeared remotely ghetto—that would simply be out and out social suicide.

She finally selected a scoop necked, cap-sleeved, cotton polyester shirt, with a patchwork pattern of olive, black, and creme. She paired that with her pleated, straight-legged, olive chino pants, and an olive belt. To complete the outfit, she accessorized it with large black hooped earrings, along with the delicate black pearl teardrop necklace her aunt gave her. Admittedly, everything, but the necklace, was inexpensive. She couldn't do anything about that. But, by teen standards, the outfit was neat and stylishly understated.

Monday morning, her first day, as the bus crossed into Richmond Heights, Twanie felt a knot in her belly. She had to admit, she was impressed. The houses were big. And so, she assumed, were the vehicles, though she couldn't know for sure, since they were all hidden inside multicar garages.

The moment she stepped off the bus, she couldn't help thinking that this must be what Dorothy felt like when she landed in Oz—confused, far from home, and out of place. Remembering what her aunt told her, she rubbed her little pearl—just in case—and headed towards the front door with her head up. As expected, the kids milling around made special note of the girl stepping off the bus. Really, who, in that part of town, takes public transportation? Twanie smiled to herself, quietly taking in their reactions, as it hit her schoolmates that the bus rider had to be a student. After all, she was heading towards the entrance and was too young to be the help. Plus, the backpack was a sure giveaway.

I guess I won't be asked to join Buffy and Barbie for lunch, she thought amused.

Happily, the first part of he day was event free. Then, after third period, she stopped at her locker to put away the books she'd been assigned that morning. That was when she discovered her new combination did not work. Twanie had her first mini panic attack for the day. She was positive of the combination. It was the first two numbers of her birthday, followed by the first two numbers of her mother's. She'd carefully keyed it in earlier but had neglected to verify it at the time. Now, all she could think to do was to try, wait, and try again. What else could she do? She only had a few minutes until her next class.

"Need some help?"

Startled, Twanie turned towards the source of the deep voice and bumped into the chest of the *Incredible Hulk*—only a dark brown dishy version. He was over six feet tall, weighing more than two hundred pounds, with beautiful smooth dark skin, a gentle smile, and dimples so deep she could get lost in them. She remembered seeing him earlier with a group of equally huge guys—probably all football players. What had struck her then was that he was the only one who bothered to smile in her direction.

"Honestly, I don't know why it doesn't work," she said. "This morning, I set it exactly how they told me at orientation. Only, now it doesn't work."

"Let me try," he said, as he gently pushed pass her.

Before she could find a polite way to refuse to give him her code, the lock had released.

"I don't believe it. How did you do that?"

"I used the default combination."

"But I reset it."

"Happens sometimes. I'm Russell Elyn, by the way. Some people call me Big Russell, but not to my face," he laughed.

She looked up at the gentle giant. And though he said it facetiously, she understood why no one would ever say anything to Russell Elyn he didn't like. The thought made her smile, which is what she assumed he intended.

"I'm Antoinette Brooks, but everybody calls me Twanie."

"Hi Twanie Brooks. Try setting it again. This time, after entering the code, make sure you release the top of the lock, turn it all the way to the right, and then push it down into the bottom half."

She did as he instructed, while carefully blocking Russell from seeing the new code she entered. She felt guilty, but she didn't know him, even if he was cute. This time she checked, and her new combination worked.

"Thank you, so much. I would've been here all day."

"No problem," he said, displaying that disarming smile again, as he continued pass her. "See you around, Twanie Brooks."

* * *

If meeting Russell Elyn was the one good thing that happened on Twanie's first day, he was the gift that kept on giving. She'd see the popular sophomore surrounded by friends and his teammates—as she'd suspected, they were all on the football team. He always had a wave, a wink, or a smile for her. Sometimes, he'd stop to tease or compliment her. He even introduced Twanie to his girlfriend, Julie—a cheerleader of course—who, if no one else was around, would also smile or speak. Neither of the two could possibly have known how much she looked forward to those random acts of civility, as she traveled the hallways.

Truth be told, she probably would never have had nerve enough to go out for the Washington cheering squad if it hadn't been for Russell.

It was towards the end of April and Twanie was happily counting down the remaining hours of freshman year. It was at the end of the day. She had been grumbling ever since third period, after sitting through fifty-minutes of Mr. Cox's excruciatingly boring Algebra-1 class—a class, in a fair world, she would have been exempted from taking.

She assumed that Mr. Cox probably had good credentials to have landed the job at Washington. His problem was that he was young, inexperienced, and lacked the confidence required to stand in front of a room of teenagers. Because he was always nervous, he'd make mistakes. Sometimes, after minutes into a solution or explanation, he'd change his mind, causing him to erase an entire board and start over. That made taking notes almost impossible. Twanie took them anyhow, to stay awake.

Not for the first time, she was tempted to skip all the remaining algebra classes and only show up on test day. Life would be so cool if she could get away with it. But, even if she aced every assignment and every last test, she'd get in trouble and probably be suspended or kicked out. That would get her out of Washington. But that wasn't how she wanted to exit.

She was in the middle of grumbling about the unfairness of it all, when the notice for cheering squad tryouts caught her eye. She'd passed it several times before, but this time she stopped. She wasn't sure why. Maybe it was boredom, general frustration, Mr. Cox, or a combination of all three.

Her thoughts went back to Debbie and Neasha, and her mother making her drop out of competition for the Banneker squad. Twanie wondered what would've happened if she'd continued to practice with her Delaney sisters. Did she ever really have a chance to make the squad? Would her grades have suffered as much as her mother had feared? Would she have been better off if they had? A couple of B's instead of A's, and she never would've been a candidate for Washington. Now that she was there, with little to challenge her or to look forward to, she wondered if this was her chance for a do-over.

"So, you want to be a cheerleader, huh?" Russell asked, from behind her.

"Just looking at the notice," Twanie said, turning to look up at him, forever amazed at how stealthy Russell could be for someone his size.

"Oh, really? From over there," he said pointing to where his friends were hanging around, "I was afraid you were in a trance or your sneakers had gotten stuck to the tiles."

"Ha, ha," she said, rolling her eyes. "You're hilarious. No, I'm not stuck. Guess I'm just a slow reader."

"I doubt that seriously. If you're curious, you should go ahead and try out. I think you'd probably be kinda cute in one of those orange and blue cheerleader outfits. And, I can definitely see you doing those flips and waving pompoms," he said as waved his arms and used the paper he had in his hands like pompoms.

"Wow, maybe you should try out," she laughed. "Actually, I used to be able to do a decent cartwheel. But the last time I tried, I had my four-year-old twin cousins, Jacob and Jason, rolling on the floor laughing."

Russell chuckled. "Jacob and Jason aside, at least you know what a cartwheel is. That alone should make you standout on that squad. Besides, you can always signup for the cheer clinic they have for the girls with less experience. That's one way to find out if the squad is for you."

"How come you know so much about the cheering squad?" she teased.

"Hey, you forget. You're looking at Russell Elyn, big-time fullback for the varsity team. Nothing gets pass me," he said. "Plus, I can read. It's written right there at the bottom."

Twanie laughed, embarrassed that she'd been staring at the flyer and had somehow missed the part most relevant to her.

"So, are you gonna do it?" Russell asked.

"I don't really know . . ."

He softened his voice, as he said earnestly, "Why not just give it a chance? Something to do, right?"

"Maybe . . . I don't know . . ."

"Look, the flyer also says that all you need is enthusiasm and school spirit. You have a lot more than that to offer. Push comes to shove, you're smart enough to fake the enthusiasm and school spirit stuff." When she still seemed hesitant, he added, "Ahh, go ahead and do it. Why not? What've you got to lose?"

"Nothing, I guess, but maybe my dignity. It'll be on you if I make a fool of myself or get hurt. Or both."

"You'll be fine," he laughed.

Twanie's smile grew as she watched Russell saunter off like agent double-o-seven exiting after successfully completing his mission.

He's right, she thought, *I really have nothing to lose. And, it would give me something to do.* Then her smile faded, as the implications of her decision hit her. *Now, all I have to do is convince Momma and the deacon.*

Her mother had changed a lot since marrying Raymond Samuels. She and Twanie weren't as close as they once were. Nor was Margie as independent as before. Nearly all important decisions were left to the deacon, which meant that he was the one Twanie had to appeal to.

Easier said than done, since she and the deacon had no real connection. As far as Twanie could tell, his opinion of her was not much higher than that of her George Washington schoolmates. Because she always had the feeling he was waiting for a signal of her imminent fall—some spiritual or social transgression—any conversation with him tended to be brief and very uncomfortable. They were slightly less awkward when Margie was there as a buffer. Which is probably why she ended up blurting out her announcement that evening at dinner.

As usual, it had been a quiet meal, with the deacon saying grace and then focusing on the food in front of him. When it looked like he was about to push the plate away, Twanie was out of time. She had to speak up. Looking from one to the other, she said, "I'm thinking about trying out for the school cheering squad."

Under no stretch of her imagination did Twanie anticipate that the deacon would seem almost pleased with the idea. When he said, "Sounds like a good way to get involved and get to know some of the other girls," Twanie almost choked on her pork chop. She was so happy and so stunned that she came close to hugging the man for the first time since she'd known him.

* * *

"Ivette doesn't like me," Twanie whispered to Julie as everyone filed out of the gym at the end of the first day of the cheer clinic. She was confident that the little group of four she'd been assigned to had done well. But, throughout the evening, she'd noticed the squad captain, Ivette, glaring at her.

"Don't pay her any mind," Julie said, hoping her fake smile was hiding her certainty that Twanie's instincts were on point. Ivette probably did not like the girl. Everybody had seen Ivette's appalled reaction when she spotted Twanie, standing in the group of hopefuls, decked out in her Benjamin Banneker tee and gym shorts.

What was the girl thinking?

Even if Julie had known ahead of time what Twanie intended to wear, she probably wouldn't have had nerve enough to discourage her. Besides, she had no idea what other options Twanie had, and Julie didn't have anything to offer from her closet that would fit the tiny, busty girl.

"By the way, I thought you did fine," Julie said, in an effort to redirect the conversation. "You are coming back tomorrow, right?"

"Yes, I'll be here," Twanie replied.

Julie waved, as Twanie went off to call her stepfather to pick her up. No matter how unfair it was, Julie had been hoping Twanie would say she wasn't returning, because everybody knew it would only get worse. What Twanie and the other hopefuls weren't told was that the clinic was not merely there to help them. It was an opportunity for the experienced squad members to weed out the truly spastic and—as in Twanie's case—the undesirables.

Of the potential candidates, Twanie may not have been the most skilled or experienced, but she was eager and determined. The leaders of the clinic were impressed that she obviously practiced following each session and returned improved. After the first couple of nights, Ivette and her two friends, Andy and Michelle, became panicked that Twanie might make it through the clinic and onto the tryouts. Instead of providing any encouragement, they went out of their way to belittle or make her look bad. Whenever Twanie made a mistake or was slow picking up a stunt or routine, the trio would roll their eyes, with knowing looks that proclaimed, "See, we knew it. She's not qualified to be on this squad." They weren't called *the-terrible-three* for nothing.

Luckily for Twanie, the-terrible-three were not the final say. Several other squad members saw what was happening and were impressed with the spunky girl and her defiance of the-terrible-three. They noted how, whenever the term *ghetto-girl*—the awful nickname Ivette had come up with—was used within earshot of Twanie, she didn't cringe. She not only ignored it but seemed galvanized by the insult. That attitude made her somewhat of a hero to them. They were thrilled when she moved on and became one of the final candidates. Because, as determined as the trio were to keep her off, they wanted Twanie as part of the squad.

* * *

Throughout the cheer clinic and tryouts, Twanie showed up every night, telling herself that it was only to prove to Ivette, Michelle, and Andy, that they couldn't get the best of her. But, at night, alone in her room, she had to admit that she loved cheering, and she wished—in some alternate reality without the-terrible-three—that she had a chance to make the squad.

On the last tryout day, after doing her best to prove she'd mastered the jumps and the required cheer routine, Twanie packed up her stuff and left. She didn't bother returning to check the selection list. It was only after Russell and Julie caught her in the hallway to congratulate her, that she realized she'd made the squad. It was like winning the lottery, so miraculously unexpected that it took several days for her to come down from the excitement.

A few months later, as she rushed to the gym for an emergency squad meeting called by Mrs. Davis, Twanie still felt pretty much the same. As she approached the gym, Iris, one of the more senior members of the squad, stopped her.

"Twanie, before you go in, can we talk a minute? It's sort of important."

"Umm, sure," she replied, curious. She didn't want to be late, but Iris was not someone who generally asked to chat with her. As a matter of fact, it had never happened before. "What's up?"

"You know about Ivette, right?"

"I heard she got hurt. Is that why Mrs. Davis called the meeting?"

"Kind of. But I wanted to run something pass you first."

"Pass me? What?"

"You're right. Ivette did get hurt. All I know is she had a bad fall while she and some others were working on new routines. It was bad enough that she was rushed to the hospital and had to be admitted."

"Oh. Is she okay?"

"She has a torn ACL. She'll probably be back at school soon, but she won't be able to return to the squad this year. And since Ivette's a senior, that's the end of her cheering here at Washington."

"Man, that's awful. I'll admit that Ivette's not one of my favorite people. But I know how important the squad is to her. And I do feel bad for her."

"Yes, it's a shame. But what I want to talk about is . . ." Iris hesitated, and nervously cleared her throat. "Well, with Ivette unable to come back, the thing is, we need a new captain. And, believe it or not, Michelle and Andy are already fighting over which one of them will take over."

"Why am I not surprised?" Twanie said, not happy with the prospect of either one becoming captain. "If you want my support, you've got it."

"No, no, no . . . I don't want to be captain," Iris said, emphatically.

"So, you're campaigning for someone else?"

"Actually," Iris said, smiling slyly, "nobody wants to run against them."

"Okay?" Twanie said. She had no idea where this was heading.

"Well," Iris said, with a strained smile, "some of us have been talking, and we thought you should run."

"You're kidding, right?"

"No, I'm serious. Nobody else is willing to chance losing against either Andy or Michelle. Everybody knows that there would be hell to pay if they ran and lost against the remaining terrible-two."

"Still, I don't get it. Why would anybody want me to run?" Twanie asked.

"You're the only one not intimidated by them. And the only one neither Andy or Michelle wants to mess with. They don't get you. They saw how, no matter how bitchy they acted at the tryouts, you ignored them, kept coming back, and kept trying. Then, once you made the squad, they got scared if they pushed you too hard, you'd go all ghetto violent on them, or even worse, you'd get your gangbanger ghetto friends to do them in."

It was so ridiculous that Twanie burst out laughing. Maybe she should've been insulted, but she understood the source.

"So," Iris continued, "you're the only one with nothing to lose. Afterall, they already hate you, but are too afraid to mess with you."

"Wow," Twanie said. "Look, wouldn't you rather have someone with more to offer than being hated by Michelle and Andy? Isn't there a bylaw somewhere against a newbie with almost no experience becoming captain?"

"No," Iris answered. "I talked with Mrs. Davis and she doesn't have a problem with it. She says that it's our squad and our decision."

"You guys are a trip. You already talked to Mrs. Davis about me?"

"Yes, because you're the best chance we have."

Twanie knew that the girls were right to be concerned. But a better solution would be for them to stand up to Michelle and Andy, and not put her on the spot. She said as much to Iris.

"Okay. Maybe we're all cowards," Iris conceded. "But, bottom-line, if nobody runs against them, one of them will become captain. It really doesn't matter which one it is, they will rule together. When she was captain, Ivette managed to keep them in check. But without her . . . Just thinking about it, half the girls are threatening to quit the squad."

"Man," Twanie said. "What happens if I say no? Or, if I quit instead? You guys are willing to let one of two people guaranteed to be bad for the squad become captain by default?"

When Iris didn't respond, Twanie shook her head. Stuck between a rock and a hard place, she made her decision. "This is bull," she said, totally bummed out by the situation and the girls on her squad. "But, even if I have no chance of winning, at least I'll have someone with some guts to vote for."

Iris again chose not to respond. She couldn't. She stayed where she was until Twanie was seated in the gym, before following her in.

Probably, if either Andy or Michelle had put her ego aside and backed the other one, the reluctant Antoinette Brooks would not have had a chance. Because they chose not to, when the votes were counted, Twanie became the new captain of the squad.

There were no high fives or victory party. Twanie received no special anything for her sacrifice. And, as expected, there were the predictable grumbles and pouts from the-terrible-two and their supporters. When that didn't seem sufficient, someone, probably one of the protestors, shifted to playing anonymous locker pranks on Twanie.

Even though she had her suspicions, Twanie could not accuse anyone of being responsible for the antics. And, while Iris and company had promised to have her back, she had no confidence that they'd help her identify or confront the culprits. So, for the sake of the squad, she endured the pranks and tried her best to ignore them.

CHAPTER 4

TWANIE WONDERED what her year would've been like if she'd have just said no to Iris and crew. She hadn't owed them anything, and like Iris said, at the time, Michelle and Andy weren't a problem for her. Meanwhile, they got what they wanted, and she was left the brunt of some type of weird revenge thing that was working on her last nerve.

"Where is that stupid bus?" she asked, checking her watch, for the umpteenth time—as if that would make it come quicker.

Twanie stretched her neck hoping to catch sight of the bus approaching, magically pulled to her by will alone. Nothing. No bus for miles. She tried not to sigh. She had found herself doing that too much lately and it didn't help. Neither did constantly looking at her watch, which she was doing once again, when she heard something. It sounded like someone calling her name.

That's when she saw it. An idiot in a black Toyota Celica had just made a crazy, and extremely dangerous U-turn. She couldn't believe that he was pulling up in front of her. The action was so reckless, it startled her and made her jump back. "Oh, my goodness," she shrieked.

She did not immediately recognize the car, but Twanie recognized the driver. It was Shaun Lacey, the hunky quarterback of the varsity football team. This close and in the sun light, the eyes that she had always thought were black, were closer to a dreamy black coffee color. With those eyes, that curly black hair, and that barely brown skin, all part of a six-foot muscular package, she saw why the girls at school swooned as he passed by.

Then again, she had to give Shaun a few extra points for taste. He was driving her car. She didn't really know much about cars, but she did know the Celica. It was on her list of cars she would buy when she made her first million. It was sleek with enough power to be considered a sports car, but small and sexy enough to be acceptable for females to style in.

However, on a day like that one, the biggest attraction was not Shaun or his car. It was the air conditioning she knew was probably blasting along with the loud rap music coming through the speakers of his radio.

"Hey, Twanie, you need a lift?"

Still not registering what was happening—not sure if he was talking to her and not some other *Twanie* somewhere outside her field of vision— Twanie looked around. Her confusion only made Shaun laugh that deep throated laugh he reserved for his worthy friends.

"Come on, Twanie, it's gotta be a million degrees out there. Get in the car before you melt," he said, as he leaned over to open the passenger door.

He was right about the heat. And the bus was nowhere in sight. Not sure what else to say, she muttered, "Hi Shaun. Uh, thanks," and slid in.

The soft leather seats and the wonderfully cold air from the vent had her impressed both with the car and him for owning such a marvelous thing. Not sure of the official protocol, she again said, "Thanks, Shaun."

After that, Twanie was quiet the entire ride, mostly nodding and responding to direct questions. Shaun did not seem to notice. He was one of those people who could fill the silence, without it seeming like much of an effort. As a matter of fact, during the ride he seemed to know an awful lot about her. Of course, being on the football team, he would know that she was a cheerleader. But he also knew that she studied a lot, made good grades, and was pals with Russell and Julie. She wasn't sure whether to be flattered or freaked out.

Then, in a lot less time than it would've taken her to ride and transfer between two buses, he was pulling up in front of her door. As he stopped the car, it occurred to Twanie that she didn't remember telling Shaun her address. But she must've. How else could he have driven directly there? It was not as if they were neighbors.

"Twanie," Shaun called out, when she had walked a couple of feet from the car, "maybe some time we can hang out together after school."

Too stunned to say anything else, she replied, "Okay," and nearly tripped as she ran the short distance to her door.

She couldn't wait to tell her beloved confidant, her aunt, about her ride home. Twanie spilled it all out in a rush. She told Dee about the heat, about Shaun offering her a ride, and how weird she thought it was that he knew so much about her. Once she finished, she waited expectantly, confused by the silence on the other end of the telephone line.

When Dee finally spoke, it was in a voice Twanie barely recognized. "Antoinette Catrina Brooks," she said, "you know I'm always behind you, supporting you. But this time I'm telling you, don't go there."

"Don't go where? I don't understand."

Her aunt again took her time, while choosing her words before continuing, "Twanie, you are a smart and beautiful young girl with loads of potential. But, honestly, you are three shades on the wrong side of the color line for the Lacey clan. For years, they have done everything short of intermarrying to keep their coloring as light as possible."

"Okay. His family is color struck. Lots of people were, back in the day," Twanie said.

"You don't understand what I'm saying, little girl," Dee said, surprising Twanie with her exasperated tone. "That Shaun boy and his family will never take serious someone as brown as you are. His father made the family proud by marrying a white woman, who, by the way, had no idea that Nathan Lacey was not perpetually tanned. To his credit, Nathan didn't lie. His family never considered themselves colored. She didn't take the surprise well, especially when Shaun was born slightly dark around his ears. The ears lightened up later, but it was all too much. Allison—I think her name was Allison—packed up and ran away with him, home to her family in Boston.

"But her family was definitely not thrilled with the little half black infant. She finally decided to give the baby to Nathan and his family to raise. Rumor has it that Shaun seldom saw her after that. She died when he was about seven. I hear it was suicide from the unbearable disgrace."

"Oh, no. Poor Shaun."

"From what I hear, the Shaun boy has his issues. But the main thing is, he will never get you through the front door."

Twanie laughed, "Dang, Aunt Dee, I didn't say I was planning to marry the guy. I barely know him. I just said that it was hot, and he gave me a ride."

Again, her aunt took her time before saying, "Just be careful, sweetie, and keep what I said in mine. Love you. Bye." With that, she hung up.

Dee needn't have worried. It was true that Twanie was flattered that Shaun Lacey even knew she was alive and, though it was a bit creepy, had gone through the trouble to find out so much about her. But what she hadn't gotten a chance to tell her aunt was that, flattered or not, she had no intention of giving her heart or anything else to Shaun Lacey. Everybody knew that he and Laila Watkins were together, and from what she could tell, they were probably matched at birth.

Like Shaun, Laila was a shining star who seemed slated for great things. She was tall, thin, smart, and popular. Plus, she was high-yellow, exactly the kind of girl Shaun's family would approve of. She wasn't particularly model beautiful, but she had the confidence of someone who was. She was also in almost every academic club imaginable, and she was on the student court. She had her future planned. First, she'd follow in the footsteps of her father and grandfather and become a lawyer. Then, she would become a judge. Given her ambition and drive, who knows where she'd end-up.

The more she thought about it, the more Twanie chuckled at how upset her aunt had appeared. Of all people, Dee should've known her better. Twanie wasn't naïve enough to think that this was some sappy movie where the smart, nerdy, socially awkward, but beautiful outcast—that would be Twanie—with wit and charm, would win the handsome, rich, and popular main character—that would be Shaun—away from his privileged, popular, but shallow girlfriend—that would be Laila.

"Paa-lease . . . be real, Auntie," Twanie said, as she burst out laughing.

CHAPTER 5

As Twanie walked through the hallways, the next day, she had no idea what she'd do if she saw Shaun. The "hang out after school" comment was random, and she wished he hadn't said it. It made things more awkward for her. And, once in the building, she dreaded the idea of running into him.

She needn't have worried. That day and for the remainder of the school term, when they did cross paths, Shaun barely acknowledged her presence. The only difference was, instead of the dismissive looks he had once given her, he'd honor her with a little nod and his eyes lingered an extra moment, as he graced her with, what she'd come to think of as, *the Shaun smile.*

While she was able to get over and move on from the awkward ride home with Shaun, there remained an unanticipated side-affect. Twanie had to make a major adjustment to her relationship with Dee. She realized that, as a teenager, she could no longer go to her middle-aged aunt with everything that went on in her life. That's what girlfriends were for.

She'd lost touch with Debbie and Neasha, and the closest thing she had to a girlfriend was Julie Prescott. Because she understood the distinction between them being true friends and Julie being friendly, Twanie tried not to push the boundaries of the relationship. But there came a time, in the fall of her junior year, when she desperately needed someone to help her with, and hopefully explain, the increasingly weird behavior of Shaun Lacey. In that situation, she only had Julie to go to.

Shaun was suddenly popping-up everywhere, even in her sanctuary from all things George Washington, the Burger Rack restaurant, in the small mall down from the school. At first, she was flattered by the attention and found Shaun quite charming. Closeup he seemed different from the entitled jock she had previously pictured. He was smart, funny, and had a smile to die for. He liked to talk, mostly about himself, and he liked that she was willing to listen. He opened up to her about things his shallow friends probably could never relate to. She was surprised and impressed how serious he was about his studies, and stunned that football was only a means to make his applications more appealing to top-flight schools, like Columbia University.

Even so, dealing with people like Shaun was unchartered territory for her. She was glad when she ran across Julie in the school library. She needed a second opinion to see if this was normal expected behavior.

"I have a question, it's about Shaun Lacey," she said, taking the seat directly across from Julie.

"What about him?" Julie said, grinning, as she put her papers aside.

"Not what you think," Twanie said, as she described Shaun's curious behavior, beginning with the ride home the previous spring.

Instead of seeing it as cause for concern, Julie found it romantic. "Like a movie," she exclaimed. "Shaun falls for you and does everything he can to win your heart. He then dumps stuck-up Laila. And through him, everybody gets to know the real you and forget all about that ghetto-girl stuff."

Twanie had to smile at the way Julie's mind worked. Real life didn't work that way. Even if it did, she did not need or want a bunch of phony friends, especially not ones who'd only put up with her because of Shaun Lacey.

"Honestly, if it was anybody but Shaun, like Jake with the thick glasses and all the acne, wouldn't you think it a bit weird, creepy even?"

"Yes, maybe. Now that you put it that way," Julie admitted.

"With that in mind, what would you say for me to do?"

"Wait, I guess. Either he'll get bored or ask you out."

Once Julie said it, Twanie didn't really know which outcome she preferred. She sort of liked the attention—maybe she'd like a little less of it— and wasn't sure what she'd do if Shaun Lacey asked her out.

The answer came on a stormy Monday, in February. School had closed early, and Twanie was waiting in the Burger Rack for the deacon to pick her up. She was engrossed in her World History assignment, when a voice she'd come to recognize, said, "Thought I'd find you here."

"Ugg," she said, embarrassed, as a glob of the special sauce, from the giant burger, dripped down her hand. "You were looking for me? Why?"

"I was wondering if you wanted to go to Chico's birthday party, this weekend," he said, handing her a napkin.

"Shaun, you want *me* to hang out with you, Laila, and your friends?"

"Not exactly. Me and Laila broke up," he said, shrugging his shoulders and looking down at his hands. "So, I thought I'd go with a friend."

"Umm, Shaun, I can't."

"I know it's short notice, but just think about it. It should be fun."

"It's not that. My parents will never agree to me going," she admitted.

"I get it. But, in case you find out that you can go, here is my number," he said, scribbling on a napkin. "Let me know. Okay?"

"Okay," she said, but she already knew the likelihood of getting permission was zero. It was the same weekend that her parents would be out of town on a church retreat. Without the deacon around to drive them, neither parent would agree to her going out with Shaun.

Since this was a true teen dilemma, she took it to Julie. And once Twanie described it, Julie squealed, "Shaun asked you out? You've got to go!"

"I don't know. With Laila on one side and my parents on the other . . . Neither of them will care that I'd be just going with Shaun as a buddy."

"Who cares about Laila or what she thinks? You say your parents will call to check on you, early in the evening, right?"

"Yes."

"So, they don't have to know. When they call, you tell them the truth, that everything is fine. Then you go and have fun at the party with Shaun."

Twanie was well aware that a lie of omission was still a lie. But this was her first party invite since starting at Washington. And, truth-be-told, she probably only discussed it with Julie to be talked into going.

* * *

The next day, right before fifth period, Twanie was surprised that Russell was waiting by her locker. "Hey girl," he said, grinning down at her. "I know you have study hall, but can we go in Mr. Tyson's lab room a minute to talk?"

Only for Russell, would she risk being late, even for study hall.

"What's up?" she said, as they both automatically walked to the rear of the room to avoid getting in trouble for the unscheduled break.

He hesitated before speaking, which was very unlike Russell. With no clue as to what was on his mind, she waited.

"I had promised myself that I would not mess in someone else's business," he finally said. "But Julie has been on this insane mission to get you and Lacey together. She means well. But I know Lacey better than she does. I also know that you're good people, and you deserve better."

Twanie sat dumb founded. Never in a million years had she expected this conversation. "Better than what, Russell? What are you trying to tell me?"

"Look, Laila's put up with a lot from Lacey. Last week, he went too far. He was messing around in one of the empty classrooms with the new transfer, Wendy," he said blushing. "They forgot to lock the door and . . . umm . . . he got caught with his pants down . . . You know what I mean?"

Twanie did. She nodded.

"I can't believe that he's already moving on you. You know that it's not just Wendy. Girls are always all over Lacey. Before, when he acted the fool, Laila forgave him. This time the whole school was laughing, not just at him, but at her too. I guess it was finally too much for Laila," he paused to let out a brief sigh, before continuing.

"You probably know for yourself, that Julie doesn't exactly see the real world. She sees things the way she wants them to be. What happens to you if Lacey and Laila get back together? And even if they don't, you deserve better than what he's put her through. I can't tell you what to do, but you need to know what's up."

"Thanks, Russell," she said, touched. "You almost sound like my aunt. But I'm not looking to be Shaun's girl or coming between him and Laila."

Russell stood up and gave Twanie's shoulder a squeeze. With nothing more to say, he left.

CHAPTER 6

TWANIE HAD ADOPTED the corner spot against the wall shortly after arriving at Chico's party. It hadn't taken long for her to conclude that, if this is the typical party for this crowd, then it and them were definitely not for her.

The music was cranked up way too loud and was hurting her ears. The raunchy lyrics were offensive and giving her a headache. She could hardly believe that the big thrill for these idiots was to do lots of drinking, get high, and pretend that they were part of the same ghetto culture that they, at school, looked down on her for. It all seemed really stupid to her. She didn't like the taste of beer or hard liquor. And she absolutely was not going to try whatever else they were passing around that was making the fools act stupid and dopey.

Shaun had walked her in and almost immediately abandoned her. He'd been huddled with two guys from the team, Ronnie and Mike, for a long time. Whatever the conversation, she sensed that they were up to no good.

Why in the world am I here? I've had enough of this party, these phonies, and Shaun.

Somehow verbalizing it, even just in her head, made her feel a lot better. Too bad there were no nearby bus stops, or she'd have left a long time ago. She was about to walk over to ask Shaun to take her home—he could always come back—when he looked in her direction. His expression put a chill straight through her. Then, in a blink, the look was gone.

The Shaun smile returned, as he strolled over to her. He took her hand, still smiling, and said, "Twanie, if I stay here another minute, I'll probably be too wasted to drive. Let's go."

She couldn't believe the relief. It was so physical that, once in the car, she felt her whole body relax. From the puzzled look on his face, at first she thought Shaun had sensed it, but he had something else on his mind.

"Twanie, I have to make a stop. My cousin, Isaac, had me pick up his stuff from the cleaner's. I have to drop it off at his place."

For the first time, she noticed the dry cleaner's bags in the back seat. *How did I miss those?* She wondered, as she shrugged agreement. She slid down in her seat, almost giddy that she'd soon be home and the night would be over.

Shaun drove about ten minutes, before stopping in front of a worn brick apartment building. He got out, grabbed a bunch of the bags, and walked around to her side. "Twanie," he said, opening her door, "I hate to ask. But it would be quicker if you helped me take this stuff upstairs."

Twanie nodded agreement. She didn't really want to be left alone in the car on the dark unfamiliar street. Plus, she would happily carry a couple of bags, if it hastened bringing the night to an end.

Handing her the remaining bags from the back seat, Shaun led her to a side stairway entrance.

As they climbed the first flight, Twanie could not contain her curiosity about a Lacey cousin that lived in a place like that. "So, who exactly is this Isaac? Are you and he close, or something?"

Instead of answering, Shaun stopped climbing, opened the door to the second floor, and stood against it so she could go through. He then led the way as they walked down a dingy hallway of apartments. When he arrived at number 214, he took out a set of keys and opened the door. He held the door to allow her to go in first.

As she entered, she noticed a bedroom that was just large enough to hold an unmade bed. Straight ahead, she could see a bathroom which she would not use on a bet. Shaun closed the door, setting a deadbolt and chain, then walked into the bedroom to put the clothes in the closet. Twanie followed him thinking that setting the security locks was a bit overkill, especially since they wouldn't be there that long.

After hanging the final bag, he covered his mouth, ran into the bathroom, and shut the door. Twanie heard what she thought might be retching noises.

"Shaun are you okay?" she asked.

Shaun, sounding weak, said "Damn, Twanie. I'm sick as a dog." He came out wiping his mouth. "I just need to lie down for a minute. Please Twanie, please help me, please."

She took his arm and helped him across the small room. "I just need to lie down," he said, as he dropped down on the bed.

Twanie took a step back, unsure what to do. "Are you all right, Shaun?"

Suddenly, without warning, Shaun reached out, pulled her down, and started kissing her. She wrestled to break out of his grip, but he was too strong for her. "Stop, Shaun. Please stop," she begged.

Once she managed to break away, she realized that running out of the apartment was impossible. There was not enough time to get through all the locks Shaun had patiently engaged as they entered. She ran into the bathroom and locked the door. Frightened and trying to catch her breath, she stood staring at the doorknob, waiting for Shaun to try it.

She had no idea what to do next. Her only hope was for Shaun to come to his senses, calm down, and take her home. She was still staring at the door when she heard a sound on the opposite side. She froze. In her panic, she hadn't noticed that there was another door. And Shaun was at it. Before she could cross the distance, Shaun had the door opened. It was like one of those old horror movies, worse than any nightmare she could've imagined.

While she'd been staring at the wrong door, Shaun had gotten a knife. It looked like the sharpest and most frightening thing she had ever seen.

"Twanie," he said, his voice menacing and his stare icy, "Let's get one thing straight. I *will* have sex with you, here tonight. Then we can leave."

He grabbed her arm and pushed her back against the wall. "It's either right here, right now, or in the bedroom. Your choice."

Twanie was too scared to cry. If he'd gone to the trouble of arming himself, she knew there was no reasoning with Shaun. She involuntarily released a moan, a sound so desolate that she did not recognize it as coming from her.

"Okay, here then," Shaun announced as he moved closer. He used his left hand to grab her around her neck. With his hand still around her throat, he said "I want you to pull your panties down. You will not scream. You will not fight me. We *will* have sex."

Hoping that any minute Shaun would come to his senses, Twanie reached down to do as he commanded.

Shaun watched impatiently waiting, his breathing getting heavier. The knife dropped as he grabbed her left breast and squeezed hard.

Twanie knew that even without the knife, there was no way of overpowering Shaun and getting away. The pain from him squeezing her breast was excruciating. His breathing was getting heavier and his maleness, against her, getting harder. She started silently crying. She was alone, in a part of town she was not familiar with, with a crazy person she did not know. No one knew where she was. She could die. No one would be the wiser.

She did not register much from that point. She did not even remember leaving the toilet and reentering the bedroom. She scarcely remembered Shaun mounting her, spreading her legs and penetrating her. All she knew was that it hurt. Thankfully, it was fast. And then it was over.

"Shit, Twanie, I never thought that you were a virgin," he said, remarking about the blood on the bed. "I thought all this time, a girl like you with a body like that . . ."

There was nothing Twanie wanted to say, in response to the implied insult. She finally knew exactly how Shaun saw her, as the *ghetto girl*—not an equal to him and his friends.

Shaun rolled off the filthy bed, handed the end of one of the smelly sheets to her, and ordered, "Clean yourself. We have to get out of here."

Everything after that was a blur. She didn't remember putting her clothes on. She vaguely remembered getting back in the car. All she could think about was that she could've died there in that filthy place and no one would know. Her family did not even know about Shaun. The only people from school who'd care, Russell and Julie, weren't at the party.

Even if she told what happened, who would believe that the wonderful Shaun Lacey would ever do anything so horrific? They would rather believe that Twanie was lying or was at fault for leading him on.

When he finally pulled up in front of her house, Twanie opened the car door and swung her legs slowly around to exit. Shaun looked over at her and said, "Umm, I'll call you tomorrow." He closed the door and drove off.

Twanie walked the short distance to her house, not knowing what to do . . . how to feel. She looked down at her purse to get her keys and said a silent prayer, thankful that she at least was alive. There was no way she would ever talk with that animal again. She would go on with her life, finish school, and go to college. She had heard about something called *the morning after pill.* But it required a prescription. She was too young to get it on her own, and there was no way she could convince her mother to go with her to get a prescription. She'd heard someone mention douching to prevent pregnancy or disease. In her heart she knew it was nonsense, but she'd try anything. She made a mental note to stop by the drug store the next day and buy a douche kit. She couldn't take any chances. Who knows what awful diseases someone as crazy as Shaun would have? And, even as quick as it had been, she definitely did not want to get pregnant.

PART TWO

Momma Dearest
(1998-2005)

CHAPTER 7

I REMEMBER THE FIRST TIME I met my mother. I was six years old. My grandaunt, Auntie Dee—the only family I had known up to that point—and I were sitting on the front porch, swinging, talking, and sipping lemonade. Which was not unusual, because we often sat swinging on the porch—our favorite place to be, rain or shine. We would watch the neighbors as they walked by. They would stop, chat with Auntie Dee, and most of them would smile and say "hi" to me. Some of them would even chat with me.

It was on a Sunday. We were relaxing, killing time after having spent the morning in church. Auntie Dee's Sunday-go-to-meeting hat-of-the-day—the purple one, with the short brim and a big flower with ribbons on the side—was still sitting on the table next to us. I loved her hats.

Though I generally preferred pants or jeans, I was wearing the one church dress that I really liked. It was the color of bubblegum, had raised soft flowers—I loved the feel of the flowers—and there was a thick shiny band around the middle, which was a slightly darker color than the rest of the dress. I had kicked off my good shoes as soon as we got home and was wearing only my white socks.

It was early spring, right after Easter, and the first few fat blue flowers were on the big bush in the front yard. Auntie Dee was a wizard at flowers, no one could work magic with only a stem like Auntie could.

We were in the middle of a serious discussion about the last of the candy from my Easter basket, when a blue car pulled-up and parked in front of our house. The color struck me, because it was almost the same as the flowers on Auntie's bush in front of the porch.

Since Auntie Dee knew everybody, I was not surprised that the pretty lady, who got out of the car, started climbing the three steps leading up to the porch.

"Hello, Twanie," Auntie Dee said softly to the lady, as she stepped onto the porch.

"Hi, Aunt Dee," the strange lady responded.

Now things were getting interesting. Why was this Twanie lady calling *my* grandaunt, *Aunt Dee?* As far as I knew, Auntie Dee and I did not have any family.

Auntie Dee's head turned from the lady to me. "Tina," she said, "this is your mother. Say hello."

"Huh?"

How could that be? Sure, when I was little, Auntie Dee had told me, time after time, that my mother would come soon. But even little kids eventually give up.

The last time any mention had been made about my mother was two years prior, when I was about four. Auntie Dee and I were spending the day at the playground. One of the other kids asked me "Where is your mommy?"

"I don't know," I answered. "I don't think I have a mommy."

"Don't be silly," she said. "Everybody has a mommy."

On the way out of the park, I started crying. "Auntie Dee," I said. "Tracy says everybody has a mommy. Do I have one? Can you be my mommy?"

The question must have broken Auntie Dee's heart. True to form, her instinctive response was to comfort me with a big Auntie Dee squeeze, before replying.

"No, sweetie," she said gently, "I can't be your mommy. You know how special you are to me and I'll always love you. Your mommy loves you too. I'm sure she will be coming to be with you any day now."

Any-day-now stretched out to be two more years—until that beautiful spring Sunday, when the mysterious woman drove up in a blue car.

"You've gotten so big!" the lady said.

I stiffened as she bent down to hug me. It might've seemed like it was the most normal situation in the world to her, but it wasn't to me.

"I know you don't remember me," she said. "But I am your mother. And guess what? You're coming to live with me from now on."

"Is Auntie coming too?"

"No," Auntie Dee interjected. "I'm staying here."

"Then, I'm staying too. You can live with us, if you like," I said defiantly to the lady.

"Sweetheart," Auntie Dee said quietly, "you have to go with her. I'll always be right here if you need me."

The next thing I knew, all my clothes and my toys had been packed up in the blue car. I was fastened in the seat next to the Twanie lady, and we were driving away. My Auntie Dee was waving goodbye with the saddest smile I'd ever seen. I, on the other hand, was secured in the shotgun seat, angry, confused, and bawling.

If I'd known what I know now, I would've jumped out of the car, held on to my grandaunt, and not let go, because that was the last time I saw my dear Auntie Dee.

CHAPTER 8

HOW DO YOU UNBREAK someone's heart? From the moment the Twanie lady walked up on our porch, it seemed that little pieces of my dear Auntie Dee's heart were chipping away. I could sense it from the weighted way she stood as she picked up her fancy purple hat. The ease and light heartedness, that was there only a few minutes before, seemed to have disappeared in an instant. When she reached to grab my hand, she held it so tight that I cried out, "Ouch, Auntie!"

"Sorry, sweetheart," she apologized. "Let's go inside."

Once inside the hallway, Auntie Dee handed her hat to me and said, "Here, sweetie, take this upstairs and put it on my bed for me."

"But Auntie . . ." I whined.

"Go on now," she said, forcing a smile, all the while pushing me towards the stairs. "Don't forget to change your clothes into the stuff I have laid out for you in your room."

At six, I was old enough to know when I was being sent away to give the grown-ups privacy, a chance to talk. From the expression on Auntie Dee's face, there was no use trying to argue with her.

I rushed up the stairs, as fast as my little legs could take me, dashed to Auntie Dee's room and gently sat the hat on her bed—I knew better than to crush or cause to be crushed any part of Auntie Dee's hat. I flew to my room, pulled off the dress and slip—Auntie Dee never let me put on a dress without proper coverage underneath—and threw them on the bed.

I was exceptionally proud of myself. Surely, I had set a new world's record in clothes changing. That done, I hurried down to check out the action, but I still wasn't quick enough. By the time I returned, Auntie Dee and the lady were waiting quietly in the kitchen.

Since the familiar smell of coffee had hit me half-way down the stairs—Auntie Dee held most of her important conversations over coffee—I was expecting to see her at the table, but she was leaning against the refrigerator with her arms crossed in front of her. The Twanie lady was sitting at the kitchen table, her head down staring at the cup of coffee in front of her, with no apparent interest in drinking it. They both turned to watch as I crossed the threshold, neither saying a word.

The Twanie lady broke the silence. "Dusty," she said, "we're going on a long trip together, won't that be fun?"

I turned to Auntie Dee for clarification. The lady likewise looked at Auntie Dee, I guess for support. But there was none coming.

The look on Auntie Dee's face was so sad that I scowled at the Twanie lady, upset at her for making my Auntie Dee unhappy. I went over to give Auntie Dee a hug, the only thing I could think of to make her feel better.

She hugged me back, gently released herself from my grip, and said, "You two talk and get to know each other." Then, to the lady she said, "I'll go and get her things together."

I stared at the door until I heard Auntie Dee dragging herself up the stairs, each step slow and deliberate.

The lady pulled out the chair next to her and indicated that I should climb up. Not liking the idea of sitting close to anybody who hurt my Auntie Dee, I chose the chair on the opposite side of the table.

"Dusty, I know things are confusing right now," she began. "But the important thing is for you to understand that I'm your mother. From now on, I want you to call me *Momma*. I've come to take you home with me."

Still upset, I turned my gaze towards the doorway that Auntie Dee had left through. Personally, I was prepared to sit and wait indefinitely for her to return. She was the only one who could fix things, so that it all made sense.

"Dusty?" the woman, who I now was supposed to call *Momma*, said a little louder, to get my attention.

"Don't call me that," I snapped, tears now flowing. "My name is Tina."

Honestly, I'm not sure what my mother expected, after being MIA for so long. She probably had this fairy tale vision of her young daughter standing each night at the door, waiting for her return. Then, on the magical day of her reappearance, the daughter would run into her open arms, exclaiming, "Momma, my dear mother, you've finally come. I forgive you everything and will love you forever."

Instead, what she got was me, a rude, impudent brat, who refused to acknowledge her or the nickname she kept insisting on calling me. Without a doubt, I was *not* giving in without a fight. Who did she think she was, anyhow? How dare she keep calling me *Dusty*? Dusty? What kind of name was that?

"Dustina Devonia Brooks," she said, raising her voice as she stood up, moving towards me with her hands on her hips. "Understand one thing, right now," she continued, now towering over me, "*I am* your mother and, as your mother, your name is what *I choose* it to be."

I couldn't believe that she was going all indignant-parent on me. Did she really think that *her* using my full name would make a difference? That trick only worked for Auntie Dee, who, by the way, knew how to make it work. When she did it, she'd end up tickling me until I laughed and ultimately gave-in to do whatever she wanted of me. This Twanie lady—I didn't care if she was my mother or not—was yelling at me and scaring me. Instead of my saying "yes ma'am", as she probably expected, her screaming only made me cry harder and louder.

"Okay, Okay," she said, putting up her hands in surrender, and returning to her seat. "It's not that big a deal . . . Dusty . . . or Tina . . . or even Dusty-Tina, if you like . . ." she said, waiting for the smile from me. I did think it was sort of funny, but I wasn't ready to give just yet.

She moved to the other chair, the one I had refused to sit in, and slid it closer to me. "You do know that *I* named you Dustina Devonia, after your grandaunt, Dee. Right?"

Duh, I thought. But I knew better than to say it out loud. Auntie Dee had taught me a few things about being respectful to adults, even when they say dumb things. So, instead, I merely nodded acknowledgement.

That must have been enough for her, because she resumed, "When you were a little baby, I started calling you *Little Dee* and sometimes *L'il Dee*. Did you know that?"

No, I didn't. So, I shrugged.

"Well, Aunt Dee didn't like it at all. You might not understand. I didn't really at the time. But she said that you needed to be your own person. That *she* was Dee. *You* were totally unique, separate from her and anybody else."

The lady paused, I guess to see if I was following what she was saying. Then she continued. "It made sense. But it seemed kinda wrong, way too formal, to call my little baby Dustina, all the time. That was just too grown-up. So, I tried shortening Dustina to *Dusty*. When your grandaunt heard me call you that, she had this look on her face. Understand, she never said she didn't like it. All she said, in a really nice way, was, 'We have plenty of time. She's only a tiny baby. We'll figure something out.'"

At that, I almost smiled. Auntie Dee was famous for saying, "Don't worry. We'll figure something out." She mostly did it when somebody did or said something clueless, and Auntie Dee didn't want to hurt their feelings.

"I'm guessing that Aunt Dee never really liked the nickname, and never intended on calling you Dusty. If Tina is what you and Aunt Dee prefer, then that's what I'll call you."

As suspicious as I was of her giving in so easily, it provided an excuse to tone down the sobbing. All the drama was wearing me out.

* * *

Everything was happening too fast. I was scared and confused, as I sat on the porch watching Auntie Dee and the Twanie lady—my mother—loading all my stuff in the blue car. Once she had finished, Auntie Dee sat next to me on the porch and started swinging.

"Tina, sweetie," she said, "you understand what's going on, don't you?"

I shrugged. Then, I asked, "Why did you put all my stuff in that car? Don't you want me to live with you anymore?"

"You know I do, sweetheart," she answered. "But your mother misses you, and she wants you to live with her now."

"Who's gonna live with you?"

"I'll be fine."

"But why can't I live with you?"

"Children are supposed to live with their parents. I love you. But, I'm not your mother. Twanie is."

"What if I don't want to go? What if I don't like living with her?"

"You'll be fine, sweetheart," she said, her eyes watering. "You have to get up now. It's time to go."

I stood up, determined to be brave. The lady reached for my hand, and I let her take it. Then, she gently pulled to lead me away. Away from everything I knew. Away from my Auntie Dee. All my good intentions evaporated, and I panicked. I couldn't do it. I was not ready. And I wanted the lady to know it. I pulled back, trying as hard as I could to get away from her. To get back on the porch. To get back to my dear Auntie Dee.

The lady surprised me. She refused to let go. And even though she wasn't very big, she was strong enough to pick me up and carry me to the car. She was smart too. She had left the door open, probably in anticipation of my resistance. That way she was able to easily slide me into the passenger's seat. Then, holding me down with one hand, she buckled the seat belt with the other, and firmly shut the door.

Just as she started up the car, she turned to me and said, in a voice that was much sterner than anything I was used to, "Stop it this instant. Do you hear me?"

The tone said reams to me and I sniffled, but quieted down. "Why did you do that?"

"Do what, Dusty . . . uhhh . . . Tina?"

"You left my Auntie there all by herself."

"Oh, I suppose it's up to you to take care of *her*, huh?" she snickered.

Now, that made me mad. I let her know it, by saying, "You're mean. I don't like you."

"I learned a long time ago, little girl, that you don't always have to like your parents. You just accept that they are doing the best they can for you."

"Was your mommy mean, like you?"

It was almost as if I had slapped her. Even as little as I was, I could see the shock and hurt on her face. Right away, I wanted to take it back, but it was too late. The lady didn't say anything for such a long time that, with nothing else to do, I closed my eyes and fell asleep.

Like the brat that I was, I'd said what I said to sting, but not to stab. At the time, Auntie Dee was my only point of reference, my only example of a caretaker. The notion of someone, who wasn't concerned whether their actions hurt the child in their care, was foreign to me. I had no way of anticipating that my rash comment, implying that my mother was like her mother, would hurt her so much. Even a brat like me would not be that cruel.

Years later, I learned a lot about my mother and her mother. Only then could I appreciate why my rash words were so very cutting.

CHAPTER 9

GROWING UP in the late nineteen seventies and eighties, my mother was an out of wedlock child, fathered by someone with more hormones than character. Her mother, Margie, my grandmother, was sure that the answer to all her problems would be solved by finding the right man to take care of her and her illegitimate child. Margie couldn't believe her luck when a reliable man, a respected deacon from her church, chose to overlook her shameless past, make an honest woman of her, and help raise her daughter.

After the union, Twanie, my mother, discovered that she had no chance of winning over her stepfather, despite the fact that she was a model child, obedient, well-mannered and smart. To make things worse for her, she was not allowed to associate with any of her previous friends, since neither the old neighborhood nor the neighborhood children met her stepfather's standards. Needless to say, she became a very lonely child.

My father was another story. Over the years, my mother would say very little about him, except that I looked like him. Most of what I learned about him was from an old school yearbook, of Momma's. As I got older, to prevent me making the same mistakes she did, she decided to fill me in on some of the details of dear old dad. In her words, "He was charming, handsome, an entitled jerk, a con artist, and an asshole." And on one of the worst nights in her life, he essentially kidnapped her and raped her.

Embarrassed, ashamed, and guilt ridden, Momma initially told no one about *the incident*. Once she discovered that she was pregnant, she had no choice. Confused and afraid, she went to Margie. Since they had once been close, she hoped to get a little understanding, support, and motherly advice.

Instead of comfort and understanding, her mother screamed at her, "Oh, Lord. You stupid stupid girl. How do I tell Raymond about this?"

Momma was shocked and hurt by the reaction. Every word she told my grandmother fell upon deaf ears. The fact that she admitted to sneaking out, only made Margie less sympathetic. Momma couldn't believe that Margie didn't really care about the facts or what really happened, that her single concern was what her husband would think. In the end, Margie became so upset that she slapped her distraught daughter and sent her to her room, to await the arrival of her stepfather, the deacon.

Momma described how, at the time, she thought she couldn't be made to feel any worse. She didn't know how wrong she was. When the deacon got home, he went ballistic. He was angrier than she had ever seen him, or anyone. He ranted for an hour on how he was not totally surprised. The real problem, the thing that was truly unforgiveable, was the timing of "the girl's mess". His upcoming ordainment ceremony was only a couple of weeks away. He couldn't have the disgrace of such a scandal jeopardize all he'd worked so hard for. He couldn't let it be known that he was a failure as a spiritual leader in his own household.

After more shouting and some whispered conversation between the deacon and Margie, they finally concluded that the only resolution was to handle *the problem* quietly. Essentially, like characters from a daytime soap opera, they were going to hide the pregnancy for as long as possible. They insisted that Momma swear to absolute secrecy, not mention anything to anyone else, and continue school through the end of the term.

Luckily the timing was such that she wasn't expected to show until the semester was over. At that point, she would be sent to live in Petersburg with my grandaunt, Dee. When the baby—that would be me—came, Twanie was expected to quietly place it up for adoption.

After the inconvenient pregnancy situation was resolved, as good Christians, Margie and Raymond graciously swore to overlook everything.

Momma would stay in Petersburg, finish out her senior year, and they'd support her financially through graduation.

But Momma's heart was broken. And she'd been betrayed not only by my father, but now by her mother, who'd made no effort to support or defend her. From her point of view, there was only one good thing that had come out of the entire situation, and it was in her belly. The idea of having someone who would truly love *her*, with no conditions attached, was extremely appealing. Except for the part about moving in with her aunt, Momma had no intention of carrying out her parents' master plan. And under no circumstances, could they convince or bully her into giving away her baby.

By the time she moved in with Auntie Dee, Momma was so dispirited, that she hardly left her room. On top of all she'd been through, taking care of a baby was hard work. Not that she didn't love her little angel, but the baby was not the constant bundle of joy she'd imagined. It was a pooping, crying, fussy responsibility, and she was grateful to have her aunt to help her through it.

That's where the story ends and the extent of what my mother shared with me. With all that she had endured, combined with the normal strains associated with childbirth, from her descriptions, it's possible Momma had some type of mental or emotional breakdown.

CHAPTER 10

WHAT HAPPENED TO MY MOTHER, at the hands of those she trusted, was unthinkable. Some of it was criminal. She was lucky to have an aunt who cared for her and was willing to help her and her baby, wholeheartedly.

I don't know what she was doing or where she was those six missing years. Moreover, I don't have a clue why she came back to pick me up on that spring Sunday. It does appear that she wanted to make up for all the years she had been gone. And, for unknown reasons of her own, she insisted on doing it alone, even without her aunt's help.

Thinking back to that day in 1998, leaving Petersburg, heading towards Richmond, I must've slept most of the way. When I woke up, the car was stopping, and we were in a MacDonald's restaurant parking lot. Auntie Dee didn't believe in fast food and I had never been to MacDonald's before. Neither Momma nor I said a word as she came over to my side and opened the door. She took my hand and walked me inside. I looked around, fascinated. This was the place where you got Happy Meals, and where Ronald MacDonald and the Hamburglar lived. I'd seen them on TV. The other kids talked about it. I was impressed.

Momma led me over to a table where a man was sitting. He was dark, big, and had a kind smile. He put out his hand and said, "Hello, Dusty . . ."

"Tina," Momma interrupted, "she prefers to be called Tina."

"Well, Tina," he corrected, "my name is Mike. I've been looking forward to meeting you."

I didn't understand the hand gesture, there was so much that was new to me. "Are you my daddy?" I asked, my arms still at my side.

Mike, flushed, not knowing what to say, he hesitated a moment before responding, "No, I'm a friend of your mother's. You can call me . . ."

Before he could finish, recognizing Mike's discomfort, Momma interjected, "You can call him Uncle Mike."

This was exciting. Even though I missed my Auntie Dee, I now had a new mother and an uncle. All in one day!

Besides being a really nice man, Uncle Mike had two kids of his own, Terri and Wanda. They lived with their mother and both were around my age. Uncle Mike would bring them over to play with me or we'd go on outings and do all sorts of fun things.

Then one day, Uncle Mike stopped coming around. I was hurt and confused. I asked Momma if Uncle Mike, Terri, and Wanda didn't like me anymore. Momma tried to explain how it wasn't my fault, and that Uncle Mike had decided to spend more time with Terri's and Wanda's mother. But that made no sense to me. Why not just bring her along? Then, we all could play together.

Nowadays, I feel sorry for my mother trying to explain grownup relationships to a six-year-old. Then again, since I'd done something that Momma didn't know about, nothing she could've said would've convinced me it wasn't all my fault that we both had lost our friends.

It started one day, while Momma and I were sitting in our apartment. There were voices coming from the neighbors across the hall. The walls and doors were paper thin and when the neighbors had their door open or someone was at their door, we could hear everything that was said. On this particular day, I heard someone yelling, "Open the f****ing door. Don't f****with me." They kept going on and on with every other word being this new jewel, that had such a special ring to it.

Fascinated, I couldn't help repeating everything the man had said. Momma, trying to be patient, told me, "Tina, that's a bad word. We don't use words like that. You understand?"

I understood perfectly and had already suspected as much. But that didn't stop me from testing how far I could go with it. Eventually, Momma lost her patience with her little darling insisting on repeating each vulgar sentence and phrase again and again—with particular vigor.

My refusing to listen or stop, brought my first introduction to Momma's *one chance rule.*

Unlike Auntie Dee, my mother's child rearing philosophy did not include overindulging her only offspring. Where Auntie Dee always saw the positive side of my juvenile antics, my mother was hardly amused.

Momma's way of thinking was straight forward. She put forth the rules and I was to obey them. The consequences for breaking the rules were always consistent and Momma did not believe in empty threats. If the offense was deliberate or egregious, she pulled out her belt.

On that day, Momma finally lost all patience and warned, "I told you to stop. As long as you live, you will do as I say. I should only have to tell you once, or else. Do you understand me?"

Again, I ignored the caution. The word and it's multitude of fun forms just rolled so easily off my tongue. I had no intention of stopping. That's when I learned, the hard way, exactly what *or else* meant.

Poor Momma. I think it never occurred to her that simply telling me to stop was not enough. That's probably why it took so long before she grabbed me, pulled a belt from the closet, and *let me have it.*

We both cried a long time, me loudly and Momma quietly. But I didn't care about her tears, she was not the one with sore legs and behind.

What Momma didn't realize was that the lesson she taught me was not the one she intended. From that point forward, I was determined to simply not get caught using my new word, by Momma. Plus, I couldn't wait to share my new gem with Teri and Wanda. To my defense, they had taught me about fart jokes and gross noises.

Even though the word wasn't new to Wanda or Terri, using it in the varied contexts was exciting. We all giggled and laughed. However, after that day, I never saw them or Uncle Mike again. It was obvious to me the reason why. And nothing Momma said could change how bad I felt.

CHAPTER 11

THERE WERE SEVERAL *UNCLES*, after Uncle Mike. I remember them all. There was Uncle Scott, who was fat and liked to read books to me. There was Uncle Gerald, who laughed a lot, told funny stories, and had a silly mustache. There was Uncle Samuel, who was polite, reserved, and spoke with an accent. Momma said that he was from Africa. Finally, there were the two who left indelible imprints on both Momma and me, Uncle Ted and Horace—who refused to be called uncle.

By the time she came to get me from Auntie Dee, the sweet naïve Twanie, of Momma's youth, was dead and buried. All that was left was a jaded woman who introduced herself as Antoinette. This harden woman of the world had one main goal, to keep her daughter from being the victim she had been or making the mistakes she'd made. Momma did not want me—through naivety or bad judgment—to be fooled, taken advantage of, or hurt as a result of trusting the wrong people, especially men.

Antoinette had learned her lesson. She never blindly trusted any of the men she dated. She was particularly careful where her young daughter was concerned. And she never, under any circumstances, left me alone with any of the uncles. All of them, until Uncle Ted, took that in stride.

When I was about ten years old, Momma was struggling. Cleaning other people's homes to make ends meet wasn't quite enough and we were evicted from our apartment. At the time, she was dating Ted Hilley, a well-spoken, kind, and friendly man, who invited us to move in with him. Uncle Ted had kinky reddish-brown hair and was not much bigger than Momma—probably about five-six, weighing about one-hundred forty pounds. He smiled a lot and was especially nice to me. I'm not sure what he did for a living. Whatever it was, he was able to afford a very nice apartment with an extra room, that he had been using for a den or office.

When we moved in, Uncle Ted cleaned the small room out for me to use. The pullout couch became my bed. There was even a small TV in there and a desk for me to use. He talked and joked with me. Something few grownups did. And it seemed to matter to him that I was comfortable and happy. I liked Uncle Ted, a lot. Which was why I couldn't understand Momma's behavior.

She and Uncle Ted shared household responsibilities and would run errands for each other. Momma never objected to doing her share. Her only stipulation was that if she had to shop or go out, I went with her. Sometimes, especially if I was watching television or asleep, I would protest. I was certain Uncle Ted could handle any situation or emergency. Momma didn't care about my opinion or what I was doing, "Get your butt up, or else," she'd say.

One night, because Uncle Ted was not feeling well, Momma offered to go out and get the pack of cigarettes he was frantic for. She was in the process of dragging me out of bed when Uncle Ted stopped her, "Antoinette, why in the hell are you taking that girl out this house this time of night? Let the child sleep."

Not missing a beat, Momma ignored Uncle Ted, grabbed her keys and walked out of my room, expecting me to follow.

Uncle Ted stepped back to let Momma pass, before saying, "Come on Antoinette, don't be silly."

"Where I go my child goes."

Uncle Ted, his temper rising, made his way pass Momma, virtually blocking the door and yelled back at her, "Are you telling me that you are willing to take that girl out this house this time of night, because you don't trust your daughter to be here alone with me? What kind of crap is that?"

Momma refusing to take the bait, stood her ground and stared.

Ted now furious, said, "If that's the case, then when you leave, don't just take your daughter, take all your raggedy ass shit with you."

He grabbed Momma by the arm, with the apparent goal of shoving her out. Momma was no fool. She must've known that once she and I were out, all our possessions would be locked inside, with an extremely angry Uncle Ted—who had no incentive to pack our stuff and get it to us. If anything, he would put it in the dumpster. So, she dug in and wouldn't be pushed out.

By then, they both were wrestling and screaming at each other. I didn't know who was right about what, but nobody put their hands on my mother. I grabbed Uncle Ted, by the waist, and tried to pull him away from Momma. He slapped me away. I lost my balance and fell. My blouse caught on something and ripped as I went down.

Momma went into mother lion mode. Uncle Ted, who was not much bigger than her, was now mostly in protective mode, struggling to get away from the insane wild woman.

"Don't touch my child," she screamed. "Bastard, you hurt my baby. Nobody puts their hands on my baby."

By then, Uncle Ted's neighbors were out investigating the commotion. Apparently, someone noticed my ripped clothing, interpreted Momma's exclamations as something more serious than a normal couple's fight, and called 911. They could put up with and ignore a lot. Men and women fought and got over it. But child abuse or potential molestation could not be ignored.

The police arrived in record time. When they started questioning Uncle Ted, by the nature of the questions, both he and Momma understood the implications.

Uncle Ted was getting nervous, not liking the direction things were going. "Hey, I didn't do anything, officers."

But the injuries on Momma and the condition of my clothes told a different story. And Momma took advantage of the situation.

She said, putting on an Oscar worthy performance, "I didn't know. . . I didn't know. . . He was in her room. . . I caught him in her room messing around with her. I couldn't have that. No man touches my child."

Momma seemed so distraught that the police allowed us to stay back while they took Uncle Ted away. They said they would send someone back to get her story.

I'm not sure how long they kept Uncle Ted, because Momma and I were only there long enough for her to gather up our *raggedy ass shit*—as Uncle

Ted had so colorfully described it—and packed it all in our car. Momma also took enough money from Uncle Ted's stash to pay for a place for us to stay.

As we pulled into the motel parking lot, Momma must have noticed the expression on my face. She pulled the car into a slot. When she gently touched my shoulder, I glared at her and pulled away.

"What?" she asked.

"Momma, we let the police take Uncle Ted. Then you stole his money."

I saw right away, from the expression on her face, what was about to happen. Unfortunately, I was too slow to duck. Momma smacked me and I fell over in my seat. Pointing her finger in my face, she spit out, "Don't you ever, as long as you're black, talk to me like that again."

I touched my hand to the cheek where she'd struck me. "Yes, ma'am," I said with my face still stinging. "I . . . I just don't understand about Uncle Ted. Is he really a bad man?"

Momma looked at me as if she might hit me again. "Look, girl. I don't know what was in Ted's head. I was planning to leave anyhow, mainly because I didn't. He may or may not have meant to do anything to you, but something had me not quite sure. And no matter what, I might not be the best mother, but I'm not gambling on my daughter's safety," she said. "My way of thinking, it's better to prevent, than to trust and lose."

The more she talked, the angrier she got. "So, *Miss Thang*. Who knows what would've happened if I had just gone to the store. Or think about it, suppose I had just let him kick us out like he wanted to. Once we were out of that door, that would've been the end. We had no way to get back in for our stuff. And about the money . . . Do you have any money that I don't know about?" She asked, leaning down in my face. "Do you?"

"No," I whimpered, as I slid closer to the door, hopefully, out of reach.

"Well, you let me handle our business. Do you hear what I say, girl?"

"Of course, Momma, I understand." I was too stunned and afraid to disagree. Anything Momma said, at that point, was definitely fine with me.

CHAPTER 12

WITHOUT US, THE POLICE had no reason to hold Uncle Ted, and Momma knew that. She had no problem with him being released, she only wanted to be a safe distance away when it happened. Uncle Ted, no matter how nice he appeared, was not known for having a forgiving nature. She assumed that, if we came across him anywhere in Richmond, it would not be a happy reunion.

She needn't have worried. Uncle Ted was no longer welcome in his apartment complex, no matter what the police could or could not prove. He'd had enough of Richmond. He packed up his belongings and moved back to his hometown, Waycross Georgia.

Momma, who should've been relieved, didn't act like someone happy that she'd possibly dodged a literal bullet. She seemed sad.

We were gathering our stuff to move to a rooming house over in Southside, when she came over and sat quietly on the edge of my bed. Since she could've talked easily from her bed or anywhere in the room, I prepared myself. And I waited.

"Tina," she said softly, "you're too little to understand, but I feel really bad about Uncle Ted."

I presumed she was talking about us getting him arrested and walking away with some of his cash. So, I said, "I guess we can find out where he lives now. Then we can save up and send him his money back. Then maybe he won't be mad at us."

"No, Tina," she said, "that's not what I mean. Like I said, you're too young to understand. Someday you will know why I feel bad about exposing you to somebody like him."

"Momma, Uncle Ted was always so nice. I still don't know why you think he was bad or why you didn't trust him."

"Believe it or not, that's probably a good thing. I really feel guilty about not walking away sooner. I should've, especially when I first started getting bad vibes. Just know that, when you get older and think back, I never-ever would intentionally put you in danger. Not if I can help it."

Her eyes started watering. She seemed to have more to say, instead she got up and walked over to continue packing our stuff. I was more confused than ever.

After that, something seemed to have happened to Momma. For the next few years, she became totally focused on us and our little family. Momma never had been the party-hearty sort of person, but now she seldom went out at all. And there were no more uncles.

At times it seemed that we were growing up together. Not that Momma implied or encouraged the notion that we were friends or equals. She still believed in established boundaries and limits for children (*me*) and made sure that I understood them (*or else*).

Even so, it was obvious that Momma had regrets about the directions her life had taken and rung by rung she was working to fix things.

CHAPTER 13

BEFORE I SAW THE PLACE, Momma had me convinced that we were lucky that she was approved for the small subsidized two-bedroom apartment, not far from the Southside rooming house we had been staying in. According to her, those apartments were hard to get into, and the only reason she was able to jump the line was by agreeing to move in "as is". It all sounded great, until I saw it. "As is", in this case, meant that the previous tenants had abruptly moved out and left the place disgusting and filthy.

"Don't worry, baby," Momma said, when she saw my reaction, "this place will be great. You'll see."

"But, Momma, it stinks," I whined.

"We can fix that with some Pine-Sol and a little elbow grease. We'll clean it all up before we move in." Needless to say, her enthusiasm and optimism were both lost on me. And I most definitely did not like that "we part".

"This really is a great place, just takes a little imagination to see it," Momma said with a level of excitement I don't think I'd ever heard in her voice before. "We're just lucky that the landlord is lazy and cheap, otherwise there would be people lining up for this apartment. We're do for some luck. Besides, someday all of this will be behind us. Trust me."

Well, dreaming of "someday" was little comfort the weeks it took to wash everything down; move all the trash out; clean out the refrigerator; clean a linoleum that looked like it had never been mopped; and scrape all the gunk off the stove, the counters, and the walls.

On the positive side, the place was better than some we had seen and, once we finished cleaning, it was home. Though the neighborhood wasn't perfect, our building was kept reasonably clean and the majority of our fellow tenants cared enough to take care of their individual spaces. Most of them were friendly and would wave and speak to us on passing.

We developed a routine. Momma worked at whatever job—oftentimes multiple jobs—she could find. I went to school, did my homework, behaved myself (*or else*), and did the lion's share of the housework.

"You need to understand, Tina," she'd say, when I dared complain. "I work and pay the bills. You have to help out and keep this apartment clean, while I keep food in the house and clothes on your back."

Knowing that Momma's words were law, I would be crazy to say anything else but, "Yes ma'am."

* * *

One day, we were sitting at our kitchen table. I was doing my math homework and Momma was sorting through the mail. She opened an official looking letter, read the contents, put it back in the envelope, and started crying. Praying that it wasn't an eviction notice or anything like that, I asked her what was wrong.

"Nothing's wrong. Just the opposite," she said. "It's only that this letter brings up a lot of memories. But it's not anything bad. It's proof that I have my GED.

"When my parents made me drop out of high school, that was one of the hardest things I've ever done. They had it all planned out. I'd move in with Aunt Dee. Have my baby. Give it away to some adoption agency. Perpetuate some lie about attending high school in Petersburg to help out Aunt Dee. And no one would be the wiser. None of the good church folk would know I shamed Momma and the deacon.

"When I refused to give you up, Momma and the deacon gave up on me. They broke my heart. And after that, I admit I wasn't the strongest or most mentally prepared person to take care of anyone. I cried all the time. Needless to say, I didn't get to finish that last year of high school. Then, a few years later, some nice people convinced me to get my GED. Now, for both our sakes, it's time for me to think about something more . . . about having a career or job that we can both be proud of. Momma's going to college, baby. I just needed this to get started."

Up until that moment, it hadn't occurred to me that Momma missed out on graduating from high school because of me. Now, looking at Momma's face, I was getting a glimpse of what the girl, Twanie, was like—all optimistic and full of hope. It made me smile.

Momma was true to her word. It seemed she was spending every free moment planning or studying something or other. By my thirteenth birthday, she was working solely at Murphy Mart, fulltime. Her bosses were so impressed with Momma's drive and intelligence that there were plans to move her into management.

The good thing was that she not only had a decent job with a future, but the store was only a few blocks away. She could walk to work, if necessary— with our car, that was a real plus. And, though the pay wasn't exceptional, it was enough. Momma was able to make the rent, buy necessities, and have a little left over.

The downside was that, since Momma sometimes worked long hours, I was left doing most of the housework, the cooking, and now I was also helping manage the bills.

The upside to it was that, in order to sign the checks and make sure the bills were paid, I got really good at imitating Momma's signature. That made it easy for me to sign notes from school, or request special considerations, without getting into trouble with Momma.

Unfortunately, we were living in, what was considered, a bad neighborhood. Sometimes when the neighborhood made the nightly news, the reality of the potential dangers was brought home. At those times, my fears about my mother walking to work were intensified, especially when she worked into the night.

Momma, however, was not deterred. She was a woman on a mission to better herself and her circumstances. She had dreams. She would move into management. And, if nothing else, the Murphy Mart Corporation had an education assistance program. She could use that to pay for college courses. She had everything planned.

CHAPTER 14

ONE DAY, AT MURPHY MART, Momma was arranging the display in the big window up front and saw this tall gorgeous well-dressed man get out of a very nice car in front of the store. Momma didn't know one car from the other, but she did know expensive. She says that she almost fell from the footstool when he came into the store. He saw her stumble and rushed over to help. She says it was like he was drawn to her. As he got closer, he was more impressive in person. With beautiful brown skin, close cut curly hair, and neat expensive looking clothes, he reminded her of a younger version of Denzel Washington. Her first thought was, *What in the world is he doing in this Murphy Mart?*

He introduced himself as Horace Franks. And when the gorgeous and charming man kept coming back to the Murphy Mart just to see her, Momma thought her luck had changed. She believed that this man, Horace Franks, was proof that someone from up above was righting all the bad things in her life, and things were permanently changing for the better.

She almost swooned when she first described him to me. "He's tall, educated, charming, and very handsome. Oh, and did I tell you? He's rich!"

Horace Franks took her to real restaurants, not the fast-food ones we normally went to. He even bought her nice things to wear to the fancy restaurants. I have to admit, Momma looked stunning in her new clothes, much younger, closer to my age than the thirty hard years she had lived. He also gave her cash money, to help her out.

Of course, my mother was starstruck, not stupid. She had enough money of her own to meet our basic needs. So, she put most of what Horace Franks gave her into the savings account she had in both our names, and a little in our emergency stash jar.

Momma had never seemed so happy. The only problem was that I couldn't stand Horace Franks, and the feeling was obviously mutual. He never let my mother know how he felt about me, and I never mentioned it to her. He wasn't mean to me. Why bother? To him, I basically did not exist.

The only time he seemed to register my presence was when I made the mistake of calling him *Uncle Horace*. Momma was in the kitchen cooking. He had been doing his normal thing, ignoring me. I was failing miserably at making conversation, trying to get along, since he was so important to Momma. Really, I don't remember what I was saying to him, but I ended it with *Uncle Horace*.

The change in the expression on his face frightened me. He glared, while speaking softly and making sure every word was perfectly clear.

"I'm not your uncle, kid. I don't know what you're used to, but never call me *Uncle Horace*. If you must call me anything, call me Mr. Franks."

"Yes sir, Mr. Franks," I said. "I'll remember."

I was terrified. People had yelled at me before. I've been cussed out. But no one had ever said such innocent words in such a menacing way.

When Mr. Franks saw Momma come in, he patted me on the top of my head, like I was a little dog or something. Momma grinned, like that was the cutest thing she had ever seen. I went to my room and didn't return until Momma called me back for dinner.

I had no idea what Mr. Franks did for a living, but he was often gone for days on business trips. Each time, I'd hope that he would not return. Ideally, he'd be a victim of a fatal car crash or a plane falling directly on him.

* * *

One day, Momma returned from visiting Mr. Franks, all giddy and excited. Mr. Franks had one of his important business trips scheduled for the following week, in New York. He had meetings all week, but he told Momma that she could meet him up there and they could have a nice weekend vacation. Momma was so head over heels, that she was positive that this would be a proposal trip, and she'd return engaged to be Mrs. Horace Franks.

She told me how guilty she felt about leaving me alone, but this could be the most important trip of her life. She hoped I'd understand and if she didn't think I'd be okay for three days, she wouldn't go. Plus, if I needed anything, I could go to Miss Hettie, the nice lady next door.

I couldn't believe how excited she was. Before leaving that Friday, as she packed, Momma declared, "Baby everything will work out fine, for both of us. Just think, I'll have a rich husband and both of us will have everything we ever wanted."

I couldn't tell her that the last thing I wanted was to spend more time with *Mr. Frankenstein.* It was like being in that old movie where the pods took over people's bodies. This was not the smart independent woman I knew. I wanted to ask, "Who are you and what did you do with my mother?"

Of course, I suspected that things would not work out the way my mother imagined. I kind of knew that it wouldn't from the minute I first met Mr. Franks. He wore nice clothes, was overly polite, generous, and smiled a lot. But to me, he was more like those creeps in the con-man movies, than Prince Charming. Even our neighbor, the nice Miss Hettie, looked like she smelled a strong stench whenever she crossed Mr. Franks' path. Why couldn't Momma see it?

Naturally, I never mentioned any of this to my mother. She was so happy and sure that we would all have a story book ending that I ignored my instincts and put my trust in her confidence. Really, I had no choice.

I watched quietly as she gathered up her things, got into her car and drove off. There was food in the cabinets and the refrigerator, about one thousand dollars cash in our combined futures-stashes—thanks to a large extent to Mr. Franks—and the rent was paid up to the end of the month. None of that was reassuring to me when, at night, I double checked the locks and left all the lights on.

* * *

Momma called to check on me several times, from the road. Then nothing. After about a week, some lady called. She said she was a friend of Mr. Franks and that Momma was delayed, and wanted me to know that she was okay.

After that call, nothing. I didn't hear from Momma or the lady. I was terrified. The good thing was that we seldom received calls. So, I dialed *69 to call back the last number that had rang our phone. I lucked out. It was the lady.   When she answered, I was so hyper that everything came out in one big burst. I told her to tell my mother that I was running out of food and that I needed clean clothes to wear to school. She curtly said that she would see that Momma got the message and please don't dial her again.

I didn't know what to think. I had no way of reaching Momma, Mr. Franks, or the lady. Though I was truly scared, I didn't want to draw any attention to my situation, get Momma in trouble, or end up with Social Services. I decided that I only needed to keep going until Momma returned from her honeymoon or wherever she was.

I hadn't lied to Mr. Franks' friend. I was running out of everything and, no matter how mature Momma thought I was, I was a kid and I was struggling. If anyone in my building noticed that I was more stressed out than usual, they did not let on. In any other district, the authorities at school might have been a problem. But, in my school, they were used to kids having bad days and, for the most part, they looked the other way. As long as I did my assigned work and showed up, no one bothered me.

When she first registered me, my mother had said, "You're so lucky Tina. You don't have to be bused back and forth to school."

Yeah, I was lucky all right. Now as I walked through the neighborhood, I was more wary. Maybe it was my imagination, but it seemed that the corner hoodlums sensed the change and my desperation. I could swear they were paying closer attention and were eye balling me more when I walked by.

I couldn't afford to waste what little cash I had going to the laundry mat. So, I washed my clothes out by hand in the bathtub. I was late to school a few days because they didn't dry in time, and I had to iron them dry.

I tried not to hate my mother, but she had deserted me and was somewhere living the *Life of Riley* with Mr. "Big Bucks" Franks, probably in some big house with servants. Meanwhile, there I was, thirteen years old having to budget what little money that was left, as best I could.

"I'm just a kid. I'm just a kid. Momma, where are you?" I'd say every night as I cried myself to sleep.

PART THREE

It Takes A Village
(2005-2007)

CHAPTER 15

I READ EVERY PIECE of opened and unopened mail that was in Momma's pile on the kitchen table, hoping to find some hint of where she might be. Then, as every new letter came in, I checked it immediately. That's how I came across a letter from Murphy Mart. They were firing Momma for "unauthorized extended absence". I felt bad for her because she loved that job so much. The good news was that there were two final checks that would be deposited directly into Momma's bank account.

Not knowing when my mother would return or how long the cash reserves would last, I set the notice down, and, as Auntie Dee once taught me, I counted my blessings.

One: Since Momma had the rental payments automatically withdrawn from her account, the apartment was taken care of. Gas, water, and electricity were included in the rent.

Two: I was on the free breakfast and lunch plan, at school. At least I wouldn't starve.

And, three: After checking the basic essentials, like soap and toothpaste, I was confident I would be fine, at least for a while. Having survived most of my life with Momma and me practically living out of a shoebox, I was an expert at using only what I absolutely needed and spending only what was necessary to get by.

The one immediate concern was toilet tissue. I was completely out. Getting through the night might be an issue. Walking to the convenience store, just for an overpriced roll of toilet tissue, was not an option, especially since it was close to getting dark.

I had used them when I ran out of Kleenex—wasting them on tears and nose blowing. What was I thinking? I'd even used Momma's little handy pack of tissues that she usually kept in her purse. *Now what do I do?* I thought.

Putting myself in Momma's shoes, I tried to picture what she would do. What came to mind were her "you think you have it bad" stories about the times she and her mother had no choice but to use newspaper for toilet tissue. Even if there was newspaper available, I wasn't quite ready for that, yet.

The question was, "Am I desperate enough to borrow from our next-door neighbor?" That would be breaking one of Momma's cardinal rules. She never borrowed from neighbors and she never encouraged them to borrow from us. Though I knew she would have a fit, I had little choice. She wasn't there. And worrying about what Momma would do, wasn't at all helpful. Besides, considering my only other options were grocery store circulars or phone book pages, I chose to swallow my pride and check if my next-door neighbor could help me out.

Miss Hettie, the lady next door, was cool. She had three kids of her own, all about my age. She and my mother were never close, but I'm certain she had to have noticed Momma hadn't been around for a while. When I asked for the toilet tissue, Miss Hettie gave me a look that said she knew something was wrong. Still, she smiled and said, "Sure, sweetheart. I just went shopping. I'll get it for you."

As she handed the roll to me, she looked at me with concern, and asked, "You okay?"

That almost made me cry. However, confiding in Miss Hettie, no matter how nice she was, might result in me being grabbed up by social workers. I had no intention of getting thrown into the system. I had heard horror stories, and I'd also seen what happened to some of the kids I know who live in the homes of professional foster parents—especially those in it for the money. No way would I chance that. So, I replied, "I'm fine, Miss Hettie."

"Say hello to your mother for me."

"Yes, ma'am. Thank you."

"You're welcome," she said, still looking at me with kind concern.

The look got to me. Tears were flowing as I struggled to open the door. I didn't turn around to see if Miss Hettie was still there. But I was sure she was. I tried to appear cool, and finally got inside. That's when I let all that had happened in the past weeks get to me. I cried for at least an hour.

When I calmed down, I made a list of all the things I needed to get on my next run to the store. Looking at the list, it was obvious, if I kept spending, even for small things, I would run out of money and options. It was virtually impossible to budget my resources, with no idea of how long I would have before Momma returned. I had a decision to make. I could sit around waiting for my mother to come save me. Or, I could go out and find myself a job. I opted for the job.

* * *

The first thing I did, when I got to school the next day, was look for my friend Paulette. I was certain that, if anyone could point me in the right direction, she could.

I'd met Paulette when I first started at Southside Middle School. She was assigned the seat next to me. At first, I thought she was making fun of me when she asked, "Girl, where you get those jeans? They the bomb."

I stared at her for a moment, trying to decide if I should cuss her out or thank her. I decided on the latter.

"Thanks," I finally said. "My mother got them from Raves at the mall."

"Girl, I got to get a pair of those. Maybe we can go to the mall sometime together and you can help me pick out a pair."

"Okay, I guess we can do that."

I hoped she'd forget. But not Paulette. She made a point to find me early the next morning to arrange our little excursion to the mall. Caught in my lie, I had no choice but to admit that the jeans were my mother's and I had no idea where she'd bought them. I confessed how, on days that my mother went in early, I would sometimes grab stuff of hers that I liked and be sure that it was back in place before Momma got home from work. To my surprise, Paulette thought this was the coolest thing she'd ever heard. She laughed and said that her mother never had anything that she'd want to grab, even if she had nerve enough to.

I had never met anyone, old or young, quite like Paulette. To tell the truth, I was both shocked and flattered that she wanted to be my friend.

After that, we would travel to the mall whenever we just wanted something to do. Most of the time we'd ride the bus. Other times, Paulette had a friend who would drop us off and pick us up. It seemed that, for someone so young, my new best bud had a network of contacts and friends.

That's why I wasn't at all surprised to hear that she had a sister that worked at the nearby Around-The-Corner drug store, who she could talk to for me.

"Yeah, girl," Paulette said. "My sister has been working at ATC for about a year now. If I ask her, I'm sure she'll do what she can to help you out. Plus, she has a boss who is a real sweetheart."

"But I'm only thirteen. Will her boss hire somebody that young?" I asked, trying not to get too excited.

"Sure. You'll just have to tell a little fib. From now on, you're sixteen." Paulette laughed, like it was the funniest thing in the world.

Paulette was like that, nothing seemed to faze her. She was bold, confident, and funny. Things that would send the normal middle school kid running off crying, would just bounce off Paulette. Take her weight. She was at least fifteen pounds heavier than the average girl in our grade. Not that she was overweight, but she was what old people called *healthy*. So, when anyone mentioned her roundness, she would just laugh and admit, "What can I say? I'm a girl who loves to eat."

Her skin was the color of dark chocolate, and she had big brown eyes that always seemed to be stretched wide, laughing at everyone around her. To those who thought being so dark skinned was a bad thing, Paulette would quote her grandma, "The blacker the berry the sweeter the juice." And she would laugh so hard that everyone would laugh with her.

It seemed that my girl was always laughing, with no shortage of people to laugh with her. Of course, it didn't hurt that, for a young girl her age, Paulette was extremely well developed, with large breasts and a round behind. She had lots of admirers. Every time I looked, there was some boy in her face, even older boys. She and I joked a lot about her behind being so big a plate of food could be placed on it and wouldn't fall off. She would just stick her butt out, shake it and burst out laughing. "Look Tina," she'd say, "it ain't good to hate. It don't look good on you girl."

* * *

Paulette lived up to her word and talked to her sister. The sister said that she'd try to get Mr. Sam, the owner, to give me a call. I didn't want to wait that long. The first thing I did after school was make my way to the drugstore to fill out an application in person.

When I walked into the store, I saw this short, dark skinned man. I assumed he worked there because he had a badge pinned to his white shirt that read, "S. Roberts". He had on a black tie to match his black high-water pants, which were about two inches above his ankles.

I said, "I'm looking for Mr. Sam. I want to fill out a job application."

The man looked me over from head to toe. "I'm Samuel Roberts, young lady. What's your name?"

"I'm Dustina Brooks."

"Who told you to come here and look for me, Ms. Brooks?"

"Jacqueline Parkes," I said giving him Paulette's sister's name.

"I think you may be too young, Ms. Brooks. How old are you anyway?"

"I'm sixteen, but I'll be seventeen soon," I lied.

"Do you have any identification to verify that?"

"Uh, no sir, I don't have my ID on me. My mother has it in her wallet and she's out of town right now with a friend."

"Okay, I do need help stocking. If Ms. Parkes sent you to me, she's a good worker and trustworthy. I'll give you a try, for now. But when your mother comes back, you must show me proper ID, okay?"

"Thank you, Mr. Sam, as soon as she steps into the house, I'll bring it right to you."

* * *

I hated lying to Mr. Sam. He seemed like such a nice man. If things were different, I could've gone back to him and admitted that I was turning fourteen, not seventeen. He might have understood and still allowed me to work. The difference would've been that, by law, he'd have to severely restrict the number of hours I could put in during the school year. For most fourteen-year-olds, that would've been fine. Unfortunately, I wasn't your normal fourteen-year-old looking to make a few extra dollars a week. I needed to work as many hours as possible, to survive.

To sort of make up for the deception, I became the perfect employee. I wanted Mr. Sam to see me as a good worker. So, every day I would rush home, do my homework, and go directly to the drug store. Mr. Sam was so impressed that he occasionally trusted me to watch the cash register during lulls, for brief periods of time.

One day, a young guy, about fifteen, came in while everybody else was in the back. I watched as he went through the aisles putting stuff in his pockets. Mr. Sam had told all of us never to challenge a thief, it would go better for us and the store. He emphasized that nothing in the store was worth jeopardizing someone's life for.

So, I waited and pretended not to see anything. When the young thief left, I found Mr. Sam and told him everything I could remember about which aisles the young guy went down, what he looked like, and described the clothes he had on, down to his Nike sneakers.

Mr. Sam made out a report. Even with me as a witness, and the video from the store cameras catching the young guy on tape, I doubt if anyone looked really hard for him or thought they would get the thief.

Later Mr. Sam said, "I'm proud of you, Ms. Brooks. You kept your head and no one got hurt. Some people twice your age may have panicked, and the Lord only knows what could have happened then."

After that, Mr. Sam never again asked me for ID. I'm not sure if he forgot, or, as I later suspected, he understood that I probably had a good reason for lying and just let me slide.

CHAPTER 16

I HAD ALWAYS ASSUMED an eviction notice would be intimidating, perhaps arriving in a flaming red envelope with bold all capital letters. There was nothing memorable about the one that came addressed to my mother. It was in a plain white envelope, with normal sized typed letters. But I knew what it was, before opening it. I was right. The letter was not the final eviction notice, but it may as well have been. It was a warning. We had all of thirty days to "pay all rent due" or "clear our belongings out" and "vacate the premises".

Bottom-line, I had run out of time. After reading every line of the letter, I put it back in its plain white envelope and sat it down next to the rest of the mail on the kitchen table. Since I didn't have any homework or school assignments to complete, I locked up, went outside to the bus stop in front of the building, and rode the bus to ATC to start my workday.

There weren't a lot of customers at ATC. I didn't see Mr. Sam right away, so I went looking for him. I found him upfront talking to the pharmacist. I hated disturbing him when he was busy, but I was out of options. I had one desperation move to play, and it involved a phone call to my friend Paulette. I excused myself for interrupting and asked Mr. Sam if I could use his phone. He nodded and I went to his office to dial Paulette.

Please be at home.

Nobody, not even my best friend, knew exactly how bad my situation was. It was time to come clean.

Paulette must have sensed something was wrong, because, for once, she didn't start off immediately teasing me. "What's up, Tina?" she asked.

"My mother is gone, and I don't have an idea where she is. Now, I'm about to get kicked out of our apartment." I was making a big effort to keep it together, but I was on the verge of tears, with every word. "I need someplace to stay, just 'til she gets back. I wouldn't ask, but I don't know anybody else to talk to. Do you think I can stay with you for a while?"

"Oh, my goodness, Tina," she said. "I can't imagine my mom saying no to you. She'll be home by the time you get off work. Come on over and maybe the two of us together can double-team her into saying yes."

We both hung up. I tried to be encouraged, but something in my friend's voice made me wonder if I had done the right thing by calling her.

I'd always envied Paulette. She had a mother and a father that were still together. Her family lived in a real house. They even had a yard.

When I got to their door, I heard loud voices coming from inside. I knocked, hoping someone would hear me, without me having to bang too hard. After a couple of minutes, my friend opened the door. As I walked in, I liked the place. It definitely was clean. I could smell the furniture wax. There was a stairway directly ahead. Down at the end of the hall, I could see straight through to the kitchen. On my left, there were a couple of old-fashioned columns that were painted white. Behind the columns was the entry to the living room.

There was no one in the kitchen. I assumed one of the voices I had heard, from outside the door, had to have come from Paulette's mother and she was probably in the living room.

It didn't take a big leap of imagination to figure out that the loud discussion had been about me. Apparently, Paulette had already told her mother what I needed, and Mrs. Parkes was not happy about it.

I followed Paulette into the living room. She pointed to me, and said to her mother, "Uh, ma, this is my friend, Tina."

"What, you think I'm blind or something? I see her." Completely ignoring me, she addressed Paulette, "I'm sorry for her problems, but your father will have a fit if I try to bring another mouth into this house. Somebody needs to call Social Services. Maybe they can find a shelter or something for her to stay in."

"Shelter? Ma'ah, we can't let my best friend go to a shelter." Paulette's frustration was mounting and her voice getting louder. "Anyhow, a kid can't go into a shelter alone. We're not talking about forever. Just until Tina's mother gets back. She can stay in my room. She already has a job. She just needs a place to sleep. You don't have to worry about another mouth."

Paulette didn't notice her mother shortening the distance between them.

"Who in the hell you think you are talking to with that tone?"

The slap, one quick motion, caught us both by surprise. It seemed to come from out of nowhere and caused Paulette to lose her balance and nearly trip over a nearby chair. Mrs. Parkes just stood over her. "If you ever talk to me like that again, you won't just be knocked down, you'll be knocked out. Now, get your ass up. Take your friend out of my house, before you both be looking for a place to stay."

Paulette watched as her mother stalked out of the room, still mumbling to herself.

"I can't believe she hit me," Paulette said.

"You all right girl?" I asked.

"Yeah. I'm sorry you had to see that. And, I'm sorry she wouldn't let you stay here, even for a little while."

"I'll figure something out," I said. At that point, I wasn't as concerned about myself as I was about Paulette. "Your mom always like that?" I asked.

"Nah, she's just having a bad day because she found out my dad is messing around with another woman."

"What?" I asked. "Did you just say your father was messing around on your mother?"

"Nah, not 'was' what I said was that he *is* messing around." Paulette said, like it was no big deal.

"Doesn't that bother you?"

"Nope."

"Why, not?' I was beginning to think Paulette was just as screwed up as her crazy mother.

"I've known about my father and that hussy for months now. How do you think my mom found out?"

"You told her?"

"Sure did. But I don't think she wanted to hear it. Ever since I told her, she's been a little crazy."

"A little?" I said, trying for a light tone.

"Hey, nobody can say that this family is boring," Paulette joked. Then she continued in a more subdued tone, "I am kinda worried about her. She's always been strong before. But I think with this, it's too hard even for her. She suspected it. But now that she knows, she wishes I'd kept it to myself."

I looked at Paulette, stunned. "I guess your father doesn't know that your mother knows?"

"Not yet. Don't want to be around when it all hits the fan," she said.

Me neither, I thought.

I didn't know what to say after that. I always thought Paulette had such a perfect family and a perfect life. I guess my mother had been right when she said that the grass is definitely not always greener on the other side.

* * *

The next day, when I arrived at ATC, instead of chatting with the other workers or saying hello to Mr. Sam, I went straight to the back and started unpacking boxes that had arrived the day before. I tried to concentrate. But in the end, I couldn't stop the tears from falling.

Jackie, Paulette's sister, came back to help me with the unpacking. I looked over at her and wondered how much of her family drama she was aware of. I gave her a weak smile, which I couldn't maintain. The tears were threatening again, so I turned away from her.

Jackie worked for a few minutes without saying anything to me. I didn't really notice that she had left until Mr. Sam came up behind me.

"Ms. Brooks, what's going on? Anything I can do?"

I wanted to stop crying, I really did. But I just couldn't. Finally, I said, "Mr. Sam, you know how I told you that my mother was out of town?"

"Yes . . ."

"Well, I haven't heard from her in weeks. And now I'm getting put out of our apartment and I don't have anywhere to go."

"Where is she?"

"I don't really know. She left for a trip with her boyfriend," I answered.

"No relatives, I assume."

"None. At least none that I know and definitely none that would be willing to help me."

"Ms. Brooks," he said as he pulled a box up to sit next to me. "You can't live by yourself. Have you talked to the people at your school? Maybe they can help you."

"No. But I know Momma will be back." I don't know why I lied. After all the time she had been gone, I didn't know anything for sure. But I didn't want him calling Social Services on me.

"I don't mean any harm, Tina, but this is serious."

Mr. Sam hardly ever called me by my first name. I knew at that moment things were going against me. I needed to convince him not to turn me in.

"I know she will work something out. Her boyfriend, well he travels a lot. This is the first time she's ever been out of Virginia. I haven't been able to reach her and she thinks that I am with friends," I said, making it up as I went along.

"So, what do you want to do?" he asked.

"I don't know," I admitted. "I guess I need a place to stay that's close enough for me to go to school and still work here to make some money."

"I don't know, Tina."

He was still calling me by my first name. Things weren't going well. I finally asked, out of desperation, "Can I just stay in the room in the back for a few days? There is a cot there and I can wash up in the rest room. I know she will come back soon."

"I don't know, Ms. Brooks. I don't think that would be appropriate."

Progress. He was calling me Ms. Brooks again. I just waited.

"I may have an idea. Are you okay for a few nights?"

"Yes, but by the end of the month I have to be out."

"Ms. Brooks, before I get deeper involved in your situation, you need to be straight with me. Do you understand?"

"Yes," I answered, my voice barely above a whisper, because I was so ashamed of the lies I had told and the position I was forcing Mr. Sam into.

"First thing, Ms. Brooks, I do know that you have not always been entirely honest with me. But I also know that you are a very good person. That's the only reason you are still here."

"You know?"

"I am not an idiot, Ms. Brooks. Though I wasn't sure of the extent of your situation before, at the time, I made a decision to not ask a lot of questions. I decided to just watch and wait before making any calls."

You did?" By then the tears had returned.

Mr. Sam paused a minute. I guess he wanted his words to sink in.

"Ms. Brooks," he continued, as if I hadn't interrupted, "I began life with a very happy, but somewhat weird, family. But things happened, and I ended up in foster homes, some good and some not so good. I was lucky, my last home became permanent and the people became my family. That's not always the case. And I did see some really bad things happen to young girls. There is never any guarantee. And it's hard, even for well-meaning people, to keep track. Since I know and like you, I have to admit that I am conflicted about just turning you over to the authorities."

There was nothing much I could say. I was putting my fate in this poor gentle man's hand, and it wasn't fair.

"Ms. Brooks . . . Tina, I have gotten where I am by making solid decisions and being able to judge people. From what I have observed about you, I knew there had to be someone who cared a lot about you. I am surprised she has not returned. It is now my goal to keep you safe until you two are reunited. I have an idea and need to check with a friend who may can help."

"Thanks, Mr. Sam."

"Don't thank me yet," he admonished. "So, as I said before, I have an idea. There is someone, a friend that I have to confer with. Until then, you go back to your home, keep yourself safe. Try and be a kid. Do kid things. You are not alone . . ." Then he hiked up his high-water pants and headed towards his office.

CHAPTER 17

I COULDN'T BELIEVE that I had turned my situation over to the grown-ups. The thought had me more scared than I had been at any time since Momma's disappearance. All my plans and all my strategies were dependent on *me* keeping *my* situation under *my* control. The point was to make sure I kept *my* head down and that I avoided doing or saying anything to bring official scrutiny on *myself.*

Now, all I wanted to do was to go back in time and stop myself from panicking and running to Paulette and her mother. Instead of freaking out, I should have taken the time to assess what I needed to do, on my own, in the time I had left. It's not as if I had no plan at all. With the help of the computers at school, I had already begun researching motels and rooming houses in the immediate area. And using the results to narrow down the ones to visit, I had checked out several to determine if they were clean and safe. Though all my efforts, so far, had revealed that only the sleaziest ones were anywhere near my meager budget, there was still time to continue looking.

Foolishly, I'd jumped the gun and made grown-ups aware of my situation. Now they would take over and make all the decisions. Mr. Sam had seriously thought that telling me to go "be a kid" was a good thing. That's the last thing I wanted. Just look what happened when I had weakened and acted like a kid. I ended up putting myself in a situation where all my options were taken away. As a result, by the end of the week, I feared that I would more than likely be in the custody of Social Services.

I racked my brain, but no matter how hard I tried, I could not come up with any idea, any miracle, or anyone to save me. Shortly before Momma's disappearance, we had discovered that the one person who loved both Momma and me, my dear Auntie Dee, had passed away from complications due to Alzheimer's disease. My grandparents wanted nothing to do with me. And the person who fathered me had no idea that I even existed. Even if he did, I doubt if he'd be willing to help.

I was thinking all this as I walked into the *All Come Inn* motel. It was the place Mr. Sam had sent me to talk with his friend, a woman named April Alexander. I did not know what to expect. With no other choice, I said a silent prayer, and went through the doors.

As I entered the lobby, though he didn't bother to look up, I could tell that the guy behind the counter had heard me come in.

"Ahem," I cleared my throat to catch his attention.

"Can I help you?" he asked, with his head still stuck in his book.

"Yes, please."

He finally looked up. He was younger than I originally assumed, maybe nineteen. My first impression was that he was the prettiest man I had ever seen. The only thing that killed the affect was the big gap in his front teeth. Aside from that, he was tall—well, much taller than me—thin and had close cropped hair. His eyes were a beautiful light brown, which stood out because of his medium brown coloring.

Standing there, in front of a stranger, in a strange motel, I felt terribly young and self-conscious. Once again, for some reason, I was close to tears.

He must have sensed that I was becoming emotional because he asked, "Are you okay?"

"No, not really. How much does a room here cost?"

He smiled. "This time of year, the rate is $35.00 a night."

"What? For this dump? I mean…"

"I know exactly what you mean," he laughed. "Don't worry about it, if I could do better, I wouldn't be here either."

"Do you think I could get a job here too, to help pay for a room? I really can't afford $35.00 a night. Especially since I don't know how long I will have to stay."

"Umm, I can't answer that, but you can wait right here, I'll go get the manager. You can talk to her. She's really understanding, a very nice person. I'm Tony, by the way."

He gave me a reassuring smile as he turned and walked towards the back. When he returned, he was followed by this exotic looking woman with black hair that flowed down past her shoulders. I assumed she was April Alexander, but Mr. Sam had said she was black, rather he used his preferred designation, African American. No matter the terminology, I couldn't see it at all. If anything, I would've guessed she was Hispanic.

The guy, who said his name was Tony, introduced her, "This is April. She runs this castle."

The woman gave me a kind smile and said, "Hello. What can I do for you, dear?"

I was tempted to lie, but I opted for the truth. "My mother disappeared, and I'm being kicked out of our apartment. Mr. Sam Roberts, from ATC, told me to come here. I just need to find a place to stay until my mother comes back."

"You're awfully young to be here on your own. How in the world do you support yourself?"

"I have a job at ATC. It's close to Southside Middle School, where I go, at least for now. That is, unless I can't find a place close enough and cheap enough for me to stay in school."

"I don't know, um . . . What is your name dear?"

"I'm Tina Brooks."

"Sammy told me you would come by, but I didn't realize just how young you were. I don't know, Tina Brooks. Seems like you will need some grown-up supervision and support."

"Miss April, my mother taught me to be independent. I've been on my own for most of the school year. I've gotten a job, on my own, and I've kept up my schoolwork. If I could afford our apartment and avoid Child Services, for the next four years, or 'til my mother returns, I would. I can't end up with

Child Services. Nothing good ever happens when kids, especially kids my age, are handed over to them."

"But that's the law, Tina Brooks, and I don't break the law. I can't."

"I know, Miss April, but my mother won't be able to find me. Plus, they probably won't let her get me back, since she's been gone so long. Like I said, I have a job. I go to school and am smart enough to stay out of trouble. All I need is a temporary place to stay for a short while."

"Can you afford $35 a night working part time at ATC?"

"No ma'am. But I'm willing to work by making beds, cleaning, anything you need."

She hesitated. Everybody I knew, felt that Social Service people were overworked and, once in a while, bad things happened. I was hoping that Miss April Alexander was aware of this too.

"Hmmm, I just don't know."

"Please, Miss April, I am a really good worker."

"Wait a moment," she said. "I'll be right back."

She left and went back through the door she had come through. Tony, the desk clerk, put his head down again. I guess he didn't have much to say to a desperate fourteen-year-old kid. I went to sit on the small sofa against the wall.

About ten minutes later, Miss April came back out. "I talked with Sammy. He, for some reason, has confidence in you, and thinks your idea is a practical solution that'll work out for us both."

"So, Miss April, can I stay?"

"Please stop the Miss April stuff. My name is just April."

I took that as a yes and jumped up to give her the biggest hug she had probably ever gotten. I would call her anything she wanted, at that point.

* * *

The next day, April showed me around. She told anyone, who seemed interested enough, that I would be staying and helping out in the motel for a short while. What surprised me was that she introduced me as her niece. I guess that was for both our protection, but I was totally taken off guard. Still, nobody asked any questions or pried for details. It was that type of place. And, apparently, Tony was also a nephew.

As we walked through the motel, I noticed that it was old but well maintained. All the people we encountered were cordial. And, what impressed me the most, was that everyone seemed to like and respect April. As the day progressed, I understood why.

She was friendly and she seemed dedicated to the place and her staff. She even knew a lot about the history of the area, particularly the All Come Inn.

Apparently, a long time ago, the motel name was changed to "All Come Inn" during a period when most places, along the bustling US Route-1 corridor, would not accept people of color as guests. The name was supposed to be a beacon to let traveling people, all people, know they were welcome. Unfortunately, when the government put in the interstate highway, a great deal of the traffic was averted, and the corridor nearly died. Businesses and residents suffered. What remained was a lot of poverty and homelessness, where there once was prosperity. At some point, people who couldn't afford apartments or who were down on their luck, began living in motels, including the All Come Inn. I was surprised to learn that there were whole families living in the motel.

When we returned to her office, April described how there were a number of desperate and even some shady people staying at the motel and, because of that, it was not an ideal solution for someone my age.

"Tina," she said, making every effort to be as gentle and as diplomatic as possible, "please understand, this arrangement must be temporary. I respect your situation, but I don't have a lot of control over transient people who check in here. More than just a bed, you need a level of security that I cannot guarantee. Starting now, we are looking at alternatives. Make no mistake, I'll do what I can to help you figure out what to do next. Hopefully, it'll all be unnecessary, and your mother will return soon."

She was nice like that. Even though I was certain that she did not think my mother would show up, April would never say it out loud to me. And for the first time since Auntie Dee, someone, besides Paulette, had my back. Needless to say, I was overwhelmed with gratitude.

* * *

Saturday, three days later, April called me into her office. Tony and a couple of guys, that I assumed were his friends, were already there. They were big guys and were around nineteen or twenty, like Tony.

She introduced them as Smitty and Jay. Neither said anything but nodded as she pointed them out.

"Tina," April said, once the introductions were complete. "I know you said that the belongings in your apartment weren't worth much, but I see no reason for you to leave them there for the landlord, or whoever, to sale or trash. Jay, here," she said pointing to the bulky tall brown skinned guy nearest me, "has a truck. He, Smitty, and Tony are here to help you move your stuff, if you're ready."

I almost cried right then and there. "Thanks," was all I could get out.

I was surprised how quickly we were able to pack up Momma and my few belongings. Every bit of it fit in a small secure cage that was inside a storage area, where the motel kept old furniture or things that needed to be repaired. April locked it up and gave me the key.

After leaving the apartment, for the final time, I recalled all the effort it took for Momma and me to make the place livable and how proud we both were of the home we had made. An overwhelming despondency came over me, a sadness that I realized would probably never go away.

When I returned to my room at the motel, I locked myself in and never wanted to leave. Of course, I cried. It wasn't so much from losing the apartment, I had prepared myself for that. What I could not have prepared myself for was the empty feeling in the pit of my stomach, a feeling of a more permanent loss. It was an acceptance, once and for all, that committing to starting a life without Momma meant admitting I might never see her again.

* * *

The following Sunday morning, I was still depressed. After securing my stuff, I should have been happy, but I had no desire to leave my room. Later that evening, April came, sat beside me on my bed, and just started talking. I was grateful that she didn't tell me how lucky I was, or that everything would be all right, or even that everything sucked and I had a right to be upset. She talked nearly fifteen minutes about the rules of the motel, guest privacy, what happened when guests checked in, and what happened when guests checked out, that sort of thing.

Then, she took my hands and made me look at her. "Tina," she said, "I can't imagine how hard this is for someone your age. It would be impossible even for someone like me, twice your age . . . plus a little."

We both smiled. Then she continued, "For now, sweetheart, the best thing for you is to keep busy. You have a lot that will help you there. There's school. There's the work you have at ATC. There's the work you have here. But I can't emphasize more, that here you must keep a low profile. You understand that, right?"

"Yes, ma'am," I said.

"By the way, I don't really feel comfortable with you walking back and forth between here, your school, and ATC. So, here are a few bus passes you can start with, along with some schedules."

There was nothing more to say. So, she placed the passes and a brochure with the public bus schedules on the bed beside me. Then, after a brief hug, she left. The strange thing was that I did feel better, not so alone.

Chapter 18

BY MY FIRST DAY at Thurgood Marshall High, I had adjusted to my new life. All summer, April and Mr. Sam were busy trying to find a permanent and more suitable place for me to stay. However, personally, I no longer saw the need. With my new support system, things were better for me than they would be anywhere else, even my old apartment complex. I liked working with and being around April. I liked having money to spend, now that I had two part time jobs. I liked that Tony and I were becoming friends. And, I liked that there were other adults around who looked out for me. With all that, I was beginning to think that April, Mr. Sam, and even Tony, were all over reacting. I saw no real urgency in finding another place to stay. At least, that's what I thought, until the day it became too dangerous for me to stay at the All Come Inn.

It was a normal Wednesday evening. I was rushing to my room to complete an algebra assignment that was due in two days. I stopped by the front desk to say *hi* to Tony.

"Tina," he said, "I need a favor if you have time."

"What?" I asked.

"One of our regulars was supposed to drop off the key to room twelve. She sometimes forgets and leaves it in the room. Can you go there and pick up the key, if it's there, and see what needs to be done?"

"That's the favor?"

"Sure, I just wanted to check before leaving. Barbara normally handles that room. She left early because of a family emergency. I don't know what she did, if anything, in that room."

"No problem," I said.

With all April had done for me, I took every opportunity to help out. I figured it wouldn't take that long to check the room and, if necessary, finish up what needed to be done. Besides, I really didn't mind putting off algebra.

Even though the guest was supposed to be long gone, I knocked first. April was a stickler about ensuring that we did not walk in on an unsuspecting guest. After knocking twice, I put my ear to the door. When there was no sound on the other side, I assumed the room was empty. I put my key in the door, while announcing, "House Keeping", just in case.

When no one answered, I continued into the room. Before I could begin my search for the keys, I saw that the bed was soaked with what looked like blood. Stunned and not knowing what to do, I started for the door. That's when I heard a noise coming from the bathroom.

Stupid me. Instead of running for my life, I decided to check to see if somebody was hurt and needed help. Common sense should've told me to get out of there, but I couldn't simply leave. As I began easing towards the bathroom, the door flew open.

A very angry man yelled, "What the hell are you doing in here?"

"Sorry," I said weakly.

Terrified, I dashed out the door. Knowing that I had to tell someone, I headed directly towards April's office.

"What in the world is wrong with you?" Tony asked, noting my panic, as I ran pass the front desk.

"I don't know," I said. "I think something really bad happened in the room you sent me to, room twelve."

"Like what?" Tony asked with all the enthusiasm of a possum moving across a busy highway.

"I just came from room twelve and the bed was covered with blood."

"Blood? Are you sure Tina?"

"I'm sure," I yelled. "Give me the damn phone, I'm calling the police." I reached for the phone.

Tony grabbed the phone before I could get it. "Look, you can't just call the police for a little blood on a motel bed. You know this place ain't the Hilton. We had better be sure before you call the cops down here. They get really upset if it's a false alarm."

"What would you prefer, the cops or me strangling your bonny ass?" I was so upset that I reached for Tony's throat.

"Okay. Okay. Li'l Bit, first calm down. Tell me what happened."

"I went to check for the key in room twelve, like you asked. It was supposed to be vacant. I went in and saw all this stuff that looked like blood on the bed. Then this man came out of the bathroom . . ."

"Man? In room twelve?"

"Yeah, a real scary looking guy."

Tony went to the computer, hit a few keys and said, "The only person signed up for room twelve is Glory Lake. I'm not saying she wouldn't have a man with her. But, normally, she should have been gone hours ago."

"You know her?"

"Let's just say that Glory is a regular. When she gets a special client she checks in here, usually for a few hours only. She should have been gone, at the latest, last night."

"Well, I didn't see any Glory Lake, just the scary guy."

"This doesn't sound good, Li'l Bit. I better get April."

Tony paged April. Together, the two of them went to check on room twelve. I followed.

When we got there, April opened the door. As she turned her head in the direction of the bed, she said, quietly under her breath, "Oh, shit!"

She and Tony stepped into the room. After noticing a trail of blood leading to the bathroom, I remained outside. I don't know how I missed it the first time. April and Tony walked around the blood to the bathroom door.

They both peeked in and rushed out. April pulled me away and we headed back to the office. Tony was almost running, it seemed like he was on the verge of being sick and wasn't going to make it.

Once in her office, April shut the door. "Tina, the man you saw in the room, did you know him?"

"No."

"Could you describe him?"

"No, April, why?"

"You're sure you couldn't describe the man at all?"

"No . . . I mean yes. I was too scared. Why, April? What was in the bathroom? You've got to tell me."

"Okay, Tina. Glory was in the tub. The man you saw probably killed her. Since she was supposed to be gone last night, he might have done it then. I have no idea why he was back in the room."

"Killed her?" I screamed. "You mean that woman's dead body is in the bathroom? That's where all the blood came from?"

"Yes. And I have to call the police."

April said all this in a manner that I can only describe as scary calm. But she was pacing around the room. I had never seen her rattled before. I'll have to admit, it was making me nervous.

"I don't think I can keep you out of it," she said. "But, since you don't really know anything, only tell them that you saw the blood on the bed, and you came down to tell me. *Do Not* . . . I repeat . . . *Do Not* mention that you saw a man in the room. If you have nothing more to offer, there is no reason to get you too involved. Too much information will only result in you getting drilled for no real reason. We don't need that. It's bad enough that the creep saw you. The good thing was that you didn't have anything on that identifies you or says that you work at the motel. Hopefully, he won't come back here looking for you."

"What does all that mean?" Now I was beginning to understand that seeing blood on the bed of a motel room was not my biggest concern.

April did not answer me. She let out a loud sigh and went to her desk to make the call. Then, she did her best to calm Tony down, before calling someone else in to take his place, since obviously he was in no shape to work the front desk.

We were all shocked when it only took the police about ten minutes to get to the motel. It must've been some type of record. The first ones to arrive only asked April a few questions. Then they headed to room twelve and told us to wait in the office.

An officer returned and questioned me with very little enthusiasm. I guess finding out what happened to a known prostitute was not high on his list. In his defense, I really did not have much to offer, especially since I could not mention the man I saw coming out of the bathroom.

Once the police were convinced that neither of us was an actual witness, they gave up and let me go.

Later, Tony told me that somebody had cut Glory's throat and stuffed her in the bathtub. We both shuddered as he described the set of industrial sized plastic bags by the tub—our young imaginations immediately visualizing chainsaws and hatchets. But, the police said that they weren't sure what the bags were for. They assumed that the person who killed Glory was probably in the process of trying to clean up when something must have spooked him. They had no idea what that could have been. We both shuddered again.

CHAPTER 19

JUST LIKE THAT, everything changed. We all agreed that the person who committed the awful crime was a threat to all of us, mostly me. The man from the bathroom had seen my face and he knew exactly where to start looking for me, even if I couldn't remember what he looked like.

April, not wanting to take any chances, no longer allowed me to work or show my face around the motel. I was essentially fired. Poor Tony was so traumatized that he quit his job and refused to return. At least he had options.

For me, the nightmares started that first night. There was this dark figure who would follow me from the motel. He would grab me on the way to the bus stop or outside the motel and slit my throat. I would wake up just as he pulled out the big green trash bags. I was so scared that I couldn't sleep with the thought of the man, from the bathroom, returning to quiet the only possible witness, me.

April doubled her efforts to find me a place to stay, and within a week she somehow managed to convince her reluctant friend, the one who ran a boarding house, to make room for me.

When she came to inform me, I was zombied-out on the bed. The television was on, merely as background noise, and I was trying hard to focus on the Social Studies textbook on the bed in front of me, but was failing.

"How's it going?" April asked, pointing to my textbook.

"I'm just sitting here wondering why I should care about the *Fall of the Roman Empire.*"

"I get that," she laughed. "I have news for you."

"What?"

"Remember, I told you that I would talk with my friend, Martha Jacobs?"

"The lady who runs the boarding house, right?'

"Yup, that's her. She's agreed to let you move in."

"She did? I thought you said that you weren't sure about approaching her, because she's so picky."

"That's true. It's her home, she lives there, and must be super careful. Since she's only doing the boarding house thing because she has the extra space, she can afford to be selective and have a pretty strict screening process. But, desperate times call for desperate measures. I appealed to her, on your behalf. I told her that you wouldn't cause problems. That I was concerned for your safety. She understood why, after I told her what happened to Glory here and how close you came to the guy who killed her. She agreed that you aren't safe here."

"I thought all her rooms were taken."

"What she has is a very small room, which she never intended to rent out. She kept thinking she'd turn it into her private exercise room. It never happened. The room was mostly collecting junk. She's willing to clean it out, put in a futon and a dresser, and turn it into a room especially for you."

"I don't care if it's small. But, will I be able to afford it?"

"Actually, it's cheaper than living here. Plus, she needs help keeping the bathrooms and common areas clean. She has a service that comes in twice a month, but that's not always enough."

"What do you think?" I asked.

"I think it's perfect for you. It's less dangerous and Martha, Mrs. Jacobs, is a good person. She's fair and will look out for you. She's raised two daughters of her own. She's not your sweet-kissy-huggy-grandmotherly type, but, like I said, she's a good person."

"She knows about me?"

"She knows that your parents are unavailable, and she thinks that we're distant relatives. Actually, in the time I've known you, I almost feel it's true."

"I don't know what to . . ." I couldn't get the words out. It seemed that I was spending a lot of time in tears.

April ignored the tears and continued, "Since, she doesn't know you, I had to vouch for you and I also had to guarantee the rent. You understand what that means?"

"I think so."

"It means, Tina, that I'm going out on a limb for you, in more ways than one. It means that if you don't pay her, she doesn't have to worry about collecting from you. She can just go after me for whatever you owe. And more than likely, that is what will happen."

"No, it won't. You know I'll do everything I can to pay her."

"I'm counting on it. But, little girl, you had better not screw me over, you hear me?"

"Yes, April, I hear you. I appreciate what you're doing and all you've done. Without you, I don't know where I would be now. I won't disappoint you, April. I promise."

"You'd better not, young lady."

"April, don't worry. Thank you. Thank you. Thank you. You have really been a good friend to me."

"You're welcomed baby. And we will be friends as long as you remember that I can't afford an extra five hundred twenty dollars a month – minus whatever you two agree on for the assistance you provide."

"I won't let you down."

PART Four

Party Hearty - Hordes of Friends
(2010-2015)

CHAPTER 20

THE SOUND MADE by the ringing phone blended nicely into the dream I was having, as I relaxed on my brand new-to-me furniture. I had been trying, but failing, to maintain interest in the latest must-watch string of prime-time sitcoms. The only thing I got out of the wasted two hours was some much-needed rest. That was why my brain didn't respond to the phone begging for my attention, until after the answering machine had kicked in.

"Hello, Tina . . . Tina . . ." I heard, through my fog. "Pick up. Come on. I know you're there."

I grabbed the phone. I most definitely did not want to miss that call. I had been waiting nearly three weeks to find out how my best friend was adjusting to college life.

Not that there was anything to worry about. Paulette would do well at any college, without breaking a sweat. Many who didn't know her, only saw Paulette as this good-natured, out-going, outrageous flake. They didn't realize that she had a world class brain which she hid well behind that apparently flakey exterior. She had this amazing talent for doing math in her head. This knack for numbers combined with her strong memory skills, and her ability to grasp and breakdown facts, was how she blew away both the PSAT and SAT. And it was also how she earned an unrestrictive-full scholarship to the University of North Carolina at Chapel Hill.

"About time," I said.

As expected, Paulette ignored my comment. "Whatcha up to, girl?"

"Nothing much," I answered. "I'm just sitting here watching TV and getting ready for work tomorrow."

"Not still nervous, are you?"

I couldn't help but smile. That was the friend I missed so much. While she was the one starting a new college career, far from home, in an unfamiliar environment, she was concerned about me and my new job as a file clerk.

"Nah," I answered. "I'm pretty used to it now. With all the stuff I've had to manage since I was thirteen, alphabetizing a few cards and typing stuff into a computer is a welcome change of pace."

"I hear you," she said. "How's the new place working out? You still speaking to Mrs. J, after she kicked you out?"

"You're sooo funny, Paulette," I laughed. "I couldn't get mad at Mrs. Jacobs. It was good that she let me stay there in the first place. She couldn't help it if her daughter needed somewhere for her and her kids to live."

"What did happen with them?"

"Don't know the details, but apparently the husband was a piece of work. Sandy, the daughter, wanted to get herself and her children as far away from him as possible."

Just before Paulette left for UNC, Mrs. Jacobs, my landlord, had announced that she was closing her rooming house. She explained that she needed the space for her daughter, who was going through a bitter divorce, and moving with her teenaged daughters from Hopewell back to Richmond.

For me, her decision turned out to be a blessing in disguise. Instead of having to travel clear across town, I found a one-bedroom apartment only minutes away from my job downtown. And that's what I told Paulette.

"You're right," she said. "That bus commute, from Southside, had to have been unbearable."

"Oh, didn't I tell you? I don't have to take the bus, I have my own car, now. Thanks to Mr. Sam."

"That sweet old guy didn't buy you a car, did he?"

"Nah, he's not that sweet," I laughed. "But he did sell me his 2000 Elantra for less than half of what he could have sold it for."

"I remember it. He loved that little car. I'm surprised he got rid of it," Paulette said.

"He bought a new car. He said I was someone he could trust to take care of his old one."

"Oh, by the way, could you use any of the stuff out of April's storage area? Last I heard, you didn't know if it still was any good," Paulette said, moving on to the next topic. That was another thing I missed about my friend. Even in ordinary conversations, it was hard to keep up with her.

"Yeah. Actually, I was surprised that it was all still in pretty decent condition. I'm using Momma's bed and the dinette set in my apartment. I sold my old twin bed to friends, one of the families from the motel. At first, I figured that I'd wait and save up some money before worrying about more furniture. At least, that was the plan, until I saw a notice from this guy, Ibrahim, who lived downstairs. He was graduating and moving to Boston. He didn't want to take his old stuff with him. I called just to see what he was selling. Since he had to get out in a few days, he offered to sell everything he had left—a love seat, chair, and end tables—for fifty dollars."

"All that for fifty dollars . . . You didn't buy it did you?" Paulette asked, dubious of the bargain.

"Actually, I did."

"What kind of condition was it in? Did you at least check for little creepy crawlers before moving it to your apartment?"

"The set's not half bad . . . *and* I did check. There weren't any creepy crawlers. But I'll admit that Ibrahim's sense of style and mine are waaay different. The tables are kinda cute. It looks like he made them himself, but I didn't ask. The chair and sofa are some butt-ugly brownish pattern. You wouldn't believe how ugly. Good thing I have Momma's old sewing machine. I went to the fabric shop, *Needles and Threads,* and got some cute material and a pattern. I'm making myself some slipcovers for the set."

"You go girl. I can't wait to see all of it," Paulette said in a way that I knew she truly meant it.

"I'm kinda proud of how it's coming along. As a matter of fact, I was stretched out—rather, falling asleep—on the sofa when you called. The cover is still held together by pins, but I'll take care of that this weekend."

"I keep forgetting how resourceful you are," Paulette said, before letting out a huge sigh, signaling that what was coming next was not going to be easy on me. "You know I've just gotta say it, right?"

"What?"

"You should be down here with me. I know that most of our high school guidance idiots were useless. But Mrs. Betts would've helped you find the right school and found you financial aid, like she did for me. She'd help anyone, whether they were assigned to her or not. Just think how cool it would've been if both of us were roommates here together."

"Paulette, I'm not like you," I said.

"What the hell does that mean?" she asked, huffily.

"Don't get testy, girl," I said. "We both know that the only financial aid I could qualify for, especially at a place like UNC, would include a lot of loans. That would mean putting myself into big time debt. Believe me I checked. Besides, even if I wanted to, I couldn't have applied for financial aid without declaring myself as an independent student. Me trying to do that would have been fun. Right? The questions that might have been raised would've made things real interesting, to say the least."

"I know, Tina. But it still seems such a waste. As smart as you are . . . Hell, you're twice as smart as half of the fools down here. You'd do great."

"From your lips to God's ears," I laughed. "Seriously, I'm not sorry about my choice. You know how tired I am of working my butt off twenty-four-seven. I've had enough of working myself half to death. For now, I need a break. Someday I'll figure out something that I want to do and then I might think about college."

"Okay, while you're thinking, you can think yourself down here and visit me. Try out your new car on the highway," my friend said, moving on again.

"Well, it's only new-to-me. Remember Mr. Sam drove it for ten years before I got it."

"Right, but I never actually saw him drive it. Knowing Mr. Sam, it probably only had two and a half miles on it," Paulette joked. "Speaking of Mr. Sam, I don't know what kind of voodoo you put on those people . . . April, Mr. Sam, and even Mrs. Jacobs. I wish my parents cared as much about me. I mean . . . Mr. Sam gave you a job, helped you get a car. Mrs. J let you stay there forever and never raised your rent. And April . . . Wow . . . April was always there looking out for you. When you needed it most, she even gave you all that money, five hundred bucks, for graduation. All I got from my parents was a handclap, as I walked across the stage. And a handshake when they met me outside. I was lucky to get that."

"Paulette, you should be ashamed of yourself, lying on your parents like that. But my protectors have been a true blessing and I don't think I'll ever be able to pay them back."

"What pisses me off is the wench that spawned you . . ." Paulette said, her mood changing.

"Come on, Paulette," I said, not liking this turn in the conversation.

"Do not *come on Paulette* me."

I just let the silence hang for a moment, which was the best thing to do when my friend got on the topic of Momma. We had had the same discussion for years and there was no calming Paulette down when it came to my mother. She was convinced that Momma was the lowest of creatures, a selfish foolish woman who had deserted her only child for a man, even though over the years I had explained why I had come to a different conclusion.

In my heart, I sincerely believed that my mother loved me. And during the time we were together, she had done everything she could to protect me. Leaving me, at age thirteen, to fend on my own, was not something she would plan to do. I was now sure of it. That's why I was convinced something terrible had happened to her. And, whatever that was, it had prevented her contacting me. Paulette, as usual, did not agree. Furthermore, this time she was not going to allow me to make excuses for my mother.

"Be real, Tina. The woman left you twice. The first time she had barely popped you out before it was *wham bam see you around kid.* You don't even know for sure she didn't run off that time with some uncle. Do you?"

"No, I don't know for absolute certain. But I do know there were no boyfriends before my dad, if you could call a psycho rapist that. And, considering her state of mind, I doubt it seriously. From conversations with Momma, it sounded like she experienced some type of nervous breakdown after I was born. No wonder. With so many of the people she trusted messing over her, it must've been too much."

"Still, girlfriend, you have to wonder where she was or what she did for those first six years."

"Yeah, I guess," I conceded. "She might have been in a hospital, for all I know."

"You mean a nuthouse?"

"I don't really know. What I do know is that Auntie Dee was protective of both of us. And Momma was very fragile. Auntie Dee would never have let her take me if it wasn't right for us both. Then again, with me being so young, I wouldn't have known if Momma was around the whole time. Auntie Dee could've just been taking the lead in raising me. Like I said, I was too young to know any different."

"Come on, Tina. Now, you're just rationalizing. You were old enough to know if your mother was around."

"What I am absolutely sure about is that, on the day she came to get me, Momma promised that, no matter what, she loved me and would be there for me always."

"We both know how that worked out . . ."

"Yeah, I know. Momma wasn't the ideal mother. But she did her best to look after me. When push came to shove, she protected me against anyone she thought could hurt me or prey on me. Look at Uncle Ted."

"What about him?" The topic swing had Paulette confused. "What's he got to do with anything?"

"I've thought about the ways he stared at me and the subtle things he did to get me alone. Momma said that someday I'd understand. Now, I'm convinced Momma was right about him. Look at what she did to protect me from him. Remember Bonita Foster and what happened to her? Nobody knew that her stepfather, a teacher mind you, was messing with her until she turned up pregnant. Her mother knew and did nothing. Remember?"

"Yeah, I remember."

"And then there were the creepy twins, Oscar and William. They weren't real brothers, but they did everything together and everybody thought they were just goofy nerds. Nobody knew what they were forcing that ten-year-old kid to do. "

"I remember that too . . ."

"So, just because I was only ten, when Momma had her suspicions about Uncle Ted, does not mean he respected my age and wasn't plotting and waiting to do bad things, hoping to get away with it."

"Okay. Okay. Maybe your mom was right about this Uncle Ted dude. But, then again, who was she protecting you from when she fell for Horace, excuse me, Mr. Franks, and threw you to the curb, big time?"

"You know that's not what I believe happened."

"You're just blind in one eye and can't see out the other one." She joked, but not with her usual gusto.

Over the years, I'd had plenty of time to think about Momma, trying to picture her as the monster who would abandon her child twice in thirteen years. No matter what it seemed like, I honestly didn't believe she would do that to me.

Not that I was delusional or blind to Momma's faults. Just the opposite. Her child rearing philosophy was straight from the Stone Age. Of that, I was painfully aware. No question, Momma's idea of discipline was extreme. She wasn't one of those parents who discussed things with kids and put them in timeouts for being bad. She'd yell and slap the mess out of me if I crossed the line. On the other hand, you let somebody else try to do me harm and she'd go into mother-lion-defending-her-cub mode.

A lot of what she did was based on Momma's single-minded determination to make me strong. Her techniques for doing that would never earn her mother of the year. But her main goal was to prevent me from becoming the victim she had been.

I think raising me, Momma became a lot stronger and wiser than she had been before. I honestly believe that given time, she would eventually have seen what everybody else suspected about Mr. Franks. She would have walked away from him, and under no circumstances would she have left her daughter alone, on the off chance that he would be so very different from all the others.

Then again, there was solid evidence that she planned on returning. When she disappeared, there were a lot of personal items that were important to her left at the apartment, things that normally she'd never leave behind. Most notable was a black pearl necklace from Auntie Dee, her prize possession. It was still sitting in her jewelry box. It was so precious to her that she wouldn't let me touch it.

Then there were her favorite clothes, her final paycheck, and the money left in our joint account that was never accessed. None of those would be on Momma's list of things to be left behind or undone.

If nothing else, she wouldn't have missed my fourteenth birthday. Ever since we'd been together, Momma always made a big deal of my birthdays. Even Mr. Franks couldn't change how she felt about that.

Finally, there was the one thing I was absolutely certain of. No matter how charming he was or how infatuated she was with Mr. Franks, Momma would not have endangered my life by intentionally disappearing without any trace. That, I believed with all my heart.

I tried, for the millionth time, to explain this to Paulette. She listened patiently for as long as she could stand it and finally, she said, "Unfortunately, girlfriend, that might be one mystery we may never solve. Maybe it's time to let her go. I'm not saying forget her. No matter what your mom did or didn't do, you have to start focusing on moving forward."

"Damn, that's deep. Maybe you should go into law or philosophy instead of math and accounting. No, I've got it, inspirational speaking," I laughed.

"Oh, shut-up. You know what I mean. Anyhow, I gotta go, Tina. There is this orientation thing all freshmen are supposed to attend. And I'm late."

"Bye. Love you."

"Love you too, girlfriend. I'll let you know if there are any big hunks at the orientation worthy of my attention."

I laughed as we both hung up.

* * *

Joking with Paulette, about her earnest *moving forward* speech, in no way meant that I didn't take her words seriously. After all, my friend was the smartest person I knew. And she understood me better than anyone. I'd be stupid to discount her advice. As a matter of fact, I agreed with Paulette that the mystery of my mother's actions might never be solved, and it would be foolish to stop living my life while waiting for answers. But, as smart as she was, Paulette was wrong to assume that I was wallowing in the memory of my poor shattered childhood. I saw no need in stressing over the past. It was gone . . . done . . . turn the page.

What I would never forget, however, are the people who rescued me, my co-conspirators. Honestly, I don't know what would have happened to me if it weren't for Paulette, April, Mr. Sam, and even Mrs. Jacobs. Just coming to my rescue put them all at risk, but they did it anyhow. Because of them, I survived the unique challenges of my circumstances in a manner unimaginable without them.

The jeopardy I placed those astonishing people in, for five years, still makes me feel guilty. Those five years, I was constantly looking over my shoulders wondering if Social Services would grab me and punish my supporters. The strain of such a heavy responsibility was enormous. It forced me to grow up much too soon.

Now grown-up, aged eighteen plus, I was free to enjoy some of what I had missed, including the one thing most kids took for granted. I finally had the opportunity to be young and worry free. That, more than anything, was my foremost reason for postponing college and not, as Paulette had suggested, being afraid to move forward. Instead, I needed time to finally be a normal happy-go-lucky young person whose primary objective was to hang-out with hordes of friends and attend bunches of carefree parties.

So, while making room in my life for the party-hearty-hordes-of-friends, I happily drove to the office each day, guilt free. I performed—what many might think of as—mind numbing duties. And then I returned home to my cute little apartment. It was my dream come true.

CHAPTER 21

A WEEK AFTER MY SEVENTEENTH BIRTHDAY, for the second time in my life, I was fired by someone I loved—for my own good. First April fired me and then Mr. Sam. It happened on the day I confided to him that I had no intention of applying to college. Mr. Sam listened patiently to my announcement. When he realized that my intent was to work forever at ATC, he gave me my notice, essentially firing me.

I was shocked because I had assumed that he would be happy. After all, I had been at the drugstore longer than most of the people working there. Not to mention, I was dependable, flexible, honest, hardworking, and smart. I was polite and well-liked by nearly everyone at ATC, including my peers, the pharmacists, and even some of the customers. ATC was home. I was comfortable there. Mr. Sam was more than an employer. He was practically family. And that, ironically, was why he said he was kicking me out, in his words, "to experience more of the world".

"But I like it here," I practically whined.

"I know you do," Mr. Sam said, sympathetically," and that's why, when it gets closer to graduation, you should look to see what else there is out there. I'd selfishly love for you to continue working here. After you graduate, until you find an appropriate position, you can do just that.

"But this place can't be a crutch. That would not be fair to you. It's best that you find out what all your options are. If at some point, you choose to come back or to make pharmacy a career, you know that I'll support you in any way I can."

"What if I can't find anything?"

"Ms. Brooks," he said patiently, "I find that highly unlikely. However, as long as you are making a genuine effort, you can stay here until you do."

Obviously, Mr. Sam had given the subject some thought. I didn't really like it. Not one bit. I looked at him and was tempted to feel that once more I was being abandoned. But I knew better. It was more like pushing the little bird out of the nest than abandoning it. So, yes, I understood his motivation. Feeling grateful for it? That would take quite a bit more time.

"Well," I said, "I at least have a year, right?"

Mr. Sam laughed, "Yes, you do, Ms. Brooks. Of course, if at any time you require a reference, I will definitely provide a glowing recommendation."

With that, he went to talk with a customer who was walking around the place looking lost.

I was numb. Watching him walk away, all I could think about was that I'd miss him and his high-water pants. "Why in the world can't that man, as smart as he is, find a pair of pants that fits properly? It's not that he can't afford them," I whispered to myself.

I wanted to feel bad, but I couldn't. I trusted Mr. Sam and I almost always followed his advice. Everybody who knew him did. He was, what April called, an *intuit,* or a person who could read people and situations just through observation. Apparently, it was a family trait. His great-great grandmother was a healer in Africa. When she arrived in this country, she practiced her craft in New Orleans and had a large following. Mr. Sam, I'm told, inherited some of her instincts. He wasn't psychic. Nor could he read people's minds. His skill was more subtle. He had a sixth sense which made him somewhat of a human lie detector.

When April first described all this to me, it answered a few nagging questions that I had never dared ask out loud: *Why had he helped me, especially since he admitted knowing that I'd lied to him? And, on that first day we met, why had April so readily accepted Mr. Sam's word that I was worth helping?*

Of course, I could've stalled or merely pretended to seek another job. But Mr. Sam would've known and, more importantly, so would I. That's why

I was one of the first to sign-up when the Citywide Youth Enrichment Program people scheduled a job fair at my school.

When the recruiter for Richmond General Medical Center accepted my application, he said how impressed he was by the accompanied recommendations from teachers and community business leaders, like Mr. Sam, April, and Mrs. Jacobs. Surprisingly, he hired me on the spot.

CHAPTER 22

ON MY FIRST DAY at Richmond General Medical Center, I soon discovered that my new supervisor, Mary Kaye Thompson, was not as easily impressed as the recruiter was. I had been hired through a job fair at my high school and understood why she would be wary. How could she not be, when she had no say-so in the screening or hiring of an inexperienced eighteen-year-old, fresh out of high school? I was literally forced on her through a process to which she had no input or control.

Though she had her doubts about me, I liked Mary Kaye Thompson immediately. She reminded me of one of those cool nineteen seventies era hippies, with her long skirt, her no fuss stringy hairstyle, no makeup, and her overall laidback attitude. She even wore the braided headband. I smiled to myself, half expecting her to raise her index and middle fingers in the universal V-for-peace symbol.

As she showed me around on my first day, Mary Kaye, not so subtly, probed to see if I was at least minimally qualified.

"I understand that you did well in high school," she said. "Apparently, you came highly recommended by several teachers, community leaders, and businesspeople. Seems they think that you are pretty smart and capable."

"Umm . . . thank you," I said, since she seemed to pause for a response.

"One thing you must know about this job is that you can't only depend on a computer. You must be good at spelling and putting things into alphabetical order. You also must be reasonably organized and good at completing tasks on time. Do you understand that?"

"Yes. The guy at the job fair mentioned all that," I answered. "I was raised by a mother who didn't believe in doing anything halfway. One thing she never got tired of saying was, 'If you're gonna do it, you're gonna do it right.' And she meant it. She pushed me to think things through, to do my best at all my school assignments, and to get those assignments in on time. As far as spelling, she insisted that I read books, magazines, sales flyers, road signs, anything that was handy. Any unfamiliar words had to be sounded out and or looked up. She had this big old dictionary that she'd had since she was in school and she insisted that I use it. I never won any spelling bees, but I never failed a spelling test."

"Hmm, your mother sounds like a good parent."

I had no response to that. I merely shrugged. There was absolutely nothing I could say.

Mary Kaye didn't seem to notice the sudden sadness that enveloped me, she had more questions to cover.

"We are the Records Management Section, a part of the Health Information Management organization for the Medical Center. While most of our data is handled electronically, that is, on the computer, we still keep hard-copy or paper records. As a file clerk, you must be able to properly manage and organize both. You also need to know how to scan paper documents into our system. Of course, we provide some training, but you must be familiar with the concepts. Are you generally comfortable with computers and do you understand about scanning documents?"

"Yes. I learned all that at school."

"Did you learn any Microsoft Office applications?"

"We had Excel and Word."

"It's not a hard and fast requirement, but we'd prefer if you are familiar enough with the keyboard to accurately type at least thirty words a minute. If this is a problem, there is software that I can recommend that you can practice with."

"Oh, no problem. They taught us typing in middle school as a prerequisite to computer class. I got up to fifty words per minute."

"Great. One more thing . . . Everyone in this office must interface with team members, medical staff, and sometimes patients or clients. Are you comfortable with that?"

"Yes."

I waited for the next question, but it seemed that she had run out. She examined the stack of papers on her desk, then looked up. Holding several of the papers in front of her, she smiled and said, "I read your application and all the references. I'll admit, I was a bit skeptical of all the high praise. If you're half as special as these papers indicate, then it seems that you will do fine here."

She stood up and said, "By the way, nobody around here ever says Richmond General Medical Center, sometimes they refer to it as *RGMC* and sometimes the *Medical Center*. Come on. Let me introduce you around."

* * *

As I followed Mary Kaye out, she pointed to the cubicle directly facing her office. "That's your space there," she said. "We will come back later for you to get situated."

I glanced where she was pointing. Right there, at eye level, white on black, was my name, *Dustina Brooks*, as big as day. I was overwhelmed. It was the coolest thing I had ever seen. There, for everyone to see, was my name on a sign marking my official cubby. Before I realized it, I was smiling like the Cheshire Cat from *Alice in Wonderland*.

Wow! This is real. I'm actually an employee of Richmond General Medical Center, I thought.

Looking from Mary Kaye's door to my cubicle, it hit me how close my cubicle was to my manager's office. I somehow managed to smile even broader, as it occurred to me that some poor co-worker probably lost their space to make it easier for my manager to watch over the new untested employee, me.

I wasn't sure if Mary Kaye had any idea why I had that silly grin on my face, but she chose to ignore it and give me my moment. Then she said, "As you can see, this is a very large workspace. It may take a day or two to acclimate yourself."

"Does everyone here work for Health Information Management?"

"No," she answered. "There are five different organizations located in this one area."

I nodded, distracted, thinking it might take more than a couple of days for me to *acclimate* myself. The room was about twice the size of my high school gym and was partitioned into sections of cubicles. On the outer walls were offices, like Mary Kaye's, with real doors. I noted that the space was so full of cubicles that there was barely enough room between the sections for walking. It must've been a bear having to maneuver furniture or office equipment through there.

"For now, I'll only introduce you to people directly associated with our section," Mary Kaye said.

"Okay," I sighed, relieved. The idea of meeting all the people in that humongous room was too scary to think about.

"Like any workplace, this one is complex with many people and personalities working together," Mary Kaye said. "By the way, you already met four from our group, *the ladies*."

"The ladies?" I repeated, confused.

"Yes. You met them this morning, in the break room."

It took a second for me to understand. Then I remembered. Before my drilling, by Mary Kaye, I had been instructed by HR to arrive an hour earlier than my normal start time, which I did. Once all the paperwork was done, the HR person, Alison, walked me to meet Mary Kaye. We found her in the break room getting a cup of coffee. She was chatting with four women who were seated around a small table.

Alison acknowledged the women in the room by saying, "Good morning, Mary Kaye . . . ladies," before introducing me.

At the time, I didn't realize that Alison was being literal, and the four women were office illuminati who were informally referred to as *the ladies*. I found out later, that the ladies—Ann, Betty, Louise, and Mae—were fixtures around the Medical Center and had worked there since the beginning of time. Together they had survived a bunch of management changes as well as a slew of reorganizations. Originally, there had been five of them, but the fifth one, Dorothy, had retired recently. Apparently, my job was created to take over some of her responsibilities.

Thinking back to the encounter, I recalled that those ladies were nice and had chatted pleasantly with us, as Mary Kaye finished her bagel and coffee, and I drank a cup of tea.

They asked the normal questions about me, like: *How old was I . . .What did I prefer to be called . . . What school did I graduate from*, etc. They didn't talk at all about themselves, but were anxious to tell me about Jaimie, a twenty-two-year-old recent business graduate from George Mason University.

They went on to explain how Jaimie was on a three-month detail, or temporary assignment, to their organization. They couldn't wait for us to meet. They were absolutely convinced that I'd love this "delightful person". They described her as pretty, friendly, and smart. They had no doubt that Jaimie would take me under her wings, show me the ropes, and we'd soon become fast friends.

After being introduced to the other members of Mary Kaye's section, I understood why the ladies made such a big deal of me meeting this Jaimie person. Everyone in Mary Kaye's section was at least in their mid-thirties. Though I was used to being around older people, it would be nice to have someone close to my age to take breaks with, to go to lunch with, to discuss common work issues with, or even to share juicy office gossip with.

Each time we entered or exited a cubicle or office, I wondered if the next person we'd meet would be the famous Jaimie. When I realized that the introductions were over, I asked Mary Kaye if Jaimie was out for the day.

Her face went blank, as she carefully enunciated each word, "Jaimie's not in yet. We passed her cubicle earlier. She sits on the side opposite your partition."

Not sure what to make of her response or her deliberate neutral tone, I quickly changed the subject.

"Alison signed me in today. But tomorrow, I'll need a badge. You said you'd show me what I needed to do to get one?" I asked.

"Oh, yeah," she said, leading me towards the nearest set of doors. "I'll take you to security and, on the way, I'll show you where the restrooms are."

"Thanks, I . . ." Before my statement was half-way out, a woman came bounding through the double glass doors. To avoid being hit with the doors or knocked down, we both were forced to jump back.

"Glass doors, Jaimie . . ." Mary Kaye said, annoyed. "You had to see us."

Looking around me, the woman, I presumed was the famous Jaimie, said, "Sorry, Mary Kaye." Then, she continued talking, as if that was all the apology necessary. "You'd never believe the traffic. I had to detour three times, coming into the city." I assumed that was her way of explaining why she was two hours late.

If this was *my* Jaimie, the one I had been waiting for, then I was sadly not getting good vibes about her. Even though that woman fit the general description the ladies had given, I hoped that there was more than one Jaimie in the office.

This person was, as the ladies had described, in her early twenties and very pretty. She had large brown eyes, pale-white skin, and beautifully styled brown hair, cut in a mid-length bob. She carried an expensive leather briefcase. In addition, I could tell that her sky blue business pantsuit cost at least twice as much as the suit I had on—the one that I could only afford by purchasing it on layaway, at the *Best for Less* discount store.

"Jamie," Mary Kaye said, pointing to me, "This is Tina, the new file clerk we've been expecting."

"Nice to meet you, Jaimie," I said, putting out my hand.

For a brief instant, Jaimie seemed unclear what to do with that hand projected towards her. The hesitation was long enough for both Mary Kaye and me to notice.

With limited polite options, she accepted the hand and unsuccessfully tried to cover the awkwardness up with chatter. "Oh, it's so nice to meet you, too. I think it's great that you can work here. It's probably different than what you're used to, but I'm sure you're like it."

Uncertain how to take any of that, I said, "I'm sure I'll like it, too."

"Oh," she said, "by the way, I just love your hair. Is it all yours?" With that, she reached out to touch my long Fulani braids, a hairstyle I had worn practically all my life.

For years, my mother spent hours doing my hair and training me   in braid and cornrow styles. Even after she disappeared, hot combs, perms, and curlers, all seemed too much effort for me. I was so used to my braids that I hardly thought about them, at least until someone, like Jaimie, tried grabbing at them.

What's with this fool? was the thought that immediately popped in my head. But given the circumstances—first day on a new job and all—I opted for a more appropriate response. I carefully maneuvered my body, and my hair, beyond Jaimie's reach. Then I gave my best interpretation of an innocent smile before giving the only possible response to her tacky question.

"Yes. It's all mine."

The answer was only technically true. God had blessed me with thick healthy hair. I often chose to style that hair in designs that could only be achieved by skillfully adding hair extensions. I paid good money to purchase those extensions. So, I could honestly say that every strain of hair, on my head, was mine—though some of it had come in little plastic bags.

As Jaimie smiled the smile of the clueless, completely oblivious to the situation, my heart sank as all my hopes for a new office bestie were dashed.

Mary Kaye gently touched my arm. Bringing an end to the awkward conversation, she said, "I still have quite a bit to show Tina today." With that she directed me through the double doors.

We had traveled only a few feet down the hall, when I noticed Mary Kaye's lips curling involuntarily. The sound she was holding back signaled how hard she was trying to stifle a laugh.

"What?" I asked, taken off guard and confused.

"You handled that much better than some people twice your age. Definitely much better than I would have."

Then, the absurdity of the situation seemed to get to her, and she couldn't hold back any longer.

"Sooo," she said, now laughing unrestrained, "what do you think? With so much in common, are you and Jaimie fast friends yet? Or should I wait a day or two?"

"Hmm . . . it may take slightly more than a day or two," I laughed, liking Mary Kaye more every minute. Obviously, she was a lot more worldly aware than the ladies were.

* * *

While Mary Kaye was not susceptible to Jaimie's charms, the ladies remained oblivious to the reality of our differences and Jaimie's attitude towards someone like me. They—with all good intentions—requested that she take me under her wings and help acclimate me to the office. This she interpreted as a license to hand over all her work for me to do—an effort, I squashed in short order. Just as much as the ladies overestimated Jaimie, she underestimated me.

Needless to say, I saw no reason to reveal my true impressions of Jaimie to the ladies. It would've been pointless to tell them that the "delightful person" they all admired and loved, was lazy and opportunistic. Since she was there for such a short time, it served no purpose to rat her out.

Anyhow, once Jaimie realized that I wouldn't do both my work and her work, she lost interest in me all together. For the remainder of her three-month detail, I found it best to simply ignore her and keep my distance. She apparently felt the same way.

CHAPTER 23

I HAD BEEN WORKING at RGMC for six months, when it came time for my first performance review. I was nervous, but I didn't anticipate any issues with my work. My boss and my co-workers seemed to like me and the job I was doing. The only blip had been the *delightful* Jaimie. Happily, she was long gone. Otherwise, she might have been vindictive enough to try and influence my appraisal, since I'd had the unmitigated gall to push back at her attempts at being manipulator instead of mentor. *How dare I?*

That morning, just before my appointment with Mary Kaye, I headed for the break room to relax, clear my head, drink some chamomile tea, and prepare myself for the meeting. As I approached the break room, I heard bits of a loud-animated conversation. The topic of discussion was the discovery of serious problems with some of the records. The conversation stopped as I entered the room, but not before I overheard that Mae and Beth, two of the ladies, had been tasked to audit an entire year's worth of data. According to the person speaking, the ladies were "ticked off", because it meant that they had to perform the audit in addition to their normal duties.

The sudden chill, as I entered the breakroom, made me rethink my need for chamomile tea. The encounter did clarify some strange vibes I had been sensing for a few days. I had brushed it off as paranoia or insecurity on my part. Now, it was obvious that my instincts had been correct and whatever the problems with the records, I was the designated guilty party. I had been tried and convicted by my coworkers. And since it negatively impacted the beloved ladies, there would be no forgiveness or leniency for me.

One minute before my assigned appointment time, I knocked on Mary Kaye's door and waited for her to invite me in. When she said, "Come in, Tina," I entered, worried that this performance appraisal could be my last.

As Mary Kaye explained the procedures guiding the performance appraisal process, I barely paid attention. I was too busy preparing myself for the point in the spiel where she'd say, "Sorry, because of recent developments we find that you are not a good fit for our wonderful and glorious organization. Nobody messes with the ladies . . ."

"Tina?"

"Umm, yes?"

"Are you okay?"

"Yes."

I could tell she wasn't buying it. But she was obviously finished with the prepared script, because she started explaining how during the previous months, she had directly double-checked my work. I had suspected as much, and it was not news to me.

"Nothing personal against you," Mary Kaye explained, "but, as you know, our section was only recently assigned the expanded functionality. That's why we hired you. As a matter of fact, you'll remember that Jaimie was doing most of it until we were able to get a fulltime person. Then, for a while, you two shared the data recording until you were able to assume full responsibility. I had no control over Jaimie. And you were totally new to what we do and how we do it. So, I did what I thought best for Records Management and RGMC. Understand?"

"Yes."

"So, though I'll admit that I have been double-checking the accuracy and quality of your work, that shouldn't insult you or hurt your feelings. It should give you confidence in the integrity of the organization you now belong to, that we take seriously everything this organization is charged with."

I nodded, since she seemed to require some type of acknowledgement.

"After saying all that," Mary Kaye continued, "I must tell you, Tina, that I am more than happy with your work. So far, you've given me no cause for concern. As a matter of fact, I'm impressed with your willingness to learn and how totally focused you are on doing things the right way. Most important of all, I like that you're dependable and get things done. This is, in essence, what I wrote in your review."

With that, she handed me the performance evaluation to take with me to sign, officially ending my probation period.

I thanked Mary Kaye and got up to leave, barely glancing at the papers she'd given me. She must've noticed something in my expression, "It's actually a good review, Tina. You should be happy," she said.

"That's not it," I said. "It's just that . . . Well, is it true that Mae and Betty have to go through a year's worth of the data entries because there were serious problems with a bunch of the records?"

"Not exactly. There were some anomalies which, unfortunately, were noticed by someone outside our department. This forced my management to request an audit of all records entered over the past year."

"That includes some of the records entered by the person who was here before me, right?" I asked hopefully.

"Yes. But, only as a precaution. Dot, rather Dorothy, the woman who previously had primary responsible for entering the data records, was an extremely thorough person. She had been here for twenty odd years with no apparent problems. Management's assumption was that the problems happened after she retired. The audit was extended to cover a year, like I said, just as a precaution."

"Which implies," I said, "that the only suspect data is the data entered by Jaimie or me."

I sighed because all I had to do was picture Jaimie with her smooth white skin, her perfect hair, her tailored suits, and how she had my co-workers wrapped around her perfectly manicured fingers. It wouldn't take a detective to figure out which of us would be voted the logical suspect in this mystery.

Mary Kaye smiled, as if she were reading my mind.

"We'll see," she said. "Read and sign your review, Tina. If you have any questions about anything in it, come talk to me. Otherwise, it's best if none of us make any blanket assumptions."

With that, there didn't seem to be any more to say. *At least I'm not fired, yet,* I thought as the door closed behind me. Before I could get too cocky, I was surprised to hear laughing behind the door I had just closed. I hoped that Mary Kaye had, that quickly, received a joke through email. I most definitely did not find anything amusing about my situation.

As I walked the short distance to my cubicle, I noticed there were several people nearby chatting. I tried to rush to my desk without making direct eye contact with any of them. I had seen the looks earlier and I wasn't prepared to feel bad about something that I knew was absolutely not my fault.

Ironically, for the previous two weeks, I had been trying to find an excuse to get out of a training session on *Excel Secrets,* that Mary Kaye had signed me up for. When she'd initially told me about it, I balked because I thought that there was not much I could gain from the training. Now, however, I couldn't wait to spend a day and a half—twelve glorious hours—staring at spreadsheets. Happily, the training started that afternoon, and since it was Thursday, I would have a long weekend away from the office.

* * *

The following Monday, I made sure to arrive an hour early, hoping to hide in my cubicle and avoid contact with my fellow workers. Just my luck, Kenny, the I.T. guy, who seemed to be there twenty-four-seven, was in the office ahead of me.

I liked Kenny. He always had a smile for me and was unaffected by anything but his computer stuff. He was friendly, obviously very smart, and had a really cute foreign accent, which I couldn't place. Best of all, he was not one of the people shunning me.

He spotted me right away. "Hey, Tina," he yelled, waving like crazy.

'Hi, Kenny," I answered, trying to rush to my cubicle before running into any other early arrivals.

"Why are you here so early?"

"No reason," I lied. "I was out a couple of days last week for training. Just thought I'd come in and get an early start."

"Liar, liar, pants on fire," he teased, waving his index finger.

"No, really . . ."

"Uh-huh. It wouldn't have anything to do with getting to your desk and avoiding the sweet ladies and their minions?"

"Yeah, well, everybody's acting weird. I think they've decided that I am the reason the ladies have to go through a year's worth of data."

"You don't say? The sweet ladies finally showing their true colors, how about that?" he said.

"Up until recently, I thought they liked me. They always complimented me on the job I was doing. Then, the first time something goes wrong, everybody looks at me cross-eyed, like I'm to blame."

"Been there. And, yes, it sucks. If it's any comfort, you're not the only one who's been the target of certain people around here and the occasional blind quickness to judgment."

"Excuse me Kenny. But, no! That is not any comfort. None of it makes any sense to me. The least someone, anyone, could do is accuse me to my face and give me a chance to defend myself."

"Doesn't work like that. Anyhow, what would they say? 'Tina, we know if there is a screw up, it had to be your fault, because you're the only young black girl in the office.' That would go over really well with Mary Kaye." Kenny said, and then he laughed.

"What's up with people around here laughing at my discomfort? The other day, I was talking with Mary Kaye. When I closed the door, I think she laughed, too. It's not funny at all."

"Sorry, about that. Nothing against you. We just know how it gets around here sometimes," Kenny said, more soberly. "Look Tina, you have nothing to worry about. That's what I should've said right away."

"How can you know that?"

"Listen, I'm going to share something that I'm sure Mary Kaye wanted to reveal to you herself. But, I'm gonna do it anyhow."

"What?"

"Mary Kaye requested that I create a special computer program to help Mae and Betty get through those records."

"Why in the world would you talk with me about a computer program? I can barely spell the word computer."

Kenny laughed. "You don't need to understand the details of this one. But . . . you *will* be glad to hear about it."

"Okay, Kenny. I can tell you're busting to tell me something that I'm guaranteed not to understand."

"Whatcha wanna bet?"

"Kenny!" I said exasperated.

"Okay. Mary Kaye had me scan the system for all the forms and data you worked with in the last six months. Since she personally had already verified those, she had me write another program that eliminated them from the list to be audited."

"And?" I uttered, still confused.

"All right, follow me. Like I said, to make it easier on Mae and Betty, I was supposed to create one program that automatically generates links to the files that need to be reviewed. In addition to that one, I designed a second program that created an exclusion list. Using these two together, Mae and Betty only have to review three-quarters of the records from the full list."

"Really?" I said, finally grasping the implications. "This means that the ladies will have a lot fewer records than they were originally told that they'd have to work with. And, it would be obvious that any processing errors, in the remaining data, were not caused by me."

"You got it. By the way, you spell computer, c-o-m-p . . ."

I laughed and punched him softly on the shoulder before he could finish.

"Thanks Kenny, for the program and for telling me about it."

He winked and went back to his area. I guess he had other computer miracles to work on.

I stood there for a moment, grateful to Mary Kaye and Kenny for coming up with such an elegant solution. But I was a little saddened by the short-sightedness of the people I had come to respect in my office.

* * *

Within a week, it was clear that the tide had turned. Through Mary Kaye and her magic, I was miraculously off the shun list. There were still a few awkward encounters for a few days. However, for the most part, everything was back to normal. The only change was in my perception of reality.

I had discovered a lot in the past two weeks. I couldn't imagine what would have been my fate if things had played out differently. In some perverse way, I was glad it had happened. It was the push that I needed—my ah-ha moment—to aim me in the direction I had, up until that point, resisted. It was in that instant of clarity that I decided to call my best friend.

"Tina," Paulette said, after I had re-counted everything to her, leaving nothing out. "I can't say for sure if you are totally right in your read of the situation. I can't judge how close a call it might or might not have been. I definitely can't say anything about the attitude of the folks in your office or what was in their heads. I'm not there."

"True."

"But . . ."

"Yes . . . But?"

"But this is the real world, my friend. Bottom-line, no matter how smart and adaptable you might be, you *are* inexperienced and new to the job. And, you *are new* to the people in your organization. Plus, you *are* young. You *are* female. You *are only* a high school graduate. And, *you are* black. Any one of those things, or any combination of them, moves the scales against you."

"So, what are you saying, exactly?"

"I'm saying, girlfriend, that you need to find a way to tilt the scales in your favor, not against you."

"How do I do that?"

"Well, you'll eventually get older, or old, if you live long enough."

"Brilliant, I'd never have guessed that."

"Shut up and listen, silly person. Eventually, over time, the people around you might get to know you and trust you more. You will get experience and be better at whatever job you're doing. But you will always be female and you'll always be black. Those two things won't change. And yes, they can work against you."

"I know where you're going. I see the breadcrumbs."

"So?"

"So, the way to tilt the scales in my favor is to go to college, right?"

"Yup. Like I said. Real world. Hope for the best. Prepare for the worst. Always CYA—always . . . always . . . always cover your ass. The stuff our parents told us, turns out to be good stuff—the best advice, when you think about it. You know, like how Mama always made me make sure that before I went outside my underwear would not embarrass her, just in case of an emergency or I dropped dead on the street."

"What?" I coughed, my friend's digression nearly caused me to choke on the water I was drinking.

"I always wondered," Paulette continued, "if she'd be more upset about my raggedy drawers or me passing out on the street."

From what I knew about Paulette's mother, I couldn't help but chuckle at the thought, not really sure of what her priorities might be. That seemed the perfect time to drop my bombshell onto my friend.

I said, "Anyhow, there's another reason I called. I wanted to admit to you that you were right all along.

"Huh?" Paulette said.

I giggled because I could tell that, for once, my chatterbox friend was at a loss for words. I'd caught her entirely off guard.

"Got your attention, did I?" I laughed. "Well, don't ever quote me on this, cuz you know I will deny ever saying it . . . But, you, Paulette Deloris Parkes, were absolutely right." The gasp on the other end of the line made me pause to enjoy the moment. Then I continued, "Yup, I said it. You, my friend, were one hundred percent on point."

"And . . .?"

"And, I was silly to think that I could magically make up all the time I lost not having an ideal childhood. That I could hit the pause button, and everything would be smiles and roses," I said, finally acknowledging my naivety. "So, girlfriend, guess what?"

"Am I supposed to say something here, or are you just pausing for dramatic effect? Just say it, why don't you?"

"Sorry about that. I just wanted to say that I'm not waiting. I'm going to college now. Well, not going, as in physically, because I need my job and have to work for a living. But I did research a bunch of online college programs. The schools I'm looking at are all accredited and will allow me to work and earn my degree at my own pace. Some will even let me fast pace. If I do it right, we might even finish up together."

That's when my friend screamed so loud that I had to move the headset from my ear. I could also tell that she was dancing and acting crazy, scaring all the nice people on the University of North Carolina college campus.

CHAPTER 24

"I HAVE A PRESENT for you," Mary Kaye said, with a grin that made me want to turn around and duck back into my cubicle.

"What kind of present?" I asked, making no effort to hide my suspicion. The words "it's probably a setup" came to mind. In the four-plus years I had worked for Mary Kaye, I knew that we had different ideas on what a present was. And when she showed up promising said presents, especially with that expression on her face, whatever the thing was, it was not to my benefit.

"I see you don't trust me, huh?"

"Well . . ."

"Okay," she said, the sly grin growing across her face. "Remember all those times you sat in for one of the girls in Patient Accounting?"

The question, of course was rhetorical. How could I forget? Once, a few years back, Patient Accounting needed a body to man the phones for a few hours. It was the end of the week, just before a holiday, and there was no time to bring in a temp. I was just about the only one available, mainly because I had no life outside RGMC. So, Mary Kaye asked if I would mind sitting in for a few hours. Since it was so close to the holiday, no one expected many calls. They were wrong. But, instead of getting overwhelmed, I enjoyed actually talking to people—even the complainers—much more than I did working on a computer or processing data.

I liked it so much that, after that day, Mary Kaye would arrange for me to shadow a few of the client reps to see what they did and how they did it. Then, whenever Patient Accounting needed backup or extra help, they would negotiate with Mary Kaye for some of my time.

Now, of course, I was curious what any of this had to do with the gift Mary Kaye had promised, so I asked.

"It's all related," she said. "At last month's Managers' meeting, it was announced that Patient Accounting had finally gotten approval to open up a new slot. I asked HR-Jodie to look out for the announcement. She just emailed it to me, and it has your name written all over it." Mary Kaye was so excited that she kept waving the announcement instead of handing it to me.

"Really?" I asked, holding my breath, not daring to imagine what that piece of paper might contain.

Mary Kaye finally handed the announcement to me. I was almost too nervous to read it.

As I scanned down the page, everything seemed perfect, until I saw that there was one requirement that gave me pause, "It says here that an Associate Degree is preferred. What does that mean exactly?" I asked.

"Don't worry about that," Mary Kaye assured me. "It's not a problem for you. It's only preferred and not mandatory. Besides, you have more than enough college credits to cover that requirement. Remember, you almost have enough credits for a full BA degree."

I was catching some of her excitement. I couldn't help it. The degree thing aside, I did have an advantage over most other applicants. I not only met and exceeded most of the job requirements, including experience doing the job, I also had a good relationship with the people in Patient Accounting.

I couldn't believe it. The job *was* perfect for me and would be a promotion, as well. She was right, it had my name written all over it. And I would be a fool not to apply. I was no fool.

* * *

Since Medical Center regulations prohibited anyone knowledgeable about the application status discussing any details with me, I had no choice but to wait patiently for formal notification.

I think at some point, the lack of feedback or communication even had Mary Kaye uneasy. She tried not to show it, but I could tell.

About a month later, she called me into her office and asked if I would do her a favor and deliver a package to the fourth floor. I had never traveled the lofty hallways of the fourth floor before. Only the highest-level hotshots had offices there.

After dropping the package off, I headed towards the elevators walking as close to the walls as possible. It was a habit Mary Kaye's secretary, Rachael, had been trying for years to break me of. She referred to it as *Tina hugging the walls*. She'd gotten on my case about the behavior because she saw it as my antisocial attempt at being as inconspicuous as possible. Actually, since I was passing through such an exalted area, she was probably right this time.

Still *hugging the walls*, with my eyes straight ahead, I didn't see Mr. Gary Greene—one of the important people who worked on the floor—until he spoke to me.

"Hello Tina," he said.

I was shocked, Gary Greene was one of the few blacks in high level management. He had been around for a long time, almost longer than I had lived. He had spoken to me a few times when he came by to talk with Mary Kaye. I knew who he was but had no idea that he would recognize me outside of my work area.

"Uh, hello, Gary," I said.

"Congratulations, I hear that you are well on your way to getting your bachelor's degree."

"Thanks," I said, not trying to figure out how he knew that much about me. After all, as big as RGMC was, the gossip pool flowed freely throughout.

"What's your area of concentration?" he asked, shocking me that he was still there talking with me.

"I'm not sure. For now, my major is Liberal Arts. Honestly, I started working here with my high school diploma and had no desire to rush into anything more. A really good friend convinced me that I was severely limiting my options. I figured I'd do the Liberal Arts thing, for now, while I figure the rest out. I guess that sounds wishy-washy. But my first priority was to get a degree."

"No, it actually doesn't sound wishy-washy at all. I admire that. A lot of young people flip a coin to choose a major and end up changing it every other year," he said. "So, how much longer do you have?"

"Not long. I have almost all my credits. I'm waiting on the results from an equivalency test for a mandatory course. If I pass, then I'm through."

"Sounds good. I'd heard that you have a good head on your shoulders," he said, and paused as if he was deciding on something. Then he added, "I also hear that you recently put in an application with Sam Monday's group."

"Yes . . ." I said cautiously.

"Personally, if I were the decision maker . . ." he paused again. "Well, I would see you as a perfect candidate. From what I understand, you are more than deserving the promotion. Let me ask you something. What would you do if you didn't get it?"

Now he was freaking me out. I wondered if he knew something I didn't, and was trying to prepare me.

I gave him the politically correct answer, "I guess I'd wait for another or similar opportunity and try again." But, in my heart, I knew I'd be devastated.

"Good attitude, but wasted around here. My honest advice to you would be to move on. And by move on, I mean to try your luck outside of RGMC."

"Excuse me, but I've worked hard and, like you said, I am a great candidate for the job. The person who knows me best, my supervisor, recommended that I try," I said, attempting not to get angry, but failing.

Gary smiled. "Good, you should be indignant. You are more than qualified for the position. My friend, Mary Kaye, is a really good person. She is smart and a great judge of people and talent. But, she has done all she can for you. Unfortunately, the deck is pretty much stacked against people like you and me."

"What does that mean?" I said, both curious and annoyed.

"Look, Tina. Let me be honest. I'm no fool. I'm smart, ambitious, I have a master's degree, and am close to earning my PHD. But I realize that I was lucky and came to work here at just the right time. It was a time when people here had gotten into trouble for some blatant discriminatory issues and were bending over backwards to prove that there were no barriers to people of color and women. That worked out good for me because I knew what the game was and took advantage of every opportunity, no matter what other people's motivations were."

"Things are different now, right?"

"Yes, they are different. The decision makers have gotten smarter about how they do things . . . Take my word for it, that position, the one you applied for, will be given to *a more appropriate candidate*. It might even get pulled altogether. That way they can get the phrasing just right for whoever they prefer to get the job, or to eliminate whoever they want to block. But there will be no obvious problems in the selection process. It doesn't matter how good you are or how much your supervisor believes in you."

Then, he pulled out a folded flier from his pocket. "Here, Tina. Take this," he said. "It's information about a new female owned health-care consulting firm. It's called MedsCon. I've worked with them. They are a startup with real potential and are seeking motivated go-getters, like you. I know some of the people there and they are fair. They care more about competency than color. Give them a call." With that he walked away.

Watching Gary disappear down the long hallway, it occurred to me that our meeting might not have been as accidental as it seemed. It also made me wonder if he was simply delivering a message, one that, as my manager, Mary Kaye couldn't deliver directly. If that was the case, then she probably felt bad about recommending me for a position that, through no fault of my own, I had no chance to get.

Still, even after that bizarre encounter, I checked daily to see if there was any response to my application. Then, nearly three weeks later, I discovered that Gary had been right. The announcement was pulled for reevaluation. Mary Kaye explained to me the reason given, and it seemed to make perfect sense. But the fact that she had trouble looking at me, said she didn't buy it. I felt sorry for her.

I still didn't want to believe what Gary had implied about the people I worked with daily. However, I couldn't totally dismiss it. Either way, I had nothing to lose by hedging my bets. So, I checked and saw that MedsCon LLC had an opening for a similar position. With nothing to lose, I made the call to set up an interview.

CHAPTER 25

MY FIRST IMPRESSION of my potential new MedsCon boss, Cheryl Scott—tall, no-nonsense, long dark hair, and confident—was that she was the spitting image of Xena:Warrior Princess, in a tan business suit. Xena was a powerful Amazonic avenging fantasy character I had seen in TV reruns over the years. The Cheryl Scott version had piercing blue-gray eyes that made me feel that she could see right through me. The total effect was chilling. Even with all I had lived through, just watching her scrutinize me across a conference table made me want to turn and run.

In the fifteen minutes, I'd been there, she hadn't smiled or made any effort to put me at ease. I think, at that point, any change of expression, even a smile, would be enough to initiate that mad dash out of the conference room and out of the building.

"Thank you for coming in," she said, pushing my paperwork aside, obviously concluding the interview. "Do you have questions or anything to add that I need to know?"

"No, ma'am," I said. While it was true, I realized—as the words left my mouth— that it was absolutely the worst possible response. It seemed that everything I'd read about what to and what not to do at a job interview went out the window, when I sat down across from Cheryl Scott.

"Okay, then," she said, with the first hint of a smile. "I've already talked with several people from RGMC. A personal friend, Gary Greene, says I'd be crazy not to hire you. And, so far, I see no reason not to trust his opinion, and offer you the position. That is, if you still want it."

That stopped me mid-rise from my seat. It took a moment, before what she'd just said sank in. All I could get out was, "Yes . . . th-th-thank you."

She sat back, crossed her arms, looked at me with those scary eyes, and said, "One thing, Tina. You may not see me much, unless you royally screw-up. Then you won't want to see me. I don't believe in micromanaging or standing over my employees. Shouldn't have to. I trust them to know what's expected and get the job done."

She paused, I guess to gauge my reaction, before continuing, "I always make sure to get that clear up front, so there's no confusion later. Okay?"

"Okay," I said.

And so ended my first professional job interview. I hadn't known what to expect. I sincerely hoped that they didn't all make you wet your pants.

* * *

I had been working at MedsCon about a month when this short, big-chested young woman approached me. One look at her toothy smile and I had a Jaimie flashback.

"Hi," she said, keeping in step beside me.

"Hi," I said, and picked up the pace, hoping she'd take the hint.

She didn't. "I thought someone said that you and Linda were good friends," she said.

"Linda who?" I asked.

"Linda Taylor. You know the dark-skinned girl on the second floor."

"Oh, because she's black, I'm supposed to automatically know her?"

"Hey, don't get defensive girl, I don't mean anything."

"And?"

"Look, I'm sorry. My mistake. Didn't mean any offense," she apologized. "I'm Denise. I work in Business Services. I heard two voices, a little while ago, and somebody was really blasting that girl, I mean Linda."

"Well, it wasn't me. I just started here a month ago. And I do not know Linda or anybody else for that matter. So, please do not get me mixed up in no he-said-she-said shit. Cause I'm not interested."

"Hey, chill out girl. I was just making conversation. Like I said, I didn't mean to offend you. But fact is, Linda is black. And, she has a dark

133

complexion. So, what I said was true, but not the way you took it." Then she giggled, "Girl, look at this nose. Lord knows, these lips are natural, too."

I turned to face the crazy woman, confused. "I have no idea what you are talking about."

"What I'm saying is that you took one look and had me typecast as . . . whatever. Then you got insulted because you assumed that *I* was stereotyping *you*. But, according to all unofficial criteria in this U-S-of-A, with one black parent, I'm the same as you are, even if one of my parents is of pure Irish descent. You really need to get that chip off your shoulder, sister girl."

"Chip? I don't have a chip on my shoulder, and I don't appreciate . . ."

"Okay, okay. Let's start over." At that, *Miss Thang* put out her right hand and said, "My name is Denise Jackson, glad to meet you."

I looked again, but what Denise Jackson's mouth said did not register with what my eyes were saying. What I saw was a very pale female, with blond highlights in her light-brown shoulder length hair. She had it pulled back into a single French braid, of all things. She also had a big chest and a flat butt. All my life, I had been told that black people could instinctively tell if someone else was black, no matter what. Well, that belief was definitely a myth, because I could not see any black features in Denise Jackson.

I shook her hand. Maybe I did it because I was embarrassed at my assumptions, and it appeared that I was the prejudiced one. Or, maybe because I couldn't believe this nut was actually trying to be my friend, even after I had insulted her. Either way, I couldn't help but smile and say, "Okay, Denise Jackson, I'm Tina Brooks. I guess I'm glad to meet you, too."

* * *

Denise was about six years older than me. But, from the start, she seemed so sweet and naive that I figured we absolutely did not come from the same side of town—in some ways the same planet. That innocent quality of hers was probably how she ended up with a guy, like her boyfriend, Reggie, who sounded like a control freak. From what she said, she'd gradually noticed troubling signs, and ignored them. By the time she accepted what the signs meant, it was too late. She was stuck—with no way out.

According to Denise, she couldn't leave out of the house without him drilling and probing about every detail. She said he would stand in front of the door and demand that she tell him where she was going and how long she would be gone.

Being friends with me couldn't have made things easier for her. In the short time we'd known each other, Denise was frequently at my apartment or out with me, which probably only added fuel to a very hot fire.

One Friday, Denise came to my apartment for movie night. It was her turn to bring the movies. I liked to make fun of her because she had a thing for all types of corny romantic films. As she pulled a video out of her bag, without looking at her choice, I picked up a plastic spoon off the table. Using it as a pretend microphone, I said, in my most deep dramatic announcer's voice, "Coming up next, ladies and gentlemen, is a tale about a mismatched boy and girl thrown together by happenstance. Immediately the sparks fly. They try to pretend there is no attraction. They spend the first third of the film snapping continuously at each other. But we all know what will happen in the end."

We both roared.

Denise's laughter dissolved into a wistful sigh. With a dreamy look on her face, she said, "Tina, as stupid as it sounds, I guess I always hoped I'd meet someone like the guys in these movies, who would fall for me on first sight and love me no matter what."

I put the spoon down and turned to her, feeling a bit guilty about my performance. "Reggie is not that guy, I take it."

"I've been with Reggie for less than a year. It feels like a lifetime. At first, everything about him was perfect. He was charming, confident, strong, and attentive. I didn't realize that under all that was a bully. He says he loves me, but I think he gets off on having ultimate control over me."

"Why don't you leave that fool?' I asked. It was the obvious question.

She just looked sadly down, glancing into the popcorn bowl, as if she could find some answers there. I noticed that my girl hardly ever looked up while talking about Reggie.

"It's not that easy. My only way out would be if he got killed in the line of duty or something. God help me. Sometimes I pray for that."

"You don't mean that Denise. It can't be that bad. If it was, I would assume you would walk away."

"Like I said, easier said than done."

I looked at Denise, waiting, because it seemed there was more that she wanted to say.

"Reggie is a very smart man," she continued. "And he knows it. He also knows that he can get away with a lot, no matter what I say or do, especially since he's a policeman."

"What? You never told me Reggie was a cop."

"Yeah, and he uses the fact that he is to the max. Every time I threaten to leave his ass, he reminds me that he has lots of cop friends. There is no place that I can hide or go where he won't find me. He makes it plain that once he does find me, I will wish I had not crossed him."

I could see tears forming in Denise's eyes and sensed just how scared she was and how powerless she felt. She wiped away a wayward teardrop and said, "Let's just not talk about it anymore. I only have a couple of hours. I have to be there when he gets home."

I reached over and hugged my new friend. I really felt for her and didn't know what to say. I was totally out of my depth. I could tell that she wanted me to promise her that everything would be fine. But I couldn't. It was obvious that, if Denise didn't remove herself from that situation, it could only get worse.

* * *

Several times over the weekend, I had to stop myself from calling Denise. It seemed better to wait for her to call me. She had revealed a great deal to a relative stranger, and it was possible that she was embarrassed and maybe regretted it. I figured that if she didn't call, I'd talk with her at work.

I went looking for her on Monday, but she wasn't in. By Wednesday, with no response to my calls and texts, I became seriously concerned. Based on what Denise had shared about Reggie and their relationship, I could only assume that her being unwilling or unable to communicate had something to do with him. My hope was that he hadn't found out about our budding friendship, and that was a factor in her being unreachable. I couldn't live with myself if I was the cause of something bad happening to Denise.

By Friday, I was near panic. As I saw it, there were only two options, call the police or go see for myself. With no proof of a crime, calling the police was pointless. That left making an unannounced visit.

Denise will just have to forgive me, if I drop in and interrupt something really private.

I was still thinking about my options, when I received a call from Jeri Bennet, Denise's boss. Jeri asked politely if it was convenient for me to come to her office. Her voice sounded strange and—giving that we didn't work together, and we'd never spoken before—her request was odd. But she was also senior management and when management asks, the only logical response from a lowly person like me is, "Okay. I'll be right there."

Her door was open. I stood at the threshold, uncertain what to do. I had seen Jeri in company meetings, and always thought that she was extremely smart and good at her job. She was a people-person who, according to Denise, cared a lot about those who worked under her. And, I knew that Denise liked and respected her boss a lot. I just had no idea why Jeri wanted to speak with me, with apparent urgency.

Before I could knock, Jeri waved me in, "Please, Tina, come in. Thanks for coming."

"No problem," I said.

"I'm concerned about Denise Jackson and I understand that the two of you are close," she said.

"Umm, yes, you might say that. We hang out sometimes."

"Since she hasn't called or contacted anyone in the group all week, I hoped you could help. I was wondering if you've heard from or been in contact with her."

"No, I haven't heard from her."

"Look," she said. "I know this might be a bit irregular and I understand if you're not comfortable talking to me. But, if she calls you or you talk with her, please ask her to call in. Tell her that we are concerned."

Jeri was right. Even though I did appreciate her concern, I was uncomfortable talking with her about Denise. Without revealing details of Denise's personal business, there was not a lot I could share with Jeri. All I could safely say was, "Honestly, I haven't spoken to her since last Friday. I was thinking about dropping pass her house today after work."

"That would be great," Jeri said. "When you see her, let her know that, if she needs anything from us, we're here."

I nodded and got up to leave. It was good to know that Denise's boss cared so much. I just hoped that whatever was happening with her would not cause my friend her job.

PART Five

If You're Not Part of the Solution

CHAPTER 26

THE CONVERSATION WITH JERI made it clear that my instincts had been correct. Something was probably very wrong. Up until Jeri called me into her office, I wasn't positive if I should be worried or not—if I was overreacting. After all, I'd only met Denise a few months earlier. For all I knew, her disappearing for days and dropping out of contact could have been part of a pattern, something she did every once in a while.

Still, why me? Of all the people around here, why ask me about Denise?

Before I could finish the thought, Mrs. Jeffries, Jeri's secretary, whose desk was a couple of feet away, said, "Tina, it was me."

"I'm sorry, Mrs. Jeffries, what was you?"

"I saw the expression on your face," she said. "I figured you were wondering how Jeri knew to call you. It was me. Denise not calling in, not responding to messages, and missing important office meetings was so out of character that several people in the group became concerned. Then, when Jeri was on the verge of calling the police for a health check, I told her to talk with you first."

"But, why me?"

"Because I know how close you two are," she stated emphatically, which caught me totally off guard.

In the short time that I had been at MedsCon, I had met Mrs. Jeffries only once. A strait-laced woman in her fifties, she was the single person in the building that no one called by her first name. Everyone respected her and understood that her one major priority was protecting and taking care of Jeri. She did not mix and she did not gossip. But, somehow, she stayed informed about what went on in the office and in the company. According to Denise, that was a big part of her protecting Jeri.

"You know," she added, "Denise doesn't have any idea how valued she is around here. She is so sweet. Everyone likes her. But she is also very private, which I admire. In the years she's been here, it seemed that I am the only person she feels comfortable opening up to, and even that's limited. You can't imagine how happy I was seeing that she finally has someone, besides an old lady, to relate to."

I had no doubt that what Mrs. Jeffries was saying was true, but it was all news to me. I had no idea that Denise wasn't as open to everyone as she was to me. After all, she had initiated the friendship. She had approached me.

Mrs. Jeffries continued, "A few months before you started working here, I was becoming extremely worried about her."

"Worried, why?"

"Denise, like I said before, is a private person. But being the professional she is, she understands the importance of attending meetings and participating in office functions. Over the past few months or so, something changed. It was worrisome. Functions that she previously made every effort to at least make a showing at, she avoided. Even when she did show, she was anxious and distracted."

I was impressed at how perceptive Mrs. Jeffries was. It was obvious she, and maybe others, cared enough to sense the effect the progression of Denise's relationship with Reggie had on her.

"Don't get me wrong," Mrs. Jeffries said. "I'm just an old lady she chats with once in a while. So, if she didn't say anything, she didn't have to. If she chose not to confide in me, then I wasn't going to ask. But, believe me, if you get to be my age, you recognize the signs of a destructive relationship."

"I guess she has more friends than she realizes," I said.

Mrs. Jeffries smiled. "Yes, she does. Lots of people respect and care for Denise. She's never come right out and told me, but I noticed her being drawn to you. For the last couple of months, she was less tense. I actually saw her laughing and chatting animatedly when you two were together. That's how I knew you two were becoming friends."

"Yeah, I guess that's true," I said. "But this week, I've been really worried, Mrs. Jeffries. I've been calling and haven't been able to reach her."

"That's our concern, too," she said. "Up until this week, Denise hardly ever missed work unless it was an absolute emergency. Everybody in the department appreciates that about her. That's what has Jeri so worried. Honestly, I hoped that you would say that everything was okay, that there was a logical reason behind it all, and we should mind our own business."

"I really don't know any more than you do," I said. "But, like I told Jeri, I will stop pass her place to see what's going on."

"Please do that," Mrs. Jeffries said.

* * *

When I told Jeri and Mrs. Jeffries my intension to stop by Denise's house, I omitted one crucial bit of information. I didn't know exactly where she lived. I'd only been to her house once. It was in the middle of the night, just long enough for her to run in and grab the cell phone and wallet she'd left behind. At the time, I was too busy singing along with the "Quiet Storm" radio hour to pay much attention. Which, after having driven around for half-an-hour, I was seriously regretting. I was hopeless at finding my way back to a place if I hadn't consciously made a mental note of landmarks and other clues.

Optimistically, I had assumed that riding around North Side, in the general area that I thought I remembered, it would come back to me. So far, that wasn't happening.

The one good thing was that, when I got to the right street, Denise's house would stand out. Her family had chosen, for some strange reason, to paint their home pink with yellowish trim. When Denise had described it to me before, I thought it would be awful. That is, until we pulled up to the curb. The pink coloring was soft, and the trim was more beige than yellow. It was actually charming, in a nineteen fifties sort of way.

I racked my brain trying to recount other details or information, besides the color of the house, she had shared that would help me. I sadly had to admit there weren't many.

Denise mostly talked about long ago family memories that had little to do with the house's location. She described how she and her brothers had been happy living with her parents in the pink and yellow house. Things, of course, changed when her father decided he didn't want to be married anymore, and her parents divorced. Her mother held on to the house for years but became increasingly uneasy about the slow deterioration of the area and their neighborhood.

At different points, Denise and her brothers left town. She finished college, started a career, and subsequently decided to return home to Richmond. And that's when she accepted the job at MedsCon.

By then, her mother was planning to sell the house. Denise couldn't stand the idea of losing the home she had grown up in, with so many happy memories. She talked her mother into allowing her to take over the mortgage and the tax bills. For all intents and purposes, the house was hers.

The irony was that her mother's concern had been about the change in the character of the neighborhood and the rough elements outside her door. With Reggie there with her, I imagine that Denise was more afraid of what would happen to her inside the house than of anything that could be done by the people outside.

* * *

I realized that I had been focusing more on my thoughts than I was on my goal, when, in the middle of the block I'd just turned into, there stood a pink house with yellowish trim. It sort of looked like I remembered it, but I could've sworn there were more flowers in the yard.

How many such combinations can there be? I thought.

I parked the car, walked up to the porch, and rang the doorbell. About a minute later, my spirits soared when I saw a shadow behind the peep hole and heard the locks being released.

The woman who opened the door was certainly not Denise. She was tall, thin, and well over sixty. She also did not resemble the short rotund woman Denise had described when talking about her mother.

"Can I help you miss?" she asked, with a raspy voice.

"Yes ma'am, I'm looking for Denise Jackson."

"Denise Jackson?"

"Yes. Does she live here?"

"No. I'm sorry, dear, no one by that name lives here," she said, about to close the door. She must've sensed my desperation, because she softened her tone. "What does this Denise look like?"

"She's short, could pass for white, and lives in a pink house with yellow trim, very similar to this one."

"Oh, I know exactly who you mean."

"I've been riding around for a while. I hate to admit that I don't have the address. Can you direct me to the house?"

"Of course. That house, the one you're looking for, is two blocks down. Make a right onto Fendall."

"Thanks." I turned to walk away, when she stopped me.

"I listen to a lot of talk around here and, if I were you, I'd get that girl out of that house."

"Why?" I asked, not sure I really wanted to hear what the woman was about to say.

She hesitated, then she said, "Now I try not to repeat things I hear, 'cause half of what I hear is wrong, in one way or the other. So, when I say something about someone you can believe that I believe it is the truth."

I was getting a little impatient. Even though I was in a hurry to see my friend, I wanted to hear what this woman had to say—if only she'd get to it.

"Well, people have talked about noises coming from that house a few times. The other day, I heard strange things myself while I was walking my dog, Sandy. The window was open and it sounded like someone hurt or whimpering. Kinda sad, you know . . ."

"Did you call the police?'

"No, dear. I didn't," she shrugged.

"Why not?"

"Wasn't my business," she replied simply. "People get upset when you meddle in their business. Plus, now-a-days there's a lot going on around this place you don't want to mess with. Not just from that house. Drugs even. I'm thinking about moving myself. God knows I can't stand the idea of anybody breaking in my house and trying to rob or rape me. They wouldn't have to kill me because I think I would have a heart attack."

I couldn't believe what I was hearing. Multiple neighborhood people noticed a problem at Denise's house, discussed it among themselves—

including this woman—and no one did anything. *What's wrong with these people?* Resisting the temptation to say or yell what I really thought—no point in making this woman feel guilty or hurting her feelings—I took a deep breath.

"I'm sorry ma'am, what did you say your name was?" I asked.

"Oh, everyone calls me Miss Nelly."

"Thank you, Miss Nelly," I said, "for the information and the directions. I have to go now and find my friend, to make sure she is okay."

I turned, waved, and continued on my way, thinking that Miss Nelly had not made me feel any better about what I might find in the other pink house with yellowish trim.

* * *

Following Miss Nelly's instructions, I easily found the other pink house with yellowish trim. Still not sure what to expect, I stood in front of the house for about fifteen seconds, gathering the nerve to walk up on the porch and knock. I took a step back, so the person answering the door could see me clearly. And, if necessary, I could make a quick getaway.

No one answered. So, I knocked again. Still no answer. I knocked again, only this time harder. I put my ear to the door. I could hear someone inside. I tried again. And this time a familiar, but agitated, voice came from inside of the house. "Who is it?"

"Denise, is that you?"

No response.

"Denise," I yelled. "Please answer me. It's Tina."

"Tina?" I heard through the door. Then it started opening, slowly.

Denise was still behind the door as I pushed my way in. For some reason, I was afraid that she would suddenly slam the door in my face.

As I stepped in, annoyed, I began, "Denise, what is wrong with you? Why wouldn't you open the door?"

Then, as I looked around from my spot inside the door, I stopped short. "Oh my God Denise . . . What the hell . . ."

Denise's face was so swollen and bruised, I could hardly recognize her. Her eyes looked like watermelons. Green on the outside and blood red on the inside. I grabbed my friend and held her to me. Both of us cried, unrestrained, before I dared let go.

"Did Reggie do this to you?"

Denise didn't answer.

"Denise, where is he? Oh, my God, he's not in the house, is he?"

I had been there for several minutes already, and it finally occurred to me that he might still be in the house. I felt the onslaught of outright panic. Denise noticed the look on my face and tried to reassure me.

"No, Tina, don't worry, he's not here."

I let out the breath that I hadn't realized I was holding and glanced around the room. It was hurricane or tornado shambled. Everything was thrown everywhere. There were even holes in the walls.

In the middle of the mess, a picture of Denise and a man was lying flat on an end table. It drew my attention because, while the man looked vaguely familiar, I couldn't place where I had seen him before.

Denise's voice bought me back to my senses, "It's bad, I know. Before he went crazy last night, Reggie promised to get someone, a friend he works with, to clean this up. He says it can be fixed in a couple of hours and I'd never know the difference. As if that's all that's needed."

"Look, we'll worry about that later. Right now, we have to get you to a doctor . . . to the emergency room."

"No, I am not going anywhere looking like this. Besides, he may come back. I have to be here when he gets back."

"But Denise, why would you want to? Look at what he's done . . . to your home . . . to you."

"This is good compared to what I looked like before. A lot of the swelling has gone down. It was healing, at least until I made him mad and he started up again."

"What do you mean, 'started up again'?"

Denise looked at me, but I wasn't sure she was hearing or seeing me.

"Look Denise," I said, "if you don't come with me right now, I'm calling the police."

Suddenly she was all focus, trembling, and panicked. With her voice still weak, she managed to raise it, "No, Tina, you can't call anyone. Please don't. If you do, he'll kill me. I know that for sure. Please, Tina, please . . ."

"Okay. . . Okay . . . But you've got to come with me to the hospital. We'll tell them a stranger attacked you or something. But you *will* be coming with me. So, let's go."

I grabbed Denise by the arm. I was ready to drag her out of that house, if I had to. She looked around the room, as if she was seeing it for the first time. And, for the first time since I arrived, I saw some of the determined spirit I knew my friend possessed.

"Let me clean myself up a bit and get dressed. I can't leave here stinking, in just a gown and slippers."

I didn't want to let her out of my sight. I wasn't sure how long her resolve would last or if she was strong enough to wash and dress herself. In the back of my head was the thought that Reggie could return before we managed to leave. But she seemed to need to do it, so I went with her to help.

As we were on our way out, Denise grabbed the picture, I'd noticed before. She opened the back, pulled the photo out, ripped it up, and threw the pieces into the mess on the sofa. That seemed to take a lot out of her, so I took her arm to stabilize her. As I helped her through the door, I said a silent prayer for her. I prayed that she'd come out of this whole. That she'd find the strength she needed to let authorities know who was responsible. And that Reggie would get what he deserved.

Securing the lock on the door, I looked at Denise barely able to stand, not sure what I would do if she couldn't make it to the car. Then a sweeping sadness came over me, as I wondered how it was possible for one human being to do such awful things to another.

Chapter 27

ONCE WE WERE OUT of the house, I saw just how bad Denise's condition was. It scared me. Just walking to the car was exhausting and painful for her. She needed more than just a ride to the hospital. She needed immediate medical attention. She needed the care that only EMT professionals could provide. Except, there was no guarantee that they could arrive in less time than it would take us to make it to the emergency room. Even if they did, could they get there before Reggie returned and made us both disappear without any trace?

It took only a couple of minutes, with Denise moaning at every bump or abrupt stop, for me to understand the other downside of me driving her in my small car. Each time she moaned, I'd turn my head towards her, feeling rotten for putting her through it. I couldn't imagine what it was like for her. For me, the short trip seemed endless.

Once we were a couple of blocks away from her house, Denise seemed to relax a bit—at least as much as anyone could, who was going through what she was. She began describing her life with Reggie.

"Remember how I told you that in the beginning Reggie seemed so perfect?" she asked, not waiting for an answer. "It only took a month. Believe it or not. Just a month for him to start acting jealous of the men I came in contact with, even men from work. And some of them are gay. You can imagine what it was like, editing everything I said to make sure there was nothing that would make him jealous. Sometimes, it was actually funny when I caught myself relating something and having to change the person's name mid-sentence." She chuckled at the memory, but I just let her talk.

"You know, at first, it was sort of cute, endearing even. I'd never had anyone that into me that they'd think every man was after me. But soon the charm of it wore off, especially when it got to the point where he had a problem with everybody I came in contact with, male or female. Sometimes I wondered if he was really bothered or just messing with me to see how I'd react. Can you imagine how awful it is being made to feel guilty about talking with your own family?"

"Denise, I don't understand," I said. "What's wrong with you talking to your family?"

"Hell if I know," she answered right away. "But, according to Reggie, they are a bad influence, and I act differently after I talk with any of them."

"I still don't understand," I said, puzzled. "Could you talk with his family? How did he act with your family?"

"I never met his family. He never met mine. At first, it wasn't the right time. Then later, as things got so confusing, I just couldn't . . ." Her voice trailed off, as if she didn't have the strength to finish.

She was silent for several moments, which scared me. I looked over to make sure she hadn't passed out. She was staring ahead with silent tears rolling down her face.

With a sigh, she continued, "At first everything was nice. Reggie was gentle and sweet. But . . . I just don't know what happened. Believe me, I'm a research person. That's part of my job. So, I had to look all this up. Spouse abuse, and all that. It's different when it's you."

At that point, I could feel her eyes on me. I guess she was trying to will me into understanding.

"You know, the first time he got physical, I was fool enough to believe it was a special circumstance thing. He had been out drinking with friends and came in while I was on the phone. He snuck up on me, absolutely sure he had caught me flirting with some man. He didn't say, 'Ah Ha!', or any such thing. He grabbed my wrist and twisted until I dropped the phone. Then he dramatically hung it up. It was so abrupt . . . so . . . well . . . out of the blue."

"What happened then?" I asked, not sure I really wanted to know.

"I screamed at him, asking him if he had lost his mind. That's when he grabbed me again and insisted that I tell him who it was I was talking with. When he found out that it was just my brother, he calmed down. He seemed really sorry and ashamed. Blamed it on the alcohol."

"Did he hurt you? How bad was it?"

"Nothing serious. More my feelings than anything. I forgave him, after he told me that he had been out drinking and comforting a friend whose wife had cheated on him. He apologized saying it made him too sensitive."

"Sensitive? More like psycho," I said, not able to hold the comment in.

Denise gave a small grunt, before she continued.

"The next day, he had flowers delivered. Everything was fine, until the next time, and the next time, and the next time. I accepted all the apologies and the gifts. I really wanted to believe that things would ease out and he would learn to trust me. . . I really wanted to believe . . . Then, after a while it didn't really matter." Denise had said the last part so softly that I could barely hear her.

I didn't want to judge my friend, but I had to ask, "It was your house. Couldn't you just tell him to get lost, kick him out . . . break up with him?"

"Yes," she answered. "Of course, I could. And I did. A bunch of times. His mood swings and jealous rages gave me no choice. Finally, about six weeks ago, I couldn't take it anymore and I ordered him to leave me alone and never come back. I threatened to take out a restraining order on him. That time he knew I really meant it. His response was one I hardly expected. Instead of his normal rant or apology, he laughed and said that restraining orders are a joke. And that he would stay as long as he wanted and would see me whenever he felt like it. If I tried anything against him, he knew how to get to my family and anybody else I cared about. And he could get away with it. I believed him."

When Denise paused again, I decided to wait her out. After a short rest, she continued as if she hadn't stopped talking at all.

"I believed him," she repeated, "and I was terrified. Not just for myself, but for all the people I held dear. I realized what I had gotten myself into and I knew that there was no way out."

I didn't want to hear anymore of Denise's awful story. I just wanted to scream or cry or do anything to release the anger I was feeling—towards

Reggie *and* towards my friend for putting up with him. But I had to keep myself together. I needed every ounce of strength I could muster to continue driving and get her to the hospital safely.

"What about your brothers?" I asked her. "Couldn't you go to live with one of them? They both live a long distance from Richmond. What about the one you told me about? The one that you said was in the Black Mafia or whatever. I'd have thought that he could help you out with a crazy like Reggie. Which brother is that?"

"That's my brother, Kennard. He's the one I'm closest to," she said. The change in her voice made me look over at her. I saw that she had the first sign of a smile on her face.

Denise had previously described her second brother, the one who lived in Chicago, as smart, handsome, strong, and as possibly having some very shady associations.

"I didn't dare tell Kennard anything," she continued. "Mainly because I didn't know what he would do. I didn't want to be the cause of my brother ending up in jail or dead at the hands of the supposedly good guys."

As I listened, it occurred to me how lucky it was that Denise had kept the fact that we were becoming friends a secret. If he'd known, Reggie would have put a halt to it, and there might have been no one to come to her rescue. My friend could have ended up dying alone in her house.

"Denise, I have to ask. I was wondering if I had something to do with Reggie going ballistic. Did you get home late last Friday? Or did Reggie find out about you coming over to my place? Is that what set him off?"

"No," she answered. "As a matter of fact, I was home in bed a long time before he got there."

"Then, what made him so angry?"

"He was already upset because some woman panicked when he tried to arrest her. She came at him with a bat. Something happened, as he was trying to avoid her. I think a table or something fell on his foot. His boss made him go to the hospital. From what he told me, they took some x-rays, wrapped his foot, gave him some pain pills, and told him to rest the foot as much as possible. It was having to be on restricted duty that had him upset. Somehow he felt it would interfere with some big thing he had planned."

Denise paused to take a breath. It seemed that the combination of it all—her injuries, the ride, and the memories—was getting to be too much for her. But she wanted to talk, so I let her.

"I tried to soothe him," she continued. "When I asked him what the big plans were, he got this look and just reached back and punched me. He had never hit me like that before. I screamed. But that didn't stop him. He just kept hitting me and hitting me."

Denise started crying again. I felt bad that I couldn't stop the car to hold her, to make her feel better. But the best way to make her better would be to get her to proper medical care. And we were still several minutes away.

She grabbed a bunch of the tissues from a box I had given her earlier, blew her nose and continued her story.

"After a while, Reggie finally realized what he had done. And it scared him. He paced around the room, saying, 'Oh shit . . . oh shit . . .' Then he started banging his fist against the walls and destroying anything in his path. At least he wasn't hitting me anymore. Know what I mean?"

She paused long enough for me to nod.

"To keep me from calling for help, he took my cell phone, and he destroyed all the phones in the house. He ranted about not letting me ruin his life and his career. At some point he came up with the idea that he would take care of me and everything would be all right."

"That's why nobody could reach you. You've been in that house alone for days with no way to communicate with anybody outside," I said, appalled.

"I think, in his warped mind, he thought he could make me all better and everything would be fine. He stayed with me the next two days, taking care of me and forcing pain pills on me. When he had to leave, he gave me sleeping pills, on top of the pain medication. I thought about the danger of mixing medications. But, at some point, I didn't really care anymore. I just wanted it to be over. One way or the other."

I couldn't take hearing anymore. "That bastard!" I blurted out, not trying to hide the disgust and outrage I was feeling. "He made sure you couldn't do anything while he lived his life, like nothing had happened."

She was leaning back in the seat, seeming to get weaker and weaker. I was afraid if she went to sleep, she wouldn't wake up.

"So," I said trying to keep her talking, "Reggie had everything under control. Why did he attack you again this morning?"

She sighed so loudly, I thought she wouldn't answer. I hated myself for asking. "I'm so sorry," I said. "That's not what's important right now. We just need to get you to the hospital, and you can move pass all that."

"I'll never move pass it, Tina," she said. "Can't you see? He'll find me and hurt me again. You know why? Because he can. You asked about this morning, but it actually started last night. He was almost giddy when he got to my house, excited about something that had happened at the station. I made the mistake of thinking that his good mood was an opportunity to tell him that I didn't think we were right for each other, that we should go our separate ways."

At that point, my friend stopped talking. Her entire body was shaking. She sobbed louder and louder.

"Why did I do that?' she cried. "Why couldn't I have just waited? I was healing. After he was gone, I could've changed the locks. I was feeling better. I was strong enough to go outside and ask someone to call 911."

Still sobbing she continued with her story. She described how Reggie lost control again. But this time hitting her wasn't enough, he raped her, violently.

She described how he had stayed the night, but he got a call and had to leave. Denise said that she was, at that point, too tired and weak to move. She just huddled in a corner, scared to move, wanting to die. That's where she was when I started banging on the door.

* * *

Once we arrived at the hospital entrance, Denise hesitated. No matter what I tried, she would not leave the car. Finally, she grabbed my arm, looked me in the eye, and pleaded, "Look Tina, I need you to promise me something."

"What Denise?" I couldn't imagine anything more important than getting her through those hospital doors.

"You've got to promise me that once we get inside you won't tell anybody what happened."

"Denise," I all but screamed, "you have to tell them what happened to you. If you don't they may not know how to treat you or what to do for you."

"Tina, you don't understand," she said. "During the time Reggie was doing his version of nursing me back to health, he told me some details about the stuff he was into. Some of it I already knew or suspected. Some was much worse than I could possibly imagine. I guess it didn't matter to him at that point. He probably figured either I was all but gone or I'd be too afraid to do or say anything against him."

"None of that matters right now," I said, almost in tears, because my friend still refused to budge.

"I know you care about me, but you don't understand. He's crazy. He'll carry out his threats. Remember what I said about the woman he was trying to arrest, and he got hurt . . . his foot?"

I nodded yes.

"He told me how she had lodged a formal complaint. From what he was saying, it seemed that she pulled out the bat because she knew how crazy he was. And after his foot got injured, he hurt her bad. Then a day later, for some mysterious reason, she dropped the complaint. But that wasn't enough for him. I don't know how or where, but I think he killed her. He didn't say so, but what he did say was, 'that bitch will not be making any more complaints against hard working officers of the law, just performing their duties.' Tina, he said that, and he actually smiled. Like it was a joke."

I'll have to admit, an involuntary shiver went through me as the reality of what she was telling me sank in.

"Tina, he can find a way to make bad things happen to my brothers, my mother, my father, and even you. You can't say anything, no matter what happens to me."

"What do you mean? Nothings gonna happen to you. We'll get you better and your family will take care of you from there."

"Maybe," Denise said staring out the car window.

"*Not maybe*," I said, stroking my friend's arm. "So, what are you going to say happened to your face and all those bruises all over your whole body?" I asked, hearing the frustration in my voice. I had to catch myself so that I wouldn't push her to the point where she would refuse to go inside to the emergency room.

"Look, at some point, the only one I might tell what happened to me is my brother, Kennard. As far as everybody else is concerned, I was attacked in my home by an intruder. Until then, I don't want you to say anything different."

Though I knew no one would believe her with a week old bruises, a swollen face, and her eyes barely open, I agreed. "Okay, Okay. I promise."

"You also have to promise not to say anything, even if I'm not around."

"What do you mean, if you're not around?"

"Just promise, Tina."

I nodded.

"You know what Tina?"

"What? "

"For the past couple of days, when I was alone, I kept thinking about this girl, Cora Winters. I knew her at Virginia State. She dated this guy that all the girls wanted to be with. But he hit her and embarrassed her in public, whenever he had a chance to. Cora was beautiful and smart and a cheerleader. At the time, I kept asking, with everything she had going for her, why she took the abuse and didn't just dump him. You know what, it's funny, but I wonder whatever happened to Cora. The last I heard, they were still together."

With that, she let me hold her up enough to walk into the hospital. After that, the efficient medical staff took over. There was nothing more for me to do but sit and wait.

Two hours passed and I know the woman at the desk was frustrated with me because I was constantly in her face. Finally, a police officer came out. He stopped by the front desk and the woman pointed my way.

"Ms. Brooks?"

"Yes, I'm Ms. Brooks."

The police officer walked closer and stood in front of me and extended his hand. "I'm Officer McDonald."

Obviously, I didn't have to introduce myself, so I stood up and took his hand and merely said, "Hi."

Officer McDonald was a tall, balding, blonde, white man, with a slim build. He had very thin lips with a thick mustache. His legs were so long I don't think it took him but two strides to get to me.

"Ms. Brooks, I spoke briefly with your friend. Can you tell me anything about what happened to her?"

"No," I said, looking down so I wouldn't be caught in my lie. "I really don't know. When I went to visit her, I found her like that, so I rushed her here. Is she okay?"

"I have to wait and let the doctor speak with you about the condition of your friend. Now how long was she in the house like this? She mentioned that some man broke in and attacked her. Is this true?"

"I guess. Like I said I really don't know. Can I speak with the doctor now? I'm really worried about Denise."

I couldn't hold the tears back any longer. The police officer put his hand on my shoulder and patted. "I'll come back and talk with you later."

The officer left and I sat back down trying to control myself. The doctor, a short man with bowlegs, came out about five minutes later. He approached me holding a clipboard in his hand. The solemn look on his face disturbed me. "Ms. Brooks, I'm Doctor Wayne Hunter."

"Hello, Doctor Hunter." I stood up. "How's my friend?"

"I'm sorry, Ms. Brooks, but she died about fifteen minutes ago."

"What?" I practically screamed. "What the hell are you talking about? She can't be dead."

Dead? The word just screamed in my head. *But Officer McDonald told me that he had just spoken with Denise. I brought her here to get better, not to die.*

All of a sudden, I just felt weak. My legs didn't seem strong enough to hold me. The doctor took my arm anticipating me falling or possibly fainting. "Please sit down, Ms. Brooks."

"Sit down? You got to be kidding. You just told me that my friend is dead. How can I sit down?" The tears were flowing steadily.

"Ms. Brooks, I am sorry for your loss, but your friend suffered some very severe injuries. I don't think she even knew how badly off she was. We tried, but there was not much we could do to save her. I am sorry."

I looked at the doctor again. I could see his mouth moving, but I couldn't hear a word he was saying. The only thing in my head was that my friend was dead. That monster, Reggie, had killed my friend, and there was nothing I could do about it.

CHAPTER 28

BY THE TIME OFFICER MCDONALD RETURNED, I was a wreck. I kept thinking about Denise and how she'd suffered such agony and had died such a horrible and unnecessary death.

I couldn't stop crying. I cried for the loss of the lovely, universally adored woman with everything to live for. For the funny woman I had met, only a few months before, in the hallways of MedsCon. For the woman who teased me about my prejudices. For the woman who refused to let me walk away with the wrong impression of her. For the woman who laughed with me about life, her family, and the silly romantic movies she so dearly loved. And, I cried for the woman I had grown very fond of and was just getting to know.

Now she was dead. And I was torn. Should I tell all that I knew to ensure she got the justice she deserved to avenge that death? Or, should I honor her final wish and withhold critical information because she believed revealing it could bring harm to people close to her?

Denise had asked so little of me and people around her, I figured the least I could do was honor her final wish. I only hoped that the police could find enough evidence, maybe from her house, that would direct them to one of their own, a monster named Reggie.

I carefully relayed to Officer McDonald only the details that I had direct knowledge of. I told him about how I had been unable to reach Denise. How her boss had expressed concern about her. And, how I had arrived at her house finding her in the condition that she was in. I told him, honestly, that this was the first time I had been in her home, that I had not witnessed anyone harming her, and there was no one else with her when I arrived.

With me having no information of substance to offer, Officer McDonald thanked me for my assistance. He gave me the name of the detective in charge, Detective Angela Robinson, just in case I had anything more to add in the future. As he walked away, I realized that, for the second time in my life, by omission, I was essentially lying to the police in a murder inquiry. The realization did not make me feel proud.

Next came the hard part, waiting for Denise's parents. I had called them when we first arrived, after persuading Denise to provide the number. At the time, I could only tell them that she was hurt and in the hospital. Now, I couldn't bring myself to call back and tell them that she was dead. The least I could do was be there, as someone who cared for their daughter, when they are delivered the awful news from medical staff and Richmond city police.

It was hard to believe that only two weeks before, Denise had been dancing around ecstatic, because her parents were finally back together, reunited after years of being apart. From what she told me, her parents' love story was straight out of one of those old romance novels.

They had met as teenagers, in the late seventies, in a newly integrated high school. Phil Jackson was utterly fascinated with the vivacious black girl. He came from an upper middle-class environment and had never met anyone like Cynthia Goodman. He pursued her.

Though, during that time, mixed relationships weren't totally accepted— it was still the South after all—being strong willed independent young people, Phil and Cindy ignored all potential obstacles and got married. They made a home together for nearly twenty years. Then, suddenly, Mr. Jackson decided he wanted something more. He accepted a job on the West Coast, and basically walked away from his family.

Only recently, after suffering a massive heart attack, did he realize that there was only one person he wanted by his side, Cynthia Jackson. He didn't dare call her. But since she was still his emergency contact, the hospital did.

Being the person she was, Mrs. Jackson rushed to his side and stayed with him, until he felt well enough to propose once again. They remarried and returned to celebrate in Atlantic City, the place they had honeymooned the first time. And that was where I reached them, with the painful news that their only daughter was seriously injured and in the hospital.

* * *

The moment I saw the distraught, stocky woman entering the waiting room, I knew she had to be Denise's mother, Mrs. Jackson. She was older, darker, and much heavier than Denise. But the resemblance was unmistakable.

The woman looked around the waiting room, and her eyes, which were red from crying, landed on me. From her pained expression, I assumed that the medical staff had already told her about Denise and where to find me. She headed directly to where I was sitting.

I stood up to meet her halfway. When she got to where I was, I stopped, unable to find any words to say.

While I was struggling with what I could possibly say to express how sorry I was, she grabbed a hold of me and held on. She squeezed me so tight, I thought she was going to crush my bones. I didn't complain, because it felt right, somehow.

Mid-hug, an extremely handsome man, in his fifties, approached us. Mrs. Jackson released me long enough to introduce us, "Phil, this is Tina, the friend Denise told us about."

Then she turned to me and said, "Tina, this is my husband, Phillip Jackson, Denise's father."

I bobbed my head slightly, not being able to speak. I recognized Denise in them both. She was the perfect blend of these two beautiful people. When Mr. Jackson, grabbed me for a hug, I broke down. I couldn't hold back anymore. I sobbed, uncontrollably, in the arms of that heartbroken man, someone I had never met, while his sweet distraught wife patted my back, trying to comfort me.

It seemed that I knew them both, this perfect, though odd looking, couple. They were just as Denise had described them. I stepped away from them both, embarrassed about losing control.

"I'm so sorry I did that," I said. "I just couldn't take you both being so kind to me, when at the same time I'm thinking that I should have gotten to Denise sooner."

"It wasn't your fault," her mother said, more gently than I deserved. "According to the doctor, she was on borrowed time."

When she couldn't finish—she was so choked up—Mr. Jackson took over. "Knowing Denise, she probably just willed herself to stay alive. I'm willing to bet, that she somehow knew that you would come. You were probably the last bit of hope she had. And she wouldn't let herself go before speaking to you."

"You know, she told us about you," Mrs. Jackson added, managing a sad smile. "She joked about the way you two met. She was impressed at your reaction and how unaffected you seemed when confronted with your assumptions about her, your own prejudice. She was sure, at that point, you were someone worth getting to know."

They both smiled, briefly, as if it were a family joke, a common occurrence that people made assumptions about Denise based on her coloring. It surprised me how the whole family seemed to take that in stride. I'm not sure I could.

"She seemed so down and depressed, but we had no clue why. It was unusual for her to not even talk to Cindy," Mr. Jackson said. "We were both worried, but being so far away there was not much either of us could do to force her to talk to us."

Mrs. Jackson took over, fascinating me how smoothly they finished each other's thoughts. "You can't imagine how relieved we were when she began talking about how you two got along and the things you two did together. She seemed more like herself."

Mrs. Jackson, nodded at her husband, looking to him for agreement.

He mirrored her gesture, as he added, "We knew something was still seriously bothering her and intended to confront Denise about it when we saw her. We still don't exactly know what was bringing her down, but we are thankful that she had a friend, like you, in the end. One who was concerned enough to rush her to the hospital for medical assistance."

I stepped back, sat down, and put my face in my hands. I thought about how long it had taken for me to go to her house. I remembered all Denise had gone through. At that point, I made a decision. I asked Mr. and Mrs. Jackson to sit down, quietly informing them that I had something to tell them. Then, after saying a small prayer that Denise would forgive me, I broke my final promise to her.

* * *

I called Jeri and Mrs. Jeffries, on Monday morning, to tell them that Denise had died in the hospital from injuries sustained from a severe beating in her home.   Confused, they both pressed, but I truly had no additional information to provide. By Tuesday morning, when I felt strong enough to return to work, everyone was aware that Denise was dead. I heard that there was a lot of crying going on in Business Services.

The one thing I deliberately did not share with any of them was the fact that, since Denise's death, everything about the situation had progressed from merely strange to Twilight Zone strange.

The Jackson's had a walk-through appointment with Detective Robinson the Saturday afternoon following Denise's death. The police had previously walked around the outside of the property. With no signs of forced entry and no witnesses or neighbors willing to share, they waited for a legally authorized individual to let them inside.

The Jackson's called me following the walk-thru, stunned. When they turned the keys to enter the house, they had prepared themselves for the destruction, I had described. But they were immediately assaulted with the smells of strong cleaners and fresh paint. Inside, the place was immaculate. There were no turned over pieces of furniture or holes in the wall. Even the torn picture, I had told them to look for on the sofa, was missing.

As they escorted the police around, they found several—apparently brand new—landline telephones functional and in place. The only telephone missing was Denise's mobile. It was nowhere to be found.

Suspiciously, there were no fingerprints anywhere, except Denise's, and those were only in places like under the sink or on her personal items. There were no diaries or anything with information about this Reggie character. And no one in the neighborhood could or would provide a physical description of any male seen routinely in or around Denise's house.

The final shocker came later, when Detective Robinson called to inform the couple about her attempts to locate the mysterious Reggie. They were unable to locate any thirty-something African American male, in the Richmond Police Department, named Reggie or Reginald, who matched the vague description given to the investigators.

Given Denise's death-bed version of what happened and no other evidence, Detective Robinson admitted, candidly, that it would be next to impossible for her to get permission to perform any aggressive investigation, particularly of a police officer that nobody, besides me, had any knowledge of. She promised that she would do her best.

With little hope of a resolution through official channels, the Jacksons were panic-stricken.

"Tina," Mr. Jackson said, "we don't know what to think. We are at a loss. Our daughter is dead, at the hands of this person, someone that the police say does not even exist."

"I am sorry, Mr. Jackson, maybe they will find some evidence and locate Reggie." I obviously had watched too many TV police procedurals, where the good guys always won in the end.

"Even if they do find him," he said. "they have no proof that it was him who beat her. That's what we are truly afraid of."

He was right, of course. I thought about what Denise had said about the power Reggie had claimed he enjoyed. From what we had seen so far, maybe he had not been exaggerating.

Nobody wanted Reggie to get away with the awful things he had done to Denise, but it looked like he might.

* * *

"Are you Tina?"

Paulette and I slowed, as we both turned to see a tall very attractive man, rushing to catch up with us. We had just said our goodbyes to Denise's parents and were headed towards my car, anxious to leave the gravesite and all that it represented.

I looked at Paulette and she was grinning so hard at the guy, I thought she would embarrass us both. But who could blame her? The man must have been what they meant, in the sixties, when they came up with the slogan, *black is beautiful.* He was over six feet tall, with smooth brown skin, sculpted cheeks, and a sexy trimmed goatee. His expensive black suit was perfectly tailored to fit his athletic build. He looked down on us with beautiful hazel brown eyes, that you could easily get lost in.

Paulette, still star struck, stammered, "Yes, th-th-th-this is Tina and um-um I'm-I'm-I'm Paulette, her-her-her friend."

"Hello, Paulette and Tina," he said. "I'm Kennard, Denise's brother."

"Hello, Kennard," I said, in that instant, reminded why we were there.

"Tina," he said. "I was hoping to get a chance to talk with you. I'm basically just getting here. I flew in from Chicago today and arrived almost too late for the funeral. Didn't mean to chase you down. But I'm told that you were the last one to talk with Denise."

Paulette gave my arm a sympathetic squeeze. Handsome man aside, she was saying that she was there for me.

"Yes," I answered. "Besides the medical people at the hospital and the police, I was the last one she spoke with."

"I guess I'm not surprised about that. Denise talked about you. Apparently, you were her best friend."

People had been saying that a lot to me, in the past few days. It was so strange to hear. I wasn't aware that Denise felt that close to me. It made me sad to think about how lonely and isolated she must have felt for such a long time. I tried to hold back the tears, but they came so suddenly that I had to turn my head, hoping he wouldn't notice.

"I'm sorry, Tina," Kennard said, apparently seeing through my weak attempt to get my emotions under control. "I didn't mean to upset you. This is really a strange situation. I'm having trouble getting a handle on it. And I'm sorry to blindside you like this. Look, why don't we talk later, at my parent's house. You both are coming, right?"

"Honestly," I said to him, "I don't think I'm up to that. What do you want to talk about? I think I told your parents everything I know."

"Maybe that's true. But all our lives, my sister was my best friend. I just want to understand what happened and get some kind of idea why."

I thought about how Denise, at her weakest point, had put so much faith in her brother, Kennard—in his finding a way to help her. Since, the police investigation was at a standstill, maybe Kennard was the only other option.

"Okay. Your parents have my number," I said. "Oh, and Kennard?"

"Yes," he said, looking at me, with those beautiful eyes, full of grief.

"I am sorry for your loss. It sounds so trite, but it's true. I wish I could've done more to help her."

At that, he hugged me, and I felt an almost electrical spark, a sensation truly new to me, one that I didn't expect. It caught me off guard. When he let go, I looked around, totally embarrassed. I hoped that no one, at this somber occasion, noticed my shameful reaction.

As he walked away, I waited for Paulette to remark on my blatantly disgraceful display. Instead, she gently touched my arm and led me to my car. It was the exact right thing to do, reminding me of what a great friend she was. Too bad Denise would never get to meet her.

Though I hadn't felt as close to Denise as she obviously had towards me, given time, that would have changed. There was so much and there were so many people we'd never get to share. I missed my friend. Mostly I missed what could have been. I wanted her back.

Suddenly, all that had happened in such a short period of time had me drained. I felt incredibly sad and all I wanted to do was to go home and cry myself to sleep.

CHAPTER 29

NEITHER PAULETTE NOR I TALKED, as I maneuvered through the lines of cars leaving the burial site. Once we were clear and heading in the direction of downtown, I broke the silence.

"Do you really think that it was possible Denise saw me as her best friend?" I asked Paulette.

"In a way you were," she said, without hesitation. "Don't get me wrong, from what you say about her, Denise was smart enough to understand the true nature of your relationship. From what you heard from her family and the people at work, she'd never really felt the need for a close female friend before. Then Reggie happened, and her family noticed the changes in her. Luckily, she met you, someone she genuinely admired, felt comfortable with, and could open-up to. I imagine that it was like a gift from heaven, because she had to have been feeling totally isolated not being able to go to her family, for the first time in her life. The extra added benefit was that it also gave her an out with her family. For their sake, she probably made a conscious decision to exaggerate her connection to someone, who was more of a friendly work acquaintance than a close friend."

"That's so sad, isn't it?"

Paulette nodded, and continued, "I think your friend had to have been really desperate and unhappy. She was in a no-win situation and hoped she could find a way to fix it, without having to admit what was going on. As hard as it is to believe, she was probably embarrassed by what was happening and couldn't tell her perfect family about it, even before Reggie started making his threats."

"Why was she embarrassed? Her family would've understood," I said.

"Tina, that's not the point. I think it was more complicated than just getting them to understand. Anyhow, once you two started hanging, she had something positive to report. She could put off exposing her shame and avoid whatever she thought would happen once her family found out—whether her fears were rational or not."

"Honestly, I don't think her family would've judged her. Knowing them, more than likely they would've done everything they could to help her."

"Maybe they would have. But nobody wants to disappoint those who care about them, especially if, from what I can tell, they idolized the poor woman. On top of everything else, I think she didn't want to let them down."

I looked over at Paulette. Her matter of fact tone made me wonder what I was missing. She seemed to have an amazing grasp of Denise's dilemma and her choices. Maybe her insight had something to do with them both being raised in big close-knit families—something I could never relate to. If I asked, Paulette would've explained best she could, but I chose to move on.

"Once Denise made the decision to open up to me, do you think that eventually she might've found a way to end it with Reggie, and maybe found somebody better suited than me to listen to her and help her out of the situation—maybe even her family?"

"Maybe," Paulette said. "Then again, she was right about Reggie. He's smart and ruthless. He probably knew that she was too strong to put up with his foolishness indefinitely. More than likely, consciously or unconsciously, he was prepared to kill her, when and if that time came. She was too much of a threat."

"Oh, my God," I said. "Once she fell for Reggie, Denise never really had a chance."

We sat silently, for the remainder of the drive to my apartment. As we got out of the car, Paulette hugged me goodbye. She had come to Richmond to help me get through the funeral. Now she had to get back to her sane life in North Carolina.

* * *

Normally, I was an early riser, but that morning, the one following Denise's funeral, I couldn't get myself to move. I barely had enough energy to open my eyes, after staying up late and thinking about the conversation I'd had with Paulette about Denise. It was still on my mind, when the phone rang.

Looking at the clock I saw that it was only 8:53AM.

"Who in the world would call me before nine o'clock on a Saturday morning?" I asked myself, reaching for the phone. The caller-id was from a Chicago area code. I recognized it because MedsCon had a lot of clients from Chicago. That meant the person on the other end was probably Kennard, Denise's brother.

Remembering my shameful reaction to him the previous day, I hesitated picking up the receiver. Assuring myself that, with the distance between us, it wouldn't happen again, I took a breath, picked it up, and said, "Hello."

"Hey, Tina, this is Kennard Jackson. I hope I didn't wake you."

"No, I've been up for a while. I'm just sitting here reading the paper and sipping a cup of coffee. What's up?"

Somehow this stranger I'd only met once, knew I was lying. He snickered and said, "I hope that coffee's not too hot, because you sound like you're half asleep and not out of bed yet."

"No, I'm up," I said, trying to make it true by jumping to my feet, an attempt which ended with me and the covers down on the floor.

"Do you need me to come over and help you get out of bed?" he teased. "It sounds like you're having a hard time?"

"Umm, you called for a reason, Mr. Jackson," I said. "I can't imagine it was to make fun of me."

"Sorry, Tina, I was just joking. The 'Mr. Jackson' thing definitely put me in my place," he said, but I sensed he was still smiling. "You have to know that Denise talked so much about you, that I forgot we've only just met. I mean, she practically had us married."

"What?"

"You didn't know? Like I said, Denise talked about you all the time. It started with, little hints like, 'You need to meet Tina.' Then, she'd say stuff like, 'Kenny, she's great, down to earth, really pretty and smart.' Finally, I called her on it, admitted I knew what she was up to. Know what she said?"

"No, what?"

"She said, 'Kenny, I have seen the women you pick out. Little brother, you need all the help you can get. You wait and see. You two will make a wonderful couple.'"

I laughed, even as the tears began to form, thinking about Denise playing match maker, without even telling me. She was gone and I would never be able to talk to her again. And now, here I was finally meeting and talking with her handsome brother, the one she obviously wanted to match me up with.

I must've zoned out, because Kennard was still talking, and I had obviously missed something.

"Is today good?" he was saying. "I can come over to your place and have a cup of that coffee you say you're drinking."

Is he flirting with me? The notion had me tongue-tied. I tried to respond, but all that came out was, "Uh, well, uh..."

I couldn't tell if he was flirting. That seemed inappropriate and weird, but not as inappropriate or weird as my reaction to him. Flirting or not, I wasn't ready to be alone with Kennard Jackson in my place.

"No need for you to come here," I said, finally getting myself together. "We can meet downtown at Burger Rack."

"Burger Rack?"

Good, something safe to talk about, I thought. What I said out loud was, "Don't tell me that you've never had a Burger Rack burger?"

Kennard laughed, "No, I'm sorry to say, I've never had a Burger Rack burger. There aren't any Burger Racks in Chicago, and when I was growing up, I never got around to trying it out."

"Well, Mr. Jackson, you're in for a treat."

"What time did you say for me to pick you up?" Kennard asked.

"You mean, what time are we supposed to meet downtown?" I said.

"If you insist. Can't blame a guy for trying."

I can't believe it. He is flirting . . . "See you at twelve thirty, at the Burger Rack on East Broad Street," I said, shamefully giggling.

✳ ✳ ✳

I spotted Kennard, as I entered the restaurant, he was sitting in a booth checking his watch.

"I'm not late, am I?" I asked, nodding my head towards his watch.

"No, as a matter of fact, you're right on time. I came early. I didn't know exactly where the place was, so I left early in case I had to drive around. Of course, we could have eliminated all of that, if you had let me pick you up."

"Not that again," I said, as we both laughed, and I slid into the seat opposite him.

The waitress came immediately to take our order, saving us the necessity to make small talk. Of course, once she had our order, neither of us knew what to say. It was hard not to think about the real reason we were there.

Kennard broke the silence. "You know, Tina, I don't think this is exactly what Denise had in mind, but I'm glad we had a chance to meet."

"Me too. She loved you so much. From what she said about you, I half expected you to wear a red cape and have a big red *S* on your chest."

Kennard laughed. "Well, growing up, we took care of each other. When we were little, from day one, she took care of me. I was her own personal live dolly. Then, from when I was a toddler on up, she was the only one guaranteed to be able to calm me down when I lost my temper. Later, most of the trouble I got into was from protecting my big sister, especially as we got older and boys started noticing her. Anybody, big or little, who got in her face or got too outrageous, had to deal with me. Nobody wanted that. They all thought I was crazy."

"What about your brother, Robert?"

"Robert always was the civilized one. I remember one time, when I was about nine or ten and Denise had to be about eleven or twelve. I was on the way home from school and walked up to this crowd of kids cheering. They were all surrounding what obviously was a fight going on. I saw Robert standing in the crowd, quietly watching. I went to stand beside my brother, to see what was happening. I loved nothing more than a good fight. What I saw, had me pushing everybody out of my way. There, on the ground, was this big girl, beating the crap out of Denise. I jumped in and pulled her off my sister, ready to take her down and anyone else who took exception to me getting involved. The thing is, it never occurred to Robert to double-bank the girl. He had this strict sense of fair play. In his mind, two against one wouldn't be a fair fight. To me, there was no such thing as a fair fight, if someone was after my family. I would've done the same thing for Robert."

"By civilized you mean that Robert was the meek one of you, the one who couldn't or wouldn't fight?"

"Not really. More goody-two-shoes than scaredy-cat. Like I said he truly believed in fair play. You see, he knew that the fight was Denise's fault. The difference was that it didn't matter to me. So, it wasn't that he was afraid or wouldn't fight. He was actually a damn good fighter, if pushed too far. Believe me I know. As the little brother, I did a hell of a lot of pushing."

I smiled at the image of Kennard as the bratty little brother.

"It seems that all three of you did well in life. You all went to college and became professionals," I said. "I know how good Denise was at her job and Robert is a medical doctor in Canada, right?"

"Yes," he said, but I got the impression that I was pressing beyond where he wanted to go with the conversation.

We both knew that we had been stalling, avoiding what we were there to talk about.

So, Kennard took the lead. "Did you ever meet Denise's boyfriend? What was his name, Reggie?"

"No, I never met him. Denise only mentioned him a few times. Then about a week before she died, we were watching movies, at my place, and the subject came up. She didn't say much then, because she said she didn't really want to talk about it. Not until we were on the way to the hospital, did she fill in the gruesome details."

I could see the pain in his eyes, and I reached over to take his hand, when I heard a familiar voice, one I thought I'd never hear again. I turned around, swiveling my head, trying to find the source. Then, I saw her. My mother was walking with the hostess, chatting.

I stood up, not sure what I was going to do, or say. Then she must've felt me staring at her.

"Tina?"

"Momma? Where in the hell have you been?" I nearly screamed, not able to hide the shock and anger I was feeling.

All the excuses, all the rationalizations, everything I'd deluded myself into believing, went out the window with the sight of my mother, obviously alive and healthy. Then she, the woman who had left a thirteen-year-old child to fend for herself, actually walked over and grinned at me.

Everyone in the restaurant turned to look at us, and the drama that was unfolding right there in the East Broad Street Burger Rack. But no one could possibly know how truly surreal the encounter was.

Momma leaned forward to give me a hug. I stepped back. I was getting angrier with each second. Instead of leaning into the hug, I pushed her away. I guess Kennard thought I was about to hit her, because he jumped between us and said, "No, Tina. I don't know exactly what's going on, but if this is your mother, don't go there."

I looked at Kennard, with daggers shooting from my eyes. How dare he?

"Kennard, you're absolutely right, you can't imagine what's happening here. Mr. Protector . . . Mr. 'family is everything' . . . Well, you've chosen the wrong family and the wrong person to protect this time."

"Baby, I am so sorry, but there is so much you don't know . . ." my mother cried.

But I didn't want to hear it. I looked at Kennard, who was staring at me, dumfounded. At that moment, no matter how handsome he was, his opinion didn't really count. I wasn't about to try and convince him about anything.

"You can't possibly understand," I said, staring him down. When he didn't say anything, I knew it was time to leave. "I'm sorry, Kennard, I've just lost my appetite." I stumbled pass my mother. She seemed to lose all her steam and flopped down in the seat that I had just vacated. I glared angrily from one to the other and said, "You two talk. I have nothing more to say."

I turned to leave as my mother tried to grab my arm. "Please Tina, don't go. I need to talk to you. There are a lot of things I need to explain. At least tell me how to reach you."

"You know what, Momma?" I said, looking her up and down. "You look well. You actually look really good. And that's the worst part of it."

I ignored the shocked expression on Kennard's face, probably at the bitterness in my voice. With nothing more to say, I weaved my way around the tables and out of the restaurant, leaving them there together in the booth.

I stormed off to my car. When I reached it, I couldn't manage to get the keys in the ignition. I just sat there, drained. I was surprised that I—normally Miss Weepy Eyes USA—couldn't cry. After a week of crying for my friend, Denise, someone who truly deserved it, I had no more tears left for Antoinette Catrina Brooks.

CHAPTER 30

I DIDN'T KNOW WHAT TO DO or what to think. I tried phoning Paulette to admit how right she had been all along. I owed her that much. After the first couple of rings, I changed my mind. I wasn't ready. I sat on my couch steaming. I was angry to the point of being totally irrational. I was mad at me because I had deluded myself for so long. I was mad at Paulette for being right. I was mad at Momma for being all the things I had denied she was. And, inexplicably, I was mad at Kennard for not taking my side.

All those years ago, I had been sad and hurt. But I had never allowed myself to wallow in the level of self-pity that I was doing then. What was the point? What would it change? At that, I made a decision. I would not allow my mother to have any further impact on my life. Nor would I sit in the apartment in the dark, brooding. Why give her that much power?

So now I knew that she was alive. All the scenarios that had occurred to a thirteen-year-old seeking answers, could be dismissed. Now I knew she had not been attacked or in some terrible accident and lost her memory. Now I knew that her car had not fallen off a bridge and was stuck at the bottom of the James River. Now I knew that she had not been kidnaped by aliens. And now, she was back in Richmond. And I knew all I needed to know.

My phone rang before I could find all the pictures that I had saved of Momma and childishly tear them up. I recognized Kennard's number on the caller-id. I wasn't sure what he wanted to talk about, but I still owed him the information on his sister that I had promised.

"Hello," I said.

"Hello, Tina. This is Kennard."

"Yes, I know. I recognized the number."

"Can we come over, to talk?"

"We? Who is included in this *we*, you are referring to?"

"Your mother and me."

"You've got to be kidding, right? Why in the hell are you putting yourself in the middle of this?"

"Don't bust a vessel, Tina. Calm down. Okay?"

"You don't know anything about this. You don't know what that woman did. You don't know what she put me through."

"You're wrong Tina. I do know something about what's going on. Your mother and I left the restaurant shortly after you did. When we couldn't find you, we sat in my car and talked. In the last few hours, your mother has had plenty of time to fill me in on the details."

"You mean you talked to my mother about me? How could you do that?"

"You told me to, when you left the restaurant. Remember? Anyhow, when you stormed out, I was left with a very upset woman—one that you called *Momma*—crying in a booth that you and I were supposed to have lunch together in."

"I'm sorry about that. I'll reimburse you my share of the bill."

"It's not about the damn bill, and you know it. Like I said, your mother has some things to tell you. You deserve to hear what she has to say, and I think it would do you both good to let her do it. If you still don't want to have anything to do with your mother after that, then that will be your informed choice."

I was silent, not sure how to respond. Kennard was right about one thing. I did deserve to have the ten years of blanks filled in. I gave him my address.

* * *

When they arrived fifteen minutes later, my mother was different. She did not look like the well put together woman I had seen at the restaurant. She looked older, tired, and deflated.

I wouldn't let myself feel sorry for her, because there was no way to forget what that same woman had done ten years prior. All the forgiveness and love had drained out of me the moment I saw her at the Burger Rack.

They both came in and Kennard sat beside her on the sofa. I sat in the chair opposite them.

Kennard spoke first, "Listen, I'm going to leave and give you two a chance to talk. I won't be far. I have some phone calls to make. Ms. Brooks, you ring me when you're ready for me to come pick you up."

With that he left.

"Okay, Momma," I said, impatiently, "say what you have to say, and then you can leave me alone. Just like you did before." It sounded childish, even to me as I said it.

My mother sat back on the sofa. "Look, Tina. You may not believe me, but I have been looking for you."

I rolled my eyes. "Yeah, right. I haven't left Richmond, even for a little while. I haven't changed my name. I lived in the apartment for months before getting kicked out. Yeah, I was impossible to find."

"What? You were at the apartment for months? That can't be true," my mother exclaimed.

"What can't be true? Momma, you knew exactly where you left me. Where else would I be?"

"You don't understand. I was told that, a week after I left, neighbors reported you to Social Services. Then you were placed in a foster home, with a family with kids your age and younger. Later, I was taunted with the fact that you were about to be adopted by that family."

"Come on, Momma, you don't have to make things up. Really, why would anybody tell you that?"

"Because they knew that I couldn't stand the thought of you being alone. Because they wanted to keep me from running away to find you or from talking with the authorities. Oh, my God! That was my worst nightmare. Oh, my God!" she said, her voice cracking.

She kept repeating, "Oh, my God" over and over. Her entire body shook with an onslaught of sobs and tears.

I was confused and did not know what to do. This was hardly what I expected. Momma was never this emotional. And, though I still wasn't certain what to feel, the Antoinette Brooks I knew, from years before, was not a perfect parent, but she wasn't a liar.

"Tina," she said, after pulling herself together. "You have to understand that, leaving you alone in the apartment, even for a few days, wasn't easy for me. I didn't go with Horace just for a few days of fun and damn what happened to you. I'd never just desert you. Horace kept hinting that he wanted to propose. I thought if we had a few days alone, I could convince him how special the three of us would be together. I knew he wasn't that thrilled with kids. I had every intention of making him understand that, no matter what, we were a package deal. If he didn't like it, then there was no chance of any life for us together."

"Momma, you don't expect me to believe that do you?"

"Please, Tina, let me finish. Then I'll be out of your life."

I rolled my eyes again and sat back in my chair. I realized that I had been leaning forward more aggressively than I probably should.

"Once I got to New York, Horace changed," Momma continued. "He said all the right things, but he was different. He took me, supposedly, to pick up friends of his and we were to leave from their place to go to dinner.

"As we approached the building, all his charm disappeared. Horace rang the bell. Instead of his old college buddy, a tall, heavyset, fifty-something, white woman, with a hard face, opened the door. I describe her, because the image sticks in my head. She was definitely not what I expected.

"Horace said, to her, 'This is Antoinette.' And he basically handed me over to the woman, Janet, like I was nothing. Then he left."

"What do you mean, handed you over?"

"Well, that's what it amounted to. She had a couple of really big men waiting, at the door. They grabbed me and took me to a room upstairs. I was a prisoner and Janet was the keeper. She locked me up in that room. Strange men came in to repeatedly rape me. And Janet made sure that I understood that they could do worse to me and any loved ones I had."

"Why?" was all that I could squeak out.

"Why did they do it or why me?"

"Both, I guess."

"It doesn't matter which, because I really don't know the answer to either question. I guess money was a big part of the reason why they did it. And, I guess, since I was a nobody with no power or influence, they did it to me just because they could."

"But why you in particular?"

"They didn't know me from Adam, until Horace discovered me. When he walked into the Murphy Mart, he realized that I was the perfect match to a request made to the group that he worked for. They provided special-order sex partners, on the QT, for rich and powerful people. Sounds a lot like a made-for-TV drama, but it's true. Horace was a scout who fulfilled those special requests. If one of the men wanted a twelve year old Asian girl; or a twenty year old Hispanic girl with blue eyes; or someone with a special mole somewhere on her body, then Horace would find the match for him."

"That's crazy. Why come all the way to Richmond?"

"Horace actually was telling the truth about why he was in Richmond. Whatever his business was, when he dropped into the Murphy Mart and saw me, he knew right away that I was just what the doctor ordered. In this case, literally, a doctor had placed the order."

"So, why didn't he just kidnap you earlier? Why didn't he just throw you in the trunk of his car and drive off?"

"He had to be in Richmond for a while, for his business, whatever that was. Plus, with the amount of money and level of power involved, he had to take his time to be sure. He had to get to know me first to make sure that I would be suitable for the rich client. He also had to find out my weaknesses, ways to control me, and how many people would look for me and how hard."

"Momma, not to sound cynical or be insensitive to what you went through, but are you saying they held you captive, with no way out, for ten whole years?"

"Not ten years, baby. Just the worst part of the ten. You see this finger?" my mother said, raising the little finger of her right hand.

"Yes," I said, waiting for her to get to the point.

"Once, when I crossed the line, one too many times, they cut off the tip of my finger. They saved the finger, put it in a container, and within a few hours, they had it surgically repaired. They were just delivering a message, a warning that they could do anything they wanted to me. But they didn't want to permanently damage the merchandise."

"Oh, Momma, is this really true?" I couldn't believe such a horrific story. It sounded even worse because of the detached way she recalled the details.

"But that wasn't enough. I guess they needed to make sure I had no reason to keep trying. While I was recuperating, Janet came to me, wanting to *chat*, as if we were best friends. She said that she would find out what happened to 'that cute little daughter' of mine, the one that Horace had told her so much about. That alone was enough to keep me in line.

"A few days later, she told me that she'd had some acquaintances, in Richmond, check out the information she had promised to get for me. She showed me a document that she said had everything she needed to know about you and about your new life. She described the foster family that you were assigned to. She said she even had a report on how it took a while for you to adjust, but you seemed to be happy. She then told me that it would be sad if something I did made something bad happen to you and your new family. Then she stared at me, waiting for it to sink in, before she left. I believed her because whatever network they belonged to was truly powerful and big. You can't imagine."

"Who are these people? How could they get away with stuff like that?"

"They are some awfully bad people, baby. The ones involved, the clients, are rich and important. That's how they get away with it. There are men out there—at least, the only ones I know about are men—who are so rich and warped, they think they can get away with anything."

"The police or the FBI can't do anything about this? It's like slavery all over again."

"It was just that, though they considered themselves providing a service. Eventually the police did raid the place and arrested everybody associated with it, including me."

"You'd think something like that would have made the news, if it involved that many rich and powerful people."

"Oh, the rich and powerful influential people, the clients, weren't arrested, just people like me. And of course, they got Horace and Janet and their bosses. As a matter of fact, I was held for over eighteen months. I found out that normally someone like me, who was accused of prostitution, is only given a fine or held for at most three months. Even though we were victims and not willing participants, the powerful people involved wanted to send a message to all of us to keep our mouths shut or else."

"Momma, that's terrible. Did you try to explain, maybe to the police, or to the government—the FBI?"

"Nobody wanted to hear what any of us had to say. Even my lawyer—who was someone who showed up one day and said that he was assigned to help me—didn't care. Anyhow, they didn't need anything from me. Horace and his crew were smart enough to fess up or were too scared not to. I was told that they did not dare give up information on the big clients. They remained protected."

"If they confessed, then why were you in jail so long?"

"Like I said. I don't know any details about what they confessed to, but apparently it did not help us, the low ones on the totem pole. Still, for some reason, the powerful clients weren't so sure about us. They wanted a guarantee that people like me didn't say the wrong things or mention the wrong names. Eighteen months later, somebody magically realized that we had been held too long without any due process. We were let go with an apology. Officially, we had just gotten lost in the system through a legal mix up. The good news was that everything about my arrest was expunged. But you see, that was part of the message, too. Those powerful people could hold us or free us or do whatever they chose. My lawyer subtlety hinted as much."

"That means that your lawyer was working against you the whole time."

Momma nodded, in agreement. "Once I was out, I was terrified. I didn't know who to trust or what to do. I was pointed to a victims' advocacy group which took me in. They talked me down because I was really on the edge. They helped me get out of New York, to relocate to East Orange New Jersey, a place where I was not a threat to anyone. Richmond was out of the question. I was advised to just lay low for a couple of years, till the dust settled. And that's what I did.

Then, I saw on a New York news station that the doctor, the one I mentioned before, had died. Horace had not lived long after his arrest. My only hope was that he lasted long enough to get raped, beat, abused, and subjected to all the things that he and his friends dealt out to us. But, when the 'beloved doctor and model citizen' died, I was finally confident that I could safely come home. I did, hoping to somehow find you."

"Couldn't you have come to get me before you went into hiding or underground or whatever you call it?"

"I honestly believed that you had been adopted into a nice family. It seemed almost cruel to pull you away from that, into my mess."

"There was no way to let me know you were alive?"

"No," Momma answered, her eyes watering. "The last time, I thought it was safe to contact you, was the first time they threatened your life. Remember, I told you about the finger? I lost it because I had tried to use the phone to call you or to reach someone from the old apartment building, who could get word to you.

"I thought I was being awfully clever and had planned out perfectly how to use the client's phone, without anyone finding out. I just wanted to know how you were doing, and to maybe get help for you. I couldn't reach anyone. I'm still not sure how Janet found out, but she was livid. She gave me a phone and dared me to dial.

"Then, she ordered me to sit the phone down on the table. When I tried to do that, she had one of her thugs hold my hand down, while she personally cut off half of my pinky with, what looked like, an extra sharp pair of kitchen shears. You see the kind of people these were . . . I couldn't compromise you. Contacting you may have made me feel better, but it could have put you in jeopardy. I might have been being overly paranoid, since I was probably not worth tracking. But I couldn't take the chance. You were safer not knowing."

"Wow, Momma," I said. "Now, I feel kind of bad for my reaction in the restaurant. But not knowing any of that, when I saw you laughing and joking with the hostess, it was like a stab in the heart. I thought what an idiot I had been all those years, deluding myself that you wouldn't deliberately just walk away from me. And that hurt."

"I understand," she said, with a loud sigh. "What I did was stupid, and I've got to live with that. What makes it even worse was that I wasn't even in love with Horace. I just saw the prospect of a better life for us and blindly dove in. I never should have left you alone like that, even if I thought it was only for a little while. There's no way I can ever justify it or make it right. I couldn't blame you for what you felt when you saw me. There is nothing I can do or say to fix any of it. There is definitely no way I can ever ask you to forgive me because I can't forgive myself."

Though I could tell how sincere she was in everything she said and how bad she felt, there was not a thing that I could say to make her feel better about what she did. In all honesty, I'm not sure I even wanted to. Actually, I agreed, whole heartedly, that what she did was stupid and everything that followed, as a result, should never have happened. Still, given the price she had paid for her lapse in judgment, telling her any of that would serve no purpose and would have just been cruel.

"You don't have to ask me, Momma, of course I forgive you," I said making my tone as gentle as possible. "I am terribly sorry for all you went through. Of course, I wish things had worked out differently for us both. But it was what it was."

My words didn't seem to make her feel any better. From the pained expression on her face, I could tell that it wasn't enough. I suppose that it must've been comforting to believe that the daughter you abandoned was safe in a home with people who loved her. Now I had taken that away, and I was afraid of what the realization might do to her.

In the middle of our conversation, Momma excused herself and went into the bathroom. I remembered how, when I was little, she would lock herself in her room at times when she didn't want me to see how upset she was. In that respect, not much had changed. Momma stayed there long enough for me to become worried. Just as I thought seriously about forcing myself into the bathroom, she came out.

"Momma, are you all right?" I asked.

"I've been wondering, what kind of mother drives off and leaves a thirteen-year-old child alone, like I did. I should've known what a phony Horace was. I should've known that Janet and crew would lie, tell me anything, just to keep me under control. The sad thing is that the lie made me feel better. I needed to think that you were okay. But now . . ."

"Momma, I don't know what to say. You survived. I survived. Yes, for a long time, I was scared and desperate. But I had friends who helped me."

"Friends? What friends? People from the complex?"

"No, I deliberately didn't let any of them know that I was by myself. If I had gone to them, then what that awful woman, Janet, said would have been true, at least the turning me into Social Services part. I couldn't chance that, but I had other friends. I don't know if you remember Paulette, the girl from school. Well, she and her sister helped me get a job at ATC."

"ATC? You mean the drug store? But you were much too young to get a job there or anywhere else."

"I was young. Originally, I lied. But, the owner, Mr. Sam Roberts, is a really good man. Even though he saw right through me, he let me work there. Then from middle school through high school, he and some of his friends took care of me. They protected me. I guess they were a foster family of sorts. I had to work hard to support myself. But with their help, I managed. The hardest and scariest part was trying to keep under the radar so Social Services wouldn't come after me."

"Where did you live? You said that you got kicked out of the apartment."

"Momma, don't worry. My protectors saw that I always had a safe roof over my head."

"You shouldn't have had to depend on strangers, like that. You say you forgive me, but I'll never be able to forgive myself. Never."

"Is that why you stayed in the bathroom so long, blaming yourself?"

"I am to blame," Momma said. "Nothing can ever change that. Look at you. You're all grown up. Now an adult. An amazing beautiful woman. And I missed my baby becoming that adult . . . So much lost time . . ."

"You know what Momma? My friend Paulette once showed me how important it was not to dwell too much on things that happened in the past. We can both spend the rest of our lives feeling bad about what happened before, or we can move forward. The only way I was able to survive was to be strong in the present, look towards the future, and not let the past bring me down. I think that's what we both need to do now."

"This Paulette, you keep mentioning, you don't mean the chubby girl who was forever getting you in trouble, do you? Not that Paulette?" Momma asked incredulously.

"Yup," I laughed. "One and the same."

CHAPTER 31

IT WAS GETTING LATE. The day had taken its toll on us, and both Momma and I were tired. Neither of us was sure how to bring it to a close.

"I have to go," she said, rising with much more energy than I'm sure she felt. "I need to get my car out of the parking lot. Plus, I have a ways to go and I don't like driving at night."

"You know, you never told me where you live. If you left now, I wouldn't know where to look for you. Do you live near the Burger Rack, where I saw you today?"

"No, I live in Petersburg, in Aunt Dee's old house. Believe it or not, I was at the Burger Rack looking for you."

"What in the world made you think I'd be at the Burger Rack, of all places?" I asked.

"The only way I had of finding you or running into you was to be at your favorite places, at least the ones I remembered from when you were little. I narrowed it down to the ones that might still appeal to a young adult. The Burger Rack and the malls seemed to be the best choices. Even though it was a long shot, I did my shopping in Richmond malls and ate at the nearest Burger Rack, whenever possible. That's why the hostess, Marsha, knew me. I was well aware that it was a silly idea. But it was all I had. And, guess what, it did work, eventually."

"You know I could've left Richmond and moved to Ohio. Or I could've become a vegetarian. Or, I could've gotten allergic to Burger Rack burgers. Why didn't you just look me up in the phone book?"

"I didn't know what your new name was. Remember? Besides, I had no right to track you down. If we happened to meet, then that's something totally different."

"Momma, that's very touching, and I'm glad you never gave up. Still, it is sort of wacky. You know that don't you?"

"Yeah, I know," she laughed. "But, like I said, it worked . . . eventually."

"What was the plan once you saw me? I figure you didn't count on me seeing you first, like I did today, did you?"

"I hadn't thought it through that far. After so much time had passed, I didn't really think it would happen. I had no idea that, after all those years, you'd recognize me."

"Really, Momma, even if it was a sweet idea, it was about as farfetched as you could get. You know that, right?" I smiled, moved to know that she'd been actually looking for me.

"Well, I don't exactly have a reputation for always thinking things through or choosing correctly between door number one or door number two," she said, referring to the game shows we often watched together, where prizes were hidden behind several doors. If you guessed right, you could win a big prize. Or choose wrong, and you could lose everything.

I thought it best to move on. To change the subject, I asked, "By the way, how come you're living in Auntie Dee's house?"

"You know that Aunt Dee never married and never had any kids, right?"

"I didn't know, but I did assume it."

"When she died, she willed everything she owned equally to my mother and me. There wasn't much to speak of, since a lot was used up to support her final years in the nursing home."

"How did you find that out?"

"When I decided to move back here, I was basically alone. I took a chance on visiting my mother. I didn't know how she would receive me. I didn't count on her wanting to see me, but I had to see her. I needed some connection . . . you know?"

"Wow, Momma. What happened?"

"Wasn't as bad as I thought it would be. Once she realized that I wasn't there to accuse her or her husband of anything or to get back at them, she warmed up enough to talk with me and tell me how well Reverend Samuels was doing. He has his own church, and it is very popular and very prosperous. She finally got around to filling me in on Aunt Dee and the will. She and the good Reverend Samuels had been taking care of the property and paying the taxes by renting it out. After the way they had treated me, all those years ago, I think they may have felt bad about their un-Christian behavior. They signed the house over to me and gave me what little was left in the account."

"That's great, Momma. Isn't it?"

"Well, it is and it isn't. The house is not in the greatest condition. I'm using what little money I have to fix it up. The area around the house has become pretty much gentrified. So, with the proper repairs, it will be worth a lot more now than Aunt Dee could ever imagine. But I'll never sell it, even though that's what I do now for a living. I love that house and the memories I have of my dear aunt."

"Did I hear you right, you're selling houses, for a living? When I saw you, earlier today, my first impression was that you looked like a lawyer. Don't ask me why. "

"Lawyer? If I knew the law, then life would've been a lot easier for me. Don't you think? Anyhow, when would I have had a chance to go to law school?" Momma snickered.

"Well, you never know. You could have been like those people on TV. You know the ones who are unjustly accused and study the law because it's their only way to get justice, while they are inside. And then, when they are released and are on the outside, they get a full-fledged degree to work for the right side of the law."

Momma let lose with her first truly spontaneous laugh. In the middle of it, she said, "Baby, I always told you that you watched too much TV. Nah, I'm not a lawyer, working to right the wrongs of society. I sell real estate. I'm pretty good at it too. I have my license and everything."

Then she smiled at me and we both burst out laughing together. It was loud and wholehearted, releasing the pent-up tension we had both been feeling. We were laughing so hard, that we almost missed the sound of Momma's phone vibrating.

She picked it up, "Hello. Everything is okay. Ten minutes would be fine."

Then she hung up and we said, "Kennard," at the same time. We both, laughed again.

"You like him, don't you?" Momma asked, with a knowing smile taking up half of her face.

"We just met, and it wasn't exactly a happy occasion. It was his sister's funeral. So, I don't really know him, and he doesn't know me."

"That's not what I said," Momma chuckled. "I just asked if you like the man. I didn't say anything about how long you've known him."

"Honestly, Momma. I was curious about him before I met him. I liked a lot of what his sister had told me about him. I'll admit some of it was scary. But, in person, I can see he is a really caring person, especially about his sister. And that says a lot. Look at the way he's been so sweet to you, how he got us together. He didn't have to do that."

"No, he didn't," she said with a strange edge to her voice."

"You don't like him?" I asked.

"Oh, honey what's not to like . . ." she said rolling her eyes, and we both laughed, again. "Just be careful, okay?"

I looked at Momma. I could tell that she had reservations about Kennard. I just couldn't imagine why. Instead of drawing out the point, I opened the door to let Kennard in.

When he walked in, the world just brightened up for me. I had no idea what it was about him, but Momma was right, I did like him. A lot!

Kennard sat on the couch next to Momma. He immediately took over the conversation. He kept it light, talking about the difference between the weather in Richmond and the weather in Chicago, and the difference between the drivers in Richmond and the drivers in Chicago. Not once did he ask anything about the deep conversation, the one he knew had taken place between my mother and me. That only made him more appealing.

Then he looked at Momma and said, "Ms. Brooks, you look like you could do with some rest. If you like, I can drive you to your car, now."

"That'd be nice, Kennard, I'd appreciate it."

"I'll ride with you," I said, before I had a chance to think about it. Maybe subconsciously I was afraid if I let her go, I wouldn't see her again.

"What, you don't trust me with your mother?"

"It's not that," I said flustered.

"I'm just kidding, Tina. I'd like very much for you to ride with us. Besides, I have a feeling that once I leave here, I won't be allowed back in here again," he teased.

Both he and Momma smiled. I turned my head, hoping they wouldn't notice me blushing.

* * *

I don't remember anything after dropping Momma off at her car. I have a vague memory of getting back into Kennard's car and adjusting the seat. The next thing I knew, we were parked in front of my apartment building and Kennard was offering to walk me to my door. I merely bobbed my head a few times, too embarrassed to speak. I don't think I'd ever just passed out like that before.

When we got to my door, Kennard stopped me from apologizing for, what must have been, the twentieth time.

"You've had a really rough few weeks." he said. "I have to admire that you have the strength to standup at all. Too bad we didn't have more time to talk and get to know each other better. Tomorrow, I've got to spend some time with my parents. Then I have to return to Chicago."

I felt my heart sink. I didn't want him to leave. Not that soon. The thought made it harder to fit the key in the lock.

I turned to look up at him, and said, "I'm so sorry that today was so crazy. We didn't finish our talk. Call me when you get a chance. I'll tell you anything I can about your sister."

Kennard gently touched my shoulder. He gazed down at me, with his sad brown eyes, and said. "The phone is too impersonal. I don't want to discuss my sister's situation over the phone. I'll contact you when I'm back in town, if that's okay."

"Sure," I said, turning my head towards the door. Forcing myself to avoid those intense eyes, I somehow managed to unlock my apartment door, with hands that were decidedly unsteady. I was surprised when I commanded enough control of them to manipulate the key to work.

He bent down and kissed me on my cheek. As he walked away, I stood there, not daring to watch him leave, afraid I'd call him back. It didn't help that he was being so kind and thoughtful.

Besides being dropped dead gorgeous and an overall good guy, I had no idea why Mr. Kennard Jackson was having such a profound effect on me. Even when Momma was warning me to be careful, I suspect that she already was too late with the advice. Kennard had barely left, and it was shameful how thrilled I was that he wanted to see me again, even if it was only to discuss his murdered sister. Somewhere, in the back of my head, was the disgraceful notion that maybe, just maybe, when he returned, we'd discuss what I believed was the beginning of a budding relationship between us.

CHAPTER 32

MRS. JACKSON CALLED. Her son, Kennard, was coming home for a few days and I was invited to attend a family dinner. "Nothing fancy," she said through the answering machine, "but we'd love it if you could come."

While I liked the Jacksons—all of the Jacksons—it was curious that they would include me, a relative stranger, in a private family gathering. I could only come up with two reasons. They wanted an opportunity, with all of them together, to get the last little bits of information I could share about their daughter. Or, and I knew I was stretching on this one, Kennard specifically asked for my presence because he was so enchanted with me.

Dream on Tina.

It had been two months since I'd seen Kennard, and I wondered if he would still have the same effect on me.

You're a big girl, Tina, I reminded myself. *You're grownup enough to not make an absolute fool of yourself in front of his parents.*

Though I wasn't totally convinced, I returned Mrs. Jackson's call to accept the invitation.

When I arrived at the Jacksons' townhouse, I'd barely touched the doorbell, when the door was opened by a young woman that I could only describe as stunning. She was not one of the Jacksons, at least not one I had met. However, the way she blocked the door implied that she belonged.

"Yes?" was all she said. But her eyes betrayed her. I could tell that she already knew that I wasn't a door-to-door salesperson or a Jehovah's Witness. From the promptness in which she pulled open the door, it appeared that she had been waiting near it. And, crazy as it seemed, I sensed that she was waiting specifically for me. Why she would do that, I hadn't a clue.

"Hi," I said, swallowing my thoughts. "I'm Tina. The Jacksons are expecting me."

"Hello, Tina. I'm Kennard's girlfriend."

Wow, I thought. *So, this is Kennard's type.* No wonder he hadn't looked at me twice. This woman with no name was gorgeous. On any given day, she was *that woman*, the one who would catch the eyes of everyone in a room, old or young, male or female. She was slender and weighed, at most, 120 pounds, while she stood at least 5 feet 7 inches tall. Me, I was 5 feet 4 inches and weighed a good 130 pounds. Her auburn hair, which appeared to be her natural color—at least I couldn't see the roots—was cut in a short style that perfectly suited her face. Her light complexioned skin was smooth and flawless. Without one damn pimple! Hell, if I was a man, I'd prefer this woman over me.

I did find it interesting that she chose to introduce herself with a label instead of a name. That implied that she, for whatever reason, felt threatened by me. Why in the world that was, had me curious.

Intrigued, I asked, "His girlfriend?"

"Yes, his girlfriend. I guess, with everything else that was going on I'm not surprised he didn't mention me. Kennard has told me a lot about you."

"He has?"

"Yes, I couldn't wait to meet you."

"Why?" I asked, genuinely curious why I would be the topic of conversation between *Miss No-Name* and her sexy boyfriend.

"Well," she said, "you were Kenny's sister's friend. And from what I hear, Kenny now considers you a friend of sorts, as well. I try to keep up with all my man's friends."

"Is that right?"

"Yes, that's right. You might say that you are one of the reasons I decided he needed me here," she said.

"Me? Why in the world . . . ? What are you trying to say?"

"I'm not *trying* to say anything. I just know that Kenny cared a lot for his sister, and he wants to get things straight about what happened to her. I also know how sometimes *certain people* might try and take advantage of that type of grief. Nothing against you, personally, but he is my fiancé."

Fiancé? It was like a gut punch. Something I did not want Miss No-Name to sense. More than likely, she was dealing those blows for effect and I didn't want her to know it was working. Even if I had felt foolish and a bit guilty about my attraction to Kennard, I was getting seriously annoyed at the bitch with no name.

Besides, even if she was Kennard's girlfriend/fiancée, why was she blocking me from entering the Jackson's home? No matter what her issues with me were, or her reasons for accosting me at the front door, it was time to remind her that I was an invited guest of the owners of the place.

"Umm, excuse me Kennard's fiancée . . . Sorry I didn't get your name."

"Oh, that's right, I didn't tell you my name. I'm Teresa. And my friends call me Tee. You can call me Teresa."

Boy is she tiresome.

I tried again, attempting to look around her for someone sane. "Excuse me, Tuh-ree-suh," I said, slowly pronouncing each syllable. "Could you let the Jacksons know that I'm here, please?"

She grudgingly opened the door enough for me to slide pass her. When I did, Miss Tee put her hands on her skinny hips and gave me her imitation of a tough girl look, designed to put me in my place. It was too much. The situation had gone from bizarre to ludicrous and I couldn't help laughing.

"Tina?" a voice above us exclaimed. It was Mrs. Jackson, coming down the stairway. She walked around Teresa to give me an enthusiastic hug. I stopped laughing and hugged her back.

"What's so funny?" she asked looking from me to Teresa.

Teresa, whose efforts at intimidation seemed to have backfired, was speechless. Her complexion had gone from high yellow to crimson.

"Nothing, Mrs. Jackson," I said. "Teresa and I were just getting to know each other. It's good to see you."

"Good to see you too, sweetheart. I didn't even hear the doorbell," she said looking puzzled in Teresa's direction.

"Oh," Teresa said, "I was right here, when it rang. I knew you were expecting Tina, so I answered the door."

"Thanks, but you needn't have done that. I was listening for the door and Kenny and Phil are right there in the family room."

"No problem, Cindy," she said. I couldn't help but smile, noting that Teresa was still at it. She was making sure I noticed that she was on a first name basis with Mrs. Jackson.

Why in the world is she trying so hard? I asked myself, as Mrs. Jackson led us into the family room, where Kennard and Mr. Jackson were waiting.

* * *

"Y'all have a seat," Mrs. Jackson said, as we entered the small dining area. Denise had often joked about what a bad cook her mother was. That's why I was surprised to see the banquet she had laid out.

I was even more surprised when Kennard and his father burst out laughing, after I complemented Mrs. Jackson on the feast.

"What's so funny?" I asked.

"You're thanking the wrong person," Mr. Jackson said. "I'll call Bev at the Soul Shack and give her your complements."

With her hands on her ample hips, Mrs. Jackson said, "You two just shut-up. At least, one person at this table has some decent manners."

That only made them laugh harder, which began a succession of reminisces between Mr. Jackson and Kennard, worthy of *The Comedy Club*. Most of the stories featured antics by Kennard or Denise or both. Apparently, Doctor Robert, the brother from Canada, was the good one and not a party to the exploits.

It was a great dinner, the type of family event I had never experienced. I was grateful to be included. Even Teresa laughed at the father and son banter.

After dinner, I offered to help Mrs. Jackson with the cleanup, but she shook her head. "There is one thing I *am* good at," she said handing a sponge to Mr. Jackson and a broom to Kennard. "Delegating!" she laughed.

Then, she gently pushed me towards the family room, as Teresa excused herself, saying she had something she needed to take care of.

That left the two of us sitting opposite each other, and for the first time I was uncomfortable in the presence of Mrs. Jackson.

She thoughtfully filled the gap. "Tina," she said, "I'm glad you're here. I see why Denise loved you so much."

Instead of making me feel better, that made me feel more awkward.

"Mrs. Jackson," I said, "I don't want you to have the wrong impression. I liked Denise a lot, but . . ."

"But you only knew each other a very short time, right?" she interrupted.

"Right," I said, relieved.

"We all know that. When she was young, the relationship Neesy had with her brothers was so special, she didn't really feel the need for a group of girlfriends. She was friendly, and people liked her, but Neesy didn't have patience with a lot of things the other girls were into. On the other hand, I think when you two met, she badly needed someone to trust. We're just glad she chose you."

As I was considering how to respond, I was spared another awkward moment when Kennard and Mr. Jackson entered the room.

Some of the joviality was gone, as they both sat down. Kennard looked around obviously searching for Teresa.

"Tee said that she had something to take care of and would come back," Mrs. Jackson said.

"Where'd she go?" Kennard asked.

"She didn't say," Mrs. Jackson answered.

"How was she going to get there?" he asked.

"I guess, your car," Mrs. Jackson responded.

"Oh, okay," Kennard said, in a tone I couldn't interpret. Then he turned to me. "Tina, Mom and Dad filled me in on what all you told them about this guy Denise was seeing, this Reggie person."

"The police still can't match an officer to the person you described," Mr. Jackson added.

"They probably don't really want to," Kennard said, the frustration evident in his tone. "It's up to us to do what we can for Neesy."

Then he turned to me expectantly.

"All I know about Reggie is that he works as a police officer," I said, feeling the spotlight on me. "I don't even know if he's RPD. He might work outside of Richmond, someplace like Henrico County or Chesterfield County, for all I know. Since Denise didn't specify, I assume he works for

Richmond police. I also assume that he's not a regular street cop, because he seems to have a lot more freedom than most uniformed officers do. The only physical description I have is that he is a tall, brown skinned man, with a strong southern drawl. He has a scar on the side of his face and possibly walks with a limp, both injuries happened when he was attacked by people who took exception to being arrested." I said, and sighed, recalling the effect Reggie's side of the stories had on Denise.

"Instead of being run-of-the-mill day-in-the-life of a cop stories, the details of how Reggie responded to those incidents were proof to Denise of how dangerous Reggie was," I said, looking around the room. "He made sure she knew that the man with the knife who'd cut him was the same person mentioned on the news, the one who was found dead in or near the James River. During the week he was hurting Denise, he became really angry at the woman who caused him to hurt his foot. She had come at him with the bat and made him trip and a table fell on his foot. According to Reggie, it was bad enough that she attacked him, while he was doing his job, she also made him miss out on something important he was planning, and then she had the nerve to complain about her treatment by the cops. Reggie told Denise that whatever happened to that woman was her own fault. He even joked about her possibly coming up missing. Denise didn't know if Reggie was messing with her or if he really had hurt and possibly killed those people to get back at them."

I paused to gauge their reactions.

Kennard said nothing. I couldn't tell anything from his expression. Mr. and Mrs. Jackson seemed less shocked than I would've thought.

"When I dropped her off," I continued, "Denise wouldn't go inside until she convinced me how vindictive and dangerous Reggie could be to her loved ones, if crossed. Considering what he did to her, she was probably right."

The room was silent. What I couldn't bring myself to do was fill them in on the details of all the awful things he did to Denise that final week.

"Detective Robinson seems to be good at her job and she seems to really want to catch this monster," Mrs. Jackson said, almost in a whisper.

"No matter how sincere she is, those above her wouldn't want the world to know that their officers are killing people," Mr. Jackson said angrily.

"He'll get his," Kennard said in a way that sent chills down my spine.

Mrs. Jackson looked thoughtfully at him. As sweet as she was, I got the impression that she would support whatever Kennard had in mind, if he caught Reggie. Sitting there in the room with those angry grieving people, I would not want to be the person on the wrong side of either of them. Denise had implied that Kennard could be dangerous. It appeared that he wasn't the only one in the family that could be said about. I would not want to be Reggie.

* * *

When the doorbell rang, we stopped talking while Mr. Jackson answered the door. He returned with Teresa, who was all grins and waving her hand around so everyone could see the humongous diamond she was wearing.

Mrs. Jackson, the first to react, said, "Oh, my."

Teresa was beaming. "I was supposed to keep it quiet until everything was settled about Denise. But I couldn't wait. What do you think?" she said walking towards her mother-in-law-to-be, so she could get a better look.

"It's beautiful," Mrs. Jackson said. "Congratulations."

"Congratulations," I said.

"What the hell, Tee?" Kennard said, unaccountably angry at his fiancée.

"Oh, Kenny," she swooned. "I know I was supposed to keep it to myself, but I just couldn't. I want everybody to know how happy I am."

Kennard fixed his eyes on his parents. Then, he went over to Teresa, took an obvious deep breath, and said, "What's going on Tee? Is this why you left? How did you get back and forth?"

"Your car, Kenny," she said with some of her enthusiasm waning.

Kennard seemed to be taking deep controlling breaths. "Umm," he said, looking from one parent to the other, "you guys mind if we take a short break? I'm giving Teresa a ride back to her hotel. What we have to talk about, doesn't really concern her. I'll be right back."

Then he turned to me, "Tina, I don't want to impose, but I hope you can stay a little while longer. Please?"

I nodded. It was all too much for me to process. There was the big diamond ring—the one that seemed to enrage Kennard—and, there was the fact that he and his fiancée were staying in separate dwellings.

As Kennard closed the door behind them, Mr. and Mrs. Jackson faced each other, but neither chose to comment on what had just occurred.

CHAPTER 33

NATURALLY, WHEN I RECEIVED the invitation from the Jacksons, I'd prepared myself for them wanting to talk about what happened to Denise. I had no problem with doing what I could to help bring her killer to justice. Under no circumstances did I anticipate the *Wacky Miss Tee Hour*. I doubt if Ann Landers, Emily Post, or even Oprah Winfrey could advise on how to respond when someone—who, by the way, is not sure if she's a girlfriend or a fiancée— misinterprets your relationship with the family of a deceased friend as some sort of threat.

After Kennard dragged Teresa away, his parents and I were left in a state of confusion and shock. I doubt if, after witnessing the strange interaction between them, anyone expected him to return as soon as he had promised. And when, as anticipated, Kennard called thirty minutes later saying that he would be a while and to give his apologies to me, we warmly separated with hugs and goodbyes.

When Paulette called to find out how the evening went, I described how in love I was with Mr. and Mrs. Jackson and how envious I was of the normal family life they'd engineered for their children. I described how comfortable they made me feel, and how they'd shared some of their special family moments. I even told her about the wacky Miss Tee and the production she made of showing everyone her humongous diamond engagement ring.

"Wow, girl, I can't believe it. One thing for sure, Tina, this kinda stuff only happens to you. That's why I like being around you. You always keep things interesting," were the insightful words of wisdom my friend offered after I finished sharing my story.

I laughed because she was right. The things that happen to me, don't happen to most people.

"But Kennard being engaged . . ." she added, sympathetically. "Damn. Now, that's a bummer."

"You know, Paulette, Kennard is cute and nice. And I'll admit that I was curious about what could be," I said. "And, even though I did like him . . . I do like him . . I am glad that he has somebody to help him through this thing about his sister. That's really good for him."

"Hmmph," was Paulette's response.

"Really," I said, "the thing with Momma, not knowing if she was dead or alive all those years, at least not knowing gave me hope. What I can't imagine is what it's like to know the awful thing that happened to Denise and not be able to do anything about it. If Mr. and Mrs. Jackson need something from me, I'll be there. If Kennard, engaged or married, needs help to get that creep, Reggie, what he deserves, I'll be there."

I was close to tears. I wasn't exactly sure why.

"Are you okay, Tina?"

"I guess so."

"Look, we haven't had a chance to get together since I got back in town. I'll be over tomorrow to pick you up. We can hang out at the mall like we used to and do some shopping. We need to get this off your mind."

"Nah. I don't feel like the mall or doing any shopping."

"Look, I've got a better idea. Why don't I pick you up later, and we can go to NightLife and have some drinks. Notice I said drinks. Plural. Lots and lots of drinks."

"You know what. I think I will . . . Oops, hold on. I have a buzz on my cell phone."

I looked at my caller-id and saw that it was Kennard. I didn't feel like talking to him, so I hit the ignore button. Suddenly, Paulette's suggestion for a night out on the town seemed right on point.

"Pick me up around nine," I said.

I hung up and sat motionless on the sofa. I hadn't lied. I *was* sad that there seemed no way to get justice for Denise. I also hated myself for not being able to forget Teresa flaunting her ring in my face. I hated the mood I was in. And, I hated that there was a tear rolling down my right cheek. I wiped it away, as I walked over to answer my ringing phone. A quick glance at the caller-id, told me it was my mother. I cheered up immediately.

"Hey, Momma. What's up?"

"I just called you before I settled in, to see how you were."

"I'm fine Momma. Paulette's in town for a few days. She's coming over and we're going to hang out for a while."

I could hear my mother yawn. "Okay, baby. Have fun. Good night and tell your friend, Paulette, hello for me. Love you."

"Love you too, Momma."

After all those years apart, my mother had taken to calling me every night. She was really trying hard to make up for her mistakes. And, after all those years, I was glad for the calls.

Chapter 34

NIGHTLIFE WAS a little hole in the wall at the far end of East Broad Street. You'd miss it, if you didn't know to look for the little red door. The food was marginal, there was never any place nearby to park, and, once you walked the multiple blocks from your car, the club was always packed. It was the rage-of-the-month place to go.

Paulette and I arrived a little after 9:00 PM. The music was blasting, and the line was already down to the end of the block. Foolish us, we had thought we were getting there early.

"Oh, my goodness. There's no way we're getting in there tonight," I said, ready to turn around and go back home.

"Oh, we're getting in," Paulette said. "I have a secret weapon."

She grabbed me by the hand and practically dragged me to the door—which, by the way, was guarded by a guy who would have made the biggest Carolina Panthers' lineman look dainty.

"Hey, Lucky," Paulette practically purred. She never ceased to amaze me. Now where in the world did she know this man from?

"Hey, Paulette, girl. Ain't seen you in a while. Where you been?"

"Been around. I'm in grad school, now. Just home for the weekend," Paulette said, as she went up to the large man. When she attempted to give him a hug, her arms barely made it around his body.

"Looks pretty crowded," she said, as she stepped back, "can we get in?"

"Sure, go on in," the big guy said, nodding towards the door.

Damn, I didn't know Paulette had it like that.

As we cleared the door, I tried to ignore the complaints and curses from those still in line. I almost felt guilty.

We both giggled as we dashed inside. Paulette turned to flash her friend a grateful smile and he nodded in return.

As usual, it was dark, loud, and extremely crowded. With the miles and miles of heads and bodies, it didn't take long to figure out that the only place to sit was at the bar.

Once we got our drinks, I looked at my friend in a new light. "Paulette, girl, where do you know that bouncer from?"

"What?" Paulette had to yell because the music was so loud.

"Where do you know that bouncer from?" I repeated louder, as I leaned closer to her ear.

"I dated him for a while."

"What? How come I don't know this?"

"Honey chile," Paulette giggled, "I get around."

I wanted to ask more questions, like how and where they met. But with the difficulty with hearing and conversing, it was better left for another day. I kept my curiosity to myself.

To our right, at a nearby table, two women were going at each other. With the intensity of the argument, it was only a matter of time before it came to blows. Others were moving away, while Paulette signaled me to move closer. Just when Lucky showed up to escort the ladies out of the club, Paulette pounced on the table. I never saw her move so fast. She had her drink on the table before I could even pick mine up from the bar.

"Damn girl, you're fast."

"I thought you already knew that."

We both laughed again.

"Thank you, Paulette, for getting me out of the house. I think this is just what I needed."

"You're welcome, girl. Now tell me more about this very interesting fiancée of Kennard's."

"It depresses me just to think about her. She's gorgeous. I hate that she doesn't have a single flaw, except for being nutty as a fruitcake, of course."

At that, I sat back. Paulette, understanding that I needed to just chill, seemed all right with us both sitting quietly, listening to the DJ, sipping our drinks, and occasionally checking out the people around us.

Several times, we noticed guys considering whether to come over or not. The first to take the plunge was a tall thin guy and his friend. They both had that college frat boy swagger, and it was obvious that they were after a lot more than a dance. So, as they approached, Paulette and I looked at each other and smiled.

Frat boy one said, "Hey ladies. . ."

Before he could get it out, we both sang out, in unison, "No thanks."

They grinned, took it in good spirits, and looked around for more receptive females. After all, the room was full of them.

A few minutes later, another guy came over and went straight to Paulette. He held out his hand like they do in the movies. It was dark, but I could see that he was well above medium height, had a decent build, and a close-cropped haircut. Unlike the college kids from before, he didn't give off the air of a dog in heat. He had one of those sexy smiles, kinda sideways, like he thought everything was just a bit amusing. I could tell that Paulette thought he was cute.

After saying 'no' to the frat boys, I finally registered that my friend had been bouncing to the music since we sat down. Of course, she was. It was the weekend, and we were supposed to be out to have a good time.

"Oh, go ahead," I told her. "You've been wiggling in your seat all night."

My girl jumped up so fast, I thought she'd knock the table over. The record was one of those extended versions that seemed like it went on forever. Watching my girl having so much fun, I thought maybe I should give it a try. But somebody had to watch the table and the purses. There's something to be said for old lady fanny-packs.

Just as I wondered if I'd be stuck alone forever, Paulette came back to the table. The record still hadn't ended. I laughed, "Too long, huh?"

"No girl. I could have danced all night, just like the old-timey song says. The guy had to stop. I think he had something wrong with his leg."

"Bad leg? He didn't have a strong southern accent, did he?" I said joking.

"Yeah, as a matter of fact he did, even stronger than some of those folks down in Chapel Hill."

My jaw dropped, and Paulette noticed. "What's wrong? What did I say?"

"Paulette, did he tell you his name?" I asked calmly, still hoping it was all a strange coincidence.

"Yeah, I thought he said it was RJ, when he threatened to pull out his RPD badge and arrest me if I didn't allow him to get off the floor." Paulette started to laugh, until she saw the expression on my face.

"Oh my God!" I said so loud that people around me turned to look. "We have to get out of here."

"Why? What's wrong?" Paulette began to look around the club. I was making a scene and frightening my friend. As a matter of fact, I was frightening myself.

"Look, Paulette, I think the man you were dancing with sounds a lot like the guy we've been looking for, the one who killed Denise."

"What? What makes you think that?"

"The man who hurt her had a strong southern accent and was a cop. And just maybe, the guy from the dance floor didn't say his name was RJ, but Reggie. Look around and see if you see him."

Paulette frantically looked around the club. I was getting to her and I could see the panic on her face. "I don't see him. I think he's gone."

Getting more and more nervous, she started rattling off questions. "Do you think it's possible he knows who we are? How would he? He's never seen you, right?"

"Right." I too tried looking around the club, but I really had no idea who I was looking for. I had only gotten a glance at him when he came to the table to ask Paulette to dance. "Paulette, keep looking around to see if you see him. I'm going to call Kennard."

"Kennard? Why are you calling Kennard?"

"He needs to know that the man who killed his sister might be in this club somewhere," I said, while I scrolled to Kennard's cell phone number.

"Damn," I said. "I'll have to go outside, there is no reception in here."

"What? You're not leaving me in here alone."

Paulette grabbed both our bags and we went outside.

I tried dialing Kennard's number again. This time it went through and on the sixth ring it was answered.

"Hello." It was Teresa.

"Hello, Teresa? This is Tina. Can I speak with Kennard please?"

"Tina, do you know what time it is?"

"Yes, but . . ." I didn't get to finish my statement.

"Talk to him tomorrow," she said, and hung up.

"Hello . . . Hello? I can't believe she hung up in my face," I said, looking at my phone in disbelief.

"Call him back, Tina," Paulette urged.

I tried the number again, but this time no one picked up. Teresa obviously was determined not to let me talk with Kennard.

"That woman is in for a good ass kicking, when I see her," I told Paulette. She just nodded.

I still had one play that Teresa couldn't block. Despite it being so late, and hoping they'd forgive me, I dialed Kennard's parents' number.

"Hello?" Mrs. Jackson answered the phone on the third ring.

"Hello, Mrs. Jackson. Sorry to call so late. This is Tina."

"Tina? Is something wrong, honey?"

"No ma'am, I just need to talk with Kennard."

"He's not here, dear."

"Mrs. Jackson. I know this is asking a lot, but can you call Kennard and have him call me on my cell?"

"Are you sure everything is all right?"

"Yes ma'am, everything is fine. I promised Kennard that I would call him about something important, and I don't think Teresa likes me."

"Oh, now I understand." Mrs. Jackson started laughing. "I'll call him right now. You just listen for the phone."

Kennard called back five minutes later. Once I explained to him what was going on, he was at the club within minutes. He saw Paulette and me waiting for him outside, pulled up in front of us, jumped out the car, and ran over to us.

"Hey man you can't park there."

Lucky was storming towards Kennard, when Paulette grabbed him by the arm. "Hold up Lucky, he's with us."

"That's all good," Lucky said, "but brother still has to move his ride." Lucky turned and walked back towards the front door.

Paulette took Kennard's keys out of his hand. "I'll move the car. You talk with Tina."

"Okay, explain to me what's going on," he said.

I told Kennard again about the man who had danced with Paulette, and how much he resembled the man Denise had described to me.

"Do you know what he looks like, Tina?'

"Not exactly, but Paulette knows what he looks like. She danced and talked with him."

Paulette came running towards us. She approached Kennard and me huffing and puffing. "Girl, I had to park three long blocks away. I ran almost all the way back here."

"Paulette, you remember Kennard?"

"Yes, how you doing, Kennard?"

"I'm doing okay. Maybe you can point the guy out that Tina has been telling me about."

"I haven't seen him since we danced together. It's like he disappeared off the face of the earth."

"Well, let's just walk around and see if we can find him."

The line wasn't as long as before, plus Paulette and I had stamps on our hands, so we were all allowed to walk in.

Kennard immediately started asking people if they knew a man who had a limp and a strong southern accent, but nobody was in the mood to answer our seemingly dumb questions.

We were getting nowhere, then Kennard decided to ask the bartender if there was a regular that was a police officer, had a slight limp, and a strong southern accent.

"Hmm, I don't know about a regular," the bartender said. "But the only one I know that comes close to that description is one of the owners of this club. He has the accent and works for the Richmond Police Department."

"Where is this guy?" Kennard insisted.

"Hey brother," the bartender said. "You've got to calm down or I'll get one of the bouncers to throw you all out."

"Okay, I'm sorry, but it's important that we talk to your boss. Where can we find him?"

"I'm sorry, but Mr. Williams left about half an hour ago."

"So, what's Mr. Williams's first name?" Kennard was trying his best to be friendly with this man.

"His name is Ray John. Everybody calls him RJ."

While listening to him talk, the bartender's voice sounded strangely familiar. I leaned closer to get a better look at him. Then it came to me. I couldn't believe it.

"Tony? Is that you?"

"Yes, my name is Tony. Do I know you?" He asked puzzled. Then this big smile came across his face. "Tina?"

I started laughing. "Yep."

Tony came from behind the bar to give me a hug. "My God, Tina, I haven't seen you in years. Damn, you look good."

"You don't look so bad yourself."

And believe me he didn't. Tony had grown hair on his face and shaved his head bald. He had closed the big gap in his teeth. He really looked good. *I mean really good.* He held me so tight, I thought I was going to explode.

"Where have you been girl? I haven't seen you since I bailed out of that death trap of a motel that we worked in."

"I left not long after you did."

Kennard had this strange look on his face. He was looking from me to Tony. From Tony to me.

"Okay, now that you two have had your reunion, let's get back down to business, shall we?"

"Look dude I ain't seen this woman for a while, since she was a kid, and we got a lot to talk about. If you want to see my boss, then you need to come back next Wednesday. That's when he'll be back."

"Look Tony, we really need to talk with Mr. Williams. Is there any other way we can reach him?" I asked, still holding his hand and looking in his handsome face. Tony looked good before, when I was thirteen. He had only gotten better looking.

"No way, once that dude leaves this club, he leaves everything in Tammy's hands."

"Tammy? Who's Tammy? Maybe we can talk with her." I could hear the frustration in Kennard's voice.

"Tammy is RJ's sister. She takes care of all the finances and handles everything when RJ is on duty at his police job."

Tony was still holding my hand. Our not being able to keep our eyes off of each other seemed, for some reason, to really irritate Kennard.

"Hey man, don't you have to go back behind the bar and make some drinks or something?" Kennard asked, breaking our hands apart.

"Oh, I'm sorry man, I wasn't thinking. I didn't mean to disrespect you with your lady. It's just that I haven't seen her in a while. But, hey, you're a lucky man."

I couldn't do anything but laugh. "I'm not his lady. He's engaged. We're just friends."

"If anybody's interested, I don't have anybody," Paulette said.

"I'm sorry Paulette," I said. "This is Tony. He used to . . . I mean, we used to work together at the motel."

Tony shook Paulette's hand. "Hey Paulette. I remember Tina talking about you. Any friend of her's is certainly a friend of mine. And, I'm sure we'll be seeing a whole lot of each other," Tony said, as he grinned at me.

Kennard seemed to lose patience with our little reunion and interrupted Tony, saying, "Yeah, yeah, all that is fine and good. We just need to know where can we find Tammy."

Tony, who was totally oblivious to the urgency of Kennards request, had never stopped scanning to see if anyone wanted something from the bar. Instead of answering Kennard, he raised his hand and said, "Just a minute, I have to wait on a customer."

"Last I looked there were three of you back there."

"Brother," Tony said, "it's my job. I'll be back."

Paulette and I looked at each other. Neither of us could figure out why Kennard was being so rude to Tony.

A couple of minutes later, Tony came back. "You asked about Tammy. She's in her office. Tammy does all the hiring, firing, and pays all the bills inside and outside the club."

"Outside?" I asked.

"Yell, they live together in a house not far from here. RJ is hardly ever there. Good thing, 'cause they don't really get along that well."

"Really?" I asked, not actually surprised, since I knew what a jerk the guy—at least the one we knew as Reggie—was.

"Yeah, RJ charms the ladies, but he's not a good guy. He's not a good cop either. He has a rep in the city as a badass cop and everybody, including me, tries to stay out of his way."

Kennard finally convinced Tony that it was important that he get Tammy to come out of the office to talk with us.

When she came out, I hadn't known what to expect. Still, her appearance caught me by surprise. I guess I assumed a club owner would be flashier. Tammy was tall, about five-eight. She was fairly attractive and had close cropped hair. She wore a practical pant suit and sensible flat shoes.

 I guess she noticed me looking down at her shoes, because she laughed and said "I just hate high heels, don't you? I'm Tammy Williams."

She extended her hand to me. When we shook, she held my hand a little too long for my comfort.

"I'm Tina Brooks and these are my friends, Paulette and Kennard."

The woman still was holding my hand as she spoke to Paulette and Kennard. "Glad to meet you both. Do I know you, Ms. Tina? It seems like I've seen you somewhere before."

I jerked my hand from her, "No, I don't think I've ever met you before."

I looked to Paulette and Kennard for some help, certain that Tammy was making a pass at me.

"My mistake, she said. "So, what can I do for you good people? I hope it's important because I have a lot of work to do."

The music was still playing, and we were all straining to hear each other.

Kennard took the lead. "We need to talk with you about your brother."

"What about my brother?"

"Can we go into your office and talk?"

"No sir. That is not possible. Whatever you have to say to me, you can say it right here. And you better be quick about it, 'cause I'm getting a little impatient right about now. So, let's get on with it."

"Does your brother, RJ, ever go by Reggie?" I asked.

"Yes!" Tammy exclaimed. "How did you know that? When he was a baby and I was not much older, my parents told me his name was Ray John. But the way I pronounced it, it sounded more like Reggie. My family thought it was hilarious. Then, when he started school, there was another boy named Reggie, and people started calling him RJ. Nobody, but close family ever calls him Reggie anymore."

Kennard and I looked at each other, realizing at the same time why Detective Robinson couldn't find a Reggie on the police force.

Kennard decided to be direct. "Okay, to get straight to the point, we think your brother was responsible for my sister's death. He killed her."

Strangely, Tammy seemed to have no reaction to Kennard's accusation. "Is that why you wanted to talk with me . . . what was so important?"

"You don't care that your brother may have caused someone's death or committed murder?" I asked, appalled.

"Look, I don't know who you people are. Frankly, I don't care. I can't accept what you say about him, just because you say it. My brother works for the police department, and people don't like the police. He, like a lot of cops, gets falsely accused of things all the time. One thing I do know, he is not capable of murdering anyone. He's a mean SOB, but he's not a murderer. So, if you don't have anything else to say, I have work to do," Tammy said, turned and walked away. A second later, she turned back, winked at me, and mouthed, "Call me."

CHAPTER 35

OBVIOUSLY, THERE WAS NO REASON for us to hang around NightLife any longer. I waved goodbye to Tony as the three of us made our exit. While I understood that my friends felt our talk with Tammy had been somewhat of a bust, personally, I was thrilled with what we had learned. To me, Tammy's confirmation that Reggie was RJ—otherwise known as RPD officer Ray John Williams—was more than we could have hoped for. I, for one, was not surprised that Tammy did not go against her brother, based on the accusations of three total strangers—no matter how evil she knew he was.

"What now?" Paulette asked, as the three of us stopped outside the club several feet from the door.

"Well, now we have a big missing piece to the puzzle," I said. "It's obvious why Detective Robinson could not find Reggie in any of the police department databases. Now that we have Reggie's full name, we can give the information to the police."

"And tell them what?" Kennard snapped. "You think anyone is going to take us seriously. They'll have the same reaction Tammy did. We have no proof of a connection between Reggie—the abuser and killer—and Ray John Williams—the police officer, businessman, and solid citizen."

"Maybe you're right," I said, understanding Kennard's frustration, while trying not to allow his logic to deflate me. "Still, it is something. It is forward progress, no matter how little. We know a lot more than we did before tonight. That's something."

Kennard was about to respond when he stopped abruptly, his attention drawn in the direction of the club. He groaned, then he said under his breath, "I don't believe this."

Our backs were to the club, so Paulette and I turned to see Tony approaching our small group, with a silly grin on his face.

"Tina," he said, "I'm glad I caught you. I was hoping to get your number. We two have a lot of catching up to do."

"Umm, Tony," I said. "We're in the middle of something really serious. I can come back some other time, and we can talk then and catch up."

"What's going on? If it has to do with Tammy, RJ, and the club, maybe I can help."

"Thanks, Tony, for the offer. It's kind of complicated, and we're all a bit frustrated right now," I said. "But, umm, thanks for how you helped us inside, getting Tammy to talk with us. We really appreciate it."

Tony took my hand. "I don't know what's going on. I can see that all of you look really upset. I hear you when you say it's serious, but maybe it can't be solved tonight. Maybe you all need to go and think about it. If you and your friend need a ride, Tina, I can sign out now and take you home."

"Look man, nobody needs a ride." Kennard said stiffly. Then he turned to me, "He's right about one thing. We can't stand around here all night. Let's go, Tina."

Paulette raised her eyebrows as we looked at each other, but neither of us moved. Kennard obviously assumed we'd follow him. No matter how cute he was, his tone did not inspire us to step in behind him.

When he noticed that he was walking alone, Kennard called in the general direction of Paulette and me, "Are you coming or not?"

Understanding that the man was going through a lot, I said, patiently but firmly, "Paulette and I rode together, remember? You go on. We can talk sometime tomorrow."

Kennard took another look at us, then at Tony. "Fine then," he said and continued walking.

"See you later, Kennard," Paulette said to his back. I could hear the amusement in her voice. "Oh," she said, "Kennard, your car . . ." He was walking away so fast, that she had to shout the instructions on where she had parked it.

Tony, seemingly unmoved by our drama, stayed with us long enough to get my number and a final hug. "Not that I don't trust you," he said, smiling. "But I'm going to ring this number later. Just to make sure you got home safely, of course."

"Of course," Paulette chuckled.

She watched him as he disappeared back into the club. For a moment, I thought my friend would chase after the handsome Tony. When she turned back to me, she had a thoughtful expression on her face. Then, unexpectedly she grabbed both of my arms and forced me to face her. She said, "I thought you said that Tony, the one from the motel, was gay."

"I thought he was."

That had my friend roaring. The remaining stragglers outside the club looked our way. But their stares had no effect on her. Paulette roared all the way to the car, as if that was the funniest thing she had ever heard.

CHAPTER 36

WE HAD ONLY DRIVEN A SHORT DISTANCE from NightLife, when I noticed that my friend, who was not generally known for her reticence, was dying to say something.

"What's up, Paulette? If you keep holding back, whatever it is that's on your mind will make you explode."

"I'm not sure this is the appropriate time."

"Since when did that stop you?"

"All right," she said, with obvious relief, "I can't believe girlfriend got two fine brothers fighting over her."

"What two? You can't possibly mean Tony and Kennard."

"Girl, where have you been for the last couple of hours?"

"What in the world are you talking about, Paulette?"

"Kenny boy almost had a fit every time Tony even came close to touching you. Didn't you see that?"

"Kenny boy, as you called him, is engaged, Paulette. And, as we speak, he's on his way back to the arms of the wacky Miss Tee."

"Well, he didn't act engaged when he jerked your hands from Tony's. He was acting like he was engaged to *you*, and Tony was trespassing on *his* very private territory."

"Honestly," I said, half-smiling, "even I saw it. I don't know what that was about. Maybe he was being protective, since I was his sister's friend."

"Paa-lease, girlfriend. I know you got this virgin thing going, but that man is only trying to keep the competition out of his way."

"What's being a virgin have to do with anything?"

"I don't know. I can't think of any other reason why you can't see what's right in front of your face," she said.

Paulette was right. I was not very experienced when it came to dealing with men. Momma had convinced me early on about the importance of choosing wisely the men I dealt with. The prime examples of bad choices being my grandfather and my father. Even before I learned the details of how the process worked, my biggest fear was that if I let any male get too close, I'd end up left alone, desperate, and pregnant. Having unwanted or unplanned babies was not for me. Needless to say, waiting for the right time and the right person limited my actual male-female interactions and the knowledge generally acquired through them. In other words, I was pretty dumb when it came to men.

"All those years ago," I said, "Tony was always a such gentleman. I never caught him ogling the women on the staff or making crude remarks, like the jerks in my neighborhood. I guess I used that as my proof of him being gay. Doesn't say much for me or my expectations, huh?"

"You poor blind baby. I'd be willing to bet that those ladies on the motel staff, even the old ones, were busy ogling Tony. Girlfriend, just watching him with you tonight, I saw nothing about him that said 'gay'," Paulette said.

"Me either," I laughed.

"Got that right, sister girl," Paulette hooted. "Wait a minute. I almost forgot about your other admirer."

"Who?"

"The sister, Tammy."

"Not my type, I didn't like her shoes," I said.

Paulette burst out laughing. She was still laughing as I got out of the car. She made one final comment that I didn't quite hear.

"What was that?" I said, leaning down to get closer to the window.

"I just said what I've been saying for years. For sure, it's never ever dull being your friend," she laughed hysterically, as she pulled away.

Chapter 37

"SOUNDS LIKE YOU all had quite a day and night," Momma said, after I gave her a brief rundown of a day which began with a simple companionable dinner and ended with a trip into the Twilight Zone.

"You're right about that, Momma," I said. "Now, I think I'm paying for it. This morning I woke up with a terrible headache that I can't seem to kick.

"How much did you girls have to drink, before all the excitement went down?" she asked, with amusement in her voice.

"Not that much, actually," I answered. "I wish all I had to worry about was a hangover, but I didn't really drink that much. For the most part, I'm not that into drinking alcohol. And last night, things started happening so fast that I didn't get a chance to overindulge. The headache is probably a combination of too little sleep, with too much drama, in too short a time."

"Sorry about that, baby. By the way, where is your girl Paulette, today?"

"I think she should be on the road or back in North Carolina, by now. She was only here for a break before she started studying for the LSAT. She's gotten it into her head that now she wants to go to law school."

"Good for her."

"Yeah, never could keep up with Paulette. I do feel kind of bad about last night, though. All she wanted was to relax, let off some steam, and not think about anything serious. Instead, because she wanted to make me feel better, she ended up dancing with the club owner, who's also a bad cop, and a killer." I said, feeling increasingly guilty. "She claims that exciting things like that only happen to her because she's friends with me."

"What are friends for?" Momma chuckled.

"Oh yeah, speaking of friends . . ." I said, and filled her in on Kennard's bizarre reaction to my reunion with my old friend, Tony.

"Good Lord," Momma said, then immediately added, "I gave up on soap operas a long time ago, because the plots always seemed so unrealistic. Man, was I wrong."

We both laughed again. Then she added, earnestly, "About the man thing, Kennard and Tony, that is. I realize that I'm not the best source for advice on that, but I can tell you what not to do."

"What?"

"Don't jump into anything blind. I haven't met Tony. I trust your instincts about him, as long as you keep in mind that you haven't seen him in a bunch of years. I have met Kennard. He seems to be a good guy, I like him." There was that hesitation again, in her voice.

"But?" I asked.

"But, don't get all wrapped up in a guy who is supposed to be committed to somebody else. Think about it. You have to be very careful when a guy gives up another woman for you. Make sure you ask yourself, 'Is it because that relationship was bad and wasn't working? Or, is it just who he is? Is he *that guy*?' You know, the guy who can't help himself and that's just what he does. Will he do the same thing to you? I've seen that too many times. Just be careful, okay?"

"Yeah. You're right. I do know all that."

"But? Now, I'm sensing a *but*."

"No, you're right, Momma. You're right."

"So, what are you going to do with your newfound information about Officer Ray John Williams?"

"I'm not sure. What do you think? Should I talk with the Jacksons or Detective Robinson about it?"

"That's really not your place," Momma said without hesitation. "Kennard has all the same information. It is his family and it's up to him to decide what to tell them. In the meantime, I think it's a little premature to talk to the police about it."

"Yeah, I get it. Everything we have is based on assumptions and no real proof. We don't have anything concrete that says that Denise's Reggie and Ray John Williams are the same person. If the picture of Denise and Reggie had not mysteriously disappeared, that would have been proof of a connection between RJ and Denise, but not proof that RJ and Reggie are one and the same."

"Exactly."

"You know, Momma, what I can't wrap my brain around is that Denise dated that guy for so long and nobody, I mean nobody, saw them together. I don't buy that. Somebody in her neighborhood had to have seen them walk to the car, or step out on the porch, or take the trash out. At the least, they saw Reggie go into the house. And, if he is as well-known as Tony says, then anyone who saw him knew exactly who he was. But according to Detective Robinson, no one is willing to admit it."

"Do you blame them? Why risk identifying somebody like Reggie? If they know he's dangerous, nobody will chance getting on his wrong side."

"I guess I can see that. And, I guess I can also see how talking to the police now would work against us, especially considering all Reggie has done so far to cover his tracks. The man scrubbed down an entire house and removed all evidence of himself in a matter of hours. I guess passing on the little we have could warn him and make him do even more to protect himself. Whatever that takes."

"That's right, baby. I don't want that animal coming after you."

"I'll talk to Kennard. If he hasn't thought about all this, he should."

"You're right. Plus, it gives you an excuse to call him."

"Don't worry, Momma. I'm not throwing myself at his feet. I'm cool."

"Okay then. Talk with you later."

"Bye, Momma. And thanks."

CHAPTER 38

MY MOTHER WAS RIGHT about one thing. It was not my place to discuss my theories with the Jacksons or the police. Since Kennard knew as much as I did about Reggie, he should be the one to decide what to do with the information and what actions his family should take.

She was also right about me looking for an excuse to call Kennard. For reasons known only to him, he had left in an obvious huff. Though I had no clue what motivated his behavior, we weren't close enough for me to call to ask him why he acted like such a jerk. Nor could I let whatever was going through his head fester. Having something specific to discuss made it easier to dial his number.

"Hello?" Thankfully, this time it was Kennard's voice on the other end.

"Kennard, it's me, Tina," I said.

"Okay. What's up?" I couldn't help but register the change in tone from our previous conversations, and the marked lack of enthusiasm in his voice.

"I just wanted to talk with you about what we discovered last night," I said, hiding my disappointment at his matter-of-fact tone. "You know . . . what we learned about Reggie. I was wondering what you thought we should do with the information. Did you share it with your parents, by the way?"

"Not yet. It doesn't make sense to build their hopes up and not have enough for the police to do anything with it. But I contacted a few people I know in Chicago. With their help, I'm hoping to get this taken care of."

This time, his voice seemed ice cold and the way he said he'd contacted "people in Chicago" to "get this taken care of" sent a shiver clear through me. I immediately thought about Denise describing how Kennard had shady connections. At the time, I'd laughed at her gangster imitations, assuming that she was exaggerating for effect. Now, I wasn't so sure.

"Umm, Kennard, what people?" I asked, apprehensively.

Kennard didn't hesitate before answering, "Just some people I know. I'm meeting with them tonight."

"I thought you weren't leaving until tomorrow."

"Tina," he said, "this is the twenty-first century. There are bunches of ways to have meetings, as long as you have access to the internet or a phone that allows conference calls."

"Oh," I said embarrassed. "I didn't think about that. Can I be a part of the conversation? You know, conference in?"

"I don't think so," he said, matter-of-factly.

"Look, Kennard," I said, getting annoyed at his brusqueness. "I just thought I could be of support. Maybe provide bits and pieces of information you might need. But, if you don't want me to be in on the discussion, then I guess that's your choice."

"Okay, I don't want you in on the discussion."

"Oh," I said, not knowing what else to say.

"Besides, I wouldn't want to take time away from your new admirer, Tony," he said.

"What are you talking about? What does Tony have to do with anything?" This was getting almost as bizarre as talking with his fiancée, Miss Tee. Maybe they were more suited for each other than I'd thought.

"Look, Tina, I have to go. I'll talk to you later."

"Oh, no you don't. You don't say something like that and just hang up. If you hang up that phone, I will be over there in five minutes. I doubt if that will go over well with Teresa. Now tell me what's going on, right now."

"Yeah? Really?" he said, I could almost see the smile on his face. "Just where exactly will you be going, to make your dramatic entrance?"

"Hell, if I know," I laughed, thinking how absurd I must've sounded.

"Right. Really, Tina, you've been a big help. But I don't want our problems to come between you and your boyfriend."

Men, I thought, *unbelievable.* "Boyfriend?" I said, out loud. "A few minutes ago, you called Tony my admirer. Now he's graduated to being my boyfriend. In the next minute you'll have us married with five kids. What in the world are you smoking over there, wherever you are?" I paused for a moment, then I added, "Or, are you just fishing because you're a little jealous? My friend, Paulette, thought you were. Is she right?"

There was a brief silence. "Jealous? Yes, I suppose Paulette has a point. I guess I am jealous. Look Tina, I know you feel the chemistry between us the same as I do."

"Doesn't really matter, does it? You do remember your fiancée, what's-her-name, don't you?"

"Yeah, *what's-her-name,* is right. You know, Tina, sometimes I feel like I don't know who she really is."

"What are you saying Kennard? Are you saying you don't love what's-her-name?" I said jokingly, but I held my breath waiting for the answer.

"No, it's not that I don't love Teresa . . ."

"So, you do remember her name?"

"Got me there," he said, but I could sense that he was smiling. "Like I said, it's not that I don't love Teresa, it's just things are a little complicated."

"In what way?"

"Okay, I see what's happening. You're determined to make this hard for me, aren't you?"

"Yup. You got that right," I said, smiling to myself.

"Okay, Tina," he said. "Why don't I come over so we can talk about this in person?"

"Umm, Kennard. I don't think that would be a good idea. I'm not prepared for company right now."

"I'll be right over." Kennard hung up the phone.

"Hello, Kennard. Hello. Oh, no he didn't hang-up on me!"

* * *

Taking Kennard at his word, I remembered that I'd been laying around all day. Bed hair and body odor weren't exactly the image I wanted to project. I jumped off the sofa and ran to the bathroom to take a quick shower. I had barely enough time to fight a comb through my tangled hair, when I heard a knock on the door.

"Now that can't be Kennard. Not that soon." I said.

I patted my hair in place, as best I could, before checking my peephole. I was right, it wasn't Kennard. Standing there, so very tall and handsome, was Tony. I backed away from the door, not sure what to think. A lot had happened the night before, but I'd never given my address to Tony. I took a quick breath and opened the door.

"Tony, what are you doing here?"

"Hey girl," he said. He then pulled something out of his pocket and handed it to me. It was my driver's license. That solved the mystery of how he got my address.

"You left this at the club," he said. "I saw it and figured you might need it. Plus, it was an excuse to drop by."

"Thanks. I hadn't even noticed it was gone."

"Since I came all this way, aren't you going to invite me in?"

"Yeah," I chuckled, stepping back. "Since you put it that way."

As Tony walked pass me, I peeped down the outside hallway. It would really be awkward if Kennard chose that moment to show up, especially after our last conversation.

"Tony," I said, "even though I really appreciate you bringing me my license, you know you didn't have to come all the way over here to deliver it. You could have called, and I would have come and got it."

"Driving without a license? I see you still live by your own rules, huh?"

"Smart-aleck. I didn't say I'd drive."

"No, you didn't," he said, softly, inching closer and placing his hands around my waste. "Either way, hand delivery was the only way to guarantee seeing you. When I knew you before, you were a cute gutsy kid, who was too young for me. Still, you were definitely someone worth knowing. Now, you've grown and . . . Well, I want to get to know you . . . see you as much as I can. I'll use any excuse to do that."

He'd caught me totally off guard. The first thing I thought was that Paulette was right, I wasn't very good at the romance thing. Even with my lack of experience, I knew I had to slow this down. Though I liked Tony, I wasn't ready for what he was offering. Not yet.

"Do you want something to drink?" I said as I tried to gently ease out of his grip.

"No," he said, not taking the hint. "Right now, I just want to be close to you, Tina."

Definitely not gay, I thought as I moved away, to avoid his kiss.

"You expect an awful lot for returning a small piece of plastic, don't you?" I joked as I pushed harder and successfully pulled away from him.

"A very important piece of plastic, remember that," he teased. "That should count for something."

I was trying to think of anything clever to say, when I heard a quick knock on my door.

Tony smiled at my dilemma, I could get in the last word or find out who was at the door.

"You gonna get that?" he said, as he winked and swaggered over to the sofa. The way he looked me up and down had me blushing.

Definitely, not gay, I thought again to myself. Out loud I joked, "You are a real trip. You know that?"

"Yeah, I know. I'll be waiting right here," he said, while he exaggerated patting the seat next to him. I rolled my eyes and then checked the peephole. It was Kennard.

"Now the fun begins," I said to myself. And opened the door. "Hey, Kennard. I see you weren't joking. Come on in."

Kennard smiled, as he walked pass me, into the apartment. If only I had a camera to capture the look on his face when he spotted Tony. It was priceless. I admit that I enjoyed the shocked expression, just a little.

"Kennard, you remember Tony. Tony, I'm sure you remember Kennard, from last night."

Tony stood up and extended his hand to Kennard, "Yeah. I remember. What's up, man?"

Kennard shook Tony's hand, and repeated, "What's up?"

There was only a sofa—a love seat really—and one chair to sit in. I wasn't going to make any obvious choices or stroke anyone's ego. So, I pointed Kennard to the other end of my tiny sofa/loveseat, and I took the chair.

"Have a seat Kennard. Tony just stopped by to bring me my driver's license. I must've dropped it at the club last night."

"Is that right?" Kennard said tightly.

With nothing to add that would deflect Kennard's obvious pouty mood, I asked, "Can I get either of you anything? I don't have beer or any alcohol, but I can offer you soda, water, or instant coffee or tea."

"I could use some water," Kennard said, and surprised both Tony and me by rising and heading towards the kitchen.

Tony, bemused, noted, "Damn, dude knows his way around, don't he?"

"Well, it's a small place and he's been here before," I said, simply.

"Okay, but where in the hell is that fiancée of his?"

Kennard, back from the kitchen, sat the glass—filled with water from the tap—on the table, glared at Tony and said, "My business is not your concern. You've made your delivery. Now, you need to step."

Men, I thought, *what's with Kennard?* I didn't know whether to be flattered, angry, or annoyed at Kennard's juvenile silliness. Thankfully, Tony chose to take the high road.

He stood up, looked around Kennard to me and said, "Tina, I'll catch you later." He started towards the door. As I stood up, he gave me a peck on my cheek. "I'll call you."

He turned, gave Kennard a nod, and walked out the door.

Kennard picked up his glass and sat back down on my sofa. "So, what's the story with you and that guy anyway?"

"Why are you here Kennard?" I asked, as I plopped back down in my seat in the chair across from him.

"You know why I'm here, Tina."

"What do you want? You think I'm going to sleep with you or something? If you think that, think again." I leaned back in my chair and crossed my arms.

Kennard rose, walked over, and looked down at me. "I love you, Tina."

"What?"

"I said I love you." He just stood there.

"You love me. You hardly know me. What about your fiancée, Teresa?"

Kennard still standing, leaned over, his long arms covering the distance between us, took my hand and pulled me from my seat. The kiss he gave me took my breath away. "Things aren't the way they seem," he said.

"I care for you, Kennard. I know it's probably obvious. But I'm not that girl. I don't have casual sexual relationships and I can't trust a guy who cheats on his fiancée."

"Tina, like I said, things aren't what they seem. Remember, I'm not the one who said I was engaged. Teresa came here without being invited. When I arrived at my parent's condo, she was already there. Our relationship was over long before I came to Neesy's funeral. That's why she wasn't with me."

I moved as far away from him as I possibly could. I wouldn't have Kennard or anyone else play me.

"Kennard, I've seen a lot in my twenty-odd years. And I'm not one of those gullible women who fall for the 'she doesn't understand me and it is over' line."

He flopped back down on the sofa. "You're right, Tina," he said. "I guess I have some things I need to handle before you and I can have any type of relationship. All I ask is that you wait for me and don't take up with Tony or anybody else. Not yet anyway."

I took my time before answering, then looking him in his eyes, I said, "I can't promise you anything Kennard. It's unfair of you to even ask that."

"You're right, Tina," he said.

He kissed me gently on the cheek, drank the remaining contents of his glass, and then he headed towards the door.

"What about the thing you were going to discuss with me about Denise? I need to know what's going on. I couldn't stand it if Reggie turned up dead and I had something to do with that."

"What are you talking about?" Kennard stopped, turned, and faced me.

"You said you had people from Chicago who were going to take care of him. From what Denise said, I didn't know what to think."

Kennard burst out laughing. "I don't believe it," he said. "She told you about that crazy Black Mafia stuff, didn't she?"

"Yes, she did. Until today, I thought she was joking and exaggerating."

"Tina," he said, and flopped back down on the sofa. "I'm not some gangster or master criminal. I work as an accountant for a company that's involved in a lot of diversified operations in Chicago. The man who started the company, my mentor, is the son of a man who *was*, for a long time, into illegal and shady stuff. He was good at it. When things got out of control and he saw that the big money was in drugs and prostitution, he couldn't stomach doing that to the people in his community. After his retirement, his son—who had an MBA and his dad's busines instincts—grew his own businesses. Unfortunately, he could never overcome people's assumption that he was a criminal like his father. Unlike his dad, Artie, my boss and mentor, has a lot of friends in law and law enforcement. That's who I called for advice. I did not call my mobster contacts to have a hit put out on anybody. You met my parents. No matter how much they loved Denise, they would disown me if they thought I'd do something like that, even if Reggie deserves it."

"Oh, Kennard, I'm sooo sorry."

"Don't sweat it. My big brother, Robert, thinks that too. Even though we've talked and argued about it for ages, he's so straitlaced that he can't stand the idea of me working with people who once had a past. He doesn't understand that people and circumstances change."

"So, what can anyone do, all the way from Chicago?"

"I don't really know. Like I said, I'm just asking for advice. They might know people here in Richmond that might can help. That's why I started before getting on the plane back to Chicago." He got up again to leave. "For now, you can give it a rest, until you hear from me. I'll call you, maybe later in the week. Give me time to work some details before sharing them with you. Get some rest."

With that, he pecked me on the cheek and walked out of the door. And with all that was happening, I was more confused and conflicted than ever.

CHAPTER 39

WAIT FOR HIM? At the time he'd actually managed to let those words slip through his lips, both Kennard and I knew how unfair the request was. Besides, exactly what did that mean? Not bother him? Indefinitely sit quietly and patiently until he called? To his credit, there was one wish he made absolutely clear. I was not to start anything with Tony. So, did that mean that I was to resist all temptation, preserve my virtue, and wait until the time was right with him—only him?

None of that made sense, and anyone with half a brain would've told him to go chase himself. Not me. I waited.

Maybe I would not have felt like such an idiot if his promise to call "later in the week" had actually happened. But it had been over a month with no call from him. No returning of my calls. No emails. No text. No African drums. No smoke signals. No communication whatsoever.

Meanwhile, their son's rudeness did not affect my rapport with his parents. No matter my relationship—or lack of it—with Kennard, we still shared the concern about progress, or the absence of it, in the police investigation into their daughter's murder. That's why I still periodically checked in with Mrs. Jackson and each time I would ask about both Kennard and Robert—didn't want to be too obvious—and each time she would respond with something like, "The boys are doing fine."

Little did that sweet woman know that with every motherly assertion that her boys were doing fine, she was reminding me that there was no physical reason for Kennard not to call me. He wasn't stranded alone on a deserted island. He wasn't captured by aliens or on a top-secret mission where he was prevented access to the outside world. Nor had he been in an accident and was disabled in some way that prevented him using any type of communications device. He just did not want to communicate with me.

Decision time. Just how much was I willing to give up for a guy who lived hundreds of miles away, was possibly engaged to a drop-dead gorgeous woman, and did not care enough to call? The phones worked in Chicago Illinois just as they did in Richmond Virginia. Maybe it was time for me to take the hint and admit how foolish it would be of me to even consider waiting for Kennard, whatever he had in mind.

With no clear reason not to, it was time for me to move on with my life. There was a really great guy close by, who was interested in a relationship with me. He had proven that he was there for me. He had been there for me years ago. And, I had no doubt that he'd still be there when I needed him.

It should've been simple. Just give in and see what could happen with Tony. He constantly demonstrated, in words and actions, how much he cared. More to his credit, he never tried to push. It would never occur to him to ask me to wait around, while he got his act together.

Then again, because Tony was such a great guy, he deserved better than to be treated like he was some sort of love consolation prize. What kind of person would that make me? No matter what was or wasn't happening with Kennard, Tony was special. It would be unfair to pretend to feel something that I didn't. For that reason, for as long as he was willing, we'd be friends.

If the time came that Tony would decide otherwise, I'd understand, but I would feel the loss. Even ten years after leaving All Come Inn, Tony had easily moved back into his role as my protector. Once he learned about what happened to Denise and its impact on me, he volunteered to be an unofficial spy at NightLife. He offered to keep his eyes open to anything that could tie Ray John Williams to Denise or any of the crimes that she had mentioned.

Unfortunately, my spy was not finding out anything useful, and honestly admitted he did not expect to. It appeared that either Reggie and Tammy were truly model citizens, or they were both extremely good at keeping their extralegal activities concealed.

Then one-night Tony and I were scheduled to watch some of his old black sitcom videos, the ones he referred to as "educational videos". When we worked at the motel, he had explained to me that he called them that because they were the result of an effort during the 1970's and 1980's to change the image of blacks on TV. The shows all featured African Americans in non-stereotypical roles: like *Julia*, which had a black woman not as a servant but as an intelligent working mother; or *The Jeffersons* and *Good Times* which had hard working total family units; or the *Cosby Show*, which had highly educated professional main characters.

When we worked together at the motel, I was the only one willing to sit and watch them with him. Honestly, I didn't care one way or the other about the history behind the videos, I frankly appreciated Tony taking the time to hang with me. Plus, I owed him for protecting me from some of the creeps who came through the motel.

That evening he brought season two of *Good Times*. I was positive that Tony had watched all the episodes so often that he could've recited the dialog by heart. He definitely knew every word of the theme song, which he never failed to sing along with during the intro. That was part of the experience. The joke between us was that he'd sing, and I'd try to stop him. Tony was cute but his voice wasn't.

This time, he was too distracted to sing and or even pay much attention to his show. When he remained unusually quiet throughout the antics of JJ, one of the more outrageous characters of the sitcom, I became concerned.

After the first half-hour episode, I asked, "What's wrong, Tony? Did something happen that you need to talk about?"

"I don't know Tina. It's just RJ. I've been thinking. I'm still not sure if we can get anything to count as proof of a connection between him and Denise. But now I believe that he might've flipped-out and killed her. I always knew he had a temper, but now I think he is just plain crazy."

"Why? What happened. What did he do?"

"Last night, he disappeared into his office with this beautiful woman. No surprise there. Then, about fifteen minutes later, we heard these awful screams coming from the office. Me, Lucky, and a couple of others rushed to the office. When Lucky opened the door, RJ had the poor woman by the throat. We thought he was going to kill her. Lucky was the first one to get to him. You know how big Lucky is, and how strong, right?"

I nodded.

"Well, Lucky could not budge RJ. It took all of us to pull him off of her. And when we did, he still didn't want to give up."

"Why was he so mad? Did you find out? Was he drunk, or drugged up, or high on something?"

"Nah," Tony said. "Nothing like that. It was just that he was so mad. Madder than I've ever seen him. Anyhow, he ran out, still steaming. The poor woman was hysterical and crying. She kept saying, over and over, 'I thought he knew . . . I thought he knew . . .'"

"Knew what?" I asked.

"That was what we were all wondering. Marty—that's her name—wouldn't say and she wouldn't let anybody call an ambulance. Lucky was putting her in a cab, paying the driver, when Tammy showed up. She asked Lucky what was going on. When he told her, Tammy surprised us all by bursting out laughing. She was beside herself. She finally stopped laughing long enough to say, 'If the person you're talking about is who I saw getting in that cab, then I know what set RJ off.'

"She again laughed so hard she could barely catch her breath. She finally got out enough for us to put together that the beautiful woman, Marty, was not born female. And, even I knew that RJ's ego could never let something like that go. But Tina, he really wanted to hurt Marty bad, or kill her."

"Oh, my goodness," I said. "Marty was lucky you guys were around."

"Yeah, really. But, for her sake, Lucky advised her to stay as far away from NightLife and RJ as possible."

* * *

The more I learned about RJ, the more I understood how foolhardy our little showdown with Tammy had been. We were fortunate that her reaction was as mild as it was. Going forward, for all our sakes, it was essential that we keep in mind that we were dealing with an extremely dangerous person. It would be smarter not to poke the bear. So, for the duration, I resolved to take Lucky's advice to RJ's date, Marty, and stay far far away from that club.

Easier said than done. Only a few days later, the following Friday, Tony needed a "small favor" which required my presence at NightLife. His car had broken down and had been towed to his friend's repair shop. He needed a ride to the shop from NightLife.

"The shop closes at six-thirty," he said, "and I was thinking you could pick me up after you got off. I wouldn't ask Tina, but your office is downtown and you're my best hope of getting to the shop on time."

It was truly a small favor and it was Tony. How could I say no? "I'll be there at five-thirty. That should get you to the shop in plenty of time," I said, trying not to let him know how nervous his request was making me.

Driving the short distance to the club, needless to say I was not happy about the prospect of running into Reggie or his sister Tammy—who would not be happy to see one of the people who accused her brother of murder. And though Reggie had never met me, he was a police officer. He was trained to be observant and to put scattered facts together. If he was tracking the progress of Detective Robinson's case, no telling what he'd discovered.

To be safe, I made sure to arrive at the exact arranged time, 5:30 PM. When Tony wasn't standing outside waiting, I crossed my fingers that he would dash out soon. Twenty minutes later, I was still waiting, and I was starting to sweat, even though the temperature was in the sixties.

I'd tried contacting Tony on his cell, but he wasn't responding to my texts or calls. Now we were running out of time and it appeared that—though I dreaded the thought—I had no option but to go inside. I simply had to convince myself to do it.

Well, I thought, *Tina, you can stay here and talk to yourself, or you can go inside to get Tony. Look on the bright side, if Tammy or Reggie comes after you, at least with the noise from the kerfuffle, Tony will know you're here. And that's the objective. Right?*

With that, I allowed myself a nervous giggle, took a few big girl deep breaths, and stepped out of my little Elantra. I put a dime in the meter, that I had been illegally parked in front of, and headed towards the door.

I took my time, hoping Tony would pop out at any moment. At the door, it finally occurred to me that it might be locked. Banging on the door or ringing a bell was not an option. I took another one of those big girl deep breaths, tried the knob—which happily was not locked—and stepped inside. Then, I looked around, hoping to find my friend quickly, and get out.

I immediately saw why Tony wasn't responding to my calls and texts. He was up on a ladder, doing something with the lights. Below him, on the stage, were two men. One was the DJ that I recognized from my previous visit. His dirty dreads were hard to miss. The other man was much taller than the DJ, and vaguely familiar. From his body language, I could tell that he was upset about something.

"What the hell do you think you're doing?" he yelled at the DJ, as Tony turned the spotlights on behind them.

I gasped.

Something about the tall man—the way the light surrounded him, his words, and the tone of his voice—sent a chill up my spine. The sense of déjà vu was much too powerful to ignore. It wasn't just a feeling. It was a memory. One that was not totally pleasant, and I knew that I had to get out of there before the tall man saw me.

By the time I reached my car, I was a mess. The thing that I had long ago buried, the source of nightmares throughout my teen years, was brought to the surface by the beam of that spotlight. The tall man had seemed familiar because his was the face of the central character of the most terrifying incident of my life. I recognized him as the individual I had come to know as *Bathroom Man,* the person who'd blocked me entering the bathroom of the bloody guestroom in the All Come Inn.

Fearing that my worst nightmares could come true, my first instinct was to run. I wanted to get in my car and drive far away. But Tony was depending on me. I couldn't abandon him. Besides, it had been a very unlikely combination of things that jogged my memory enough for me to recognize the tall man as Bathroom Man. Since, way back then, he'd only seen me a brief moment, and most of that was from the back, it was unlikely that he could identify me as the terrified kid, from so long ago. Even Tony didn't know who I was when he first saw me at the club.

Not running away did not mean I couldn't take precautions. I had originally parked my car for a quick getaway. Now, the great spot, close to the club, near the door that everyone would use to exit the place, left me totally exposed. Assuming Tony would be out shortly, it seemed silly to drive around looking for another parking spot. So, I opted for invisibility. I slid down in the driver's seat with my head only high enough for me to see when Tony walked out.

Periodically, I'd stretch my neck for a better view. The third time I did it, I saw the tall man step outside with Tony. They chatted a quick moment, before Tony hastened to the car.

"Hey Tina, saw you as you were walking out. Good thing you came in. I had lost all track of the time. If you hadn't come in, I'd never have gotten off that ladder." He stopped short, as he registered the expression on my face. "What's wrong?"

"Tony, you're not going to believe this."

Before I could finish, there was a tap on my window. As I turned, my heart dropped. The tall man was motioning for me to let the window down.

I lowered my window very slowly, my hand unsteady on the button, and stammered, "Can . . . can I help you?"

"I just came over to meet the woman who's got my boy running out the place like it's on fire. Hi," he said, extending his hand. "I'm RJ. My sister and I own this club."

No, it couldn't be. I thought. *Reggie and Bathroom Man the same person?*

I was stunned and terrified. Any doubt, I had about how dangerous Reggie could be, vaporized. Not sure what had happened in the case of Glory Lake, but it was obvious Reggie had killed more than once—terminating anyone that got in his way—and he'd been doing it for a long time.

The last thing I wanted to do was touch the hand that was still there waiting. It took a monumental effort for me to reach out the window and shake that hand.

"Hmm, soft hands, as well as a beautiful face. Lovely lady, you know what? You look kind of familiar. I know this sounds weird, but have we met somewhere before?"

"No, I don't think so." I was hoping I didn't sound as nervous as I felt.

He kept staring, making me feel increasingly uncomfortable. "I know I've seen you somewhere before, Miss . . ."

"Hey man. Her name is Tina. And I'm sitting right here," Tony was joking, but I hoped it would be enough of a distraction. I just wanted to get out of there before Reggie remembered where he'd seen me.

"Okay, okay . . . I get the hint. Nice meeting you, Tina."

He turned and walked back towards the club.

I let out a massive sigh. I couldn't wait to get out of there. I pulled out, driving too aggressively, but I didn't care. Tony kept telling me to chill. That whatever had gotten into me, I needed to calm down or I'd kill us both.

I knew he was right, and after I was sure I was far enough away from NightLife, I pulled over to the curb to get myself together. Besides, I'd been so panicked that I hadn't thought about where I was headed.

"What's going on, Tina? Did meeting RJ freak you out that much? If so, I'm sorry I put you through that."

"Remember why we both left the motel?"

"Hell yeah! I'll never forget that. Guess my running away like I did, did not exactly help my image as a macho man."

That made me smile. "Macho man? You do know that I thought you were gay. Right?"

"Can't gay guys be macho?"

That did make me laugh.

"Why in the world did you think I was gay? Because I didn't hit on you?"

"Nah," I said. "Honestly, I think it was because I thought you were pretty. And I had never seen a pretty man before. Young as I was, I associated that with being gay."

"Hmm, not sure whether to be complimented or concerned about that."

I smiled as I turned to Tony—amazed at how he was able to make me relax. Unfortunately, that feeling was not going to last for either of us. It was time to reveal what I knew. I felt bad because I remembered the impact that night had on him.

I said, "RJ or Reggie, or whatever you want to call him, he is the guy from the motel room."

"You think RJ is not only the person who beat your friend to death. You think he was the person you saw that day? The one who killed Glory Lake?"

"I'm sure of it. I've been remembering things since I saw him in front of the spotlight inside the club. It all came back to me, and I remembered the face, as clear as day."

"Shit," Tony said. For the first time, he looked really spooked. "What do we do now?"

"I don't know about you, but I can't leave him on the streets to hurt more people. Heaven knows how many lives he's ended or destroyed."

"You say that to say what?"

"I have the card the Jacksons gave me with Detective Robinson's info. I'm going right this minute to tell her all I know about both murders."

"You sure that's what you want?"

"No, but that's what I'm going to do."

I put the car in gear, pulled out in the street, and headed for the address on Detective Robinson's card."

* * *

"What are you going to tell them?" Tony asked, as I landed a space to park. We had both been quiet, lost in our thoughts for a while.

"I don't know, but I'm going in there."

I stormed into the police station and went straight to the counter. "I need to talk to Detective Robinson. I want to tell her about a murder."

For some unknown reason, I was shaking, tears were dropping, and I was so emotional that Tony decided to speak for me. "Hold on a moment Tina, let me handle this," he said, then he turned to the officer behind the counter. "Like my friend says, we need to talk with one of your detectives, a Detective Robinson." Tony handed the man the detective's card.

"What is this about sir?" the officer asked, as he returned the card, apparently not moved by my excited proclamation.

"Like I said, we need to talk to the detective about a murder. What about that is so hard to understand?" I said, beginning to lose my cool.

"Look young lady," he said, leaning forward. "You'd better check yourself. Being a smart ass will not get you what you want any faster."

"I'm sorry, officer. Can we speak with Detective Robinson? Please?"

"I'll check if she's available. Just give me both your names." The officer wrote down the information and then said a few words, quietly, into a phone behind him. He turned back to us. "The detective will be out in a moment. Wait over there," he said, pointing to a bench on the other side of the room.

Just as I began having doubts about being there and was ready to grab Tony's hand to leave, a tall Caucasian woman approached the counter. The officer at the desk pointed in our direction, and she walked over to us.

She was almost six feet tall. Her neatly styled short cut hair, with bangs, was dyed blonde, and was the only concession to vanity about her. Everything else was sensible and almost masculine—like she was trying too hard to not appear feminine. Her brown leather jacket was old and worn, as were her loose-fitting pants. Her shoes were the kind of grandma leather sneakers I hadn't seen since I lived with my Auntie Dee. She wasn't wearing any makeup and looked like I felt after a long hard day. And, she didn't seem particularly happy as she stood in front of us.

"Hello, I'm Detective Angela Robinson. I understand you want to tell me about a murder?"

"Umm, yes, I think so." Tony answered because, suddenly my mouth didn't work.

"You're not sure?" She looked at us both. Considering what we must've looked like and us summoning her like we did, I couldn't blame her for being a bit annoyed.

I looked up at the tall no-nonsense woman and decided I was making a big mistake. *Suppose that creep, Reggie, walks in here right now? Suppose this woman is a good friend of his? After all he is a police officer. They may be best friends. They may even be sleeping together.* At that point, I just wanted to get the hell out of there.

"I'm sorry, Detective, I see now that we made a mistake. Years ago, I worked in a motel where a young woman was murdered. Her name was Glory Lake. I thought that I saw the man who might have done it. Now that I think about it, I have no proof and may be mistaken. It would be wrong for me to accuse him, especially if I'm not absolutely sure."

"But you think you saw someone who favored this man recently, is that it?" she asked, forming each word carefully.

"I'm not sure anymore. Sorry to bother you."

I grabbed Tony by the hand, and practically dragged him out of the police station. We didn't look back.

I couldn't get in the car quickly enough. I unlocked the doors, prepared to get behind the wheel when Tony stopped me. He put his hand out and pointed to the keys, "I'll drive."

I handed the keys to him, walked around to the passenger side of the car, got in and just stared forward, not sure exactly what had just happened.

Tony started the car.

CHAPTER 40

"THAT WENT WELL," Tony joked, only after we were forced to stop because of a red light. This being unchartered territory, we had no idea what to expect or how to act, that's why we had traveled aimlessly for blocks with one single goal. Get as far away from the police station as possible. During those minutes, we rode mostly in silence, obeyed every possible traffic rule, and I checked constantly to ensure no one was following us. Paranoid much?

"I guess going to the police station was not one of my best inspirations," I admitted.

"Honestly, Tina, what did you think would happen?"

"I don't know. I had to do something. I can't stand the idea of that man literally getting away with murder . . . murders." I said, staring in the direction of the side window, but not really looking through it.

"So, Nubian Nancy Drew, what do you want to do now?"

I smiled at the reference, because we both knew that I was way out of my depth.

"Go get your car as we planned, if it's not too late," I said, feeling guilty about totally forgetting the reason for picking Tony up. "Is it too late?"

"Maybe not. I'll call Rod," Tony said, reaching for his phone. "He sometimes stays late at the shop. If he's around, he'll let me get it."

"Great," I said. "At least something good can come out of this evening."

There was not much more either of us could say. Tony made his call to his friend—who thankfully was still at the shop—and promised that we would be there within fifteen to twenty minutes. We made it there in exactly fifteen, riding the entire distance in silence. The only sound was the background noise from my little Elantra.

The shop was on a dark back street, in a small industrial complex. There were cars in obvious need of repair on both sides of the narrow road, and no place to park. The only space that would fit my little car was in front of the driveway of the business next to the repair shop. Since it was late and the business was obviously closed, we chanced blocking the driveway.

A short dark man waved at Tony, as he stepped out of the car. I assumed it was his friend Rod.

"Be right back," Tony said. "Keep the doors locked."

Next thing I knew, someone was tapping on my window. "I have my car," Tony said, looking concerned. "You didn't even notice me pulling up next to you. I'll follow you home, to make sure you get there safely."

"You don't have to do that. I'm okay."

"No, you're not. I'll back up, and then you lead."

I smiled to myself at Tony's take-charge bossiness. Once he was no longer blocking my way, I pulled out.

Tony drove behind me. When we arrived at my apartment complex, the lot was so full that it took a few minutes to find open spaces near the rear of my building. Normally, I was careful to park under or near a light. This time, I just didn't care. I couldn't muster up enough initiative to search pass the first available slot. I honestly didn't know what to do, what to feel. It must've been the shock of discovering Bathroom Man, followed by the fiasco at the police station, because I had no idea what to do next. I couldn't move.

Tony waited in his car a few minutes before walking over to check on me. "You okay?" he asked, his face full of concern.

Deciding that I wasn't, he made me open the door and remove the keys from the ignition.

"Come on," he said. "You can't sit here all night."

He was right. I let out a deep sigh and walked with him to my apartment.

"Why the hell did I do that?" I blurted out the moment I entered my apartment. "Did I really think the police would welcome me with opened arms, happily handcuff Reggie, drag him to prison, and all would be right with the world?"

"It'll be okay, Tina, really," Tony said, continuing his well-meant, but hopeless, attempts to calm me down.

A thought hit me and made me abruptly stop the panic pacing, I had been doing. Turning around and nearly bumping into poor Tony—who was having trouble anticipating my erratic behavior—I said, "You know what this means? The Jacksons have a right to know that it's partially my fault that Reggie is still walking the streets. I need to call Kennard and fill him in on what just happened and what we discovered. I only hope that he and his family understand."

"Why would you do that, Tina? You don't really have any new facts about his sister. For now, all you can do is make it worse for him *and* his family. Maybe first you and I need to figure out what to do. Then, when the time comes, we can decide who all to talk with." He paused to see if I was at least tracking what he was saying, before adding, "Tell me, honestly, Tina. Why is Kennard the first name you think about? What can he possibly do from Chicago?"

Probably nothing, I thought. But I didn't dare say it out loud. I knew exactly what Tony wished I'd say. He wanted me to tell him that I didn't need to talk with Kennard tonight or ever. He wanted me to say that as long as I had him, I didn't need Kennard or anyone else. If I said any of that, it would be untrue and unfair to him. In the preceding couple of months I'd tried to feel what he felt towards me, only to come to the realization that, though Tony was handsome and a wonderful guy, I couldn't get pass the image of the big brother he had been to me when we worked at the motel.

"Tony," I finally said, choosing my words carefully, "that family has been through a lot. They are trying to put together information, to pass on to the police, in order to get the abuser of their daughter and sister punished. In the meantime, there was a reason for Denise keeping her abuse secret from them. Reggie had not only threatened Denise with harm but also her entire family.

"As it stands, her family assumes that Reggie is just your run-of-the-mill bully, who went too far, and all they need to do is to get proof he killed her. They have no clue what kind of person they are dealing with. If I keep quiet and Reggie starts to feel threatened . . . Well, he's already killed twice that we know of. You have seen him near choke a person to death, just because she bruised his ego. Even if it makes me look bad, I have to share what I know."

Tony listened without interrupting me. When I finished, he made no attempt to dispute my argument. From his reaction, or lack of it, I could tell that he was disappointed by my insistence on talking to Kennard. He doubtless assumed that the long speech was just a rationalization. Probably, from his point of view, the phone call was merely an excuse for me to get in touch with Kennard and obtain solace and reassurance from him.

What Tony didn't know was that, days before, I had at long last taken Kennard's less that subtle hint—being ghosted has a way of bringing the message home—and given up any notion of a special relationship between him and me. Needless to say, knowing how Tony felt, this was not something I could share with him.

While he was trying his best not to show it, I could sense it was Tony that needed reassurance from me. The strained expectant look on his face signaled that he was still hoping I would make the right choice.

If it was a test, then I failed miserably. Without even pausing to consider Tony's feelings, I made the call. Rather, I tried to. There was no pick-up on the other end. I was forced to leave a message, assuming that, despite him not responding to any of my previous messages, Kennard at least opened up or listened to them.

"Kennard," I said to the machine on the other end, "this is Tina. I have some important information that you and your parents need to know about Reggie. Call me when you get this message."

When I finished recording, like a balloon that had been punctured, Tony seemed to deflate. He retrieved his keys and his phone from the end table, where he had left them earlier. After trying so long to be supportive—to keep me from going over the edge—he stood up to leave. I guess he'd come to the conclusion that there was nothing more he could do for me.

As he collected his stuff, he looked over at me and his eyes fell on the traitorous phone, still in my hand. I can't imagine what his thoughts were. He merely said, "I'll call you in the morning to check if you're okay."

As much as Tony had been there for me, I'd let him down. We both understood that he wanted and deserved more from me. Unfortunately, I didn't have it to give.

"Thanks, Tony, for being there for me. I know I'm a mess right now. I'll just go to bed and try and rest and clear my head," I said.

"Okay. See you," he said. He kissed the top of my head and then he left.

* * *

In your typical suspense, thriller, or horror story, the tension builds. Then, when it seems as if nearly all hope is lost, there is the dramatic resolution. And the world is put right again—at least until the next sequel. However, in my real-life tale of terror, there is no gradual unfolding to a guaranteed payoff. I lay on my bed haunted by the possibility that the monster in my tale, unlike King Kong or Godzilla, might never get stopped or caught, simply because when given the opportunity, I had not come forward. I wondered what would have happened if I had just tried harder at the time, or any time in the interim years, to remember more details about Bathroom Man. All I ever saw in my head and in my nightmares was a shadow.

With sleep not happening and nothing much else to do, I started thinking back to something my high school Social Studies teacher, Mr. Hall, always said, "You're either part of the solution or you're part of the problem." Mr. Hall, a great believer in civic responsibility, told us that there was no in between. He felt that apathy or just waiting for someone else to make things right was unacceptable and was only a way of enabling the bad guys, and, more-often-than-not, helped make things worse and not better.

Now I saw firsthand, how right he was. When I'd stood back and insisted to myself and others that I had no useful information to provide to the authorities about Bathroom Man, I'd been worried about the repercussions to me, and not about getting justice for poor Glory Lake. And guess what? Ten years later, the bad guy was still out there, free to hurt people.

How could I happily close my eyes and drift off to sleep when, in my head, Mr. Hall was screaming, "If you had helped put Reggie away ten years ago, Denise would still be alive today."

When I looked at the clock and saw that it was already 2:15 AM, I gave up on trying to sleep and looked around for some type of a distraction—any way to defocus. Otherwise, I'd never get any rest.

My inspection settled on the light dust coating on my bedside table. It seemed that it was always there, no matter how often I cleaned. The table had been a constant dust magnet ever since Momma brought the set home from J.C. Penny's, years before.

Okay, something I can fix, I thought.

I hopped up and headed into the kitchen to look under the sink for the soft cloth that I reserved for the purpose. According to Momma—who had at times cleaned other people's houses for a living—a damp soft cloth was better and cheaper than store brought furniture polish.

Once that was done, I decided to tackle the rest of the apartment. By eight o'clock, my apartment was sparkling—all dishes washed, furniture dusted, clothes put away, floors swept, and carpets cleaned. There was nothing left to clean *and* nothing to keep me in the apartment.

Before making any decisions on what to do next, I checked my phone to see if I had missed a response from Kennard to my second message. About an hour after Tony had left, I'd made one final attempt to reach him. Instead of leaving another vague *call me* message, I described the circumstances behind Bathroom Man and how I knew it was Reggie.

Even before making the call, I had no doubt that Tony was right. Nothing I had to say was directly relevant to the search for justice for what had been done to Denise. Truly, it provided insights into the kind of person Reggie was, but everybody already knew he was pond scum. So, why make the call? I had to admit that my actual motivation was selfish. It made me feel like I was doing something.

At long last, I could sense myself winding down and went back into my bedroom and fell across the bed. I swore to myself that I would find a way to make things right, that I had no intentions of shoving the facts about Reggie—to be fair, the assumed facts—under my now sparkling clean carpet. But, at that moment, I was drained. I was in no shape to make any decisions about anything beyond whether to take my clothes off or just stay as I was.

I opted for not moving and closed my eyes and immediately dozed off.

Chapter 41

I BARELY MANAGED a couple of hours of sleep before being startled awake by mechanical noises outside my window. Building maintenance would pick that time to suddenly become efficient. Why on a Saturday morning?

Too wired to go back to sleep, I stripped off all the clothes from the day before and hopped into the shower. My mind went back to where it was prior to my brief nap.

Maybe, I thought, *if I'm careful, I'll be able to watch the club without getting caught. Even if I don't have enough now to narc on Reggie, I can watch him. If he looks like he's about to hurt someone else, I'll be there to call the police.* Mr. Hall would be proud.

I pulled my straight legged black jeans from the closet and matched them with a black t-shirt, socks, and shoes. I placed a couple of water bottles and some ice in a lunchbox cooler. Then I grabbed my camera.

The camera had been a present from Paulette a few Christmases back. Her family found the camera among her grandmother's things, after she died. It was one of those old 35mm Nikons that no one could afford, back in the day. It was old and worn, from years of use. With all the other cool things for the members of the family to fight over, Paulette was the only one who saw any value in an old beat up camera. Even if it wasn't new, it was something her best friend had wanted for years but could never afford.

With the camera hanging from its black strap around my neck, I topped the outfit off with a black baseball cap. Then I pulled out a black windbreaker and dark glasses to go with my dark clothes. Finally, I was ready to head out—the embodiment of: *How to Be a Reckless Clueless Spy in Just a Few Easy Steps*. Thankfully, I didn't get very far.

I was searching around the building's lot for my car, when a voice behind me said, "And where do you think you're headed this time of morning?"

It was Kennard. I'd almost forgotten how handsome he was. He stood there, in fitted black jeans, a black hoodie, and a tan t-shirt. Except for the shirt, it was almost as if he was dressed to accompany me on my stakeout. And at that moment, I was never so glad to see anyone. I let go of the mini cooler, threw my arms around him, and just held on.

"If I'd known I'd get this kind of reception, I would have come back sooner," he said.

As the initial elation wore off, I let go of him, took one step back, and soft punched him on the shoulder. "Where the hell have you been all this time? Why haven't you called me or answered any of my calls?"

"Ouch!" he said, exaggerating rubbing his shoulder. With both palms forward, he jokingly backed away to avoid any further physical attacks, nearly tripping over the cooler. As he gained his footing, he seemed to notice, for the first time, my faux-James-Bond-look. Pointing to the cooler, he asked, "Were you on your way out? Going on a Goth picnic or something?"

His observation forced me to take stock of myself—the dark clothes, the baseball cap, the camera dangling from my neck, and the water bottles in the cooler. I realized how hard it would be trying to explain my intensions to anyone who was remotely sane. What I had planned now seemed reckless and totally irrational, even to me. What in the world was I thinking?

Embarrassed at my foolhardiness, I daren't mention the truth of what I had been about to do. So, I did what any red bloodied female would do in a similar situation. I lied.

"Umm," I said, stalling to come up with something remotely plausible. "I was getting a little claustrophobic in my apartment and was just going for a little ride."

"I guess I can understand that. But, if you can spare a few minutes, we really need to talk. If it's okay with you, I'd like to do it inside."

"No. I don't think so," I said, vigorously shaking my head.

"Tina . . ." he said, taking a careful step towards me.

I reflexively tried to step back, but my efforts were thwarted by the brand new shiny red Corolla behind me.

"You know what, Kennard?" I said putting up my hand to force him to stop advancing. "I took to heart all the stuff you said to me. You know, the crap about how I should wait while you went off to make things right. You can't imagine how foolish I felt when you ghosted me, and I did not hear from you for over a month. If it hadn't been for your parents, I wouldn't have known if you were alive or dead."

"I am so sorry you were worried or thought I was, as you said, ghosting you. It was nothing like that," he said.

"Sometimes saying you're sorry is not enough."

"You're right. Before you punch me again or run off, I have something that I want you to see," he said, removing a folded piece of paper from his pocket and handing it to me. "This explains what really was going on. I'd prefer we go inside before you read it. Trust me, it is a lot to take in."

No way was I going to agree to that. "You gotta be kidding me," I said defiantly. I was in no mood to wait for answers when I had some of them right there in my hand. I unfolded the paper and started scanning the official looking contents.

Kennard, clearly trying to give me as much space as possible, leaned against a Malibu parked next to the Corolla. It seemed more a family car. There were toys, a child car seat, and various miscellany strewn about. Luckily, both owners were enjoying their weekend, and neither came out to yell at us.

"I don't understand. What does this mean?" I asked after reading the document twice.

"It means, basically, that it was impossible for me to respond to any of your calls or attempts to contact me, because I never got them. It means that my phone was cracked or hacked or whatever you want to call it. Bottom-line, someone, who wasn't me, planted something in my phone that intercepted all calls and text between you and me. The effect was that it made us both think that our messages were being ignored." Kennard explained all this as he reclaimed the document from me and replaced it in his pocket.

"You mean somehow somebody put something like a virus on your phone? I've heard of people planting viruses and stuff like that on computers.

But how could someone do something like that on a phone? Who would want to? And why?"

"That's where it gets really interesting. So, now can we go inside? I can tell you all I know about it," he said. "Come on. I think whoever owns these cars would appreciate us moving on."

Anticipating a positive response, he picked up the cooler in his right hand, and held out his left for me to take.

We walked companionably quiet for a few moments. Then Kennard broke the silence.

"Tina, while I didn't ghost you—as you described it—I do owe you an apology, of sorts."

"For what?"

"Losing my sister was one of the worst things that has ever happened to me," he said, staring straight ahead. "It did get to me a lot more than I'd be able to admit. But I think if Neesy is looking down, she'd probably slap me across my head for the way I behaved towards you and your friends."

"What do you mean?" I asked, not at all sure where he was going with the confession.

"I've had time to think about the way I acted," he said. "I did some pretty childish things. I did have a lot on my mind, but it was no excuse for the way I behaved, especially towards your friend, Tony. I acted pretty lousy."

I nodded, "Yeah, you definitely did."

He laughed. "Can't give a guy any slack, huh?"

"Hey, I was a November baby. Us Sagittarians tend to be honest to the extent of being blunt. Look it up," I laughed.

"You could cut me just a bit of slack, in this case. I could see Tony had a thing for you. That bugged the hell out of me."

"Why?"

"Have you seen that guy? If I was into men, I'd go for him!" he joked.

"It's not always about looks, you know."

"Well, you have to see it from my point of view. With this hunky guy hitting on you, and with you thinking that I was committed, it didn't look good for my chances."

"Thinking? Did you say thinking you were committed?" I all but shouted. "Teresa was wearing your ring. That says committed to me."

"You don't understand," he said, emphatically. "I never gave Teresa a ring and we were never engaged. I don't know where she got that damn ring."

"Well, at the time, you never said anything different. Now you're saying it was all a figment of everyone's imagination?"

"Not everyone's. Just Teresa's."

"You're not *that guy*, are you Kennard?"

"You mean, the guy who says whatever he can to get his way with women? No, I'm not *that guy*," Kennard said, shaking his head, as he looked me directly in my eyes. "And I swear, Teresa was never my fiancée. We'd broken up a long time before she showed up here. You have to understand. My folks were going through a lot. I didn't want to add to it. That day was not the time to call Teresa out on her lies. I figured I'd go along and straighten it all out later."

"Kennard, that makes absolutely no sense. For one thing, you sold your parents short by underestimating them. And, if what you say is true, then you couldn't possibly make things right by letting that big a lie go unchallenged."

"Yeah, I learned that the hard way. When she went off and came back waving a ring around, I realized that trying to be nice or ignoring it was not going to work. I was not only encouraging what was going on in Teresa's head, I was also lying to my parents by allowing the situation to go the way it was going.   That's why I rushed Tee out of my folk's place with every intention of dropping her off, telling her to take the next plane to Chicago, and coming right back, like I said. But nothing's ever that easy with Teresa."

"Kennard," I said, "you were gone a long time. Even late into that night. When I first called you from the club, Teresa picked up your phone. So, you were still there. How hard is it to say, 'Good night, Tee, I have a life?'"

"I didn't know about your calling me and Teresa picking up. I was there so long because Teresa got emotional and it didn't seem right to leave. We talked, but I wasn't getting the feeling we were on the same page. By the time my mother called to tell me to call you, I was done. There was nothing more to say. When I left to meet you and Paulette, Teresa had promised to head back to Chicago."

"I'm just curious. If you didn't give her the ring, where did she get it?"

"I don't know, and I didn't ask. Honestly, men are always falling for Teresa. She was engaged before. Maybe that guy, Clarke, or some other guy gave the ring to her. Teresa is not poor. She's very smart with her money. She might've bought the ring herself."

He paused talking long enough for me to get my keys into the lock and open the door.

* * *

I had barely closed the door behind me when, with the cooler still in one hand, Kennard somehow managed to enwrap me with his available arm. I was so happy to be with him that I didn't think about resisting. I don't remember thinking about anything. After all that had happened in the previous few days, I needed the distraction of being close to him. For the first time in my life, I didn't want to be in control.

The kiss was not like the chaste one he had given me before. And honestly, it made me nervous. An annoying alarm went off in my head. It reminded me to be cautious and not yield to his charm. No matter what I was feeling inside, I had to be sure that this thing—whatever it was that we felt for each other—was more than just a physical attraction. Regardless of how happy I was to see him, there were a lot of questions that remained to be answered.

I put the palms of my hands firmly on his chest and pushed him back, forcing some safe distance between us, and said, "Slow your roll, big boy. You said you wanted to talk."

"*Big* boy?" he said, with a sly grin.

"Don't get cute. You know what I mean," I said, thinking that I needed to put much more space between us.

I turned away from him and led the way to the living room area. I flopped into the chair—leaving only the couch for him. Instead of sitting, he continued towards the kitchen. I smiled, thinking that Tony was right. Kennard did seem to make himself at home. I wasn't sure how to take that.

"Umm, is there something I can get for you in my kitchen?"

Not taking the hint, he replied, "No, I'm fine."

"Make yourself right at home, why don't you?"

"Really. I'm just putting your cooler on the counter. I assumed you didn't want it on the floor or on one of your tables. Plus, if I needed a glass of water, I can see where the sink is. You have plastic cups sitting right there on the counter. Why bother you? It's not rocket science. Besides, you seem tired under all that crankiness," he said, making it to his spot on the couch.

"Crankiness? I may be a little tired but I'm not cranky. I'm never cranky."

"Yeah, sure," he said.

"Okay, you win," I said, now impatient to bring the conversation back in focus. "You want to tell me about the document now?"

"Right. First, you have to believe me. I never invited Teresa to my parents' place and neither did they. She just showed up at their door. She told them some cockamamie story about how she originally was supposed to work that night but had gotten out of it. Instead of flying in with me, supposedly, she decided to surprise me. My parents had no idea that I had broken it off with Teresa, and they didn't question her fairytale."

"I don't understand. If you didn't invite her, how did she know about your plans with your parents?"

"Good question. "

"Do not tell me she's psychic," I joked.

"Something like that," he answered in all seriousness.

"You're kidding, right?"

"Yes, sort of. She didn't get her info from the psychic realm or tarot cards. But she had her own set of skills that would make you believe she did. There is a lot you don't know about Teresa."

"Like what? No wait. Now I think I need some water. If it's okay with you, I'll get some from the kitchen."

"Nobody likes a smart-aleck. You know that don't you?"

"I've been told once or twice. Go on, continue," I said returning with one of the bottles of water from my cooler.

"Anyhow," he said, rolling his eyes, "Newal Johnson, the company I work for, has its hands in a lot of pots. Remember how I told you the owners got their start?"

I nodded, recalling how Denise had had me thinking the people he worked for were gangsters or hardened criminals.

Kennard continued, "Since they did not exactly start off as your run-of-the-mill mom and pop organization, they knew firsthand that there are some really bad guys out there. Two years ago, they decided it was time to upgrade their security management to a more comprehensive firm. They chose

Adams, Lowell & Lowell Security Services. I imagine you haven't heard of them, ALLS Services?"

"No," I said, rolling my eyes as I shook my head.

"Okay, maybe you wouldn't have," he said. "They are mainly in Chicago and specialize not only in the physical stuff—like keeping people from breaking down your doors—but also in network and internet—keeping them from breaking into your computers.   Like a lot of the major security firms they hire ex-military and ex-law enforcement. But they also claim to have the best and the brightest in computer security experts. They recruited Teresa right out of college."

"Really? Somehow I never pictured Teresa as a computer nerd."

"Actually, nobody does by looking at her. When ALLS came on board, the first thing they did was go through all our computers and networks with a fine-tooth comb. Imagine my surprise, when the computer guy, scheduled to check and setup the machines in my department, turned out to be Teresa. I had been expecting a geeky guy with taped up glasses."

"Instead, you got Teresa who'd give Tyra Banks a run for her money."

"Yeah, something like that. When Teresa walked in, it seemed that all work stopped on the entire floor.   I'll admit that I was flattered when she seemed interested in me.   When we started dating, I became the hero of the accounting department. And for a while, I was awestruck. Not only did she look good, but she was genuinely smart, and great at what she did."

"What happened?"

"Unfortunately, for someone with all she has going for her, Teresa has always been terribly insecure—extremely needy and jealous. After a while, I have to admit, all the drama got old. Even though I liked her, I finally broke it off when it became obvious that she was way more serious about me than I would ever be about her. It didn't seem fair to lead her on. I thought we had parted as friends."

"But she didn't want to be your friend?"

"I found that out much later. As expected, things were a little awkward, at first. But it seemed we had gotten through it. When she called to say how sorry she was about Denise. I thanked her . . ."

"You thanked her, how?"

"Nothing like what you are implying. I thanked her over the phone. Like I said, I had broken it off and I was happy about it. Then, she showed up here, acting crazy. It was too much. I tried hard to be cool, but. . ."

"So, what does any of this have to do with your phone?" I asked. It was getting hard to track. I wanted to be sympathetic, but still wasn't sure where all this was going.

"The one unpredictable thing in all of this was Teresa's jealousy. Nobody would have found out to what extents she'd go to, if she hadn't been away causing havoc in Richmond. The security company she worked for was in the process of checking out some strange network wide problem, when the person who was substituting for Teresa found a spy program on my computer. It was not related to the network problem. It was just sitting on my computer monitoring my activity."

"It was only on yours?"

"Just mine. First, they thought I had let a virus in. You know how that happens by opening a strange email message or something. They brought in an experienced security expert—this time it was really a guy. His name is Lee. Lee checked out the suspicious code. He somehow, I have no idea how, isolated the source of the code to Teresa. Normally, when you are suspected of something like that you are immediately terminated, and sometimes turned over to the authorities. But between her company and mine, the decision was made to handle it quietly. They gave Teresa an option, quit or be fired. She resigned."

"Kennard," I said, "I'm barely following what you are telling me. What I don't understand is why they checked your phone. Maybe I'm dense . . . They found the problem in the computer in your office at work. What did that have to do with your personal phone?"

"The way Lee explained it, they had seen stuff like this before—cases where the hacking was in a place of business but was strictly personal. They could tell almost immediately that this was very personal and the objective very specific. She wasn't after company information or trying to steal secrets. Teresa was focused on communications from specific sources, none of which were related to my job. That's when they warned me that my personal phone was at risk. Once they found there was an issue, the plan was to keep the phone active to see if they could hack the hacker. "

"And what exactly did they find?"

"They found that on my phone the main target was calls between you and me. Like I said before, the objective was to not only monitor our communications, it was also to make us feel, as you said before, that we were ghosting each other. If the security guys hadn't found this all out, I would still be thinking that you had given up on me. I came by last night to talk, but you weren't in. Stands the reason, I tried again this morning."

"So, Teresa did all that. And nobody's telling the authorities? I think they should lock her butt under the jail."

"Obviously, neither company wanted the publicity associated with what she had done. Both had a lot to lose if it got out. And I, honestly, just want her out of my life."

"She's a criminal. She deserves to go to prison. You know, for all intents and purposes, she might not give up that easily. Remember, I met her and walking away is not an option with someone like her. If you don't do something, she will make you regret it."

"As far as the companies are concerned, Lee says that they have their suspicions, but they don't have the right type of solid proof they would need to take to law enforcement. If they did it wrong, Teresa could sue them."

"So, that means that your crazy ex gets off scot-free," I said, not happy with what I was hearing. "Don't you think she should be punished?"

"Probably . . . I don't know . . . I think that there is actually a difference of opinion on that. Personally, I think that being an attractive woman is working in Teresa's favor. It's hard for even the toughest of those guys, especially the ones who worked with her, to see her as a villain. Anyhow, it's a moot point. No one knows where she is."

"Aren't you afraid with that crazy woman out there? She's already shown how far she'd go because of her obsession with you? If you aren't, I am."

"I doubt if Teresa wants to do anything to bring attention to herself. She, more than anyone, knows that so far, she has gotten off easy. At least that's what Lee says. Teresa is smart and is probably laying low, for a while. Given that all her ties are in Chicago, I doubt if you personally have anything to worry about."

"Yeah," I said, "from your lips to God's ears."

* * *

I couldn't get over how comfortable it felt to be sitting and talking with Kennard. Denise had obviously thought that we would be perfect for each other. She was at least half right. He seemed perfect for me.

"You know Tina," he said, "Denise talked about you a lot. After a while it was like I knew you and we were discussing a mutual friend. Sometimes she'd say something and end it with, 'Well, you know how Tina is. . .' I'd laugh because somehow I did." He looked over to see how I was taking all this. I just nodded.

"Anyhow, when I finally met you, it was in no way like meeting you for the first time. Everything my sister had mentioned, your body language, your expressions, your smile, your laugh, even the little quirks, were all familiar."

"Quirks? What quirks?"

He just smiled and continued, "You know, Tina, the strange thing is that I think Teresa knew before I did, or she somehow sensed exactly how strongly attracted to you I could become. That's probably why she felt compelled to risk her job by monitoring and blocking us communicating."

"Yeah," I said. "Your girl is a real trip."

"She's not my girl anymore."

I laughed at that. Though I did not like her, I could understand how hurt she must have been.

I was almost lost in my concern for Teresa, when I looked up at Kennard and saw that his eyes were watering. "What's wrong?"

"I was just thinking about my sister. She hated Teresa and always said that she didn't trust her."

"And that makes you sad?"

"No. Neesy and I shared everything all our lives. We were that close. But she never told me about what was going on with Reggie. I guess she was afraid of what I might do. And she was right."

At that, the tears rolled down his face. I was at a loss at what, if anything, I could say to make him feel better. I moved closer so that I could cover his hands with mine.

"In a weird way," I said. "I think Denise may have actually loved that creep. And, yes, I'm sure she did not want a showdown between you and Reggie. I don't blame her for hoping that things would work out and you two would meet and be, if nothing else, friendly."

"You are way too nice Miss Tina Brooks. I think I do love you even if we haven't known each other long," he said, giving me a look that sent tingles right through me.

He held my eyes for what seemed like a lifetime, but it was only a moment. Then he leaned forward and kissed me. It was a gentle kiss, but it most definitely was not one between sister and brother. I happily returned it.

Before that kiss, I had been able to maintain some distance—a reasonable level of detachment. Now, I was becoming very nervous thinking where this all might lead. I got up and walked over to the table, where I had left my water bottle. I took a sip of water. I wasn't thirsty but it was a way to physically distance my body from his.

Instead of returning to my seat, I pretended to suppress a yawn, as I said, "You know what? I'm being really selfish to make you do all this talking and bringing up all this stuff. You must be worn out. I know I am. I got next to no sleep last night and I probably should crash."

"Listen, Tina Brooks, there are a lot of things I could say at this point—like, I'll gladly leave and see you tomorrow. But that's not what I want to do right now and we both know it. Do you want me to leave?"

"No, not really"

"So, you want me to stay?"

"Yes."

"Not sure what you are saying. So, I'll break it down some. You want to get some rest. You want me to stay so that we continue the conversation after you're all rested up?"

"Yes," I said barely able to get the word out. I said it so softly, I'm surprised he heard me.

"You do know that this couch is much too short for me," he said, as he stretched his long legs out to demonstrate the difference in length between my little love seat and a full-sized Kennard.

"I see," I said laughing nervously. "I don't think that'll work too well."

"So, do you want to get a few blankets and pillows for me to stretch out on and make a pallet on the floor?"

"No, you don't have to do that either?" I can't believe I giggled.

"Then, that leaves the bed."

I couldn't bring myself to answer, so I just nodded weakly.

"Understand Tina, not a thing will happen that you do not want to happen. You trust me on that, right?"

There was nothing more to say as I turned and signaled for him to take my hand and led him into my bedroom.

"You sure?" he asked. I want your first time to be right for you.

I once again soft punched him in the shoulder, "You know too damn much about my business, Kennard Jackson. You know that?"

He laughed. "Like I said, my sister and I were besties. We had really long and detailed conversations."

Suddenly, I was really nervous and unsure what to do. Then he pulled me to him and cupped my face in his hands. "You can't imagine how I've thought about this . . . Being with you." Then he gave me another one of those toe tingling kisses.

CHAPTER 42

"SO, MY BABY GIRL is all grown up," Paulette teased.

"Oh, shut up, Paulette," I said, feeling my cheeks getting hotter and hotter, glad that we weren't in the same room.

I should have known when I made the call, that Paulette would guess the one thing I had resolved to keep from her. Foolish me, I figured a call to my best friend would distract me. I had barely gotten through mentioning Kennard when she squealed—an awful sound that hurt my ears—before saying, "Oh, no. My goodness. I don't believe it. You finally did the do!"

How she figured that out merely from my mentioning his name was a mystery to me. But I chose to brave it out. "No," I said, pretending a calm that I was not feeling. "What makes you even think that?"

"Girl, don't you lie to me. I will hang up on you."

"That's not what I wanted to talk about."

"So, you did do the do?"

"Paul-lette, cut it out."

"Okay. Okay," she said. "I won't mention it again, unless you want to."

"Good," I said, relieved.

"So, is that good-seven or good-nine, on a rating of one to ten?"

"Paulette!"

"All right. I'll stop."

"Ten!" I blurted. Not being able to contain myself any longer."

We both giggled like junior high school girls.

"So, where is Mr. Wonderful? Why in the world are you talking with me on the phone?"

"Denise named him executor, and his family needs him to get into her safety deposit box. They've decided it's time to just get everything over with. Up 'til now it's been too painful going through her stuff, especially when it meant revisiting the place where their daughter was so brutalized."

"I can understand that," Paulette said, softly.

"Kennard called earlier today, to tell me he had an appointment at the bank, and he would get back to me later."

"Are you going to get a chance to see him?"

"Depends. He has to catch a flight back to Chicago and I haven't heard from him since I've been home."

"Hmmm," Paulette said, stretching out the word.

"What?"

"Now that that's settled," she said, "tell me how you went from, 'My-o-my, Kennard is ghosting me. I'm so over him . . .', to sleeping with the man."

"Okay, I know it looks bad, like I'm some lovestruck idiot that forgave him everything the moment I saw him. And I'll admit I was glad to see him, at first . . ." I said. Then I redeemed myself by telling her all Kennard had explained to me about Teresa.

"That B-i-double-itch!" Paulette exclaimed. "She is one crazy-scary person. I hope Kennard is right and she keeps her psycho butt in Chicago."

"Me too," I said. "Now, I have to tell you the worst part."

"What do you mean by 'worst part'? What more is there?"

"Friday, I finally got a good look at Reggie. Remember how I kept saying that he seemed familiar, but I couldn't put my finger on why?"

"Not really, but go on."

"I was doing Tony a favor." Paulette swooned when I mentioned his name. We both giggled. "Anyhow, I was giving him a ride to pick up his car from the repair shop. I had to go in the club because he wasn't answering my messages, letting him know that I was outside waiting. When I went inside, I recognized a man on stage as the same person I saw coming out of the bathroom in the motel, the one who'd killed that woman. Paulette, I almost lost it when the man came outside with Tony and introduced himself as RJ."

"Oh, my goodness, Tina. Are you sure it's the same man?"

"I was sure enough to drag poor Tony to the police station to tell them. But I lost my nerve."

Paulette was quiet on the other end. I could only imagine that she was thinking how lucky she was to be far-far-far away from the madness that was my life.

"Paulette," I said, when she hadn't spoken in at least ten counts. "I seriously don't know what to do now."

"Nothing."

"What do you mean, nothing? Don't you understand what recognizing Reggie as the Bathroom Man means?"

Paulette waited a beat, before asking, "In all your post-coital bliss did you mention this to Kennard?"

"Yes," I answered. "We spent most of Sunday, just relaxing and talking. Late in the day, I started feeling guilty and knew I had to give him a chance to decide whether to hate or forgive me. I had to tell him everything."

"What did you say?"

"I first told him about my working in the motel. He already knew about Momma disappearing. So, it was more like adding details. You know . . . about how I handled it and how you, April, and Mr. Sam came to my rescue."

"Me?"

"Hell, yeah. I wouldn't have made it without you. I'd never have met Mr. Sam. I definitely would not have had the nerve to approach him. God knows I never would've ever thought about lying about my age."

"So, essentially you told him what a corrupting influence I was on sweet little Miss Dustina Brooks."

"The truth is the light, sister girl," I laughed. "Anyhow, when I got to the part about Bathroom Man, he was stunned. He hugged me and said that he couldn't imagine going through that at fourteen, or any age."

"I'm liking him more and more. Then what?"

"I told him about how I was sure that Reggie was Bathroom Man."

"What did he say to that?"

"What could he say? I waited for the implications to sink in. And asked him could he ever forgive me?"

"And?"

"He looked at me like I was crazy, and he said to me, 'You were fourteen years old, a kid who had just been deserted by your mother. Then you are frightened to death by some wild man in a room with blood everywhere. None of that was your fault. There is nothing to forgive you for.'"

"Hurray for Kennard," Paulette said. "I hope you listened."

"I was relieved that he saw it that way. But I still feel guilty. That's just how I feel."

"You need to get over it, girlfriend," Paulette said with surprising vehemence.

"I can't help the way I feel."

"Yes, you can. Take your hint from Mr. Wonderful. Did he get up and run out screaming when you confessed to being such a terrible person?"

"No, he didn't. He was quiet for a while, then he said, 'Tina, let me make this perfectly clear. No one can blame you for Reggie. What Reggie did, then or later, is not your fault.' Then he hugged me again and we just sat for a long time not saying anything. Know what he said, when he finally spoke?"

"What?"

"He said almost the same thing you always say. He said, 'You have had an interesting life, Tina Brooks.'"

"Well, the man is right. You have."

"Then he asked if Denise knew about any of this."

"Did she know?"

"No. I never had any reason to tell her. But, Paulette . . ."

"What?"

"I still don't know what to do. We can't have someone like RJ Williams, alias Reggie, out there getting away with so many awful things."

"Listen to me Dustina Brooks, and you listen good," Paulette said, now all seriousness. "You stay as far away from that man as possible. He might see you and remember, just like you did. There's no telling what someone like that would do. I can't lose you. Promise me you will stay away from him."

"I promise," I said. And I meant it.

CHAPTER 43

I STARED AT THE TV screen scolding myself for once again sitting around and waiting for a call from Kennard. My brain told me that he and his family had a lot of business to get settled. Then, he had to prepare for his flight back to Chicago. His flight left at 8:15 PM and it was already after six. If he didn't call soon, there was no way I would get to see him before his flight.

Even to me I was acting disgustingly needy. I tried to figure out who was this pathetic female that I definitely did not recognize. I remembered what Kennard had said about Teresa being too needy. Was I headed in that direction? Was it something about Kennard that brought this out in previously stable females? Was I doomed to go to the App Store and purchase software to track Kennard's every movement?

Thankfully, I was brought out of my funk by the ringing phone. As I caught myself rushing to answer it, I said to myself, "You are just too pathetic Tina Brooks. You know that?"

I sighed when I saw from the caller-id that it wasn't Kennard, but Tony. I picked up the receiver to answer. "Hello?"

"Tina, it's Tony."

"Hi, Tony. What's up?"

"I have some interesting news. I think I have evidence, on tape, that might can be used against RJ. You seemed so upset the other night that I knew I had to do something to help."

"What did you do, Tony?" I asked, hoping he had not done anything to put himself at risk, because I'd had an emotional breakdown.

"Don't worry, Tina. I didn't do anything crazy or stupid. It's just that, yesterday I saw an opportunity and took advantage of it."

"What opportunity?"

"Well, not many people know that Tammy records everything that goes on in her club. I mean everything, but the bathrooms. She trusts no one. Except for special occasions, she keeps the one to the backroom turned off. That's where they, mostly Reggie, have private meetings."

"Don't tell me you were crazy enough to steal the recordings, hoping to get something. If Tammy's that paranoid she will definitely miss them."

"No, better than that. I knew from the way the room was setup, that Reggie would have some people in. So, I went out and bought a couple of those little media cards just like the one in the machine in the backroom. I replaced the one that was in the machine and just waited for the action to start. Don't worry, I'm not stupid enough to do something like that with no one to cover my back. I hope you don't mind, but I told Lucky about what's going on. I needed his help. You remember Lucky, don't you?"

"The bouncer . . . the big guy?"

"Yeah, that's him. He's also a good person and he's smart enough to want bad dudes like RJ to get what they deserve. Anyhow, he agreed to make sure no one became suspicious or walked in to catch me messing around with the machine."

"What about Tammy?"

"She took a few days off, so I knew she wouldn't be around."

"How did you know what time to record?"

"I didn't really, so I set it to record when someone entered the room. I just had to make sure we removed that tape before Tammy returned."

"And Reggie had some type of meeting?"

"Yeah. I thought it would be a waste, when I saw that it was just his cop buddies. I have to admit, even though I had multiple media cards, I really didn't want to go through that whole thing more than once," he said.

"Tony, I'm not sure about doing it one time. More than once, that's too big a risk," I said.

"That's the thing, Tina. It wasn't a waste. Not at all."

"Really?"

"Really. Man was I surprised at what got captured on the tape. I have it with me and I'll be right over."

Before I could say anything else, he had hung up. "Damn," I mumbled, "now how am I supposed to deal with this?"

Thirty minutes later, Tony knocked on the door. He was so excited that he couldn't wait for me to see what he had recorded.

"From what you said, I take it you already looked at it?"

"Yes. I checked it out. That's why I called," he said, with a nervous smile. "It's really scary stuff. Honestly, Tina, I had no idea . . . Reggie and his cronies are real bad cops. It was like your everyday police strategy meeting. But instead of real police work, those guys were talking about shaking people down and stealing from people they arrest. Really bad stuff."

"Do you think there's enough to lock Reggie and his crew up for good?".

"Who knows? But, first . . ."

Tony put the little disk thingy in the slot on my laptop and started playing it. Sure enough, Reggie and the other men were admitting to crimes and planning more. Watching them, I had to remind myself that most police are not like those guys.

"Do you know who these men are?"

"Yeah," Tony said, with a note of triumph in his voice, "even the ones who aren't called by name. Between us, Lucky and I created a list."

"Too bad, with all the bad stuff they admit to, there is no way to associate any of it with Reggie's side crimes—his killing innocent people."

"I'd be willing to bet that those guys are mostly thieves and bullies. They might not know about Reggie's side crimes. Some of them might. If they do and they're caught, somebody might give up Reggie."

"Maybe. Who knows?" I said, not at all convinced. "So, what do we do with the video? Who can we give it to, without getting ourselves hurt, arrested, killed, or whatever? You know Reggie has a habit of dumping people who cross him in the river."

"That's why we have to be smart. I'll think on it. And, like I said, Lucky wants to help," Tony said.

"I don't know, Tony. Now that just adds one more person, who might be in danger behind this mess."

"That's why we all gotta be careful and smart," he said.

"What are you going to do with the tape, in the meantime? Where are you going to keep it?"

"I'll find someplace. First, I'll make a copy to leave on your computer. We can make other copies from it, once we decide who to send them to. That, of course, will have to be done anonymously. And, when we send them out, the copies must not have our fingerprints or any way to identify us."

"You have really thought this through."

"Me and Lucky did together. You're right, we don't want to get ourselves hurt, arrested, killed, or whatever. I don't know about the other cops, but Reggie scares the shit out of me. We don't have everything planned, but we will be careful."

Tony waited until the recording was copied onto my laptop. The entire time, his head was bobbing with his efforts to stay awake. Up until then, I hadn't noticed how exhausted he was.

"Thanks, Tony. This is great. Thank Lucky for me too. You seem really beat. Maybe, you should get some rest," I said.

When he hesitated, I knew what he wanted me to say. But an invite for him to stay was definitely not going to happen. So, he put the original disk thingy in his pocket and left.

CHAPTER 44

TONY REALLY HAD ME ANXIOUS, with all his talk of fingerprints and deep throat operations. That's why I decided to make an extra copy of the video and set it aside, just in case. They always did that on TV. I even put on a pair of rubber gloves before unwrapping the little miniature drive from its pack and placing it in the slot on my laptop.

I was watching the progress of the copy operation when there was a loud rap on my door. Thinking it was Kennard or Tony returning, I was so annoyed at the banging that I didn't bother with my slippers. I walked barefoot to the door and checked the peephole, prepared to chastise whichever idiot it was for knocking so hard. It wasn't Kennard or Tony. The shock of what I saw on the other side had me recoil and step back. Standing at my door, as bold as day, was Ray John Williams.

Reggie? What is he doing here?

My only hope was that he had missed the momentary darkening of the peephole. The temptation to take a few more steps back was strong, but the thought of the floor creaking kept me in place. I held my breath, praying he would just leave. It didn't work. Reggie resumed banging on the door.

"Tina Brooks, I bet you're in there," he said. "Had to stop by because a little bird called me and reminded me where I had seen you before. Makes me wonder about your boyfriend, Tony. Gotta figure he can't be trusted.

Probably been all up in my business. Too bad. I like the guy. Don't you worry, I'll take care of him. Have a nice day, now. You hear . . ."

With that, he gave one final hard pound on the door and walked away.

"Little bird? What little bird knew anything about that day in the motel? Oh, my God. This man knows me. He knows where I live. Tony? I need to get in touch with Tony," I said as I rushed to my landline phone.

I dialed Tony's apartment. There was no answer. I hung up and dialed his cell phone. Still no answer. I didn't know what to do. I was too scared to leave my apartment.

I dialed Kennard's cell phone. For once, he picked up right away. "Hey," was all he said.

"Kennard, oh my God, he was here at my house." I must've sounded absolutely nuts.

"Calm down, Tina. What's wrong? Who was there?"

"Reggie . . . Reggie was here." I lowered my voice, just in case he was still close by. "He was here at my apartment. I didn't let him in. I didn't let him know I was here. But he talked through the door at me. He said that some little bird told him about me seeing him in the motel. I have no idea who . . . who would know to do that."

"He didn't know that you were in the apartment?" Kennard asked, his voice full of concern.

"No. I kept quiet. Never said anything back to him. I'm sitting, staying quiet, and not turning on any lights that weren't on before he showed up. I'm really scared. He threatened Tony and I can't reach him to warn him."

"Keep as calm as you possibly can. I'm here with my parents. I've already canceled my flight because there's a lot that happened today that we need to talk about. I'll head out now. Bolt your door. Stay calm. Put your cell phone on vibrate and keep it handy. If Reggie had planned to do something, he would've done it. Give me Tony's number and his address. I'll go and see if I can find him to warn him."

"Oh, my God, Kennard. Tony has an incriminating video of Reggie and some other cops. If Reggie gets a hold of that, he definitely will hurt Tony."

"Tina, just give me his information."

"I have it in my address book. I'll text it to you."

Considering how flustered I was and that I was sitting in a half-dark apartment, it was a miracle I found the little black imitation leather address book. After texting the information to Kennard, I called his number again.

"Did you get the message?"

"Yes, I got it. I'm heading out now. Whether I find them or not, I'll let you know what happens. Okay?"

"Okay. Kennard?"

"Yeah?"

"I've never been so scared in my life."

"I know, Tina. I'll call you later."

* * *

I must have dosed off, because the next thing I knew it was eight o'clock and the phone was ringing. I stared at it but didn't recognize the caller-id. The first thing I thought was that it was Reggie calling to see if I was home. I froze. I couldn't pick up, even if I wanted to. I didn't dare reach for the phone. It would require me moving and I couldn't do that, in case he was outside the door listening. I waited for the answering machine to kick in.

"Hello, Ms. Brooks. This is Detective Angela Robinson of the RPD, we met a couple of nights ago. I realize that it's late, but I would like to come over and talk with you, if it's convenient."

Detective Robinson? What could she possibly want to talk with me about?

Of course, staring at the phone would not get me any answers. I'd never find out anything by sitting on my hands, refusing to move. Anyhow, I probably owed her. I had barged in and interrupted whatever police things she was doing. I had wasted her valuable detective time, while she could've been serving and protecting. Bottom-line, I had gone to her house—the police station—unannounced. The least I could do was let her in mine.

I picked up the receiver, "Hello, Detective Robinson. I'm here."

"Ms. Brooks?"

"Yes."

"I'm only a couple of minutes from where you live. If you don't mind, I'd like to come over now, to talk with you."

"Okay, Detective."

"See you in a few," she said, and then she hung up.

It was the jolt I needed. The call forced me off the couch. I was tired of hiding in my house. I got up. Brushed my teeth. Combed my hair. And waited until I heard a knock on my apartment door.

I eased to the door and peeked through the peephole. Sure enough it was Detective Robinson, looking pretty much as she had before.

I opened the door. Not sure what the proper protocol was, I stood inside the opened door and said, "Hello, Detective."

"Hello, Ms. Brooks. May I come in?"

Not sure if, like for the vampires in the movies, I had to specifically invite her in. If I didn't say the words, *come in,* did it count? Just in case, I merely stepped aside to allow her to walk through. That way it couldn't be used against me in court.

"Umm, what's up Detective? How did you know how to find me?"

She pointed to the badge, dangling from her neck, "I'm a detective. Remember?" she laughed.

That caught me completely off guard. I never imagined the no nonsense woman from the police station making jokes and laughing.

"I guess I meant to say, why are you here?"

"Ms. Brooks, your visit had me curious. After you left, I looked up the case you mentioned. There was a young girl referred to in the report of the murder of the prostitute, Glory Lake, at the All Come Inn. The report listed her as the niece of the manager. She would've been about your age. Interesting enough, the name matched that of the person who came by the station Friday night. Once I made that connection, I tried to remember where else I had heard that name. It was also mentioned in a case I'm involved in. That all got me curious. I don't like unanswered questions. They annoy me. So, I thought I'd come talk with you and see if I can get some answers."

"Come on through Detective," I said. *To heck with the vampire curse thing.* "I think we might have a lot to talk about. Hopefully, I'll have some of those answers for you. Do you want some coffee or tea or something?"

"No thanks. I'm good."

I led her into my little living room. She chose the chair and I sat on the couch opposite her. I figured I better start talking or I'd panic again.

"Detective, do you know a colleague named Ray John Williams?" I asked.

"Yes. He's part of a special major crimes task force."

"Now that's just hilarious," I said, "because the Ray John Williams I know about is behind several major crimes. Even though I can't prove it, I know for a fact that he's guilty of extortion, intimidation, and murder."

"Some very serious accusations, Ms. Brooks."

"I know that. I also know that I'm tired of keeping quiet. What it didn't say in the report that you read was that I was a homeless fourteen-year-old. I was being aided and protected by some very kind people, who saw that I had a place to live—the motel—and the opportunity to support myself doing small jobs. One day, while checking out a room in the motel, I saw blood everywhere. Then I heard something in the bathroom and thought someone might be hurt. I was approaching the door when this scary man popped out. I ran. Later, I learned that Glory Lake had been left in that bathroom with her throat slashed. There was evidence of someone being interrupted while attempting to clean up after the crime. I was that interruption. At the time, I was so traumatized that I couldn't remember anything about the man. With no concrete information, we kept quiet about me seeing him."

"You couldn't identify him?"

"Right. For years, I still couldn't remember anything but a shadowy figure. In my nightmares he chased me. Then, the other day, I had to meet my friend, Tony, at NightLife. While I was there, the entire incident was literally brought back to me in a flash of light, and I recognized Ray John Williams as the man I saw coming out of the bathroom."

"And that was what you came to tell me?"

"Yes, exactly. But, like I said then, I had no real proof. I didn't know what would happen to me if I accused him, at that point. I was confused and scared. I panicked. That's why I ran away."

"I can understand that. And you know Ray John Williams, how?"

"I don't really know him. We're not friends or anything like that. I was looking for a man named Reggie, who had beat my friend, Denise Jackson, for days and left her to die. I found her like that and tried to get her help."

"But it was too late?"

"Right," I said, looking for judgement in her expression, and not finding any, I continued. "Anyhow, I had never met Reggie. I only knew the things Denise had said about him. I had caught a quick glimpse of the person, I assumed was Reggie, in a picture in her house. So, the only solid thing I knew for sure about Denise's boyfriend was that he worked for the police. A few weeks back, a friend and I went to NightLife, she danced with Ray John. It seemed a strange coincidence that he matched everything Denise had described, including working for RPD. The only thing we didn't have was the connection between RJ and Reggie. We got the answer to that from his sister, Tammy. She told us that his family sometimes called him Reggie. That was it. We were then positive that Ray John, RJ, and Denise's Reggie were the same person."

Detective Robinson didn't say anything the entire time I told my story. I couldn't tell if she believed any of what I was saying, but she did take notes.

"Well, Ms. Brooks," I came for answers and you provided some surprising ones, I have to admit."

I couldn't tell from her body language or her voice if she believed any of what I had said. At least I had gotten it out.

"You may find all this hard to believe," I said. "I don't know if saying any of this will make a difference. I'm just tired of not telling what I know. One thing you might keep in mind. A short while before you called, Ray John Williams came to my door and practically admitted to being the person in the bathroom, years ago. He threatened me and Tony, the man who was with me at the police station. I haven't been able to get in touch with . . . with him since." I didn't want to lose it in front of the detective. Still, the thought of what could've happened to Tony, was making it hard.

"Why would he threaten your friend?" she asked.

"Because Reggie thinks my friend was trying to help me get evidence against him."

"Really? What evidence could your friend find ten years after the crime?"

"Nothing. But there is something I think you should see." I said, as I turned to my laptop and played her the video.

Detective Robinson, for the first time, lost her cool demeanor. "Where did you get this?"

"I can't tell you that. But I'm willing to bet someone can use it to build some kind of case. And maybe, just maybe, one of those servants of the law in that video can help with information on Ray John's other activities."

Detective Robinson sat there staring at the screen, even after the video had stopped. I had no idea what was going through her head. Though I still wasn't absolutely sure if I could trust that she'd do the right thing and make Reggie pay for any of his crimes, something about her told me that she would at least try.

"Here, Detective, you take this," I said, as I ejected the copy I'd made of the video and handed it to her. "You know, Detective, I've been thinking a lot lately about a favorite saying of one of my teachers, from his long-ago days as an activist. It was, 'If you are not part of the solution, you are part of the problem.' He told us that it was originally an African Proverb, but it was adopted by a man named Eldridge Cleaver. In the past few days, I saw how my inaction may have contributed to Ray John feeling that he's invincible. So, even though I was a kid—and I do know that Ray John's actions are all on him—I have a lot of guilt for not doing all I could when I had the chance. I feel that I am part to blame that he was still around free to kill my friend."

Detective Robinson nodded, and got up to leave. I couldn't tell what she was thinking. But I liked that she didn't give me the "you can't blame yourself" speech or try to convince me one way or the other about Reggie.

As she stepped through the door, I said, "Detective, I think you're a good person. I'm trusting that you will be part of the solution here."

Detective Robinson looked at me, gave a brief nod, and left.

I locked the door and engaged the dead bolt. At that moment, I decided that I wasn't going to let the possibility of Reggie being near make me a prisoner in my own apartment. I turned all my lights on and walked into my kitchen to find something to drink. Suddenly, my throat was very very dry.

I looked at my cell phone. While I was telling the detective my story, I had missed a text from Kennard: *On my way over. Found Tony and Lucky. Both ok. Will fill you in when I get there. See you soon.*

CHAPTER 45

I BARELY HAD TIME for a bathroom break when my phone rang again. "What is this?" I grumbled. "When did I get so popular?"

Not recognizing the number, I waited to hear the caller through the answering machine.

"Hello, Tina," the voice said. It was a woman, and she sounded familiar. "This is Teresa," she said. "You remember me, don't you? If you're in, please pick up. We need to talk."

Teresa? Why would she be calling me? I thought.

"Come on, Tina. If you're there, we really need to talk. Don't you want to know how you're being lied to? Pick up. You owe me that much."

This woman is truly crazy, I thought. But curiosity got the best of me, and against my better judgment, I hit the speaker button, and said, "Hello Teresa. What exactly do I owe you?"

"Oh, hi. Glad you decided to take my call," Teresa said in one of those sing-song voices used my telemarketers.

"I repeat. What exactly do I owe you, Teresa? And, for that matter, what could we possibly have to talk about?"

"Not on the phone, Tina. I need to see you in person."

"What? You intend to fly all the way from Chicago just to have a one-on-one conversation with me?"

"Chicago? I'm not in Chicago. I'm in Richmond."

"In Richmond? Why?"

"Don't stress your little brain with so many questions. You might hurt something," she giggled. "Anyhow, is it all right if I come over?"

"No."

I could sense, even over the phone line, her surprise at my response. Why she'd be surprised, or even why she would think I'd want to meet with her, was way beyond me.

"Look, Tina, I think it's in both of our interest if you let me come over, now," Teresa said.

Her insistence only solidified my resolve, and I said, firmly, "Teresa, I don't know you. I don't know what you want. Actually, at this very moment, I could care less. Believe me, this is not a good time for whatever you want to talk about. Goodbye and have a nice life." I hung up.

"Wow, that felt good," I said, and headed towards the kitchen for something to drink.

Five minutes later, I received a text. It was a picture of a little boy that appeared to be about two years old. It was beautiful and was the perfect blend of the best of Teresa and Kennard. The message text said, *He tell you about Little Kenny? Now can we talk? I'm in your parking lot. Be up in 2 minutes.*

The text hit me like a brick in the face. Who could not look at that kid's eyes and not see Kennard? The nose was the perfect nose I remembered, from when I saw Teresa. I originally thought it was too perfect and had been surgically created. Now, looking at that little face, I knew that it had to have been natural.

Or was it? I didn't know much about Teresa, but I did know that she was manipulative, unscrupulous, and she was a computer expert. Given the right software, even I could create the picture of perfect *Little Kenny* and give him any nose I chose. Plus, even if Kennard was louse enough to try and hide the fact that he had a kid, Denise or her parents would have mentioned the child, at some point. So, if the kid wasn't real what exactly was Teresa up to?

I had a decision to make and I had to do it quickly. There was a seriously crazy woman on her way to my apartment and I'd already been foolish enough to answer the phone and reveal that I was home.

Maybe, I thought, *the smart thing to do would be to leave now. Run down the emergency stairway, get into my car, and drive off. It's probably not smart to wait for the wacky Miss Tee to show up.*

On the other hand, it occurred to me that it might be best to play it out and get it over with, especially since Kennard was on his way. If Teresa didn't murder me when I opened the door, I could stall her until he arrived. There were obvious unresolved matters between them that had nothing to do with me. Bottom-line, regardless of what Teresa had to say to me, it was up to her and Kennard to work their issues out.

With what seemed like the logical decision made, I texted Kennard: *Teresa on her way up to my apartment. Just wanted to warn you. Hope you're close.*

He must've been stopped at a light or something, because he sent an immediate response: *5 minutes.*

Will leave the locks off the door. You can come right in, I texted back. Then, I sat and waited for the wacky Miss Tee.

* * *

Nobody looks that good all the time, I thought, as I opened the door for Teresa. She had on black stretch jeans, a black top, one of those long below the knee cardigans—beautiful goldish color—slouch socks and high heal ankle boots with trim the same color as the sweater. Even casually dressed, she looked like she was ready for the catwalk.

"Hello, Teresa, come in," I said, leading her into my cherished little apartment. I could tell from the expression on her face that she was less than impressed. I imagine, to someone like her, it must've seemed too bargain basement tacky than anything she'd like.

"Hi, Tina. Thanks for having me," she said, as if I'd invited her over for tea and cookies. The woman had problems, that's for sure.

"So, what was it you wanted to talk to me about?" I asked, not really interested. Just trying to buy time until Kennard arrived.

She walked with her bag on her shoulder, while she kept her hands in the big pockets of the sweater. It crossed my mind that if she had a gun in one of those pockets, I was done for. We continued through. She sat on the couch and looked around without speaking. I couldn't imagine what was going through her head, so I chose to wait her out.

271

."You know, Tina, I still can't figure it out. What exactly is it that Kennard and his family find is so great about you?"

"Excuse me?"

"I really tried to, you know, figure it out," she continued, as if I hadn't spoken. "I studied everything I could about you. You grew up in one of the worst areas of the city. You graduated with okay grades. You seem to be reasonably competent at your jobs. Got your little Liberal Arts degree over the internet. No debts. And you pay your bills on time. Nothing really special that I can tell."

I was speechless. This woman had invaded all aspects of my life and she sat there as if I was on the wrong side of a job interview. Then it hit me. "You are the little bird." I couldn't help but raise my voice. Catching myself, I said, in as calm a manner as I could muster, "You called and told Ray John that it was me in the motel. I'm not sure how you figured it out, or how you made the connection to make the call. But it was you."

"What?" she asked, looking at me as if I had suddenly grown horns.

"You made a call that was almost guaranteed to get me seriously injured or killed. Why did you do that?"

"I don't know what you're talking about."

"Yes, you do. You tried to get me killed, without it coming back on you. That's why you made that call . . ." I said, standing up, my voice again rising.

"Made what call? What do you mean she tried to get you killed?" It was Kennard. I was so absorbed in the shock of my revelation that I hadn't heard him come in.

"Hello, Kenny," Teresa said, her face lighting up, her voice softening, and her entire demeanor changing.

Kennard walked over to where she was sitting. "What is she saying, Teresa? What exactly did you do?"

"Nothing, Kenny," she said shrugging. "I have no idea what Tina is talking about."

I couldn't take one more minute of that awful woman. "Get out of my house, please," I said with as much calm as I could muster.

"Kenny," she said, facing Kennard, in all innocence. "I have no idea what's going on. I just came to have a girl to girl talk with Tina. Then she goes all crazy talking about little birds and me trying to get her killed. I have no idea what's wrong with her."

"Oh, no," I said, as the answer to my question suddenly hit me. "Now, I get it. I know how you knew about the motel. That long message I left on Kennard's phone. I described everything I'd learned about Ray John. Kennard never got it, because you got it first. You got it from some spy stuff you put on his phone, didn't you?"

Teresa looked at me, as if I was totally crazy. She turned to Kennard, as if to say, *This girl has completely lost it. Call the bus.*

"Please, leave," I said, weary of Teresa. "You are just evil, and I don't want you in my house."

I was so angry that I was close to tears. I couldn't stand being in the same room with her one moment longer. When she showed no signs of moving, I did. In my haste, my toe caught on the edge of the carpet and I found myself stumbling, grabbing blindly to gain my balance. Before landing face first, Kennard was there.

I sunk into his arms. Until Kennard began making soothing noises and stroking my back, it hadn't registered that I was crying. Even though he was being gentle with me, I could feel the heat of his rising anger.

"Umm, I think it might be time for me to take my leave," Teresa said, master of the obvious. This was not how she had planned it. The situation was too much out of her control. Plus, I doubt seriously if she cared for Kennard's solicitous behavior towards me.

"I'll walk you out," Kennard said, through clinched teeth. "We can chat on the way to your car."

"That would be just fine, Kenny," Teresa said. Then she looked at me, "See you around, Tina."

Not if I see you first, I thought. What I said was, "Goodbye Teresa."

Happy to see the back of Teresa, I sat down on the couch to wait for Kennard to return and fill me in on what he knew about Tony, and what the other news was he wanted to tell me. I thought about turning on the TV, for noise value. But after the wacky Miss Tee, neither the imaginings of Hollywood nor the horrors and wonders of the daily news could distract me.

When I heard the door open, I was surprised to hear two voices, Kennard and another male. I went out to the door, and Kennard was there with a man that I recognized from seeing him around the apartment complex.

The man saw me and said, "Brother here, says he's okay. But I walked with him here, just in case."

I had no idea what the man was talking about. Then my eyes were drawn to several big red spots visible on Kennard's black hoody that weren't there when he left.

"What happened?" I exclaimed.

The man took the lead to answer my question.

"Was taking a smoke on my balcony," he said. "Saw brother here and a sister leave the building. Brother was talking real serious like. She wasn't saying nothing. Brother turns to walk away. Next thing I know, sister is moving fast towards him. She's charging like she's about to do some real damage. I couldn't see exactly what she had in her hand, but I figured it had to be a knife or something like that. I shouted, 'Look out, man . . . I think she's got a knife!' He turns and waves his arm to block her. I ran outside fast as I could. By the time I got there, sister was long gone, and brother man here was standing there with the knife in his hand. He seemed kind of out of it. So, I walked him here. Looks kind of bad to me, but he says he's okay."

"Oh, my God, Kennard," I said.

"Umm, I think you need to call somebody," the man said. "Brother doesn't look too good. I was about to get ready for work. But I'll be home all day tomorrow if you need a witness. Apartment 304."

"Thank you, Mr?"

"Byron. I'm Byron Jones," he said, and left.

Kennard hadn't moved or said anything. I didn't know what real shock was like. I was getting concerned.

"Kennard?" I implored.

"I'm okay, really, Tina. It's just taking me a minute to process. That's all."

"That looks like a lot of blood," I said. "I think Byron is right. You're not okay. Come on, let's go into the bedroom. There's more light there. You can stretch out and we can better check you out."

CHAPTER 46

KENNARD STILL HELD THE KNIFE in his right hand. I doubt if he realized it was there. I gently touched his arm. He stared down at the point where I touched him and allowed me to ease the knife from his hand to mine.

The thing was small with the blade folded in. It was nothing like the little pocketknives Boy Scouts used or twelve-year-olds received for Christmas. Closed, it was at least four inches long and a lot heftier than your run-of-the-mill pen knife. From the amount of blood on Kennard's clothes, I assumed it was razor sharp. The handle was painted gold. I couldn't help noting how well it matched Teresa's outfit. Just the item for your run-of-the-mill fashion-conscious psychopath. Not sure what to do with the thing, I placed it on the kitchen counter.

Why would Teresa carry something like that around in her pocket? I wondered.

As if he read my thoughts, Kennard said, "It's an OTF knife, kinda like a switchblade. Teresa has them in different colors. One of the uniquely Teresa things that never quite sat right with me. She says she got them for protection, to ward off jerks at client sites that didn't take no for an answer."

"A switchblade is a little extreme. Most women, in her situation go for a whistle. Or, pepper spray. Or, at the most, self-defense training," I said, as I made my way back to gently grab his arm to get him moving in the direction of the bedroom.

He nodded, and said, "After she overheard the guys she worked with talk about them, she looked them up—research is more Teresa's style than even considering sweating in a room with a bunch of other women. Why they appealed to her? Only she can say. Maybe the idea of a weapon made her feel badassed, or she just liked the fact that they came in designer colors. Still, as far as I know, before today, she'd never actually used one against anybody."

We continued slowly towards the bedroom. Obviously, at some point, I'd have to come to grips with the fact that she'd brought one of those deadly things on her surprise visit to me. At the moment, my priority was checking out the extent of Kennard's wounds. I agreed with my neighbor, Byron Jones. Kennard saying that he was okay was not at all convincing me.

I helped him up onto the bed. Then, together we gently removed the thick hoodie and t-shirt. Teresa had connected in several places, his arm, his side, his stomach, and his back. She had done a surprising amount of damage in such a short amount of time. The fact that nothing was gushing out, made me feel better.

I located my little first aid kit. It seemed woefully inadequate, and it didn't take a rocket scientist to see that I was way over my head. Ignoring Kennard's protests, I dialed 911. I was not going to make the same mistake I'd made with his sister. This time I wanted the certainty of qualified professionals for the best possible outcome.

After a few minutes of instruction from Hazel, the unflappable emergency operator on the line, I knew I had made the right decision to make the call. The only thing left was to wait for the professionals to arrive. In the meantime, she told me to keep him talking.

"What do you think Teresa will do next?" I asked, simply because this psycho-jealous-crazy-ex-girlfriend thing was new to me, and I didn't know what to expect.

"I don't really know. Until today, I had no clue how sick she was . . . *is*."

"Sick or not, she has to assume that the police will probably be looking for her," I said.

"Not necessarily. Teresa knows me and how hard it would be for me to call the police on her," he said. Right away, he raised his hand to quiet my protests, when he saw the expression on my face. "But . . . if she really wants to disappear, she might think she's smart enough to get away. The experienced security guys she's worked with might have passed a few tricks on to her, trying to impress the pretty computer nerd."

"So, the crazy woman, with a trunk full of colorful designer switchblade knives, just gets away safely while she outsmarts the police?"

"I didn't say she would. I just said that Teresa might think she can. But no matter how smart she thinks she is or how tough she seems, Teresa is fragile. *Annnd,* I am sure that she's probably really scared right about now."

"You know. To hell with the fragile Miss Tee. I could care less how fragile she is. I don't care if she's scared. I don't care if she was in some sort of trance, when she did the awful things she did, and wakes up and regrets what she's done. I really could care less about *poor* Teresa. I just don't want her walking around. I need to be absolutely sure that she's off the streets. I don't think I'll be able to sleep again until I know for sure."

Kennard, a bit taken off guard by my vent, said, "Tina, no matter what else she does, I do think that she is probably too smart to show her face anywhere near either of us."

Yeah, where have I heard something like that before? I thought.

Still, after what he'd just been through, his attempt to make me feel better, only reminded me of my part in the drama. "I hope you're right," I said. "I can't believe I allowed her to manipulate me into letting her into my house. I couldn't leave well enough alone. I had to find out what she was up to. My curiosity about that crazy woman's motives almost got you killed."

"Tina, this is all on Teresa. You did nothing wrong," Kennard said. "You have to know that it wasn't me she originally intended to hurt, right?"

He paused to wait for my nod, my acknowledgement of the giant elephant sitting there in the room with us.

"Maybe if I'd handled things differently, she would've gone about her business," Kennard mused. "After what she did, calling Reggie to set you up, she'd gone too far. Instead of my normal trying to talk sense to her, I ranted on about how you were the one I cared for, that I have no feelings for her, and that I absolutely want nothing to do with her ever again. You know . . . that guy, Byron, was right. She never said anything. She almost seemed bored . . . until I turned my back on her. Then again, if I hadn't come here, you'd have been the one she struck out at. Without someone, like Byron, to warn you of her coming at you, you'd be dead. I could never live with that."

"Think about the effect it would've had on me," I joked. When he didn't crack a smile, I continued, seriously, "Sorry. I know it's not funny, but it's hard to wrap my head around someone hating me that much and wanting to do me harm, especially someone I hardly know or who hardly knows me. Then again, she claims she cares for you and look what love means to her. I don't get it . . ."

Before I could finish, we heard the distinctive "eeeoooeeeooo" of sirens approaching. The police and ambulance had arrived. I went to the door to wait for them.

* * *

By the time we arrived at the hospital—Kennard in the ambulance, me in my little Elantra—Kennard's parents were there waiting, and his brother was on his way from Canada. As the doctors rushed him to the back, with his parents in tow, I had one of my déjà vu flashes.

But this time, no doctor came to tell me that we had gotten there too late. It was Mr. Jackson who came out with good news. Fortunately, Teresa had missed all major organs. Kennard would only have to be in the hospital for a couple of days. Then he could go home to the loving care of his parents to continue his recovery.

While he was in the hospital, someone in his family would be with him at all times. There was really no reason for me to hang around. I was not family, spouse, or even official love interest. But I couldn't go. There was so much going on in my head that I couldn't bring myself to leave.

For one thing, there were two extremely dangerous people out there gunning for me, and they both knew where I lived. Unlike on TV, nobody offered to watch my place around the clock or relocate me to protective custody. I was on my own. Whatever that meant.

I stretched out on the hospital waiting room sofa and bundled up in a blanket that was supplied to me by the kindly nursing staff. I was rolling deeper and deeper in self-pity, when I looked up and saw Detective Robinson entering the waiting room. I knew for a fact that Teresa's attempt on Kennard's life was not her case. So, why was she there?

"Hello, Ms. Brooks," she said, and headed directly to where I was sitting.

"Hello, Detective. Since we seem to be keeping such regular company, maybe you should just call me Tina."

"Okay, Tina. I'm Angie. How is Mr. Jackson doing?"

"He's going to be fine. His parents and his brother are in there with him now. There's normally a limit of two visitors at a time, but they made an exception for his brother. I'm not a blood relation."

"What, if I may ask, is your relationship to Mr. Jackson?"

"Funny, Angie, I don't have an answer to that question. We only met at his sister's funeral but, because of his sister's feelings for us both, we already had this undefinable connection between us. We both sensed it."

"Soul mates, matched souls . . . that kind of thing, huh?"

"You never cease to surprise me, Detective."

"Yeah, I'm a riddle, wrapped in a mystery, inside an enigma," she joked, as she sat down.

For the first time since Kennard had been attacked, I laughed out loud. "Thanks for that, Detective . . . uh, Angie. Why are you here?"

"I guess Mr. Jackson didn't get a chance to tell you what we discovered."

"What you discovered? About what?"

"Apparently, Mr. Jackson's sister was a very smart woman. She was in an abusive relationship, but she didn't break. She was concerned, not only about the abuse to her, but other questionable activities she noticed that this man was involved in. She began noting things and recording observations. She collected facts, documented little bits of information, and hid them, just in case they would mean something later. For some reason, she even felt it necessary to document that she and this person actually had a romantic relationship. It was as if she anticipated that at some point, he would deny even knowing her." Detective Angie said all that with not a small bit of admiration for my deceased friend, Denise.

"How exactly do you know any of this?"

"She told us," Detective Angie said, with a sly smile.

"She told you? How?"

"She left a note in a separate safety deposit box, that only her brother, as executor, had access to. In that note she told him to go to their secret hiding spot, the one they used growing-up. Mr. Jackson called me immediately and we checked it together. She had hidden, under the porch, a bunch of stuff—papers, pictures, and documents—that she wanted only him to find."

"She knew," I said, my voice quavering. "Denise knew that if something happened to her, Reggie would do exactly what he did. Go through her house and clean everything up. Damn, Denise. I had no idea she was that smart."

"Yup. For someone in her position, she was awesome. We now have proof, in her handwriting, of the relationship she had with one Ray John Williams of the RPD, also known to her as Reggie. We have proof of an increasing pattern of emotional, physical, and psychological abuse. We have notes and letters indicating that Ms. Jackson feared there was a real possibility she would not get out of the relationship alive, that there would be repercussions to her friends and family if she came forward."

We both set quietly, while I sobbed and absorbed all that Detective Angela Robinson was telling me.

"With the information and evidence that we found, plus the video tape you provided, we now have Mr. Ray John Williams officially being questioned, as we speak."

"Will any of that be enough to make sure he gets what he deserves?" I asked. "Sometimes facts don't guarantee justice."

"You're right about that, Tina. But we have a lot. With an aggressive District Attorney and help from the Feds too—by the way, some of the allegations are of federal crimes—we have a really good chance. Plus, with the video you provided, some of his associates will probably be willing to work a deal for testimony against Ray John. I'd say we have a pretty good chance of Mr. Ray John Williams spending a great deal of time locked up. Given the nature of some of his alleged crimes, Ray John had better get himself a really good lawyer."

She stood then and put out her hand, which I took gladly and shook it energetically, until she couldn't take it anymore and pulled away.

"I have to go now," she said.

"Oh, Angie?"

"Yes?"

"Umm, does anyone have a clue where the woman who attacked Kennard, Teresa, is? Kennard thinks that she might be clever enough to hide from authorities for a long time."

"Apparently," Detective Angie said, amused, "she thought that too."

"What do you mean, *she thought?*"

"It appears that when the security company she had worked for, heard about Miss Teresa Norman's latest exploits, it was the last straw. Evidently, from what I gather, she'd recently been caught messing around with one of their client's computers. She'd used the company's resources to spy on one of the client's employees, one Mr. Kennard Jackson. For that, they let her off easy and forced her to resign. They drew the line at her trying to do bodily harm to Mr. Jackson. Not good for business. That's when they decided to use their resources to help the police locate Miss Norman. They are the real deal, by the way. I am seriously impressed. They went to work, found out quickly where she was hiding—still in Richmond, for heaven's sake—and they pointed the authorities to her. Miss Norman is now in RPD custody."

"Thank God," I said.

"By the way, Tina," she said, "I came here to talk with you because I want both you and that family to know that, for most of us in the department, it is important to us to be part of the solution, too."

"Good to know," I said, smiling. "And thank you for listening. Thank you for caring . . . for everything."

With that, Detective Angela Robinson nodded her head, resumed her no-nonsense detective persona, and left.

I couldn't believe it was over. I sat there, numb, for several minutes before gathering my stuff. I texted the Jacksons that I was leaving, and that Theresa was off the street. Then I went in search of my little Elantra. It was time to go home.

CHAPTER 47

I WAS SURPRISED TO FIND a parking space directly in front of my apartment. That hardly ever happened. Lucky me, because it was questionable if I had the energy to walk any distance to my door. For some reason, the elation one would expect to feel with closure—after all, the bad guys were caught— hadn't set in yet. Instead, I felt drained, sort of empty and sad. I guess the effect that people like Teresa and Reggie have on their victims is so profound that the devastation, horror, and fear do not all go away by putting the bad guys in jail.

I'd had a lot of time for thinking while lying in the waiting room, and I'd come to some honest conclusions about myself going forward. The Jacksons were a very sweet and a very close family, but I wasn't one of them. Whether any of them would admit it, my presence would always be a reminder of what happened to Denise. Of course, I believed them when they said they appreciated my role in making Denise's last few months more bearable. Still, it ended tragically. Bottom-line, I did not save her. We, not a one of us, got there in time.

I wasn't sure where that left Kennard and me. How we met, why we met, and the part I played in why Teresa attacked him, were not things he could easily forget. That was an awful lot of baggage to bring into a new relationship. Physical attraction and Denise's confidence that we were a perfect match might not be enough. But that was a question for another day.

As I stepped into my apartment, I let out an involuntary groan, at once reminded that it wasn't completely over yet. Dried drops of Kennard's blood were on the hallway carpet. Seeing that, brought back the image of my first sight of Kennard and Byron Jones coming through the door.

"I'll deal with that later," I said. But, even as I said it, I knew there was no way I could put it off. There were many more blood-stained reminders in my bedroom. I couldn't close my eyes, walk around the stains, or pretend it all away. Miss Tee was in jail, but the remnants of her handy work, her attack on Kennard, remained.

I gathered what little energy I could and went to tackle my bedroom. Even as physically and mentally exhausted as I felt, I wanted Miss Tee and all signs of her and that night gone, eradicated, expunged, obliterated, out of my sight, and out of my life. If I had my druthers, I would've burned all the bloody traces. Instead, I gathered up the sheets, towels, wash cloths, and clothes. I put them in a large plastic trash bag to dispose of them. And, on my way out the door, I rolled up that blood-stained hallway runner. I dragged it and the trash bag out back to the dumpster; and tossed them in. That simple act gave me some of the feeling of closure I needed.

When I got back inside, I was tired, but not sleepy-tired. So, I went into the kitchen and turned on the radio. Maybe some tea, a salad, and the public radio station would take my mind off all things Teresa and Reggie.

The station was in the middle of an all blues hour. When the DJ announced the next song, I didn't recognize the title or the artist. Once it started playing, I stopped cutting my carrots and stared at the radio.

I laughed and said out loud, "Damn, that's one of Auntie Dee's songs."

The selection, the caller had requested, was from an old blues singer, Wynonie Harris, and was called *Buzzard Luck*. Listening to it, I recognized it as one of Auntie Dee's favorites, from her record collection. Sometimes when Auntie played her old LP records, she'd turn up the volume, grab my hand, and we'd dance. At the end of the song, we would clap, as if to congratulate each other on such a terrific performance. Then we would fall down together, laughing.

I smiled to myself. Listening to *Buzzard Luck*, the song about a guy with really bad luck, reminded me how lucky I'd been to have the time I had with

Auntie. And even with all the bad and scary things that had happened in my life, I'd always have the memories of her to balance them out.

I was still listening and reminiscing when my apartment phone rang.

"Hello Momma," I said, recognizing the caller-id.

"Hey, baby," I'm on my way up there, anything you want me to stop and get for you, on the way?"

"Nah, Momma. I'm good."

"So, how are you doing, baby?"

"I'm fine, Momma," I said, stifling a yawn. "Knock hard when you get here. I may be asleep."

"Did you get a chance to make the calls you said you were gonna make?"

"Yes, I did," I said. "I talked with Paulette and Tony. I explained as much as I could to the people in my office, including Jeri, Denise's old boss. I texted all the Jacksons and got them updated on progress as reported by my new friend, Detective Angie. I even called April and Mr. Sam. I figured they'd want to know that Bathroom Man was finally caught."

"Speaking of your Mr. Sam, did you share with him, the decision you made about graduate school?"

"Yes, Momma, I did," I said. "It was so funny. Mr. Sam had kicked me out and told me to go find myself. But all the time—just like any adoptive father—he was hoping that what I found would lead to a career in pharmacy and back with him at ATC. When I told him about my decision, he did his Mr. Sam 'hmmph' grunt, which is equivalent to everybody else's happy dance. He had so many suggestions and ideas that, for the first time, I had to stop him talking and say we would talk later."

Recently, I had been thinking about ATC. I had never gotten over my initial desire to be a part of it. When I thought about it, I had never enjoyed any of my jobs or found them as fulfilling as I did my first one. I liked that Mr. Sam and ATC were an integral part of the community. He didn't just dispense pills or sell goods. He devoted his life, in and out of his building, to helping people. I knew this firsthand. I could do worse than to model my life after him—minus the highwater pants, of course—starting with a graduate degree in pharmacy.

"Sweetie," Momma said, "I'm glad you had people like your Mr. Sam around, to help and mentor you. I wish . . ." She didn't have to finish. I knew what she wished.

We were both silent for a moment, and then Momma said, "Baby, I was thinking, why don't you come back with me to stay in Petersburg for a while? You can have your old room. I've converted it into a guestroom. It's different from what you remember. More grown-up. But I think it'll be good for you."

"Might not be a bad idea. Kennard's family has him covered. If need be, even in traffic, I can be back in less than an hour. Plus, my apartment does not feel much like home, right now. It might be nice to be in the one place that I felt really safe. Thanks, Momma. I can't think of anything better you could possibly do for me now."

"Something else I wanted to tell you, but I figured I'd better do it while I was out of arms reach," she said, with a nervous chuckle.

"Okay, Momma, what is it?" I asked, preparing myself.

"Umm, how would you like to meet your father?"

"Whoa, didn't see that coming," I said.

"Well?"

"Well, what?"

"How would you feel about meeting, the distinguished Virginia State Senator Shaun Lacey?"

"Why now?" I asked, genuinely curious.

"He wants to meet you," she said.

"I thought he didn't even know about me. Momma, what's going on?"

"Well, he didn't know about you before. At least, he didn't know for sure. Most likely, in high school, he didn't want to know. It would have complicated his achieving his goals and affected his efforts to get into Columbia. I imagine that the admissions people at that Ivy League school would've looked cross-eyed at a rapist/baby-daddy as a freshman candidate."

"I guess you had your reasons for not facing him down, or going to the police, or even going to his family about what he did."

"Yes, I did. No matter what he says now, Shaun wouldn't have admitted what he did. Me accusing a Lacey of fathering a child through rape, in public or private, would've been worst for me than Shaun. That was something Aunt Dee and I agreed on, long ago.

"So, all this time, he never even knew that you'd had a baby? He didn't even suspect that you were pregnant?"

"I'm not so sure that's true. Shaun was a smart guy. He had to have suspected it was a possibility. He knew what he had done. When rumors started going around school that I was pregnant, he had to have heard them. Though everybody else at that school would've assumed any father of my child was probably some gangbanger from the projects, he knew better. Besides, the signs were there for him to see. I quit the cheering squad. I stopped speaking to anyone at the school. I moved around like a zombie. I gained weight. Even my counselor heard the rumors and called me in to find out what was going on. Of course, I couldn't talk with her because I'd promised Momma and the deacon not to tell anybody."

"Oh, Momma, that must've been awful," I said.

"It was. But, by the time you were born, Shaun had disappeared. I assume he was in school, in New York. His ghetto girl conquest was the last thing on his mind."

"So, I ask again. Why now?"

"I went to see him."

"What? When? Why?"

"Like I told you before, when I got back to Richmond, I had no idea how to find you. I finally came up with the plan of accidently running into you. After a while . . . well, let's just say it wasn't working and I got desperate. I couldn't afford to pay anyone to help. I was hoping Shaun, with his influence, could find a discrete way to help track you down. I wasn't out to ruin his life, so I sent a generic note saying that I needed his help locating someone precious to me. When he didn't get back to me, I figured that was my answer."

"And something happened recently to make you go see him?"

"Yes. I don't know what went on behind the scenes when my note first got to his office. But last week I got this call. It was Shaun. He said he was sorting through some old papers and saw my name. He recognized it immediately. He apologized for his staff. But, according to him, they have to filter all correspondence and, because my letter was so vague, they just sat it aside."

"Uh huh, sure," I said, sarcastically. "By then you'd already found me. But you guys still met. And then what happened?"

"I showed him your picture and told him about you."

"Momma," I said, "he just believed you?"

"He more than likely already had his suspicions about who that 'someone precious to me' was, that I'd mentioned in my note. Add that to the questions he probably had in his head for a long time. He wanted answers. I think the picture convinced him. You do look a lot like a darker version of a young Shaun. Plus, I'd made it clear that I wasn't asking anything of him."

"Did he apologize for what he did to you?"

"No."

"Wow, Momma," I said, "what a special guy. Good thing I'm not in his voting district. That's all I can say."

"Well, baby, he is who he is. But he did ask a lot of questions about you and me. Of course, I didn't go into details about the bad things that happened to us, since 1992. What would that serve? I just emphasized how smart, and pretty, and strong you are. And always have been." I heard a crack in my mother's voice.

"Momma, really, I'm not sure how I feel about this," I said.

"It's your decision, kiddo. I told him about you working and paying your way through college. I told him that you were looking into graduate school. He says that he'd really like to help you in any way he could. I'm sure he meant financially. So, like I said, it's up to you. But, if taking advantage of his guilt will help you achieve your dream, then forget your pride and take the money and run. Think of it as back child support."

"But. . ."

"He was actually excited about what he heard about you. He does seem to have grown up a bit. Matured. Baby, he wants to meet you. Like I said, it's up to you. You can talk with him. Then see where, if at all, you want to go from there."

"Okay," I said, "I'll think about it."